GARVEY'S CHOICE
The Graphic Novel

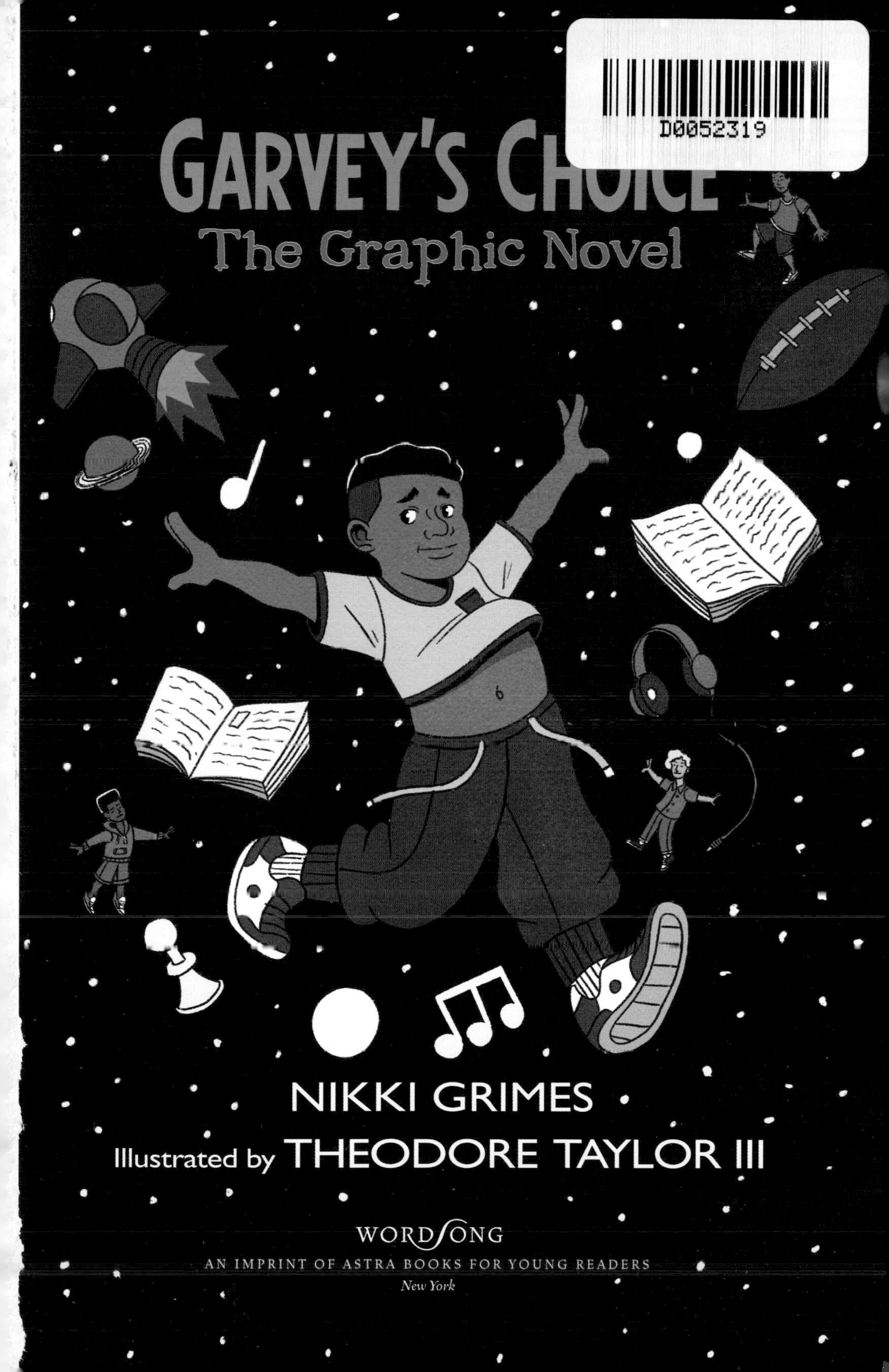

NIKKI GRIMES
Illustrated by THEODORE TAYLOR III

WORDSONG
AN IMPRINT OF ASTRA BOOKS FOR YOUNG READERS
New York

For Deborah Taylor
and all librarians who labor
on behalf of our children —*NG*

Dedicated to my father,
Theodore Taylor Jr.,
who will always inspire me to be me —*TT III*

Garvey's Choice: The Graphic Novel is based upon the novel *Garvey's Choice.*

Wordsong
An imprint of Astra Books for Young Readers, a division of Astra Publishing House
astrapublishinghouse.com
Printed in China

ISNB: 978-1-6626-6002-3 (hc)
ISBN: 978-1-6626-6008-5 (pb)
ISBN: 978-1-6626-6009-2 (eBook)
First paperback edition, 2023
10 9 8 7 6 5 4 3 2 1

Library of Congress Cataloging-in-Publication Data

Names: Grimes, Nikki, author. | Taylor, Theodore, III, illustrator. | Grimes, Nikki, Garvey's choice.
Title: Garvey's choice : the graphic novel / Nikki Grimes ; illustrated by Theodore Taylor III.
Description: New York : Wordsong, an imprint of Astra Books for Young Readers, 2023. | Audience: Ages 9-12. | Audience: Grades 4-6. | Summary: "Award-winning author Nikki Grimes's beloved novel in verse Garvey's Choice is now a graphic novel, imaginatively and dramatically illustrated by Little Shaq artist Theodore Taylor III"-- Provided by publisher.
Identifiers: LCCN 2022042526 (print) | LCCN 2022042527 (ebook) | ISBN 9781662660023 (hardcover) | ISBN 9781662660085 (paperback) | ISBN 9781662660092 (epub)
Subjects: LCSH: Graphic novels. | CYAC: Graphic novels. | Fathers and sons--Fiction. | Hobbies--Fiction. | Singing--Fiction. | LCGFT: Graphic novels.
Classification: LCC PZ7.7.G778 Gar 2023 (print) | LCC PZ7.7.G778 (ebook) | DDC 741.5/973--dc23/eng/20221014
LC record available at https://lccn.loc.gov/2022042526
LC ebook record available at https://lccn.loc.gov/2022042527

Design by Barbara Grzeslo, Theodore Taylor III, and Symon Chow
The text is set in Anime Ace 3BB.
The illustrations are digital.

Contents

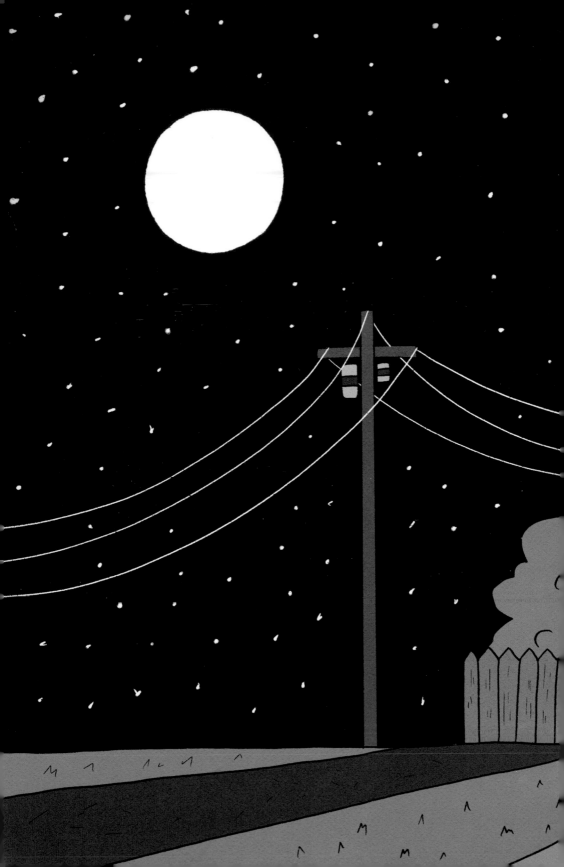

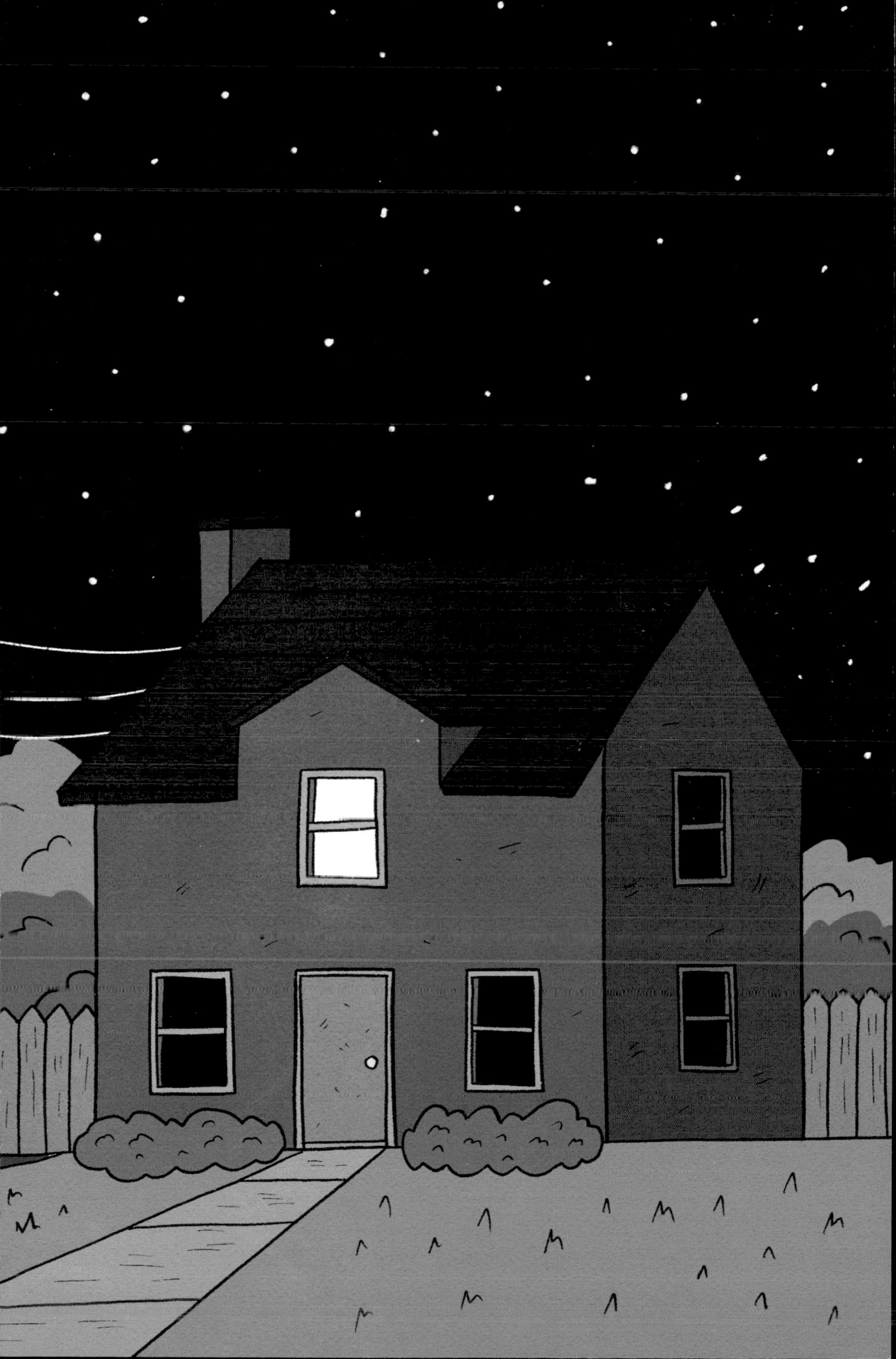

ORIGAMI

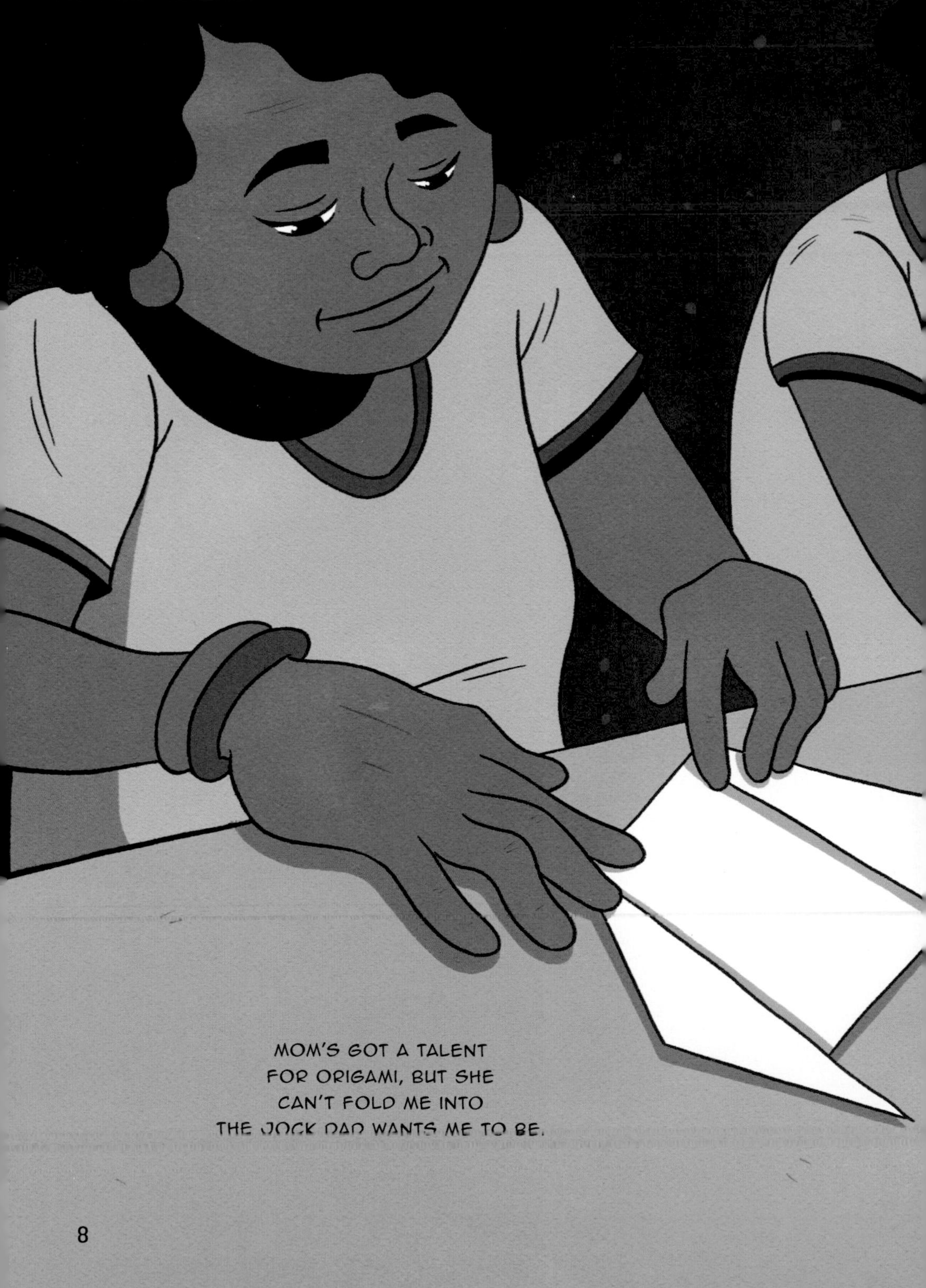
MOM'S GOT A TALENT
FOR ORIGAMI, BUT SHE
CAN'T FOLD ME INTO
THE JOCK DAD WANTS ME TO BE.

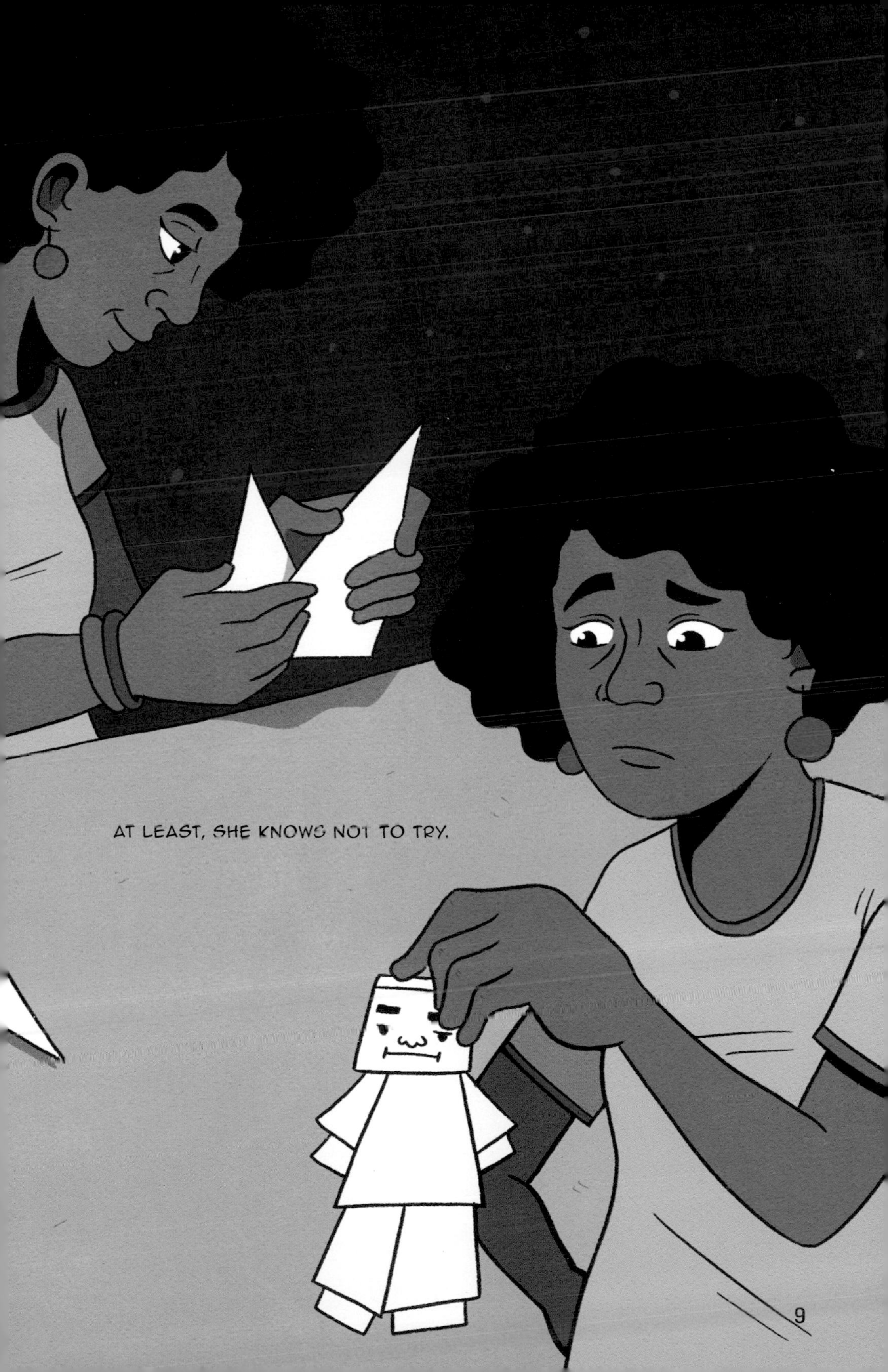
AT LEAST, SHE KNOWS NOT TO TRY.

IT FIGURES

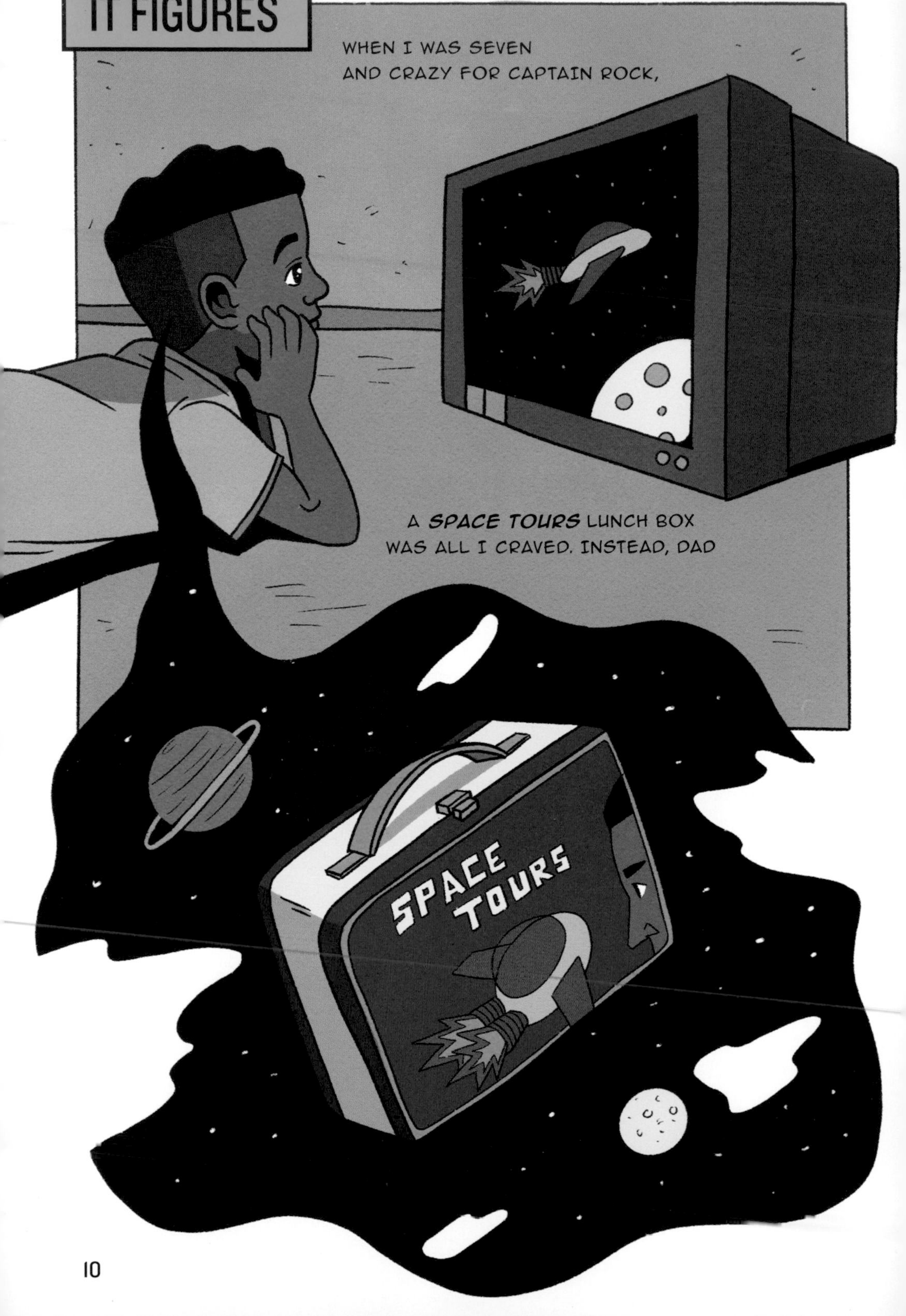
WHEN I WAS SEVEN
AND CRAZY FOR CAPTAIN ROCK,
A *SPACE TOURS* LUNCH BOX
WAS ALL I CRAVED. INSTEAD, DAD
SPACE TOURS

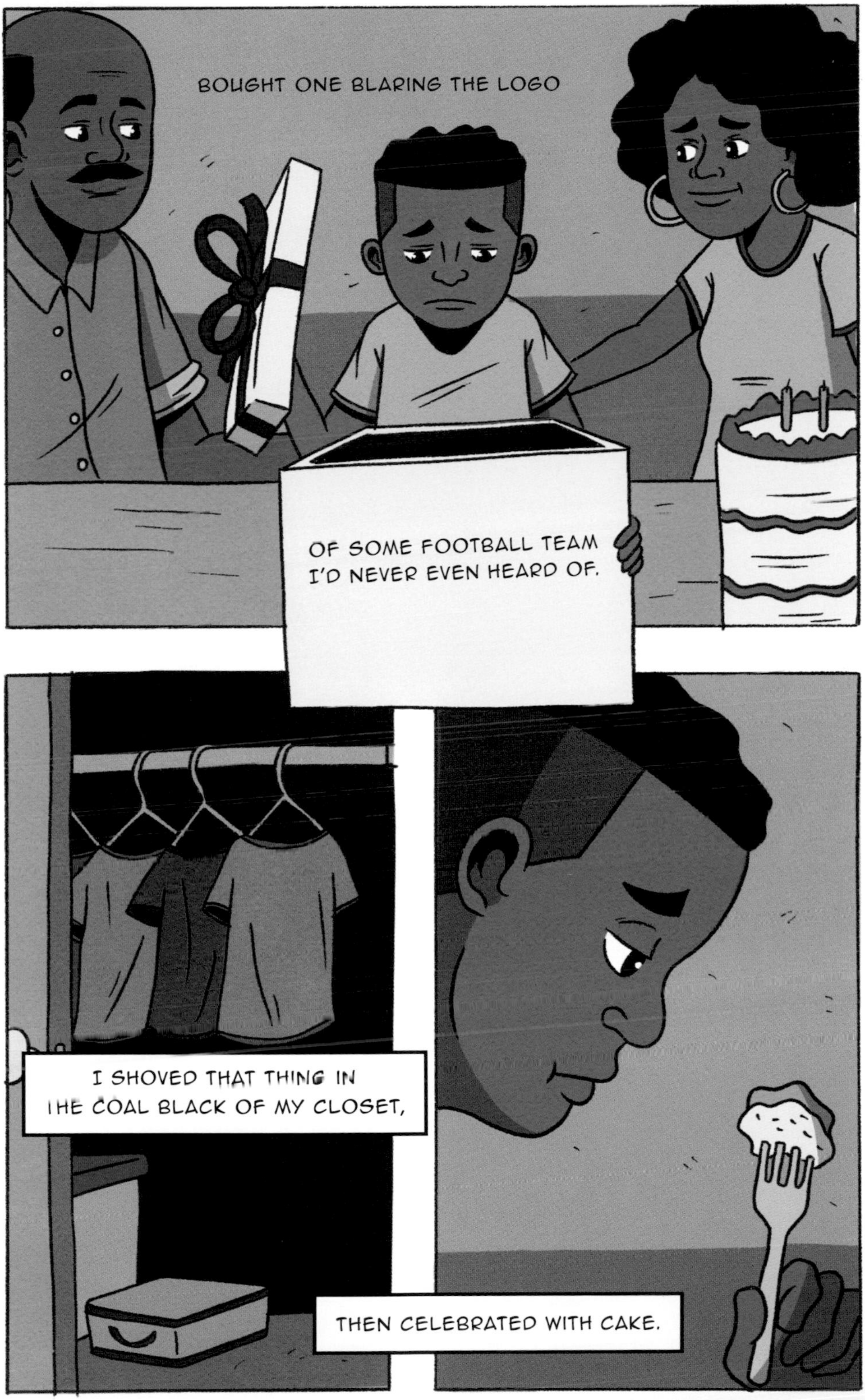
BOUGHT ONE BLARING THE LOGO
OF SOME FOOTBALL TEAM I'D NEVER EVEN HEARD OF.
I SHOVED THAT THING IN THE COAL BLACK OF MY CLOSET,
THEN CELEBRATED WITH CAKE.

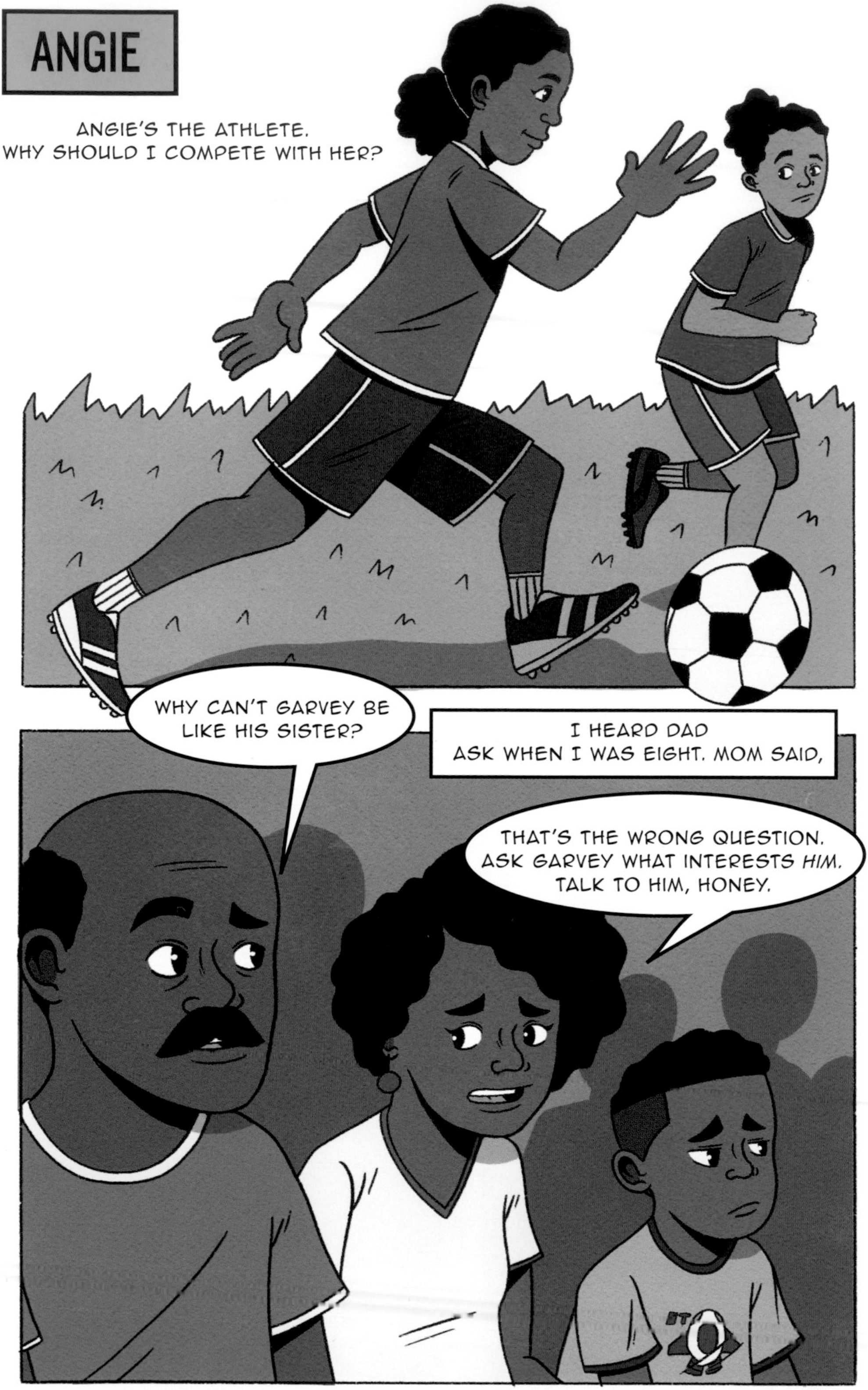
ANGIE
ANGIE'S THE ATHLETE. WHY SHOULD I COMPETE WITH HER?
WHY CAN'T GARVEY BE LIKE HIS SISTER?
I HEARD DAD ASK WHEN I WAS EIGHT. MOM SAID,
THAT'S THE WRONG QUESTION. ASK GARVEY WHAT INTERESTS *HIM*. TALK TO HIM, HONEY.

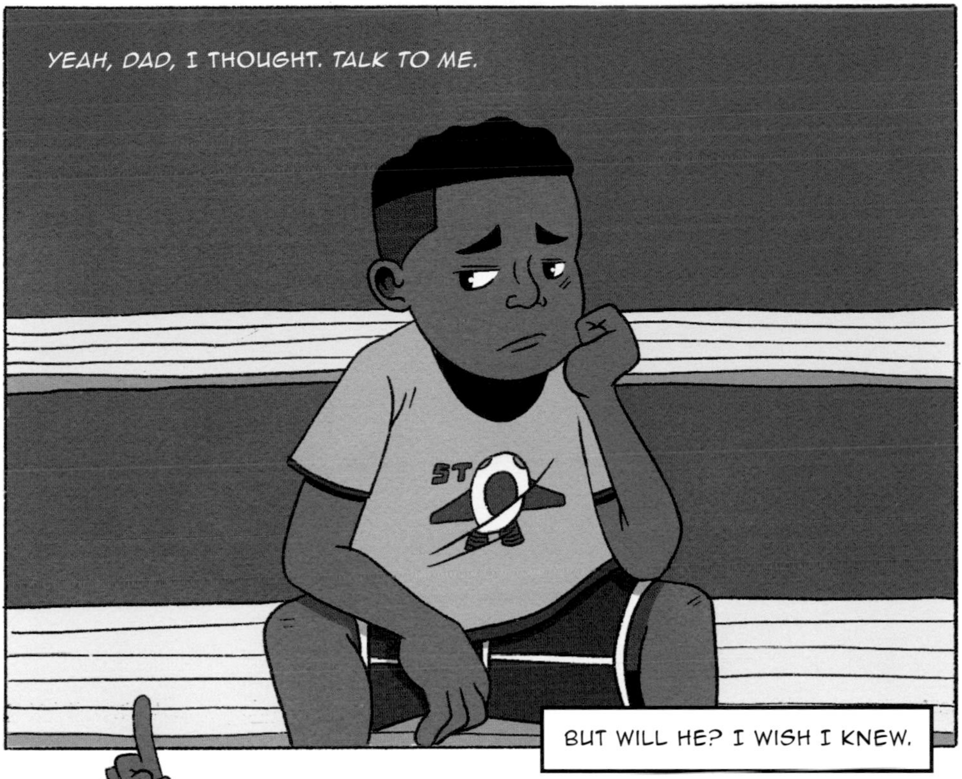
YEAH, DAD, I THOUGHT. TALK TO ME.
BUT WILL HE? I WISH I KNEW.

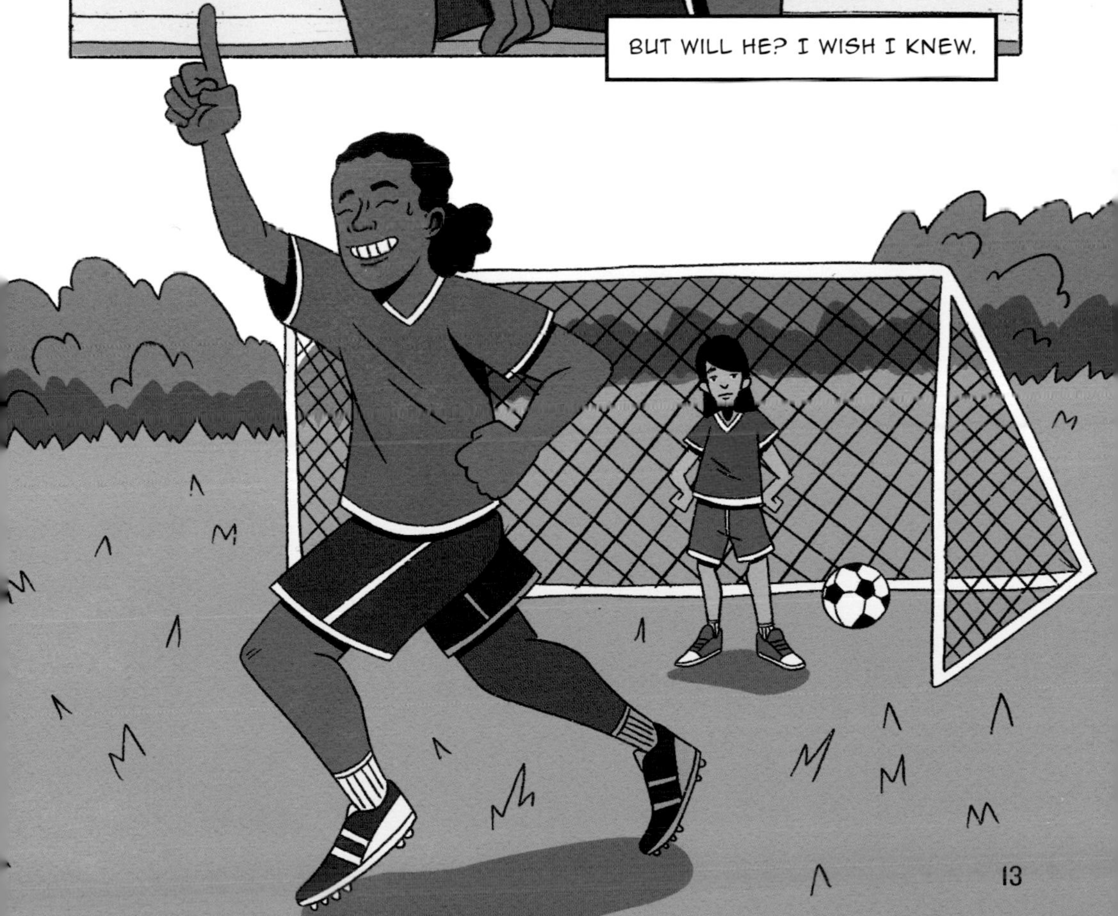

SUMMER LOST AND FOUND

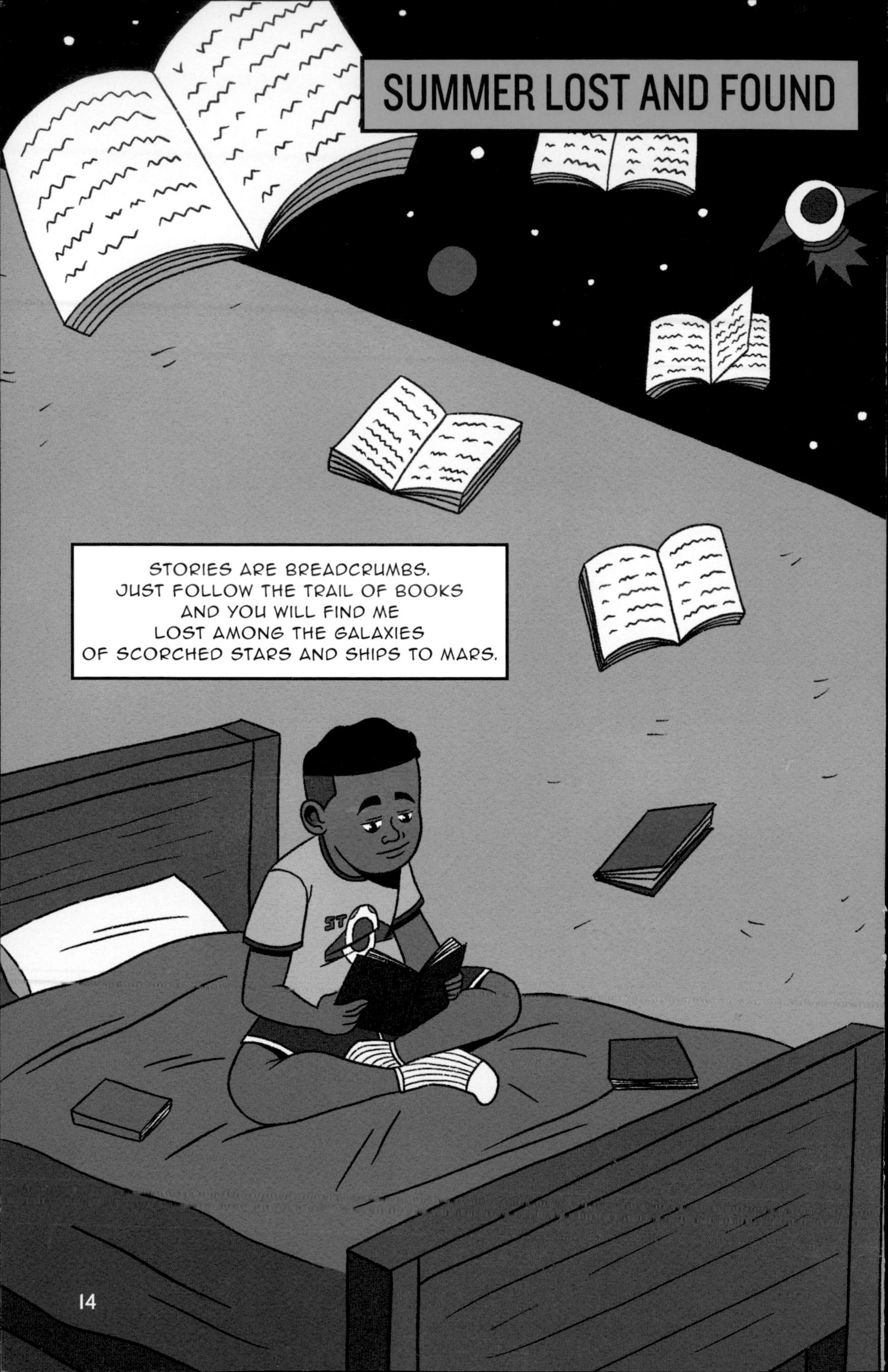
STORIES ARE BREADCRUMBS.
JUST FOLLOW THE TRAIL OF BOOKS
AND YOU WILL FIND ME
LOST AMONG THE GALAXIES
OF SCORCHED STARS AND SHIPS TO MARS.

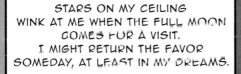

STARS ON MY CEILING
WINK AT ME WHEN THE FULL MOON
COMES FOR A VISIT.
I MIGHT RETURN THE FAVOR
SOMEDAY, AT LEAST IN MY DREAMS.

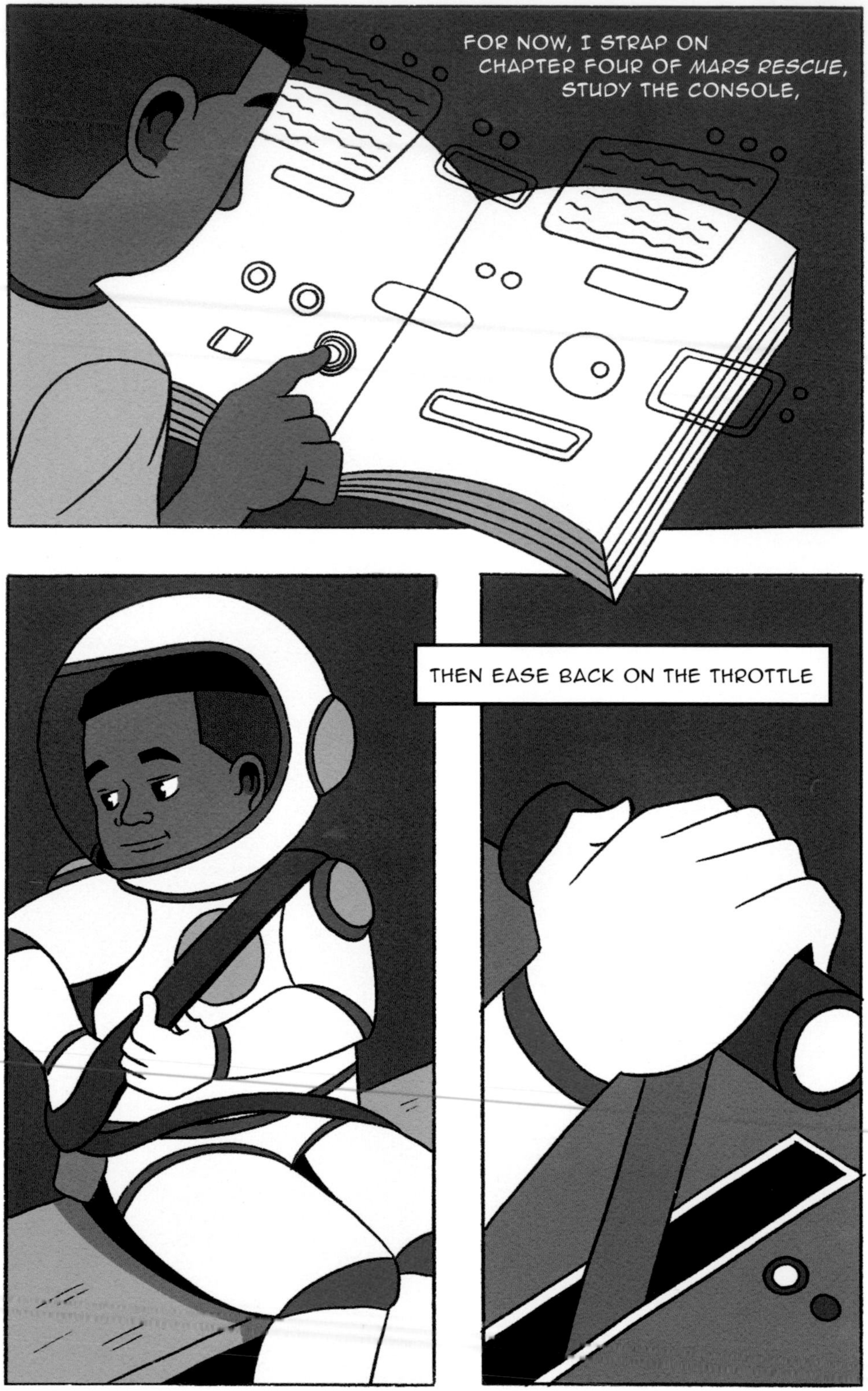
FOR NOW, I STRAP ON CHAPTER FOUR OF *MARS RESCUE*, STUDY THE CONSOLE,
THEN EASE BACK ON THE THROTTLE

FOR A SMOOTH FLIGHT THROUGH STAR FIELDS.

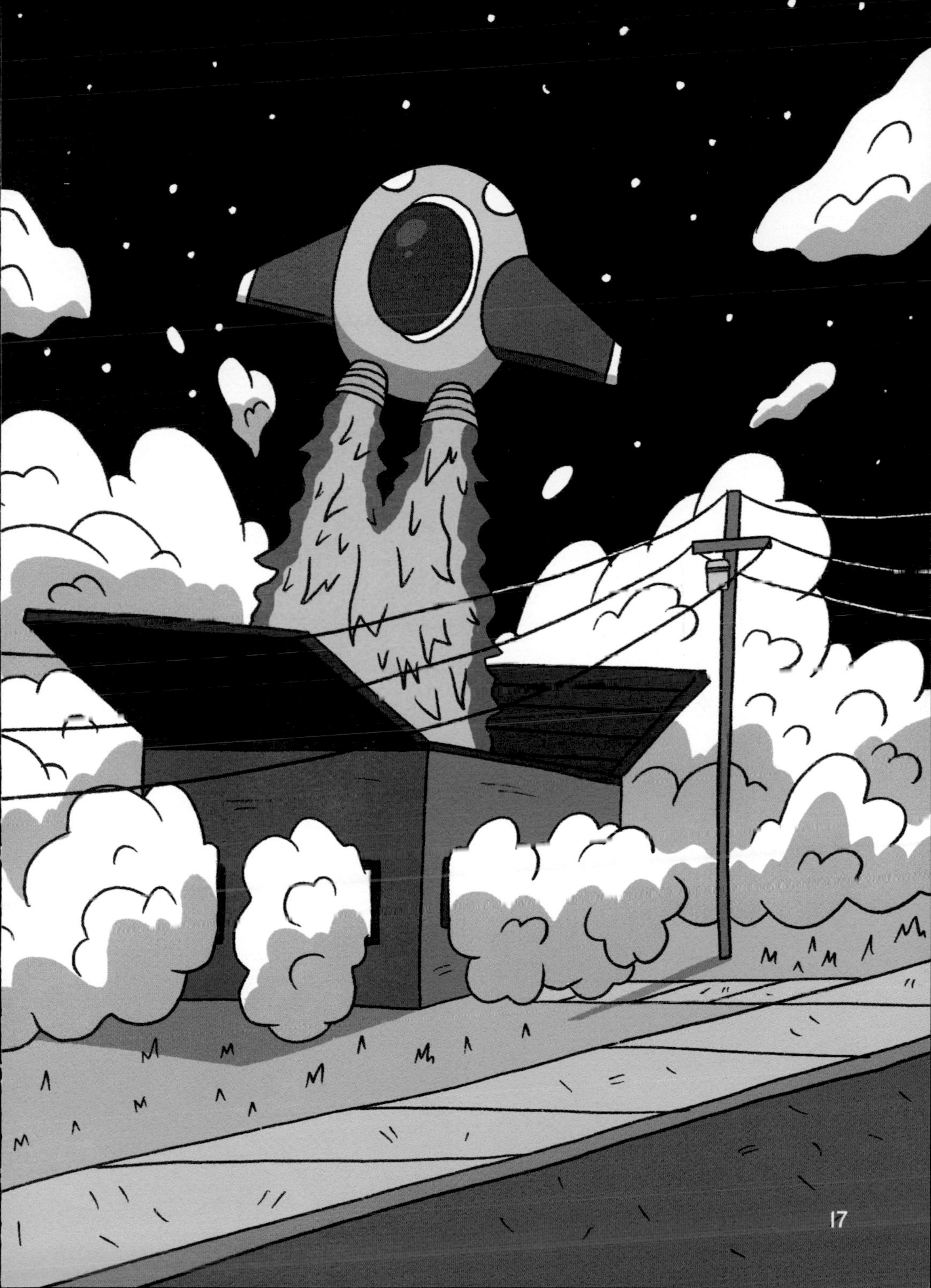

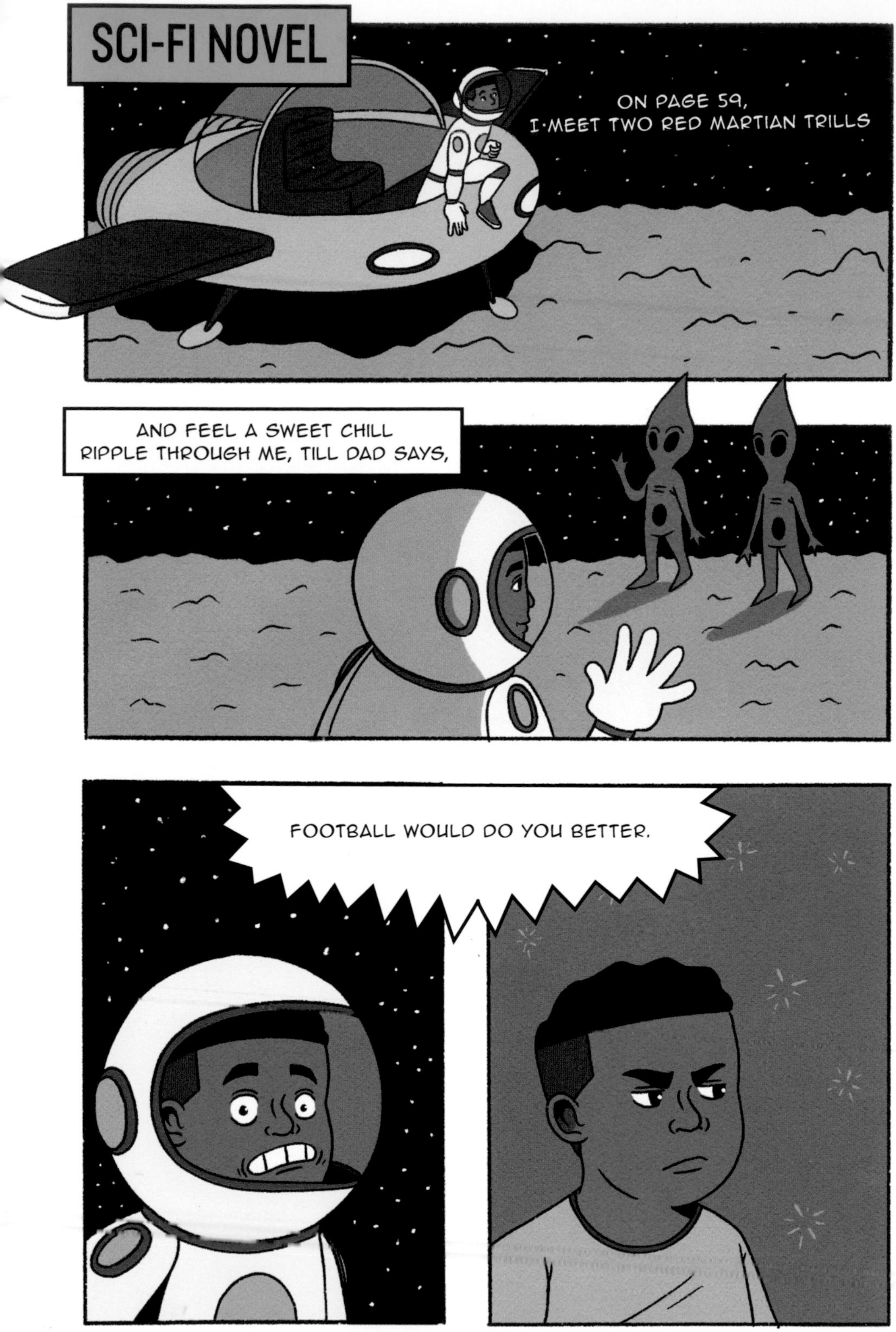
SCI-FI NOVEL
ON PAGE 59, I·MEET TWO RED MARTIAN TRILLS
AND FEEL A SWEET CHILL RIPPLE THROUGH ME, TILL DAD SAYS,
FOOTBALL WOULD DO YOU BETTER.

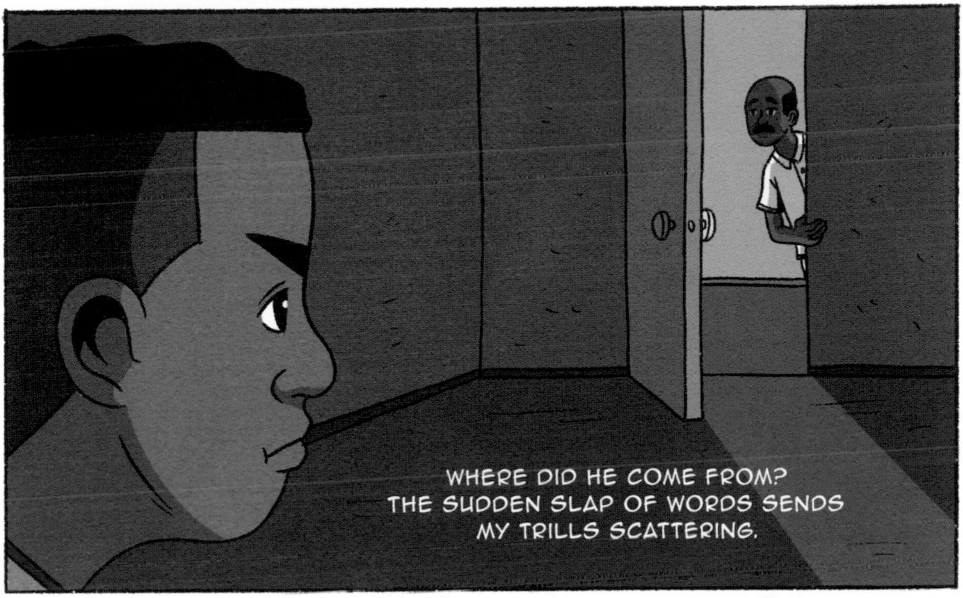
WHERE DID HE COME FROM?
THE SUDDEN SLAP OF WORDS SENDS
MY TRILLS SCATTERING.

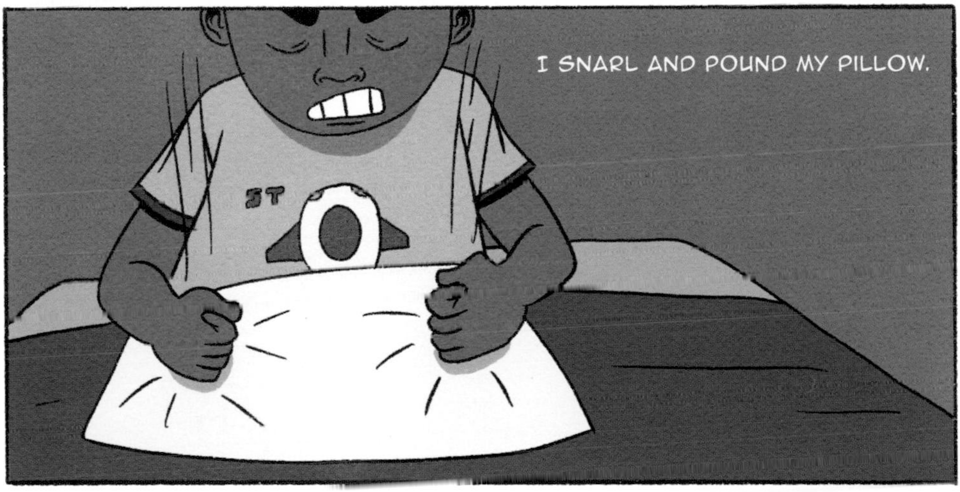
I SNARL AND POUND MY PILLOW.

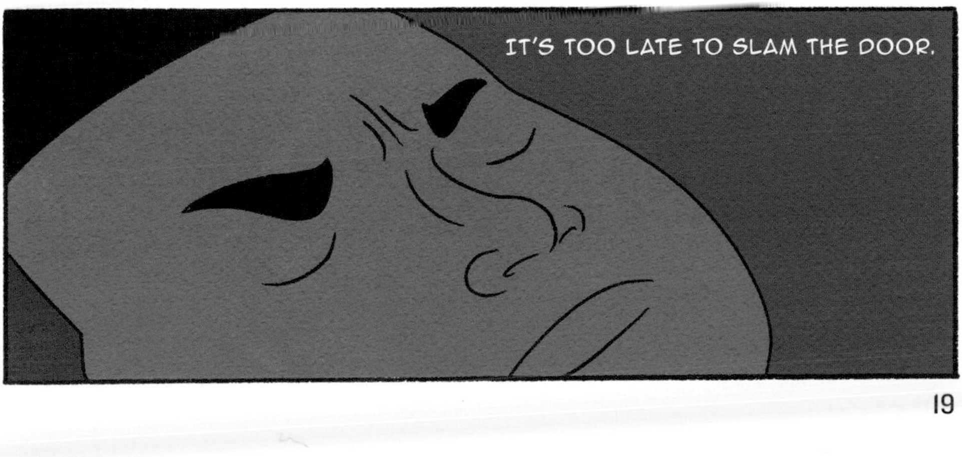
IT'S TOO LATE TO SLAM THE DOOR.

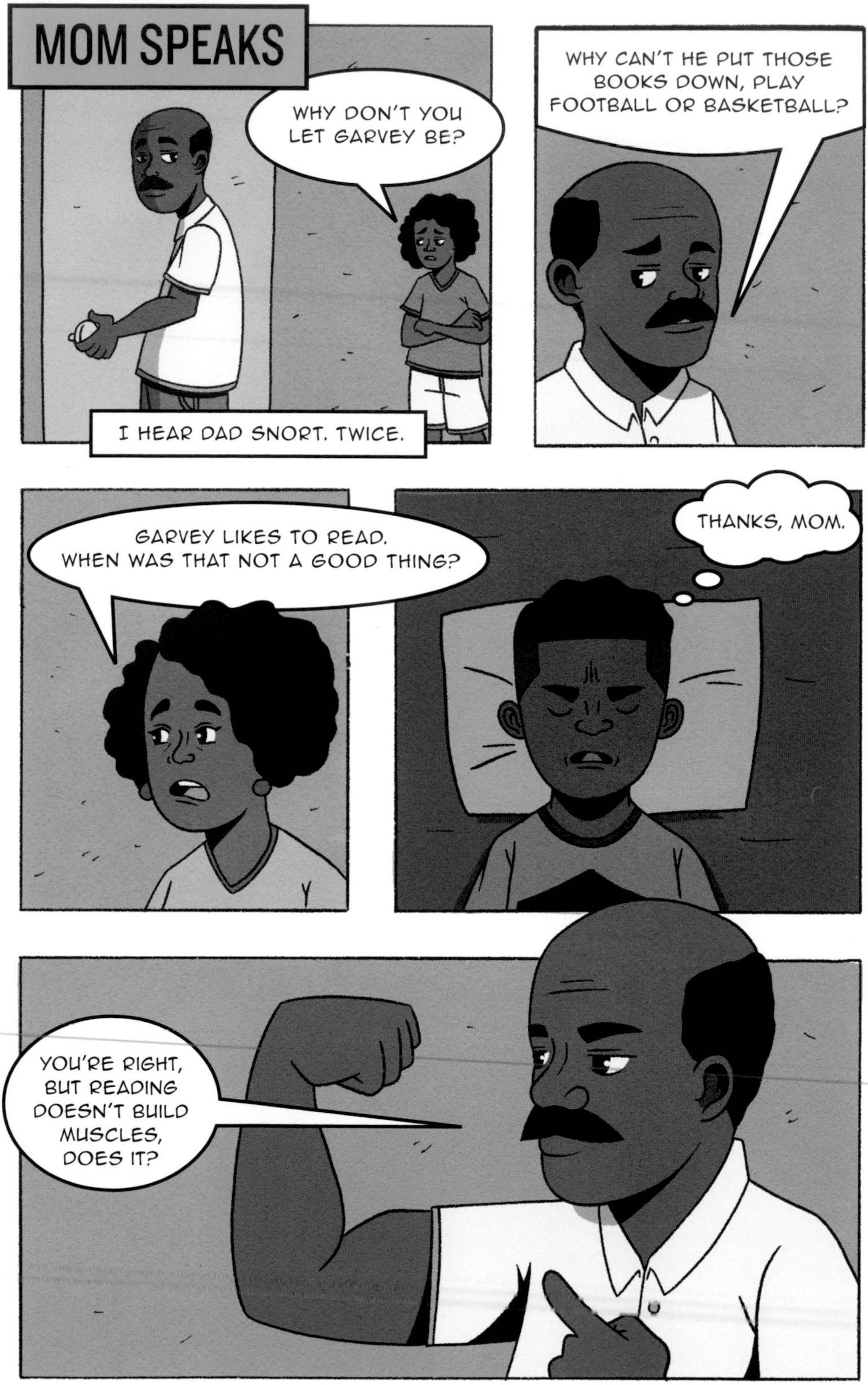
MOM SPEAKS
WHY DON'T YOU LET GARVEY BE?
I HEAR DAD SNORT. TWICE.
WHY CAN'T HE PUT THOSE BOOKS DOWN, PLAY FOOTBALL OR BASKETBALL?
GARVEY LIKES TO READ. WHEN WAS THAT NOT A GOOD THING?
THANKS, MOM.
YOU'RE RIGHT, BUT READING DOESN'T BUILD MUSCLES, DOES IT?

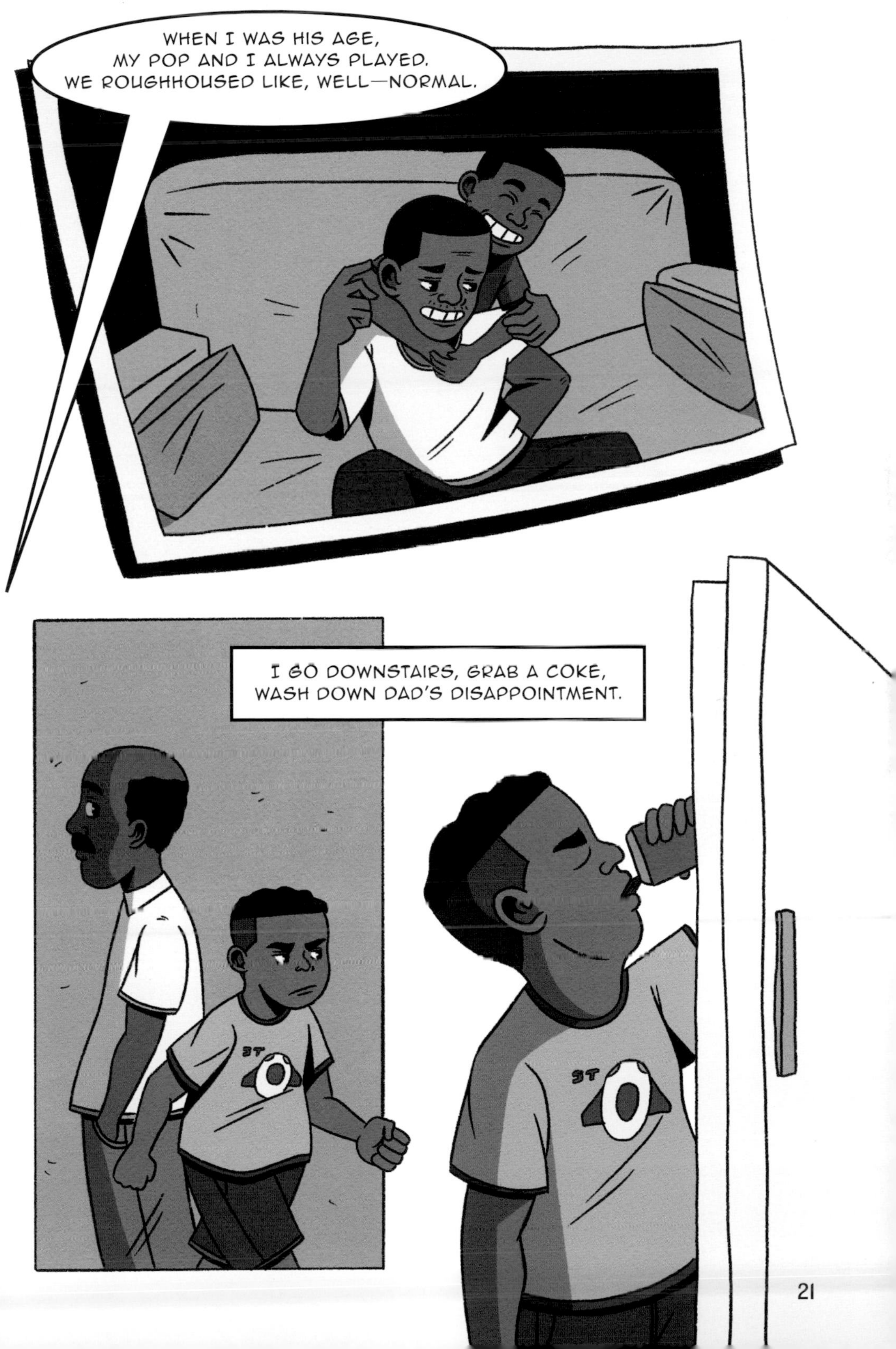
WHEN I WAS HIS AGE, MY POP AND I ALWAYS PLAYED. WE ROUGHHOUSED LIKE, WELL—NORMAL.
I GO DOWNSTAIRS, GRAB A COKE, WASH DOWN DAD'S DISAPPOINTMENT.

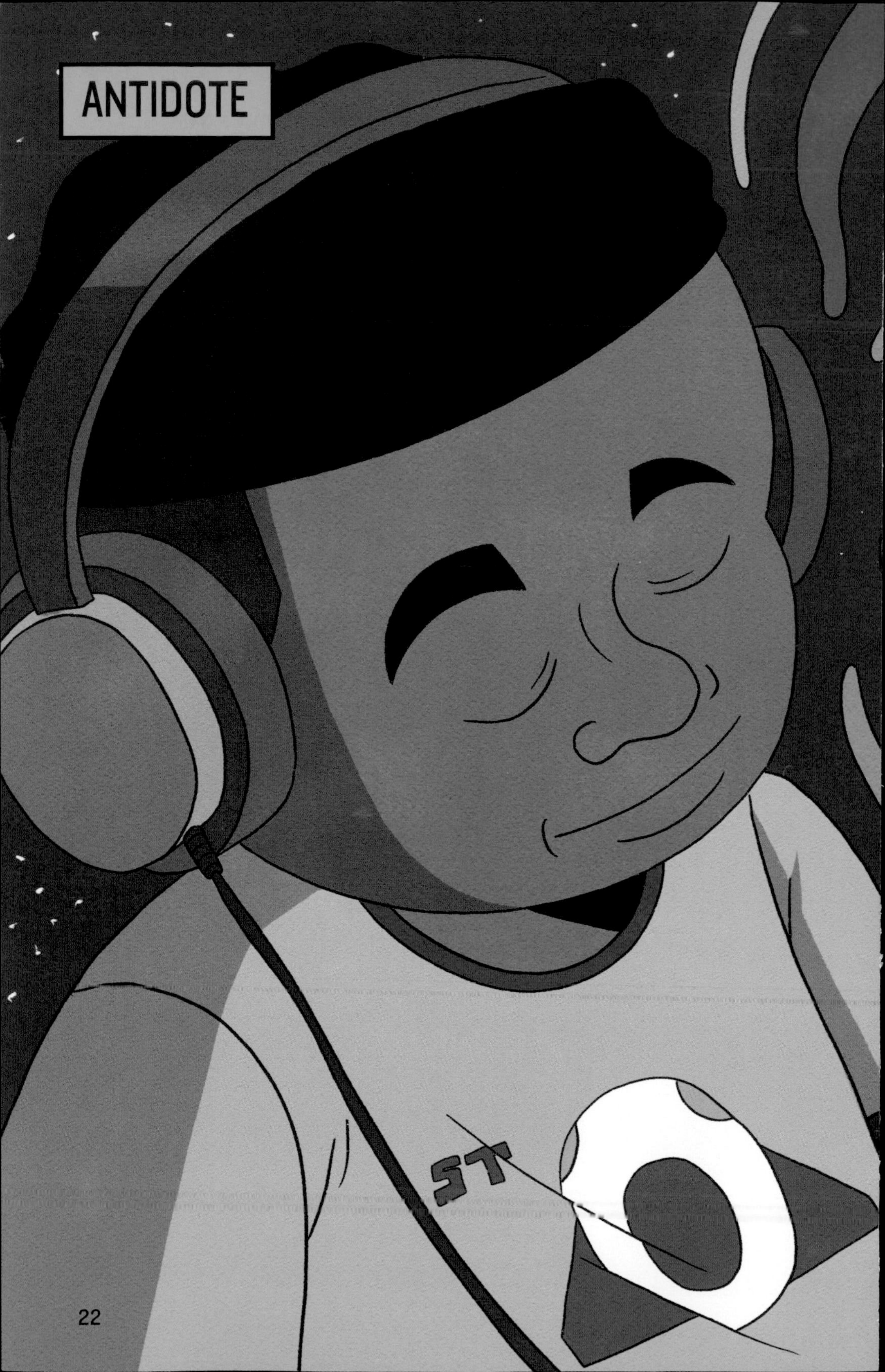
ANTIDOTE

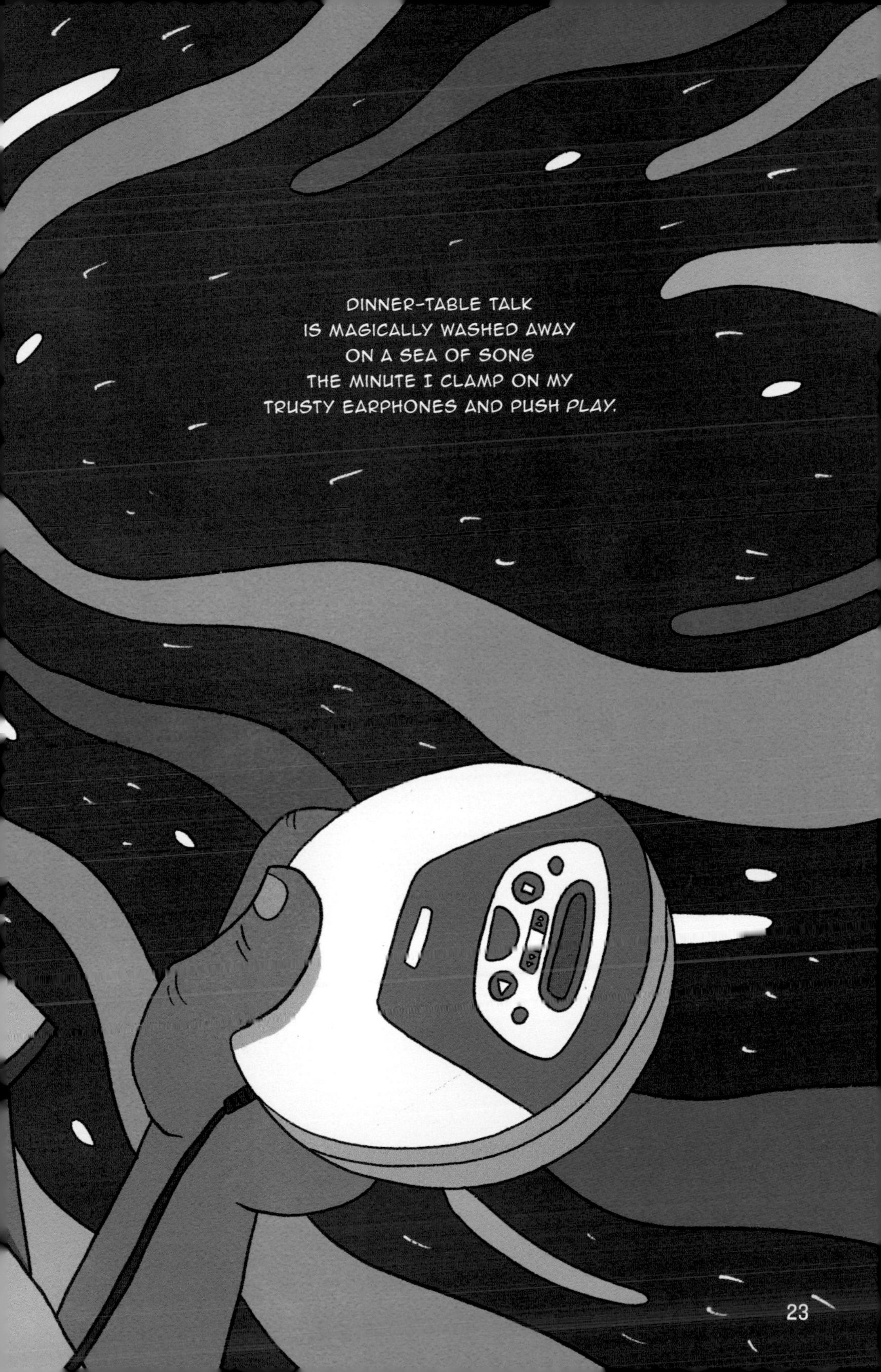
DINNER-TABLE TALK
IS MAGICALLY WASHED AWAY
ON A SEA OF SONG
THE MINUTE I CLAMP ON MY
TRUSTY EARPHONES AND PUSH *PLAY*.

RHYMES WITH HARVEY

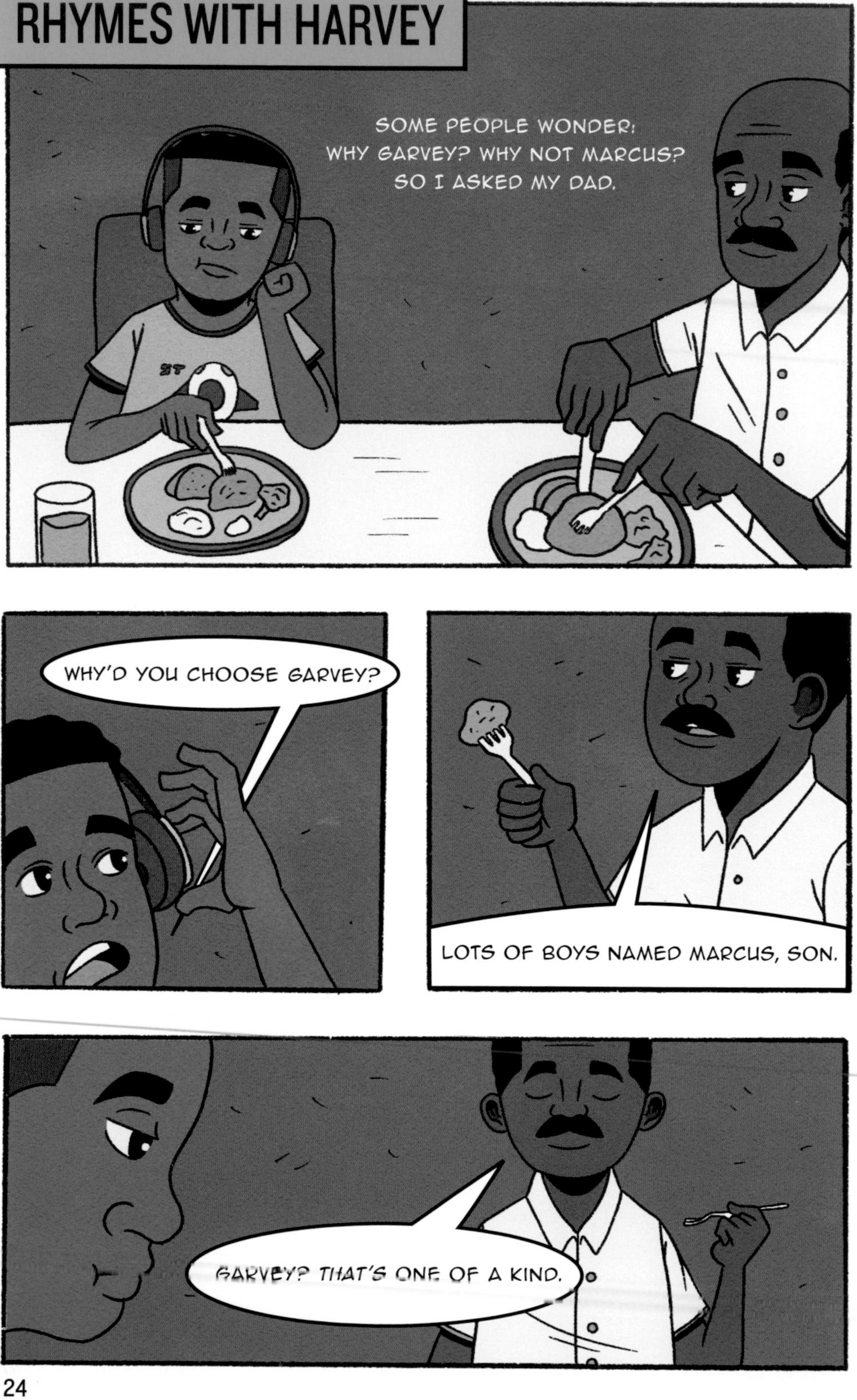
SOME PEOPLE WONDER:
WHY GARVEY? WHY NOT MARCUS?
SO I ASKED MY DAD.
WHY'D YOU CHOOSE GARVEY?
LOTS OF BOYS NAMED MARCUS, SON.
GARVEY? THAT'S ONE OF A KIND.

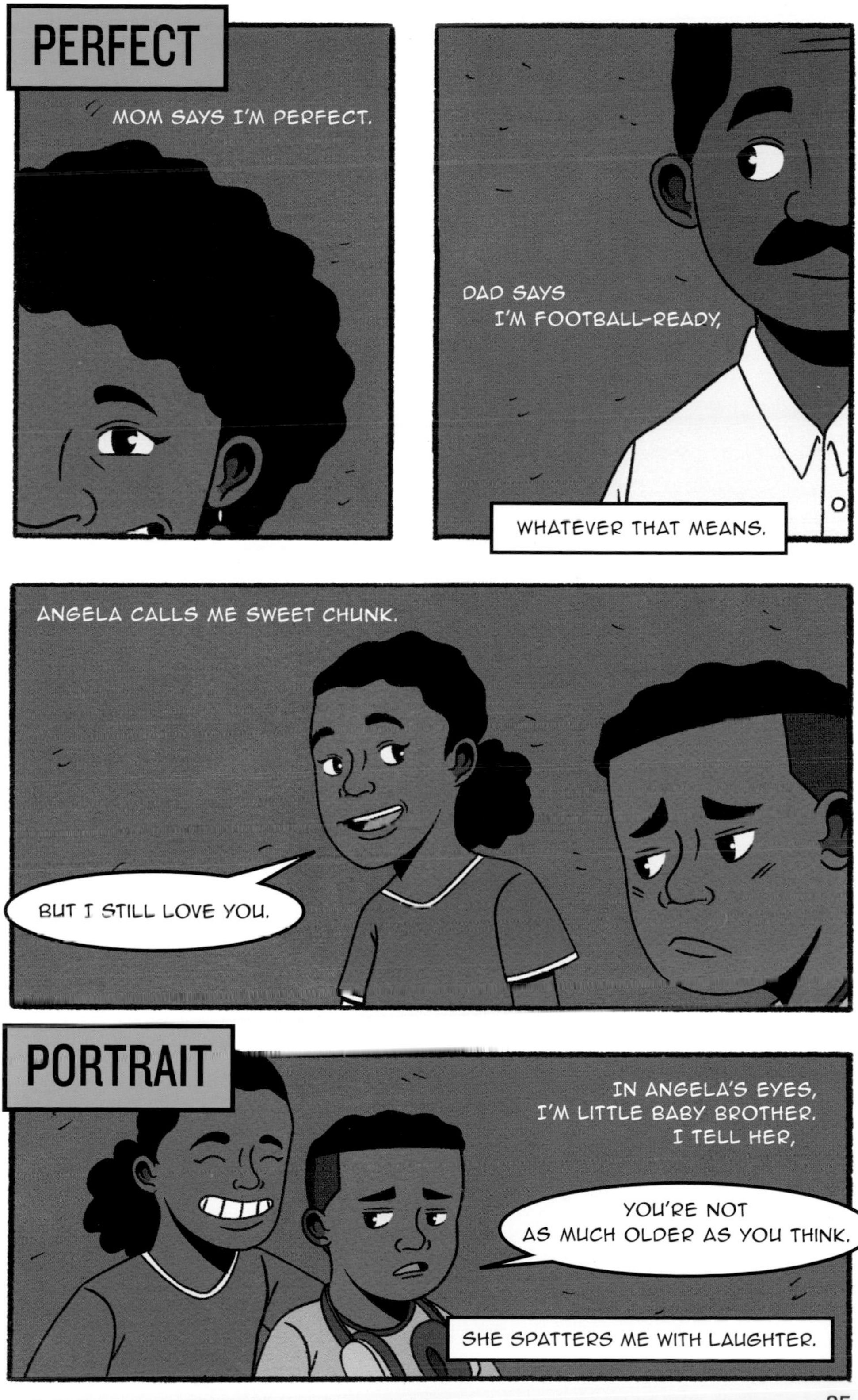
PERFECT
MOM SAYS I'M PERFECT.
DAD SAYS I'M FOOTBALL-READY,
WHATEVER THAT MEANS.
ANGELA CALLS ME SWEET CHUNK.
BUT I STILL LOVE YOU.
PORTRAIT
IN ANGELA'S EYES, I'M LITTLE BABY BROTHER. I TELL HER,
YOU'RE NOT AS MUCH OLDER AS YOU THINK.
SHE SPATTERS ME WITH LAUGHTER.

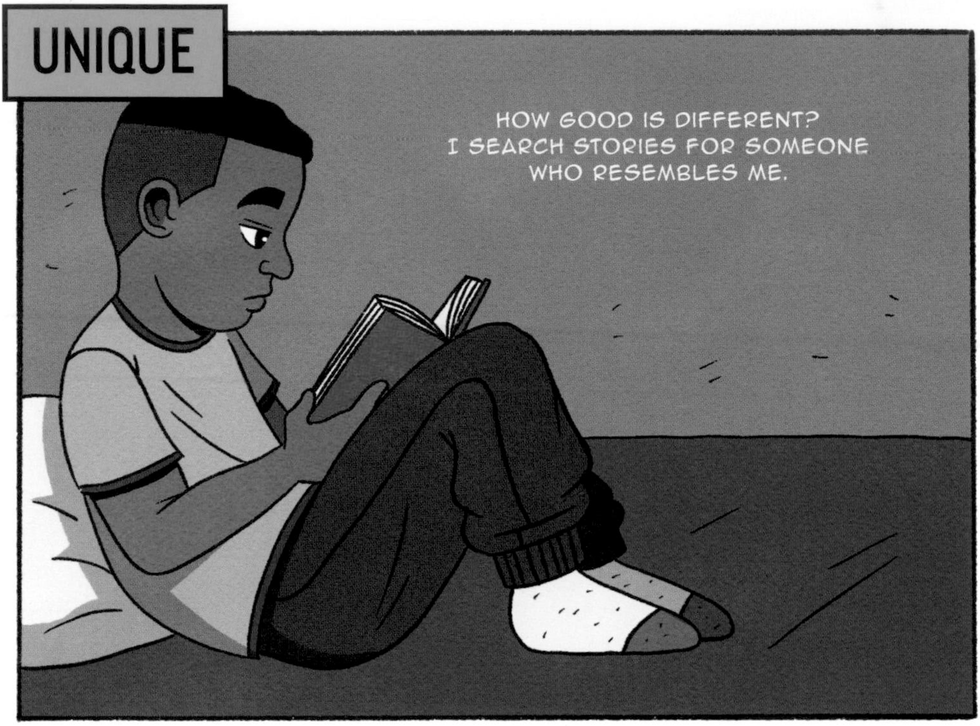
UNIQUE
HOW GOOD IS DIFFERENT? I SEARCH STORIES FOR SOMEONE WHO RESEMBLES ME.

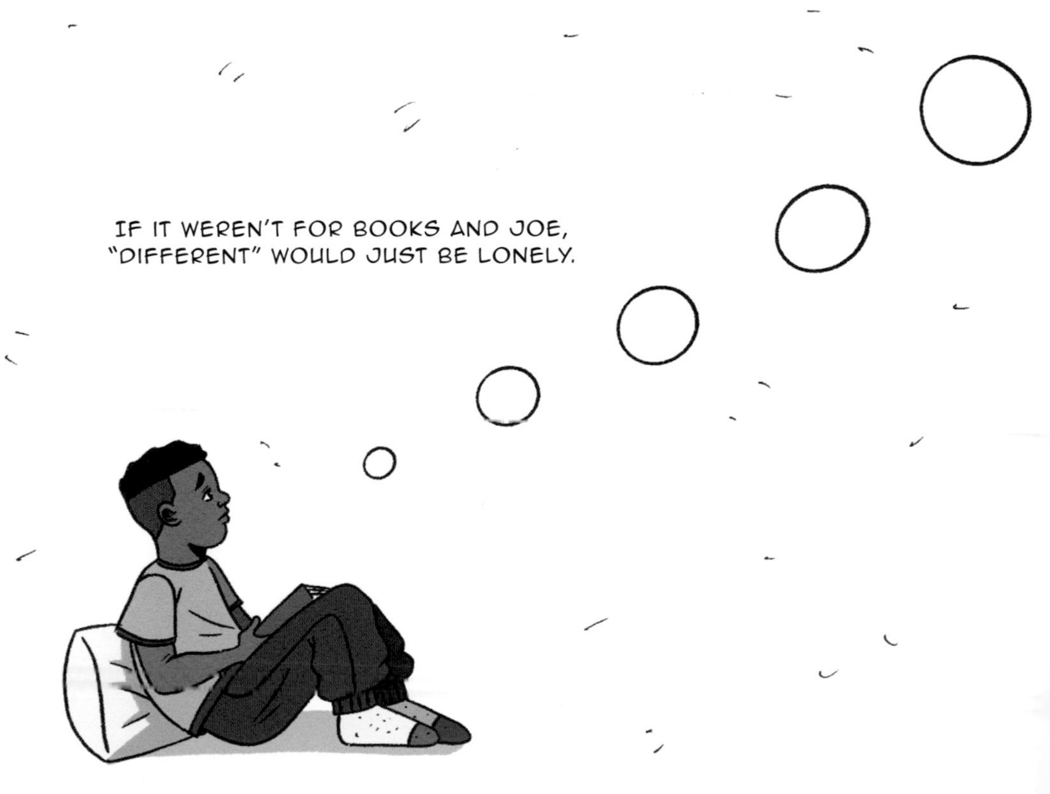
IF IT WEREN'T FOR BOOKS AND JOE, "DIFFERENT" WOULD JUST BE LONELY.

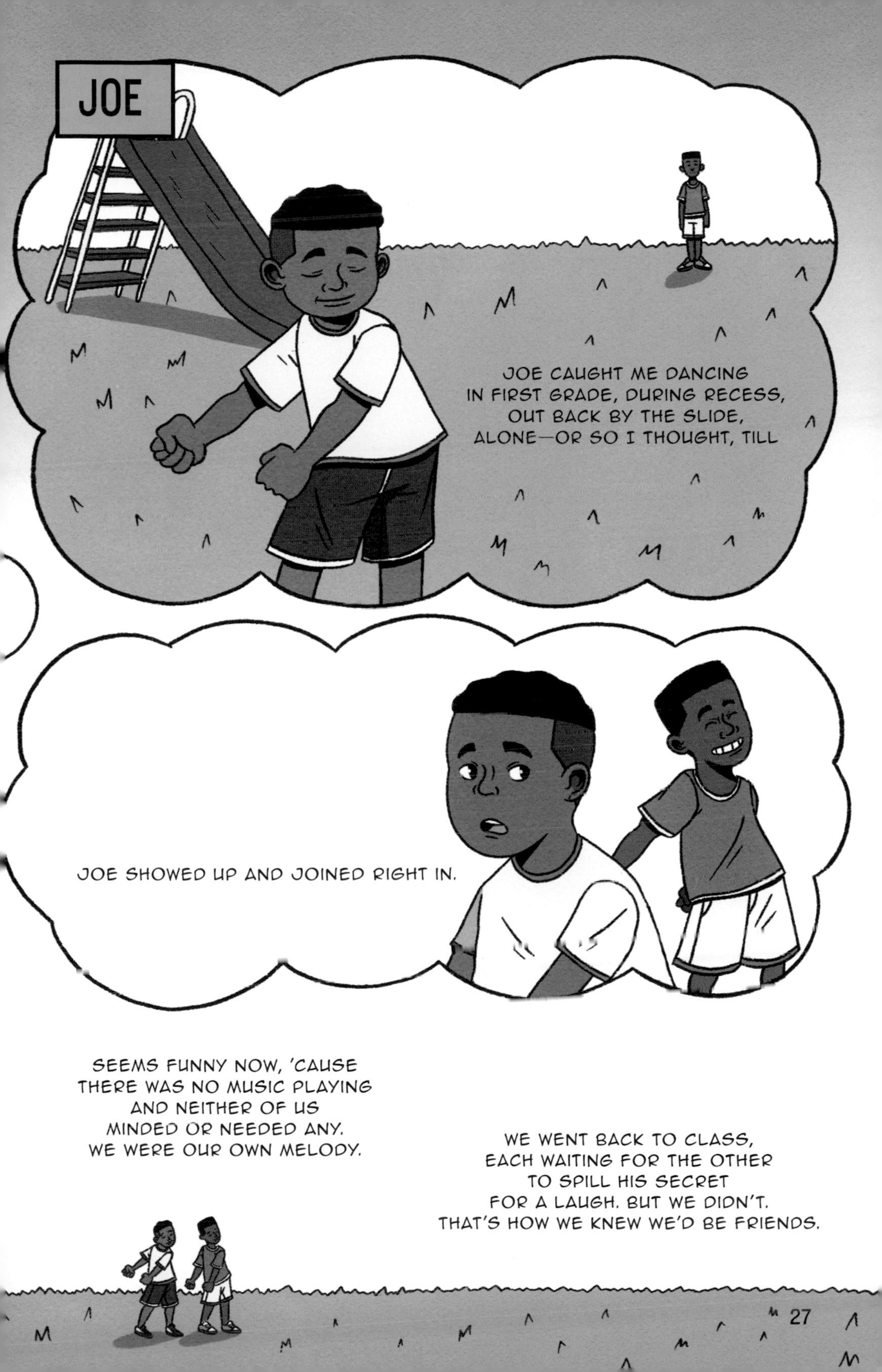
JOE
JOE CAUGHT ME DANCING IN FIRST GRADE, DURING RECESS, OUT BACK BY THE SLIDE, ALONE—OR SO I THOUGHT, TILL
JOE SHOWED UP AND JOINED RIGHT IN.
SEEMS FUNNY NOW, 'CAUSE THERE WAS NO MUSIC PLAYING AND NEITHER OF US MINDED OR NEEDED ANY. WE WERE OUR OWN MELODY.
WE WENT BACK TO CLASS, EACH WAITING FOR THE OTHER TO SPILL HIS SECRET FOR A LAUGH. BUT WE DIDN'T. THAT'S HOW WE KNEW WE'D BE FRIENDS.

BEST FRIEND

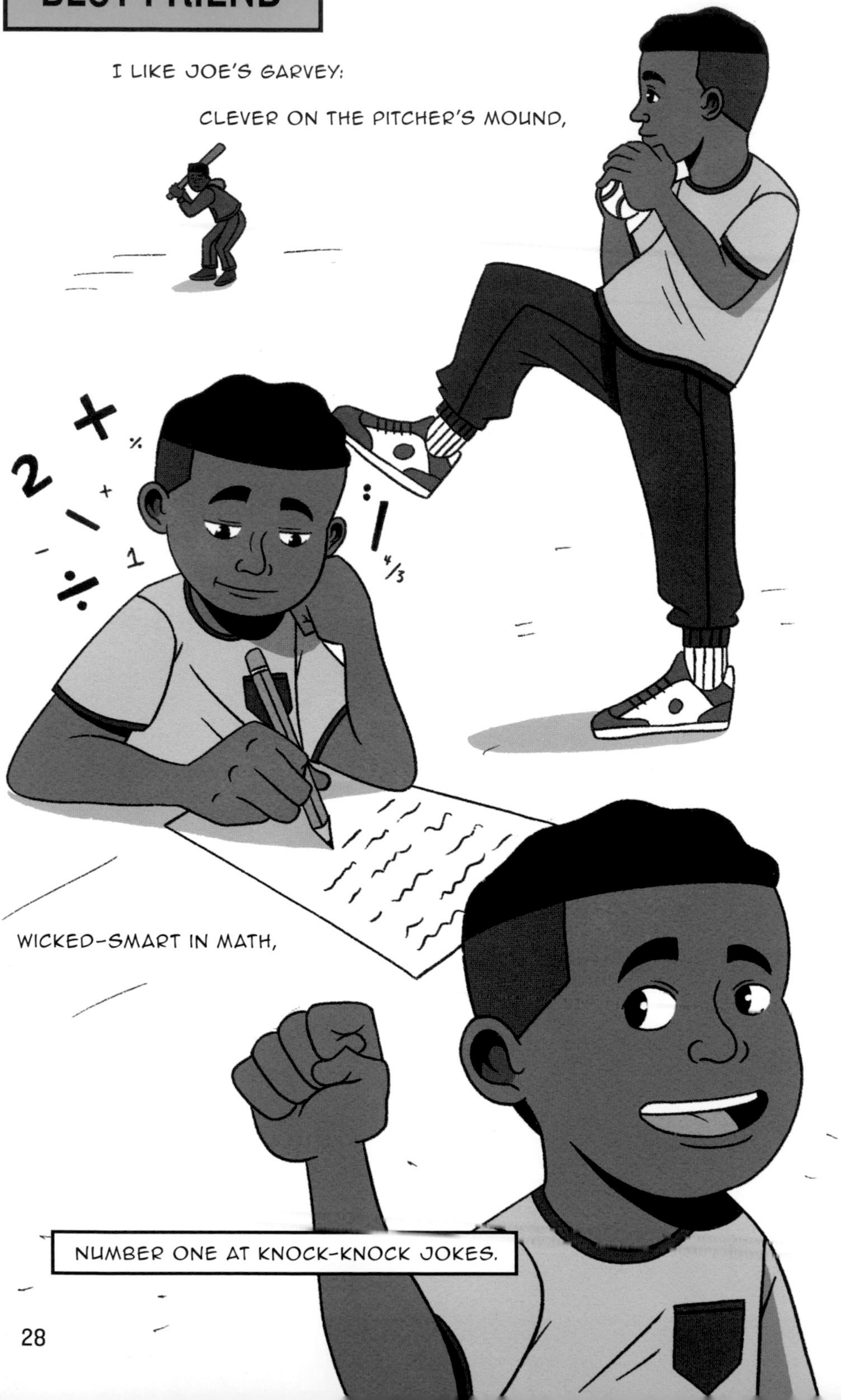
I LIKE JOE'S GARVEY:
CLEVER ON THE PITCHER'S MOUND,
WICKED-SMART IN MATH,
NUMBER ONE AT KNOCK-KNOCK JOKES.

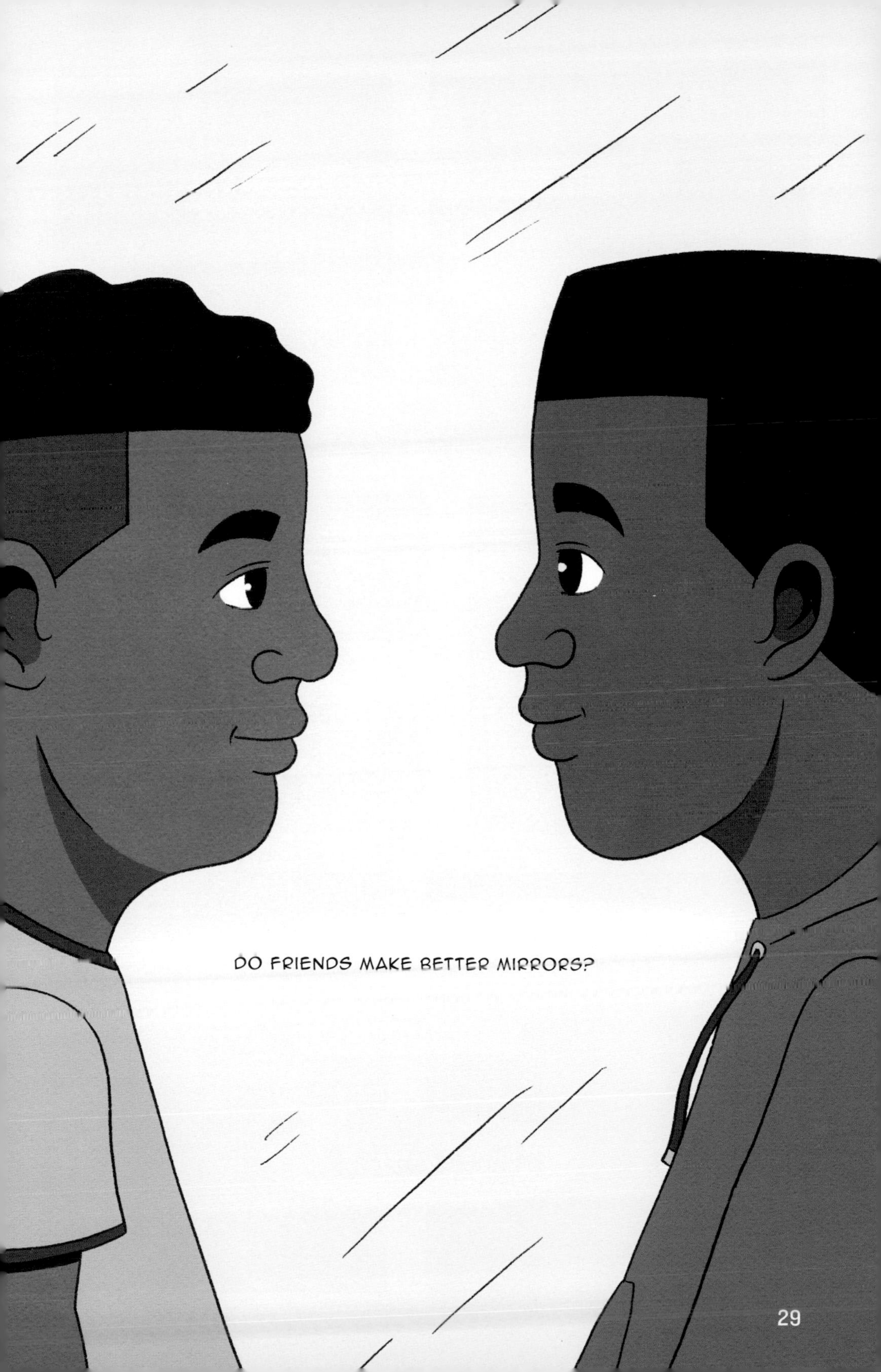
DO FRIENDS MAKE BETTER MIRRORS?

KNOCK-KNOCK

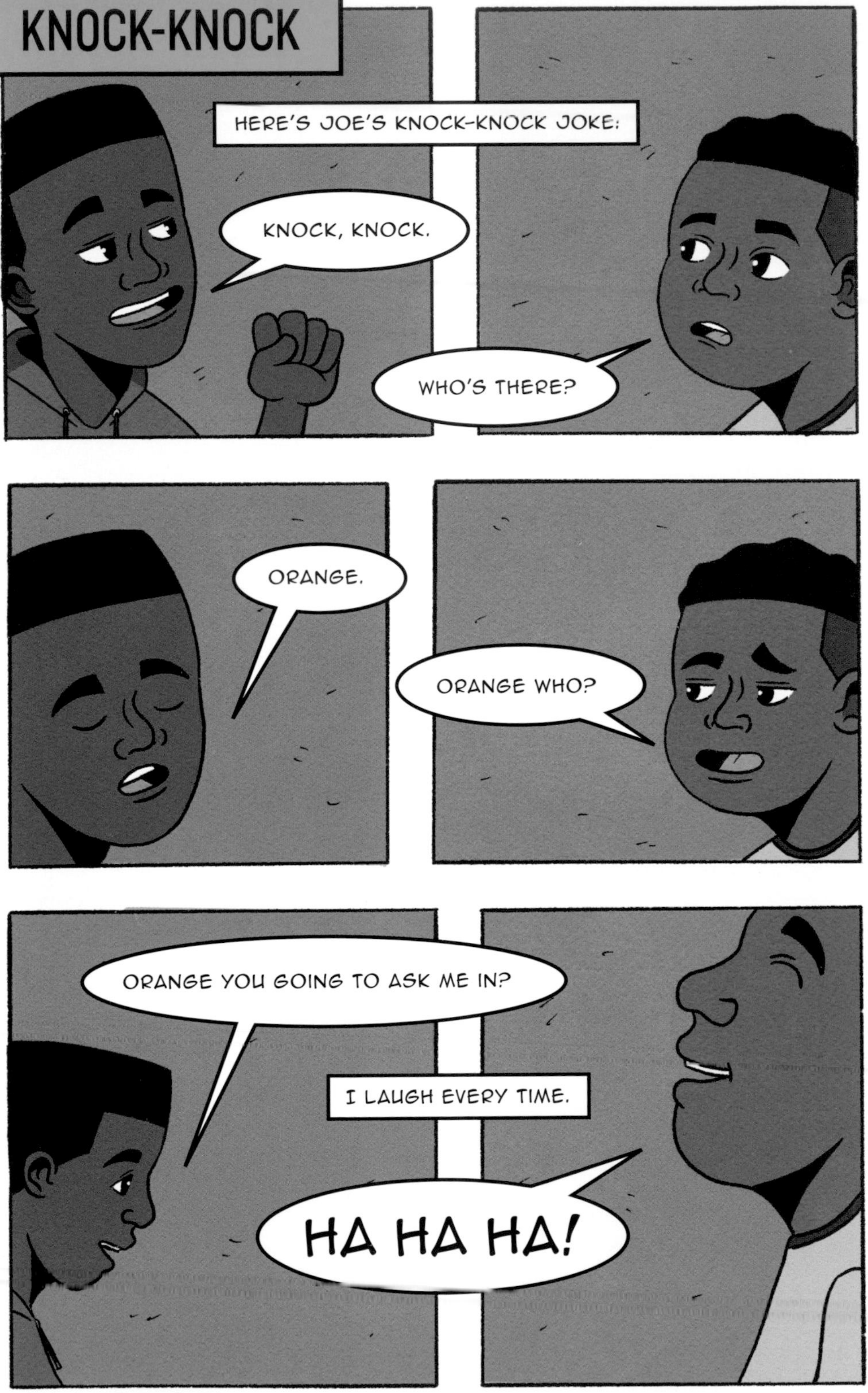
HERE'S JOE'S KNOCK-KNOCK JOKE:
KNOCK, KNOCK.
WHO'S THERE?
ORANGE.
ORANGE WHO?
ORANGE YOU GOING TO ASK ME IN?
I LAUGH EVERY TIME.
HA HA HA!

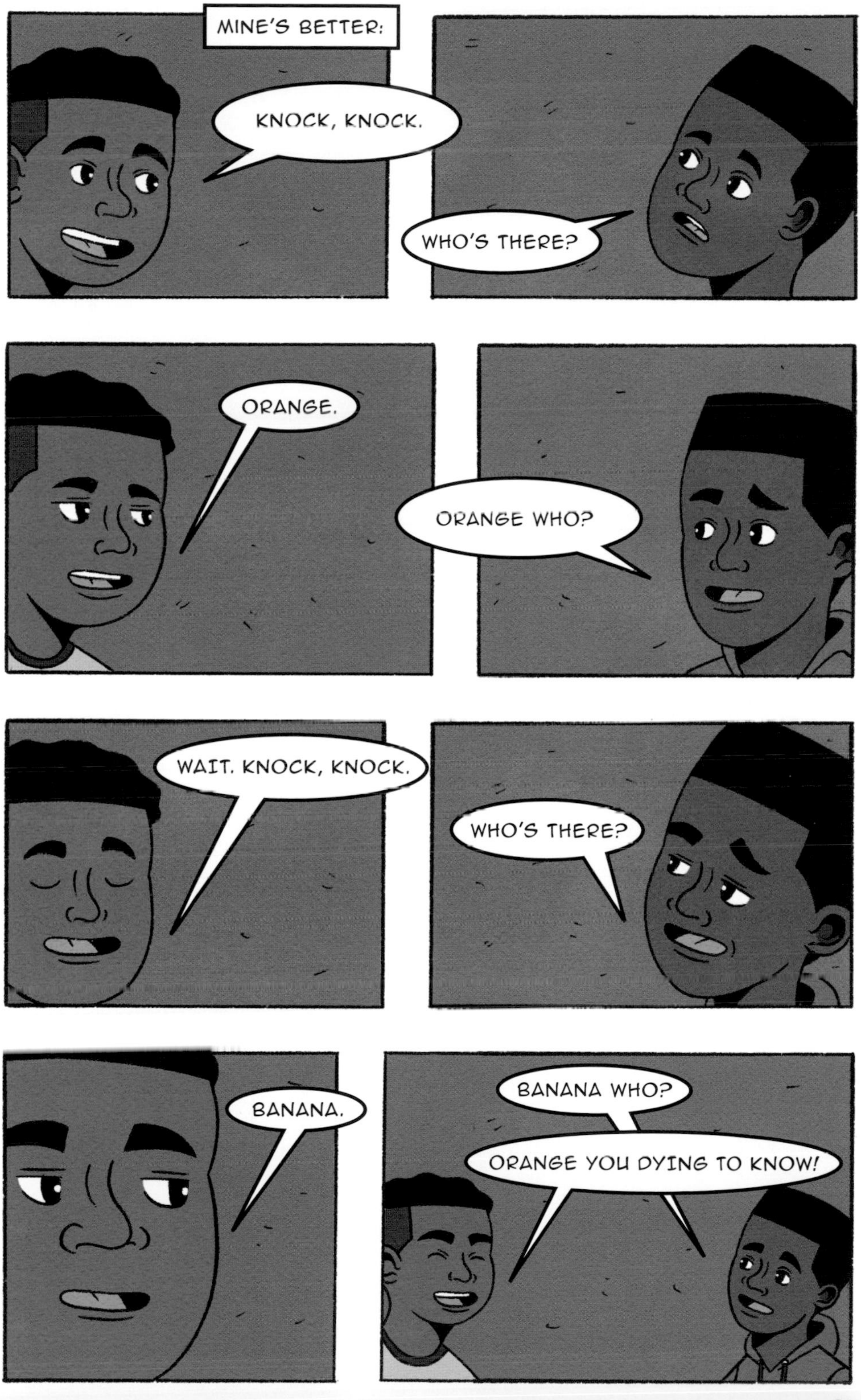
MINE'S BETTER:
KNOCK, KNOCK.
WHO'S THERE?
ORANGE.
ORANGE WHO?
WAIT. KNOCK, KNOCK.
WHO'S THERE?
BANANA.
BANANA WHO?
ORANGE YOU DYING TO KNOW!

ME AND JOE

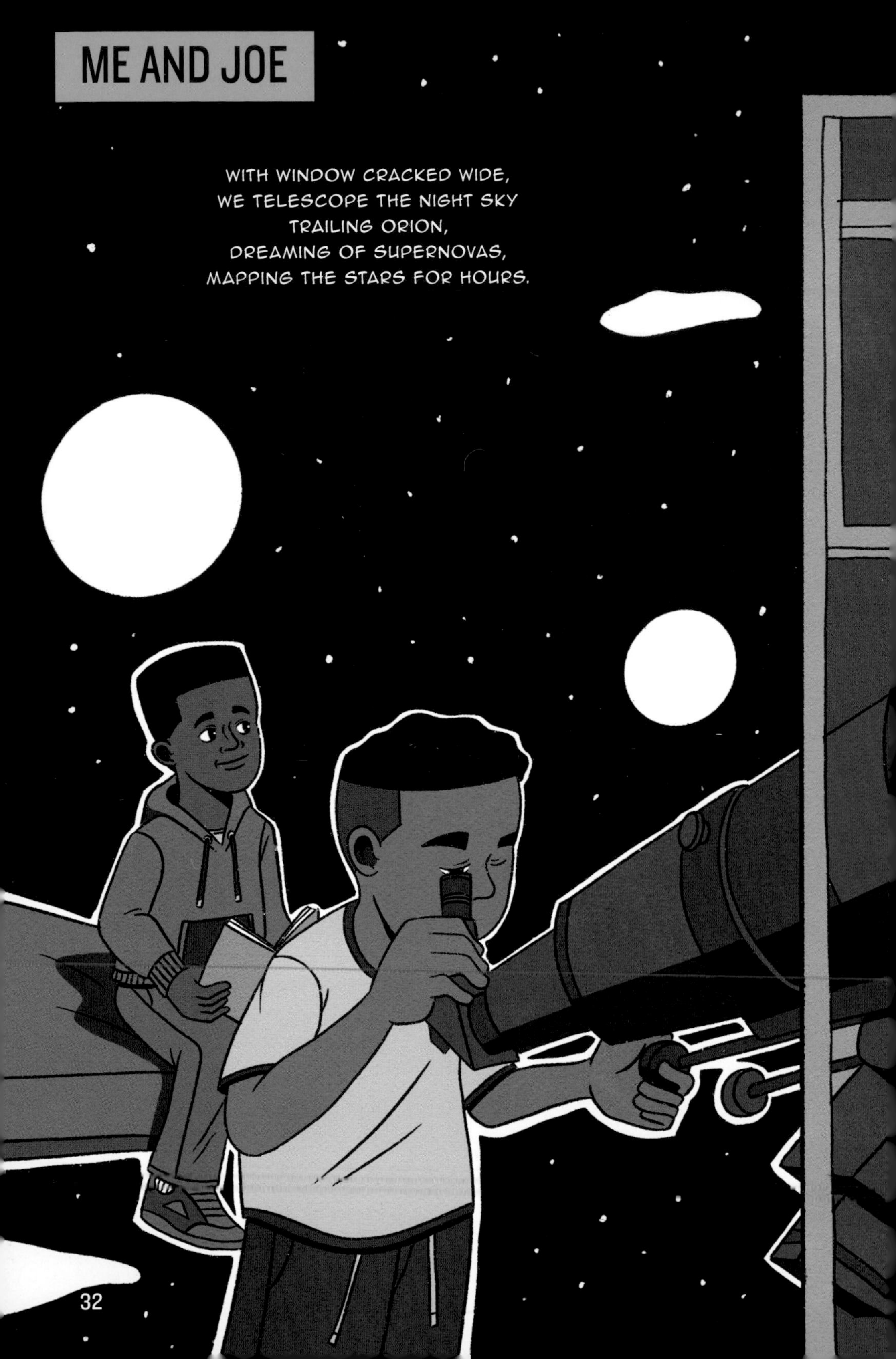
WITH WINDOW CRACKED WIDE,
WE TELESCOPE THE NIGHT SKY
TRAILING ORION,
DREAMING OF SUPERNOVAS,
MAPPING THE STARS FOR HOURS.

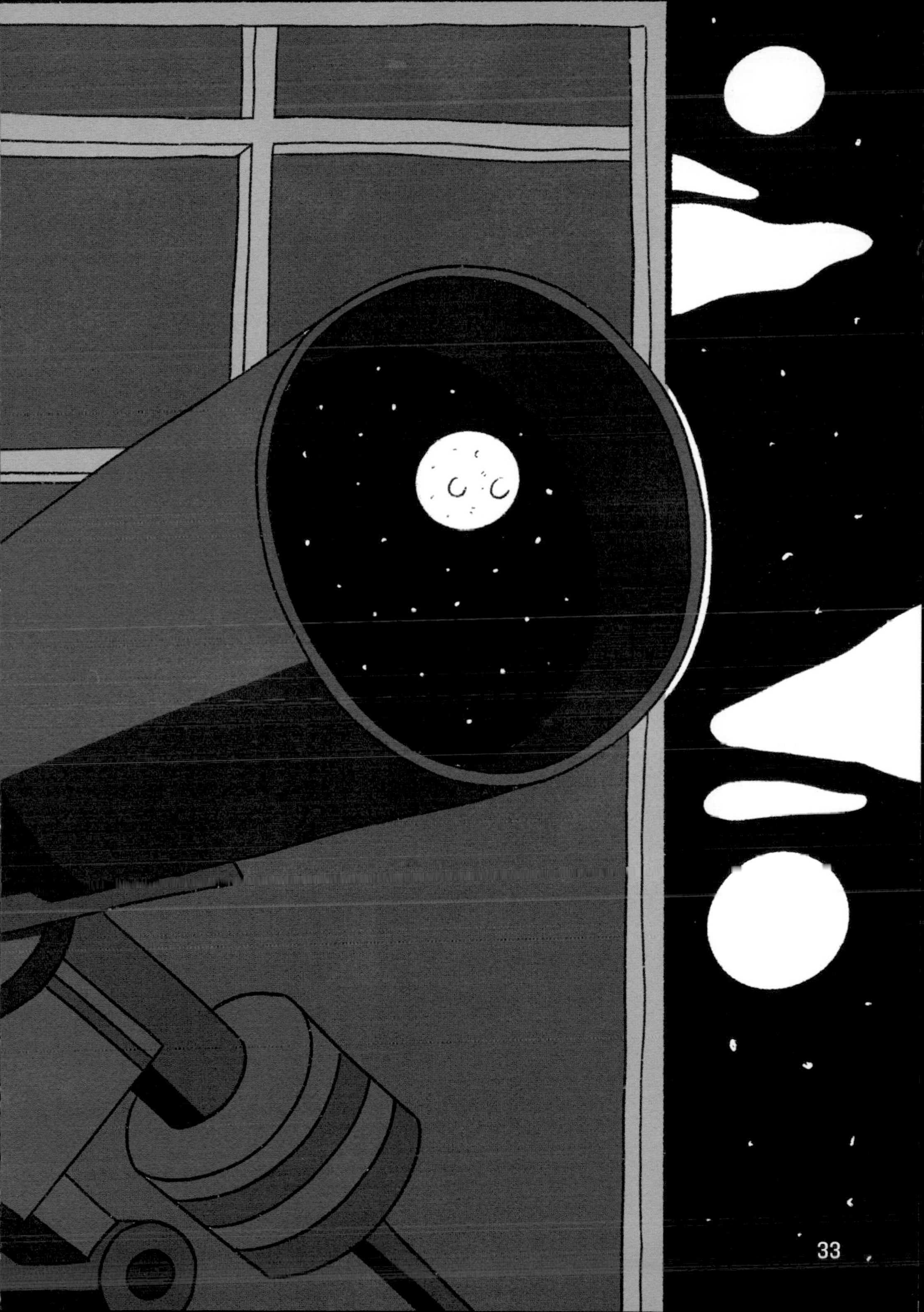

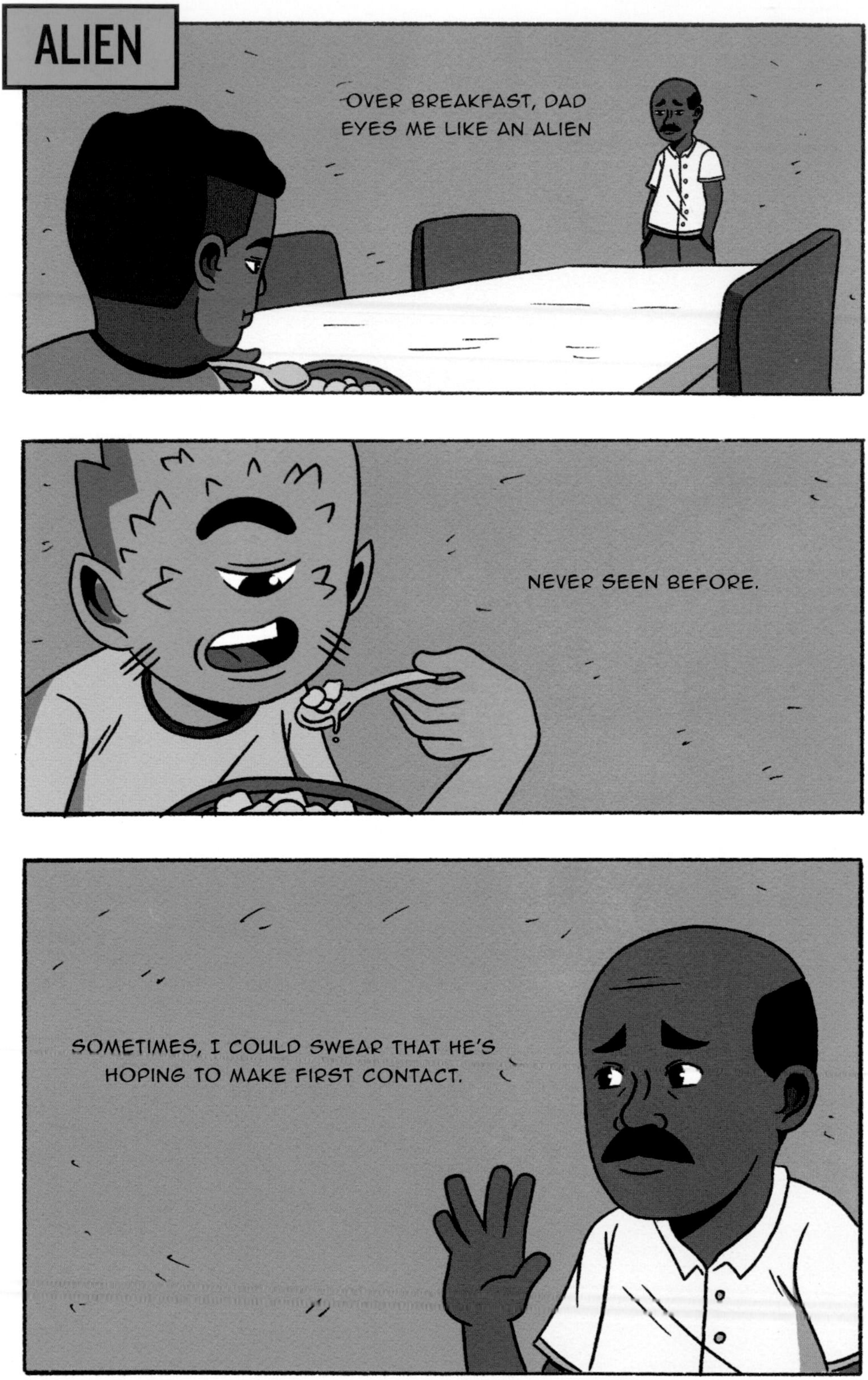
ALIEN
OVER BREAKFAST, DAD EYES ME LIKE AN ALIEN
NEVER SEEN BEFORE.
SOMETIMES, I COULD SWEAR THAT HE'S HOPING TO MAKE FIRST CONTACT.

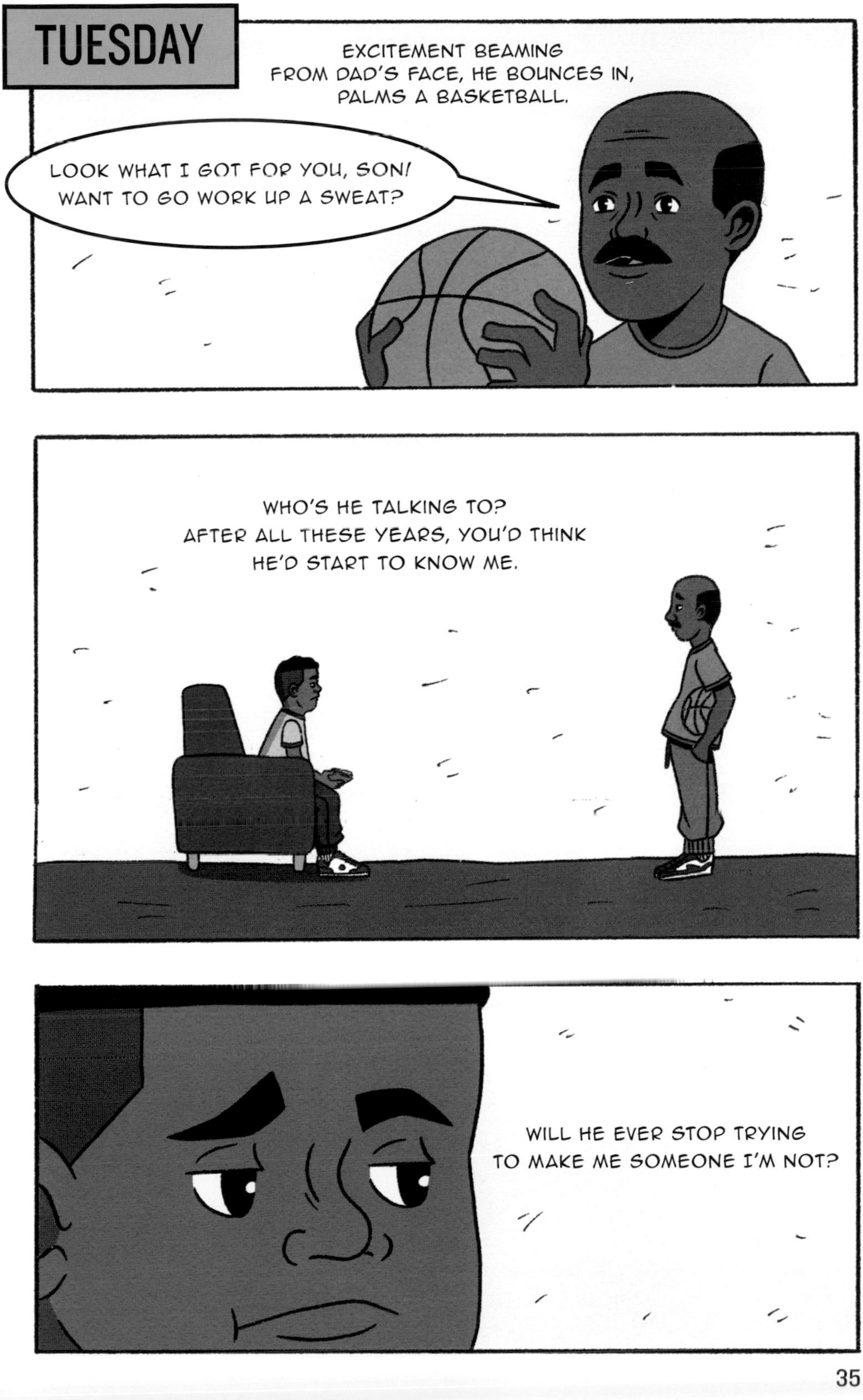
TUESDAY
EXCITEMENT BEAMING FROM DAD'S FACE, HE BOUNCES IN, PALMS A BASKETBALL.
LOOK WHAT I GOT FOR YOU, SON! WANT TO GO WORK UP A SWEAT?
WHO'S HE TALKING TO? AFTER ALL THESE YEARS, YOU'D THINK HE'D START TO KNOW ME.
WILL HE EVER STOP TRYING TO MAKE ME SOMEONE I'M NOT?

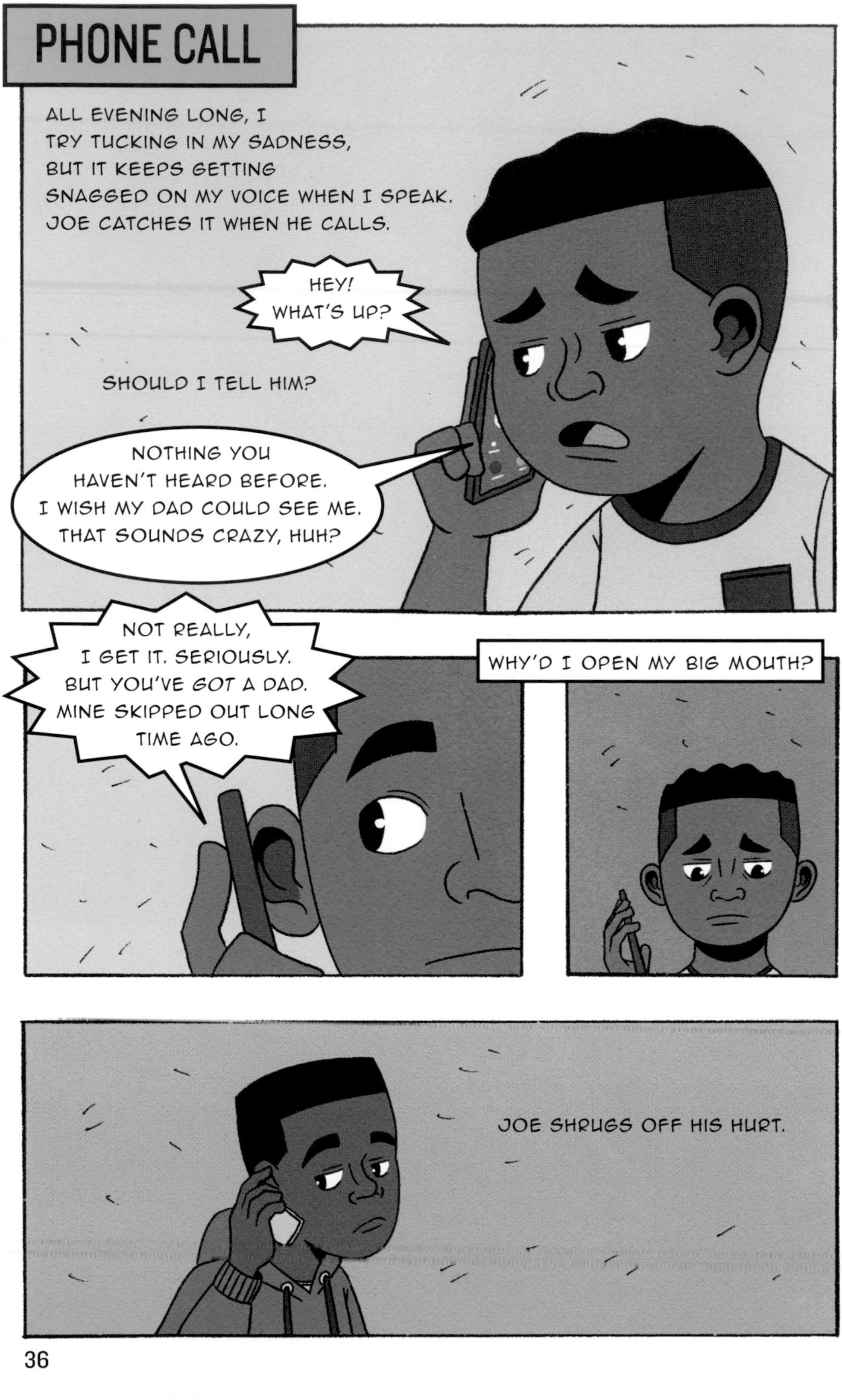
PHONE CALL
ALL EVENING LONG, I TRY TUCKING IN MY SADNESS, BUT IT KEEPS GETTING SNAGGED ON MY VOICE WHEN I SPEAK. JOE CATCHES IT WHEN HE CALLS.
HEY! WHAT'S UP?
SHOULD I TELL HIM?
NOTHING YOU HAVEN'T HEARD BEFORE. I WISH MY DAD COULD SEE ME. THAT SOUNDS CRAZY, HUH?
NOT REALLY, I GET IT. SERIOUSLY. BUT YOU'VE *GOT* A DAD. MINE SKIPPED OUT LONG TIME AGO.
WHY'D I OPEN MY BIG MOUTH?
JOE SHRUGS OFF HIS HURT.

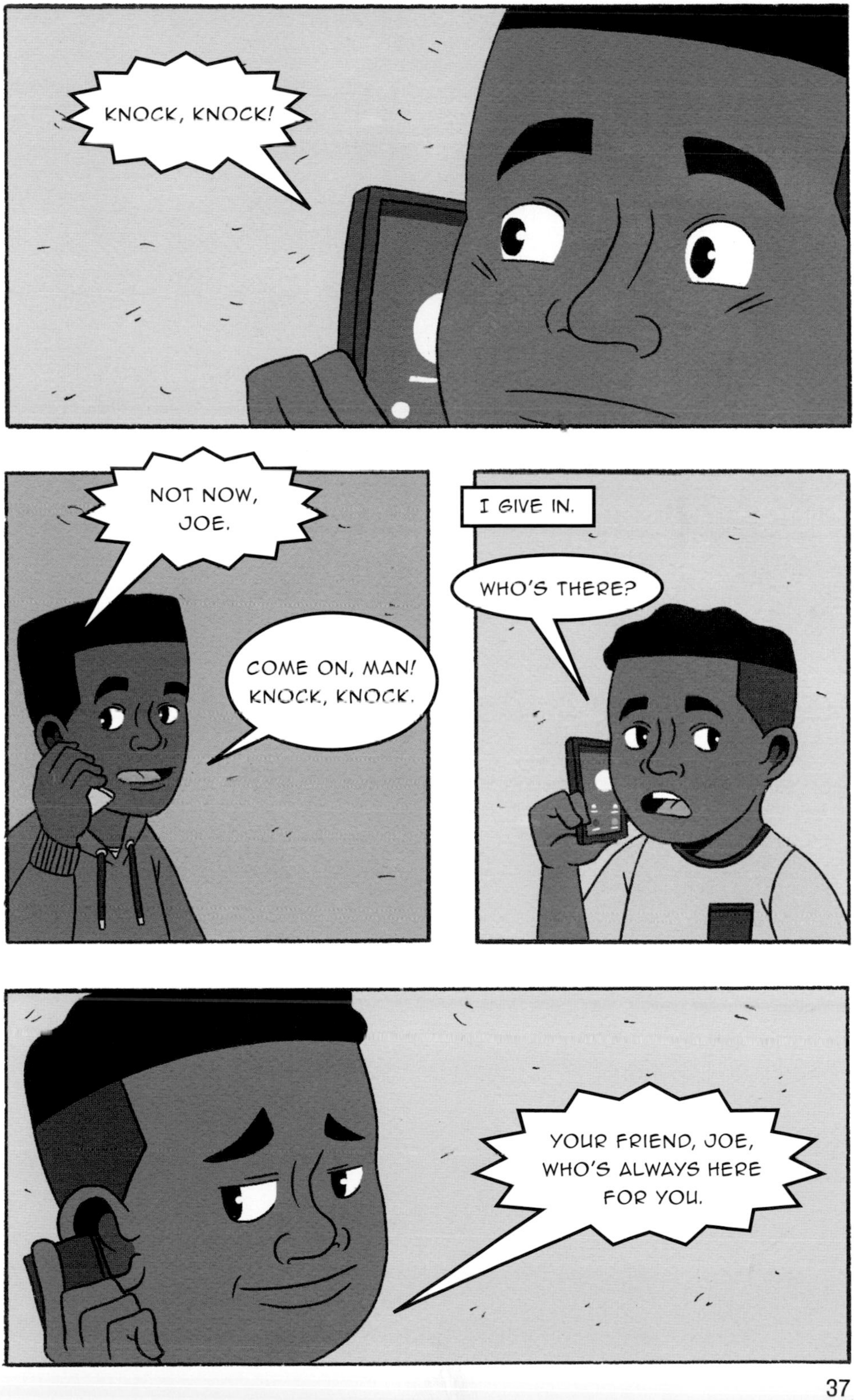
KNOCK, KNOCK!
NOT NOW, JOE.
COME ON, MAN! KNOCK, KNOCK.
I GIVE IN.
WHO'S THERE?
YOUR FRIEND, JOE, WHO'S ALWAYS HERE FOR YOU.

DANCE WITH MY FATHER

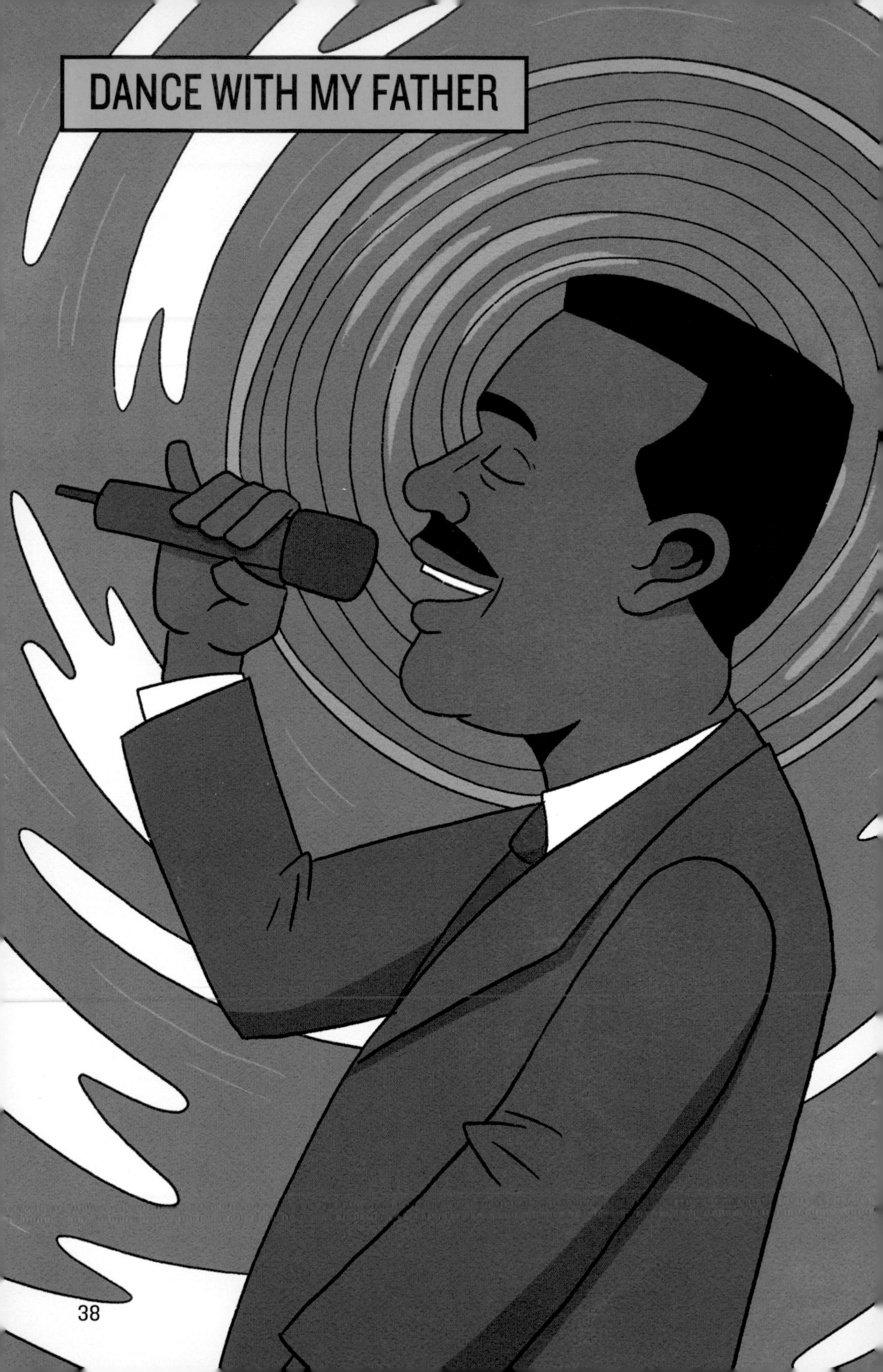

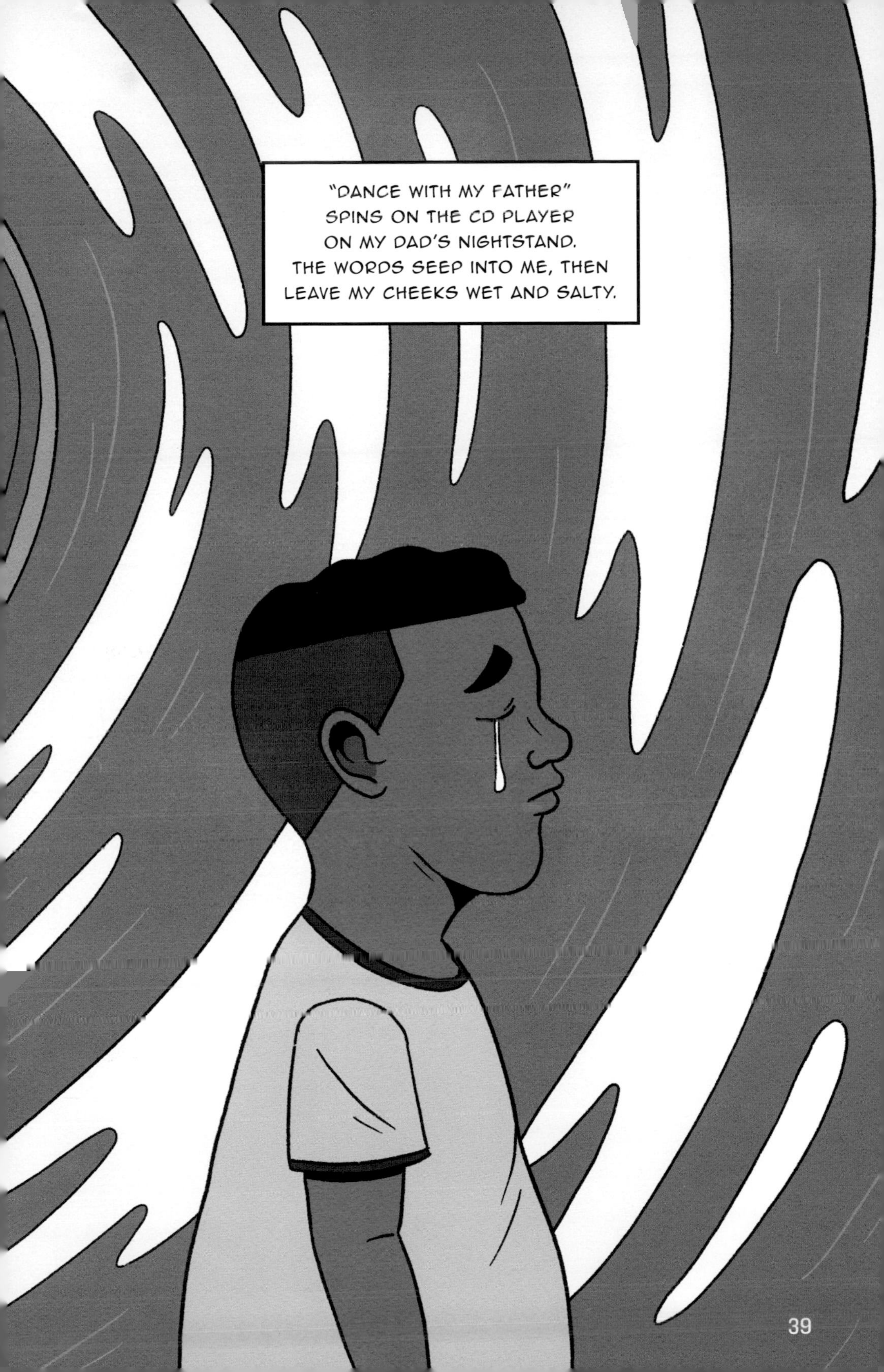
"DANCE WITH MY FATHER" SPINS ON THE CD PLAYER ON MY DAD'S NIGHTSTAND. THE WORDS SEEP INTO ME, THEN LEAVE MY CHEEKS WET AND SALTY.

SATURDAY PLAY

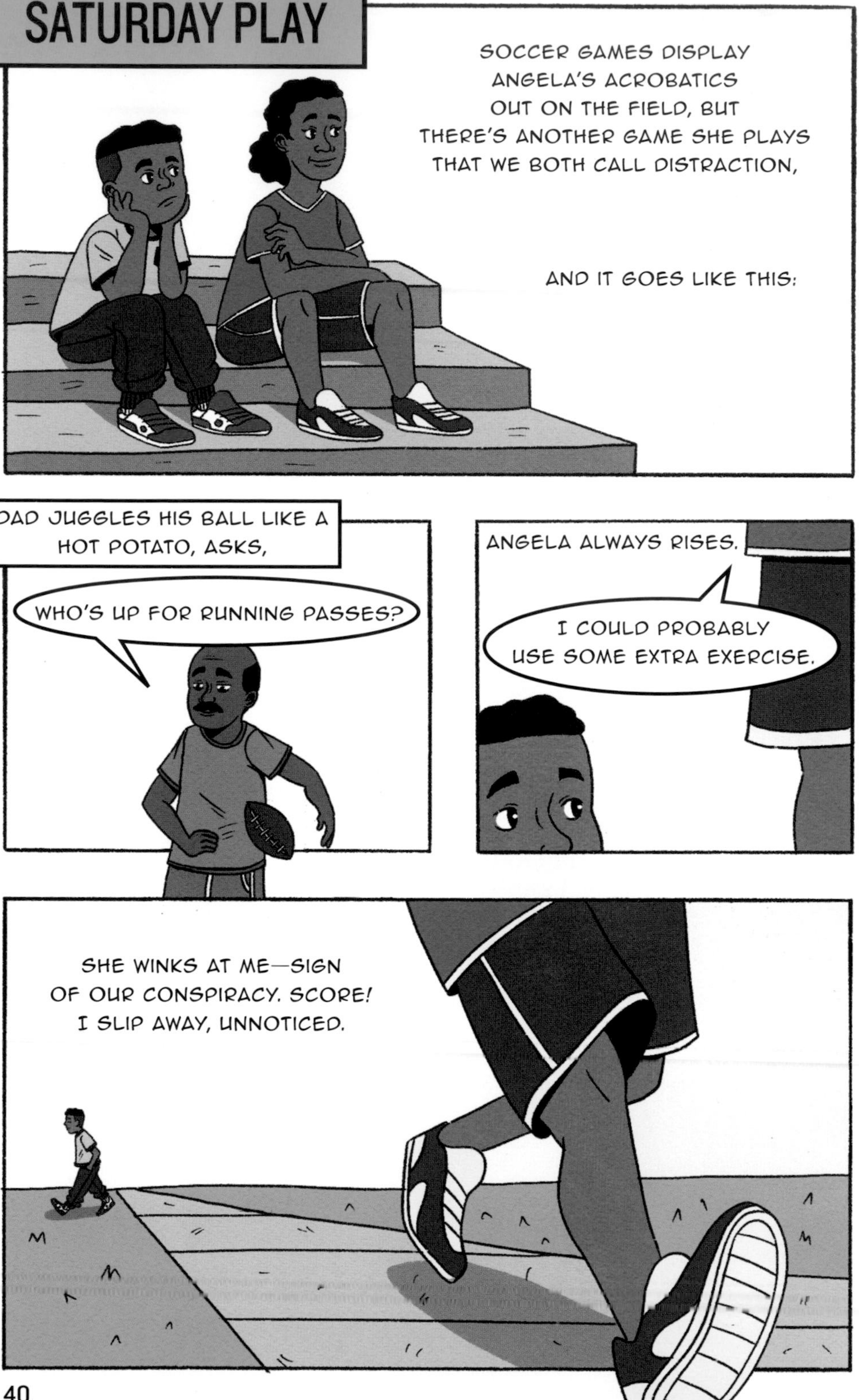
SOCCER GAMES DISPLAY
ANGELA'S ACROBATICS
OUT ON THE FIELD, BUT
THERE'S ANOTHER GAME SHE PLAYS
THAT WE BOTH CALL DISTRACTION,
AND IT GOES LIKE THIS:
DAD JUGGLES HIS BALL LIKE A HOT POTATO, ASKS,
WHO'S UP FOR RUNNING PASSES?
ANGELA ALWAYS RISES.
I COULD PROBABLY USE SOME EXTRA EXERCISE.
SHE WINKS AT ME—SIGN
OF OUR CONSPIRACY. SCORE!
I SLIP AWAY, UNNOTICED.

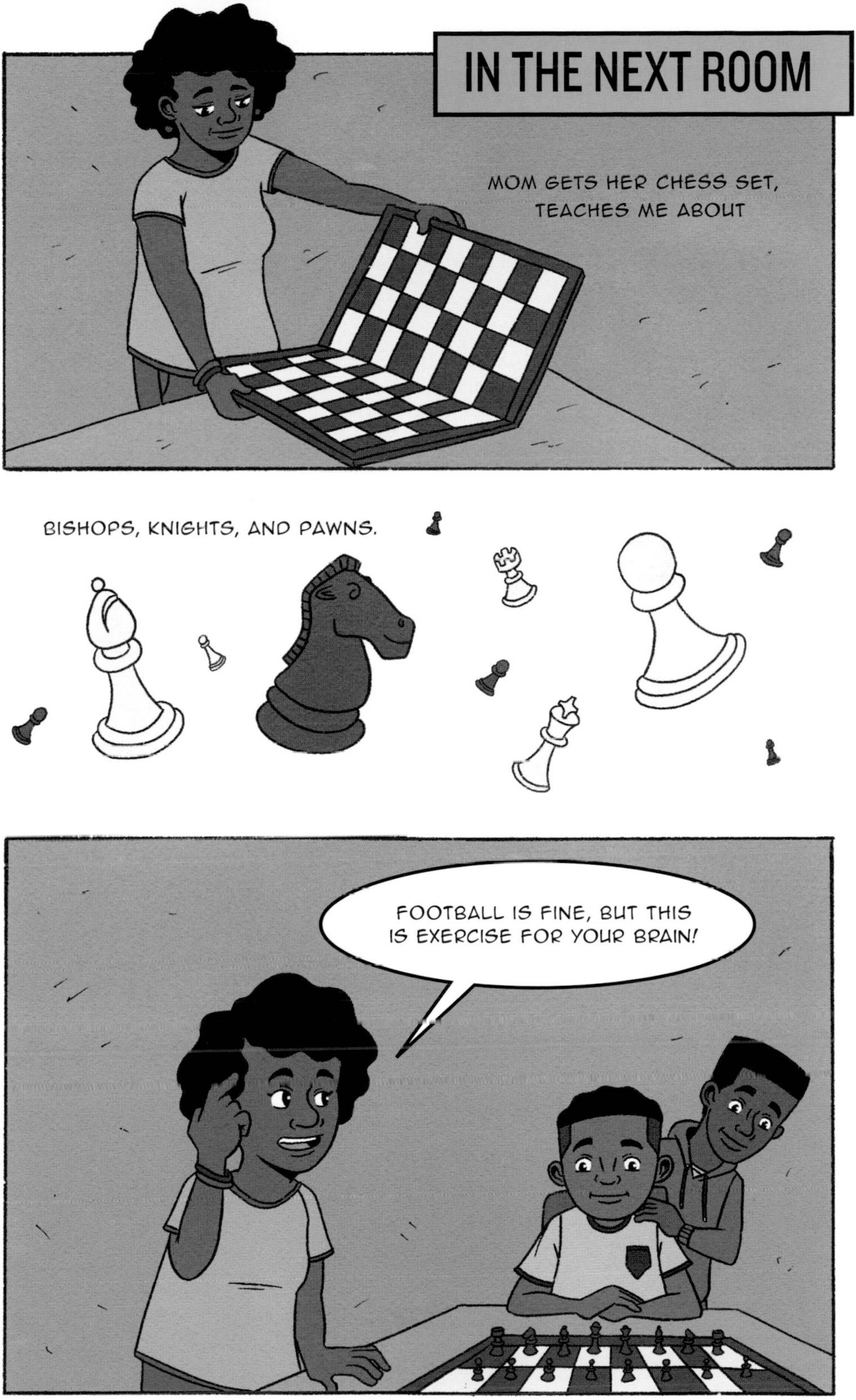
IN THE NEXT ROOM
MOM GETS HER CHESS SET, TEACHES ME ABOUT
BISHOPS, KNIGHTS, AND PAWNS.
FOOTBALL IS FINE, BUT THIS IS EXERCISE FOR YOUR BRAIN!

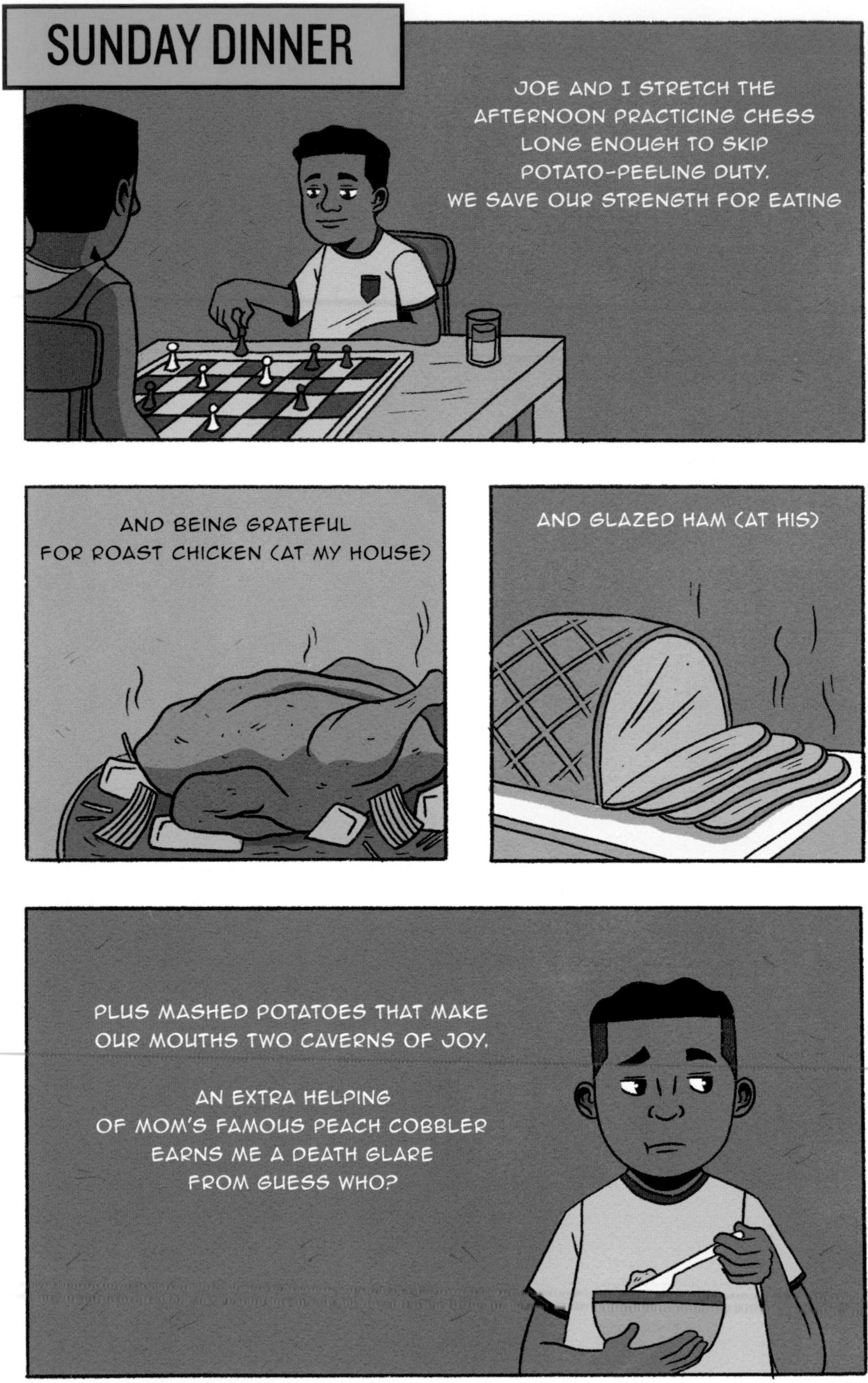
SUNDAY DINNER
JOE AND I STRETCH THE AFTERNOON PRACTICING CHESS LONG ENOUGH TO SKIP POTATO-PEELING DUTY. WE SAVE OUR STRENGTH FOR EATING
AND BEING GRATEFUL FOR ROAST CHICKEN (AT MY HOUSE)
AND GLAZED HAM (AT HIS)
PLUS MASHED POTATOES THAT MAKE OUR MOUTHS TWO CAVERNS OF JOY.
AN EXTRA HELPING OF MOM'S FAMOUS PEACH COBBLER EARNS ME A DEATH GLARE FROM GUESS WHO?

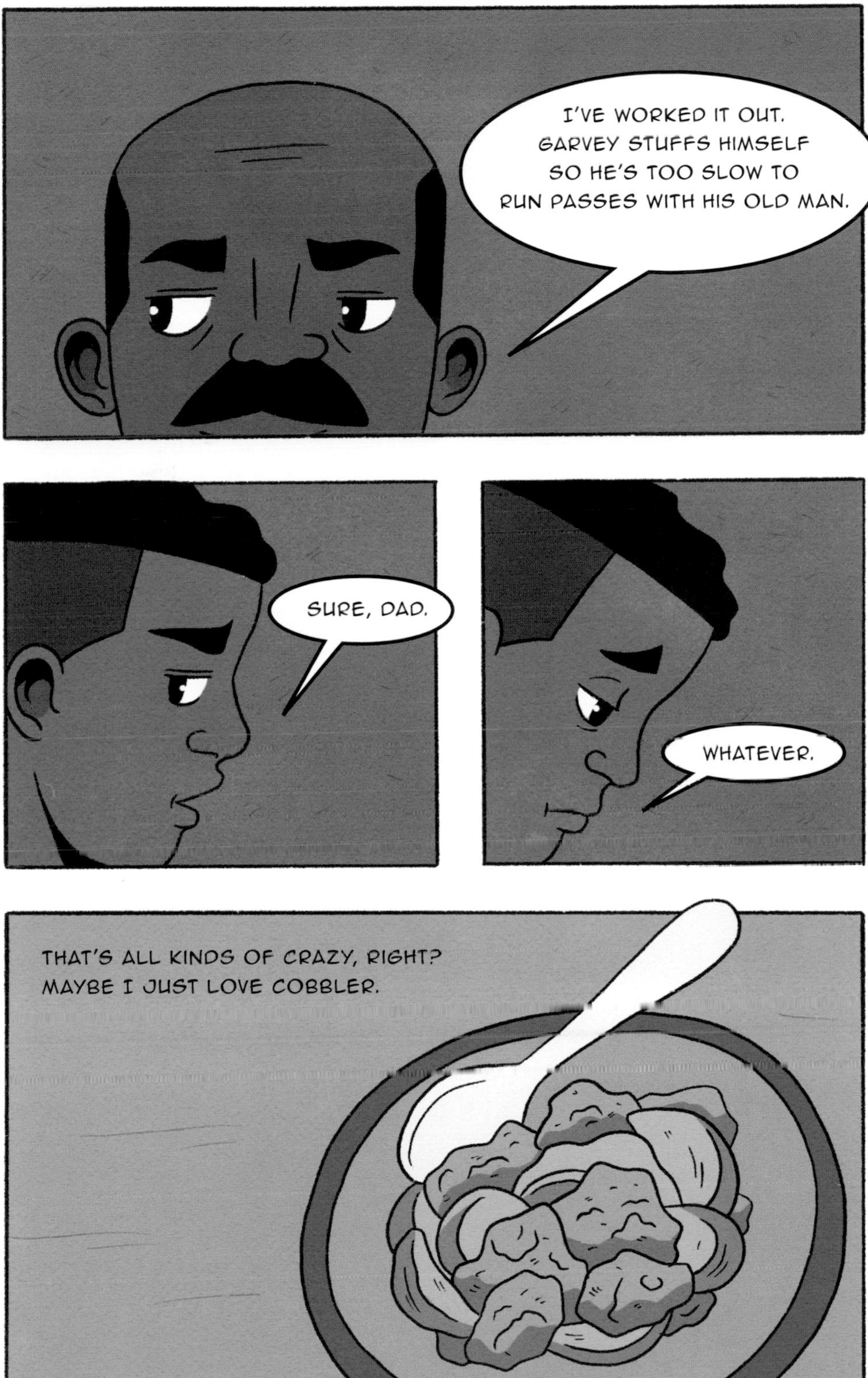
I'VE WORKED IT OUT. GARVEY STUFFS HIMSELF SO HE'S TOO SLOW TO RUN PASSES WITH HIS OLD MAN.
SURE, DAD.
WHATEVER.
THAT'S ALL KINDS OF CRAZY, RIGHT? MAYBE I JUST LOVE COBBLER.

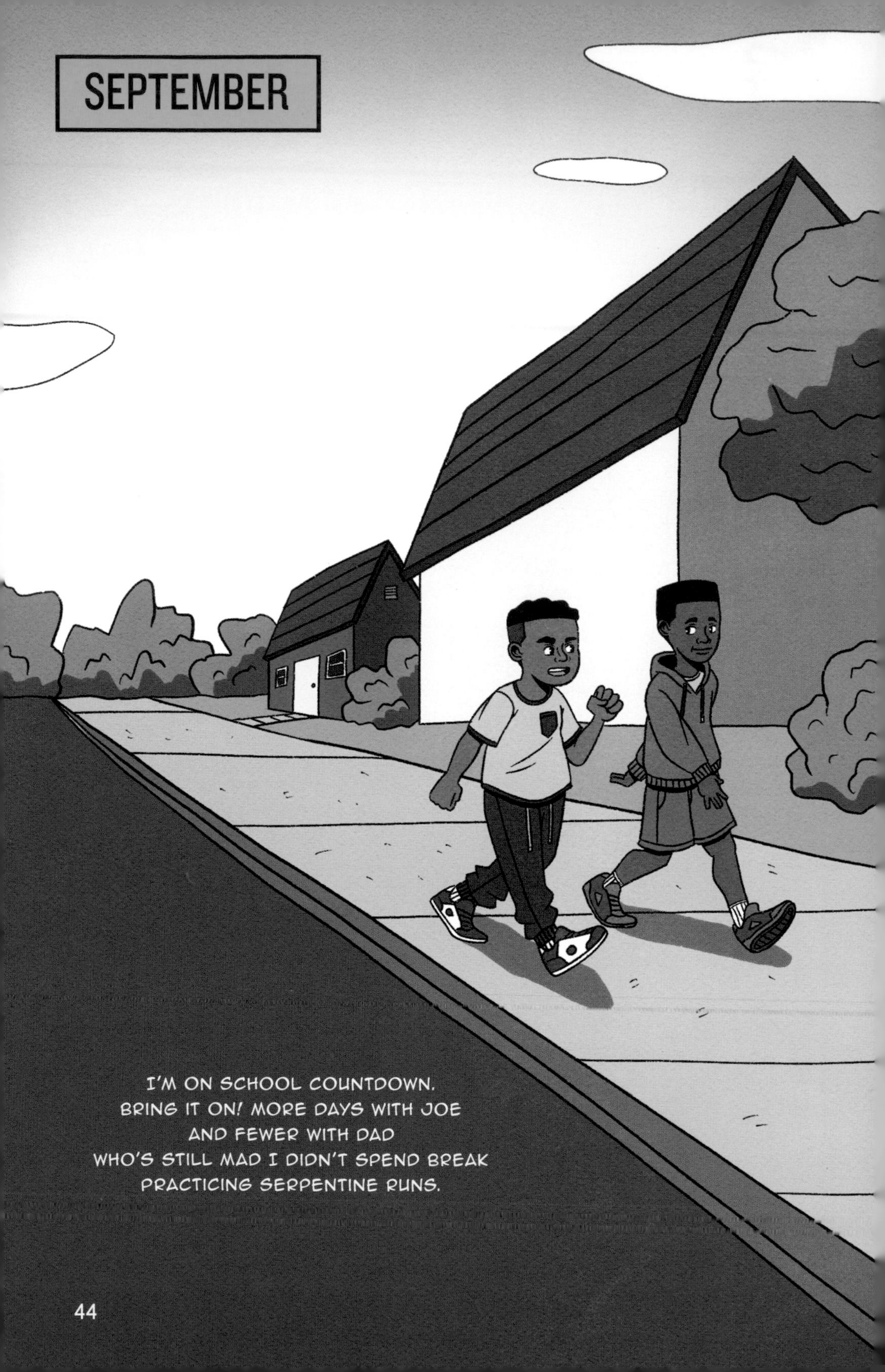
SEPTEMBER
I'M ON SCHOOL COUNTDOWN.
BRING IT ON! MORE DAYS WITH JOE
AND FEWER WITH DAD
WHO'S STILL MAD I DIDN'T SPEND BREAK
PRACTICING SERPENTINE RUNS.

CHECKMATE

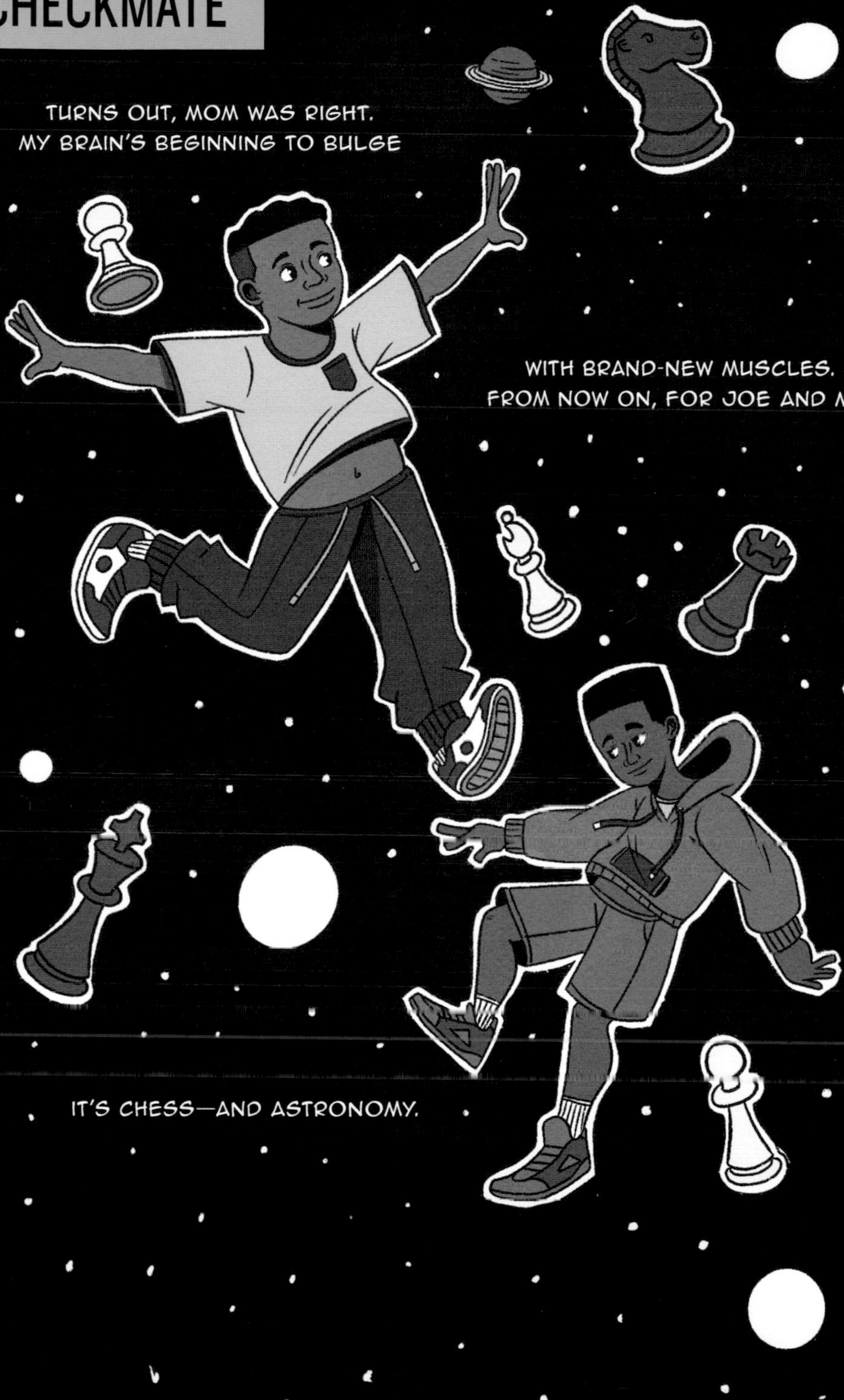

TURNS OUT, MOM WAS RIGHT.
MY BRAIN'S BEGINNING TO BULGE

WITH BRAND-NEW MUSCLES.
FROM NOW ON, FOR JOE AND ME,

IT'S CHESS—AND ASTRONOMY.

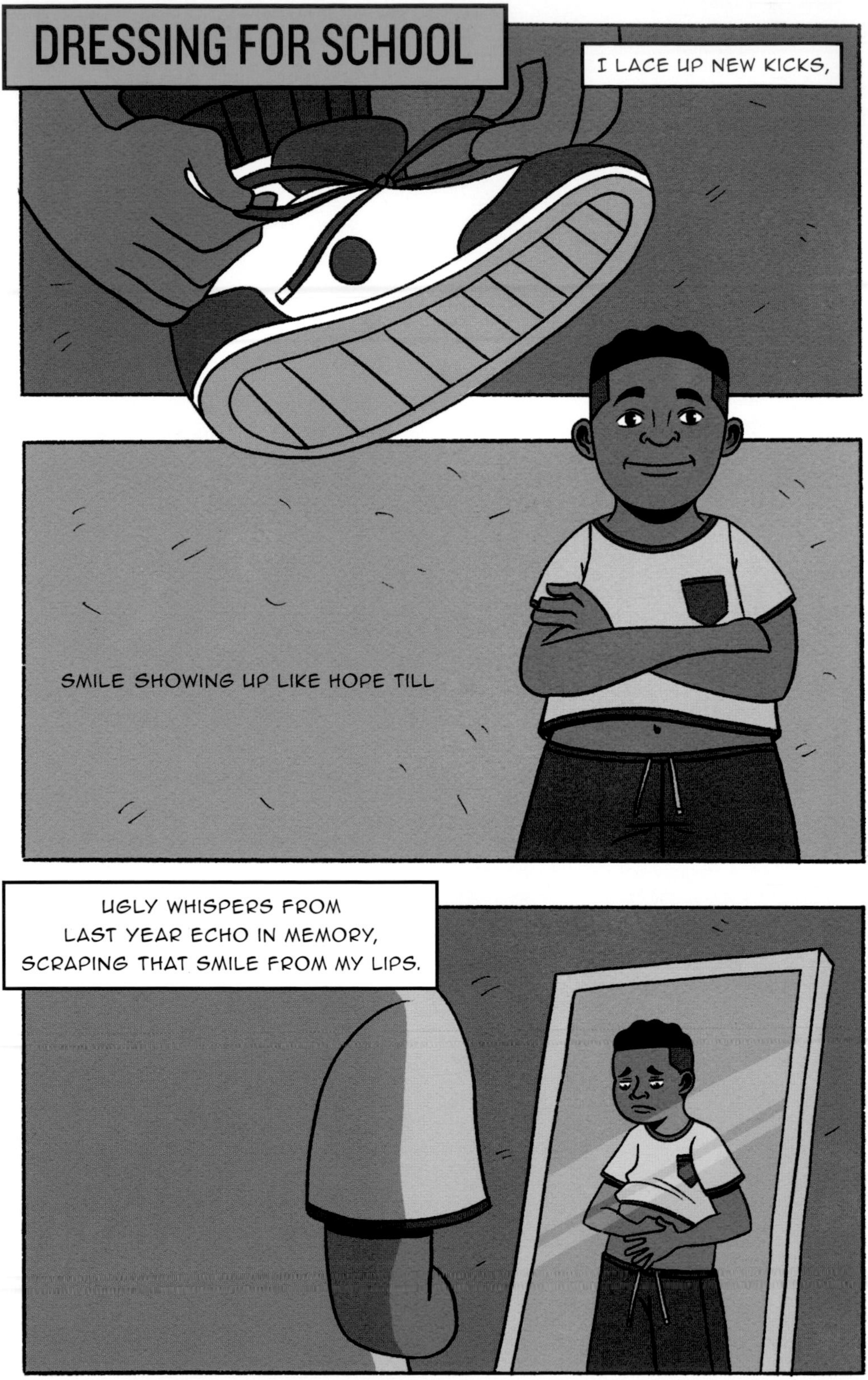
DRESSING FOR SCHOOL
I LACE UP NEW KICKS,
SMILE SHOWING UP LIKE HOPE TILL
UGLY WHISPERS FROM LAST YEAR ECHO IN MEMORY, SCRAPING THAT SMILE FROM MY LIPS.

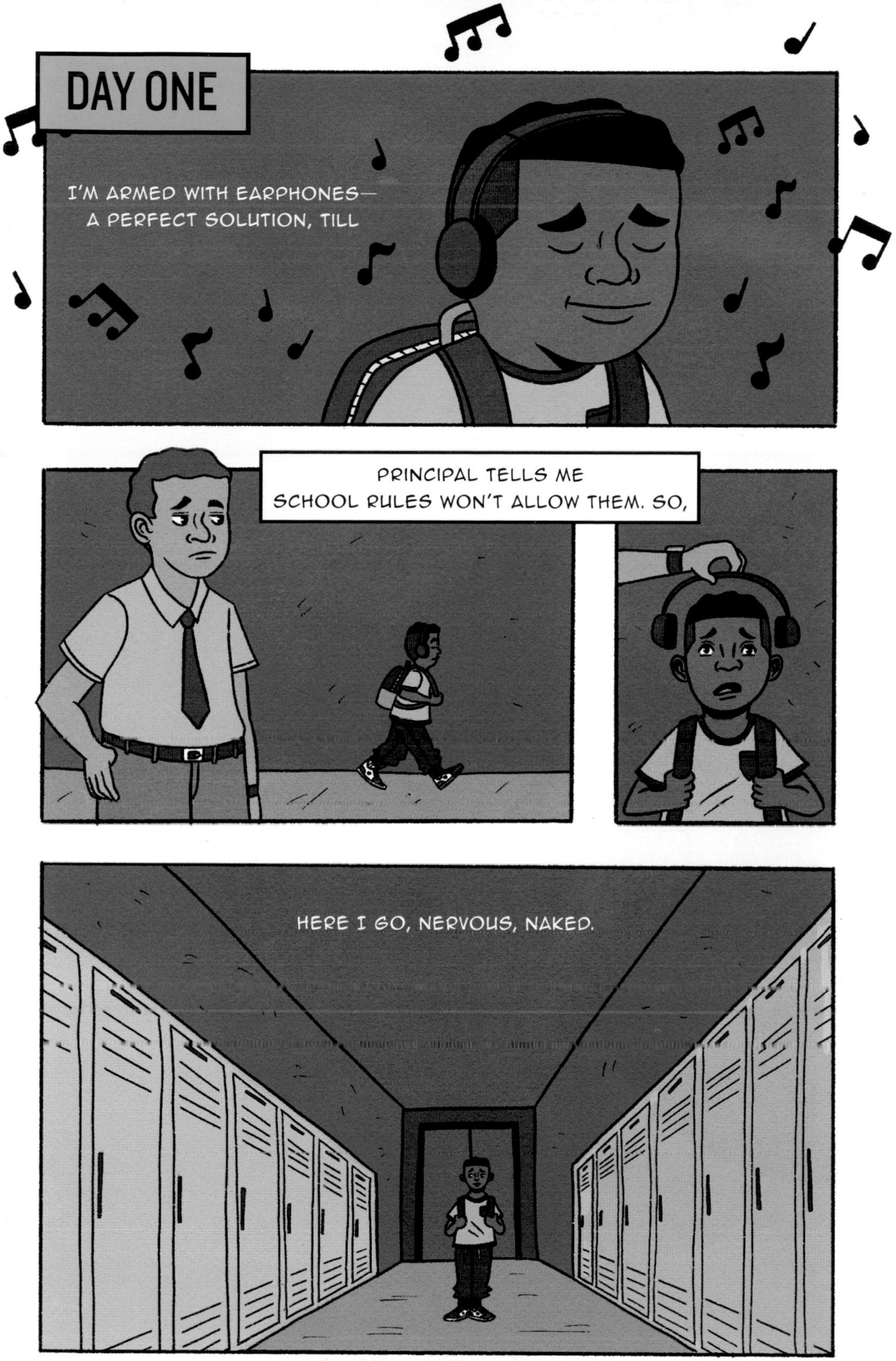
DAY ONE
I'M ARMED WITH EARPHONES—
A PERFECT SOLUTION, TILL
PRINCIPAL TELLS ME
SCHOOL RULES WON'T ALLOW THEM. SO,
HERE I GO, NERVOUS, NAKED.

TOO-SKINNY-FOR-WORDS

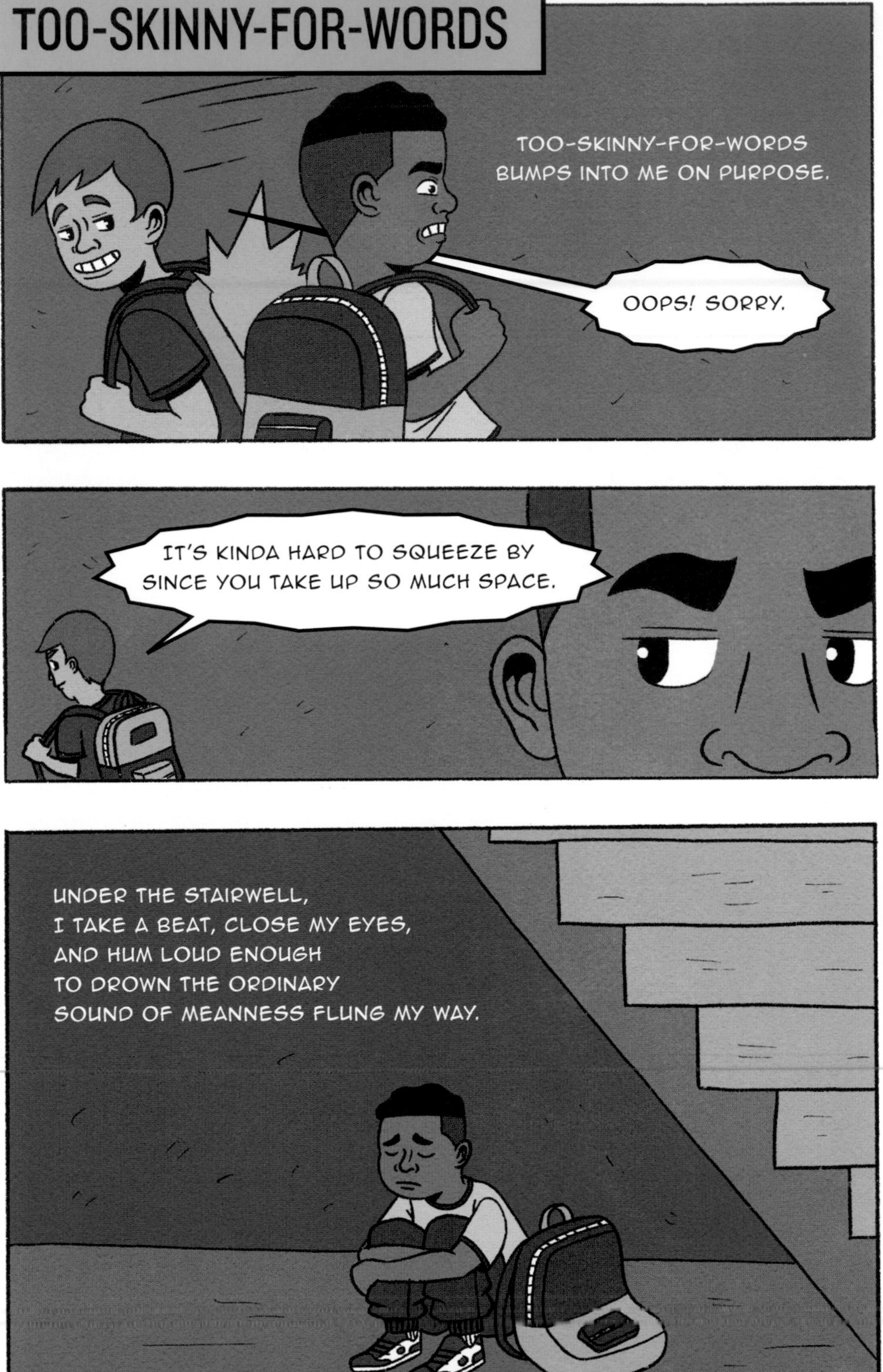
TOO-SKINNY-FOR-WORDS
BUMPS INTO ME ON PURPOSE.
OOPS! SORRY.
IT'S KINDA HARD TO SQUEEZE BY
SINCE YOU TAKE UP SO MUCH SPACE.
UNDER THE STAIRWELL,
I TAKE A BEAT, CLOSE MY EYES,
AND HUM LOUD ENOUGH
TO DROWN THE ORDINARY
SOUND OF MEANNESS FLUNG MY WAY.

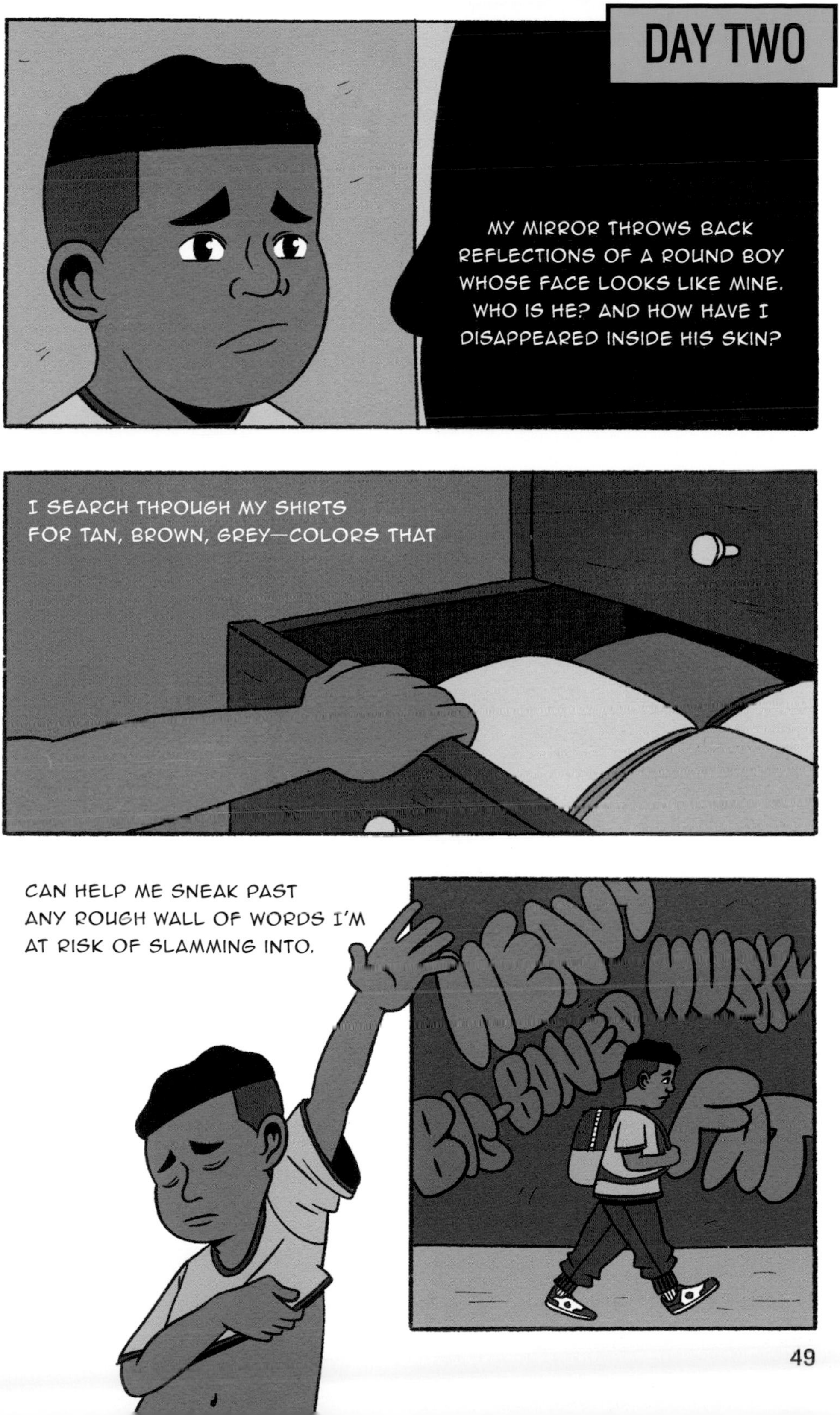
DAY TWO
MY MIRROR THROWS BACK REFLECTIONS OF A ROUND BOY WHOSE FACE LOOKS LIKE MINE. WHO IS HE? AND HOW HAVE I DISAPPEARED INSIDE HIS SKIN?
I SEARCH THROUGH MY SHIRTS FOR TAN, BROWN, GREY—COLORS THAT
CAN HELP ME SNEAK PAST ANY ROUGH WALL OF WORDS I'M AT RISK OF SLAMMING INTO.
HUSKY
BIG-BONED
FAT

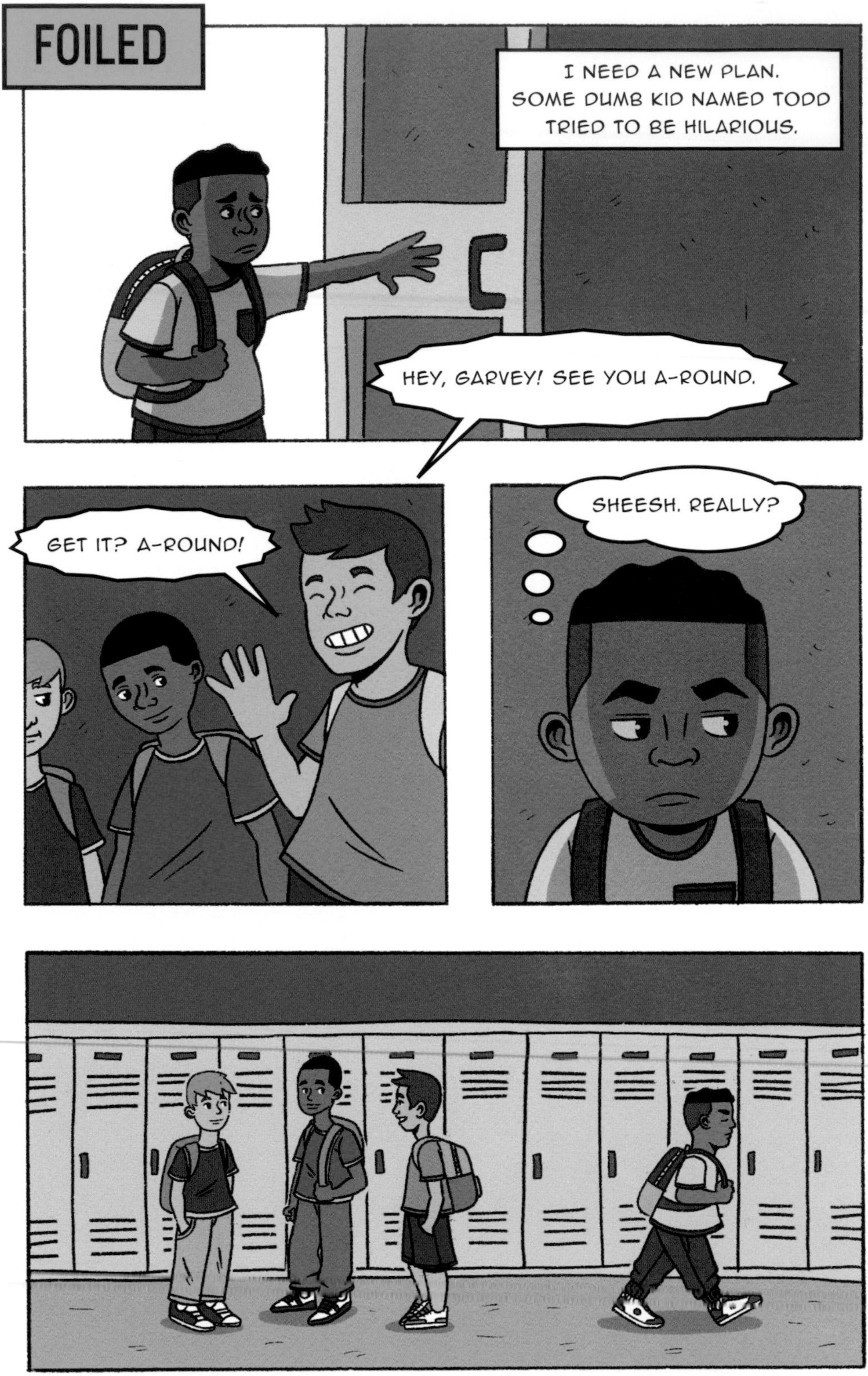
FOILED
I NEED A NEW PLAN. SOME DUMB KID NAMED TODD TRIED TO BE HILARIOUS.
HEY, GARVEY! SEE YOU A-ROUND.
GET IT? A-ROUND!
SHEESH. REALLY?

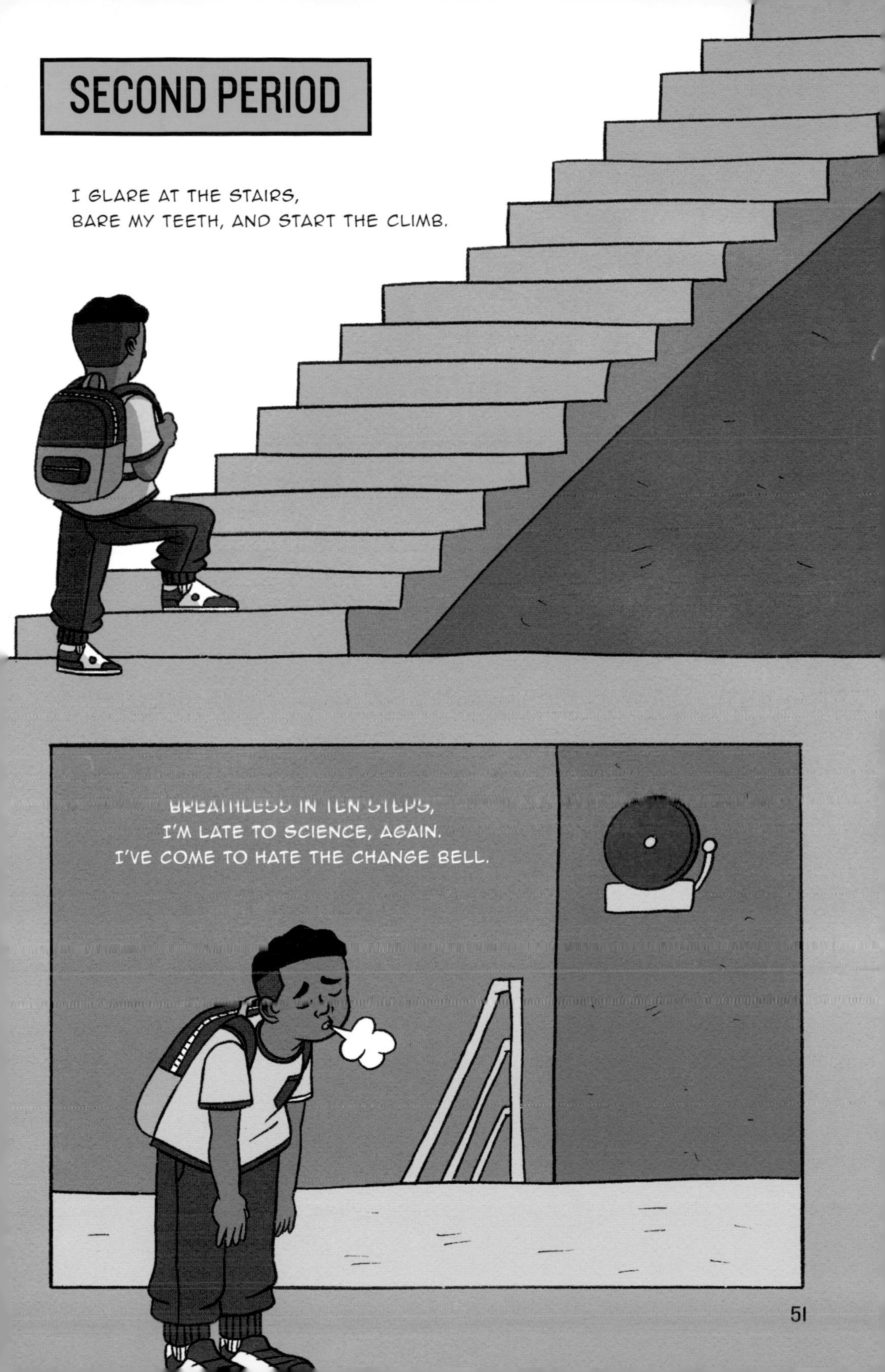
SECOND PERIOD
I GLARE AT THE STAIRS,
BARE MY TEETH, AND START THE CLIMB.
BREATHLESS IN TEN STEPS,
I'M LATE TO SCIENCE, AGAIN.
I'VE COME TO HATE THE CHANGE BELL.

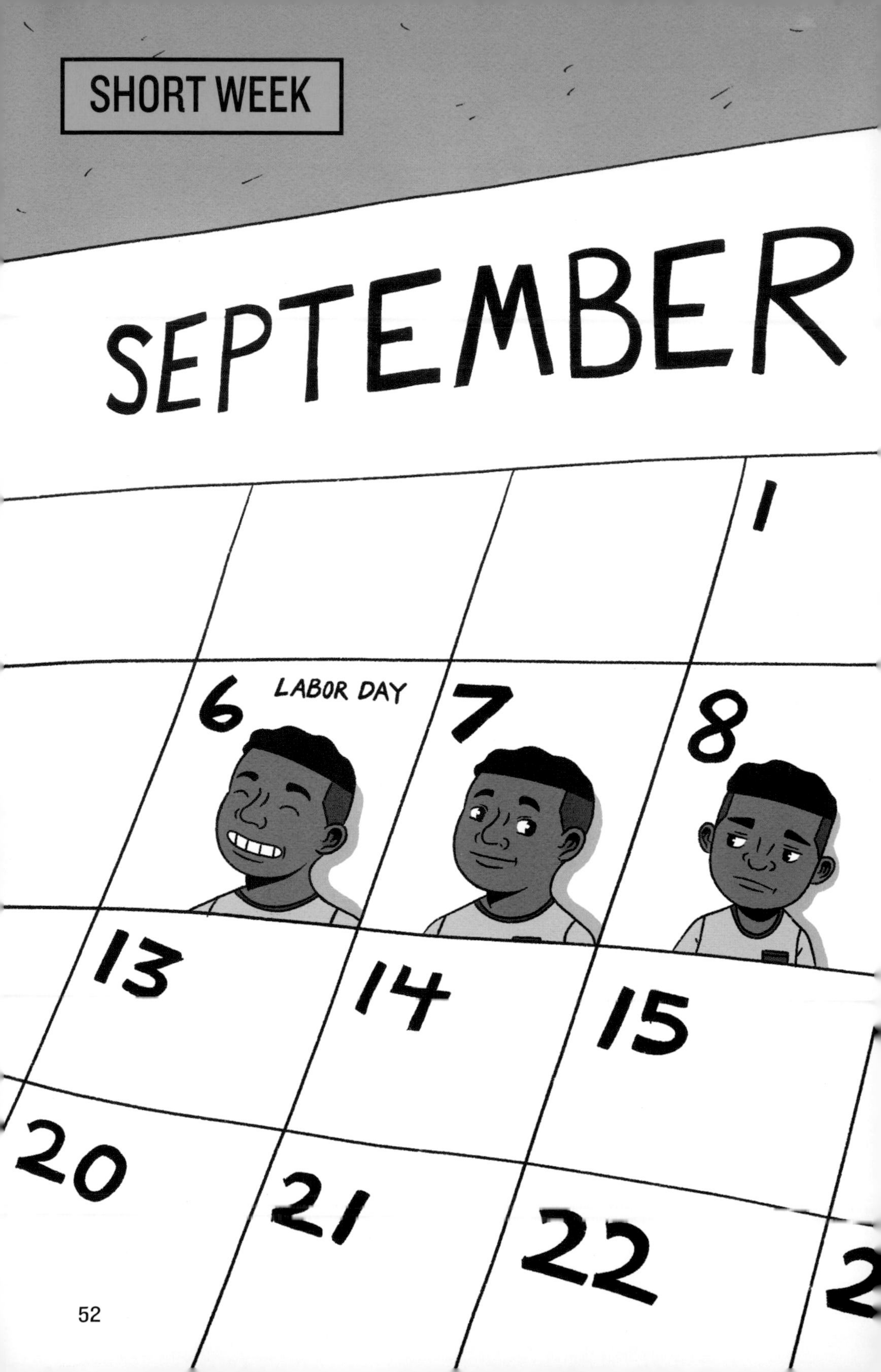
SHORT WEEK
SEPTEMBER
1
6
LABOR DAY
7
8
13
14
15
20
21
22

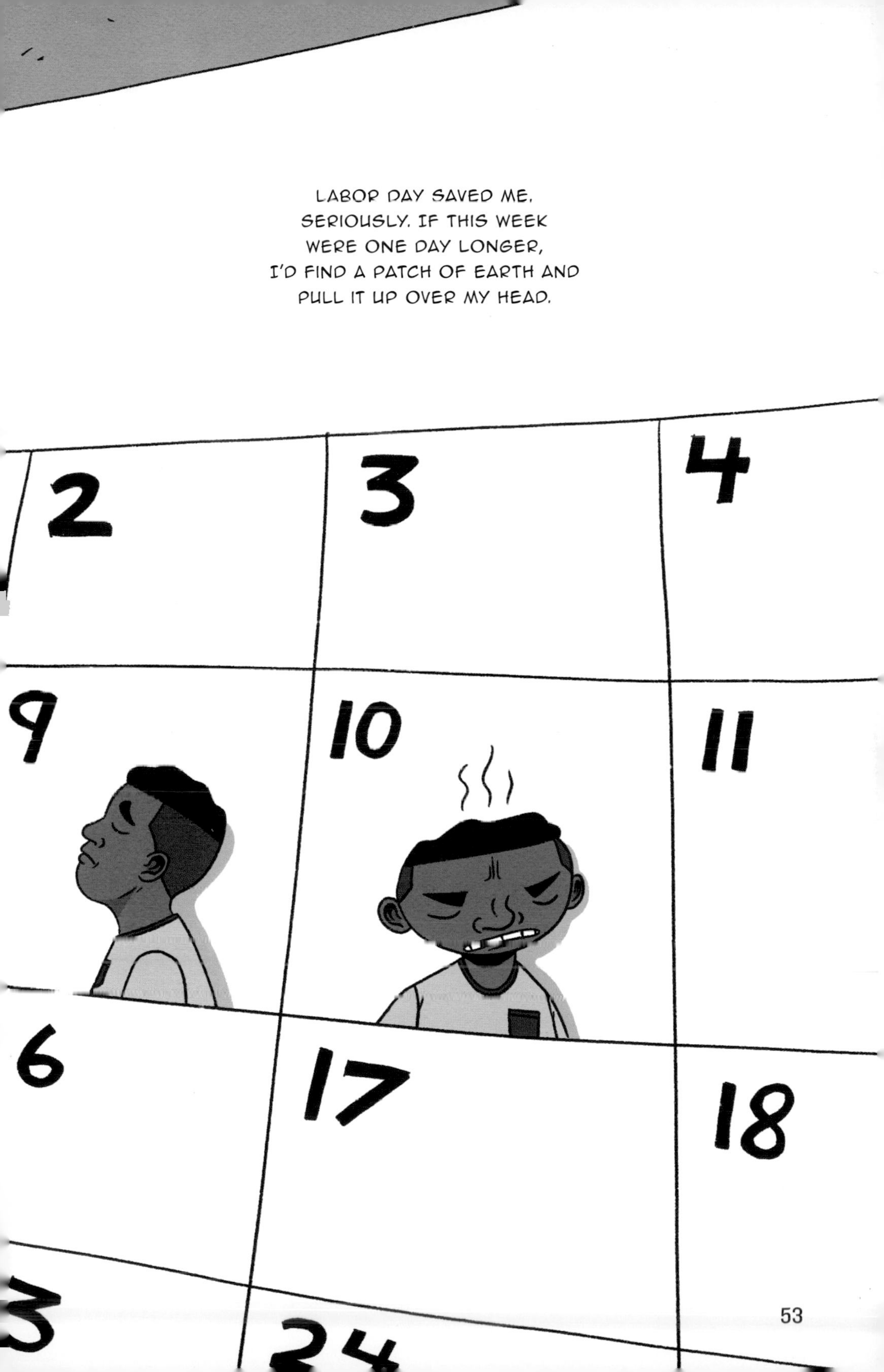
LABOR DAY SAVED ME. SERIOUSLY. IF THIS WEEK WERE ONE DAY LONGER, I'D FIND A PATCH OF EARTH AND PULL IT UP OVER MY HEAD.
2
3
4
9
10
11
6
17
18
3
24

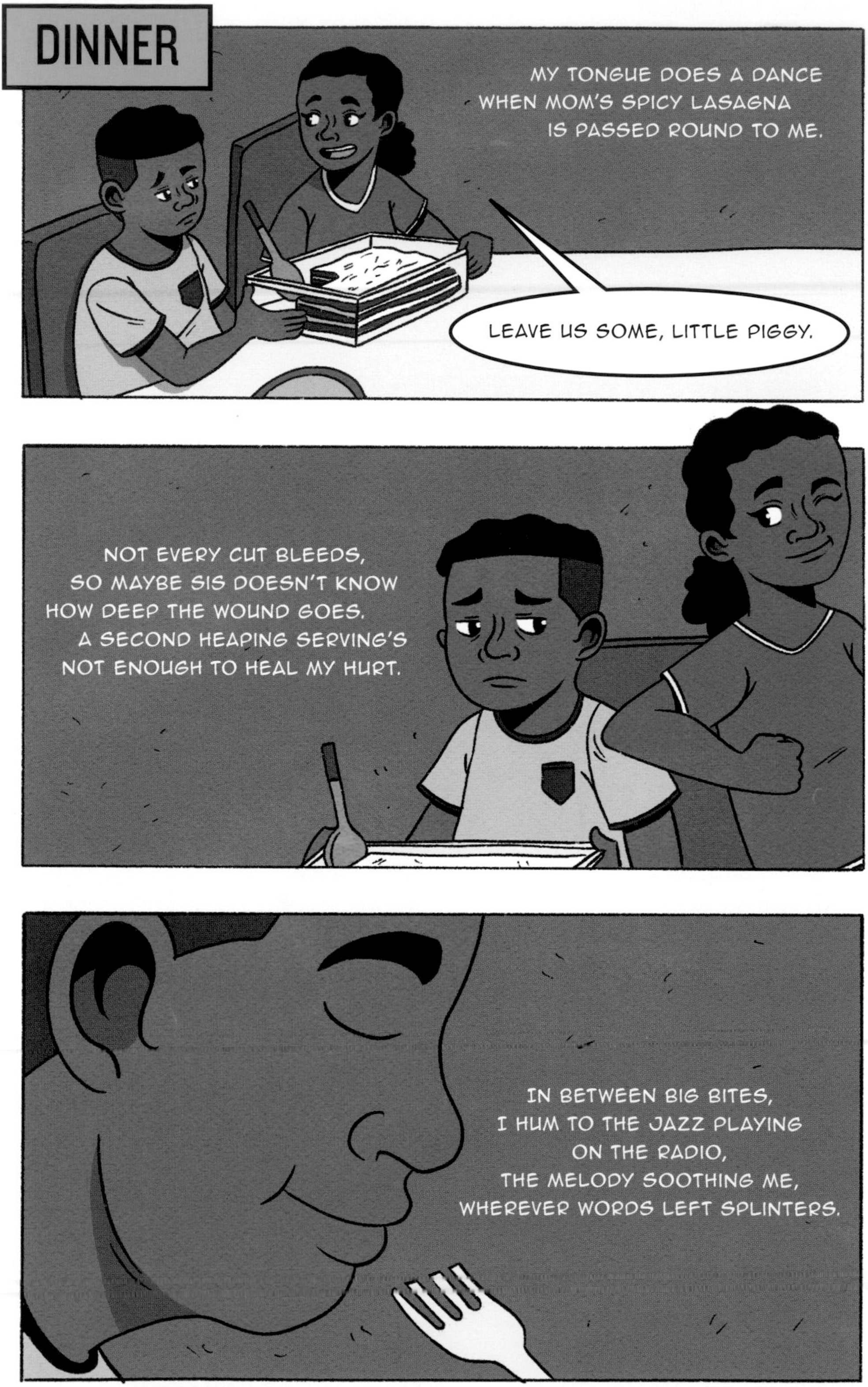
DINNER
MY TONGUE DOES A DANCE WHEN MOM'S SPICY LASAGNA IS PASSED ROUND TO ME.
LEAVE US SOME, LITTLE PIGGY.
NOT EVERY CUT BLEEDS, SO MAYBE SIS DOESN'T KNOW HOW DEEP THE WOUND GOES. A SECOND HEAPING SERVING'S NOT ENOUGH TO HEAL MY HURT.
IN BETWEEN BIG BITES, I HUM TO THE JAZZ PLAYING ON THE RADIO, THE MELODY SOOTHING ME, WHEREVER WORDS LEFT SPLINTERS.

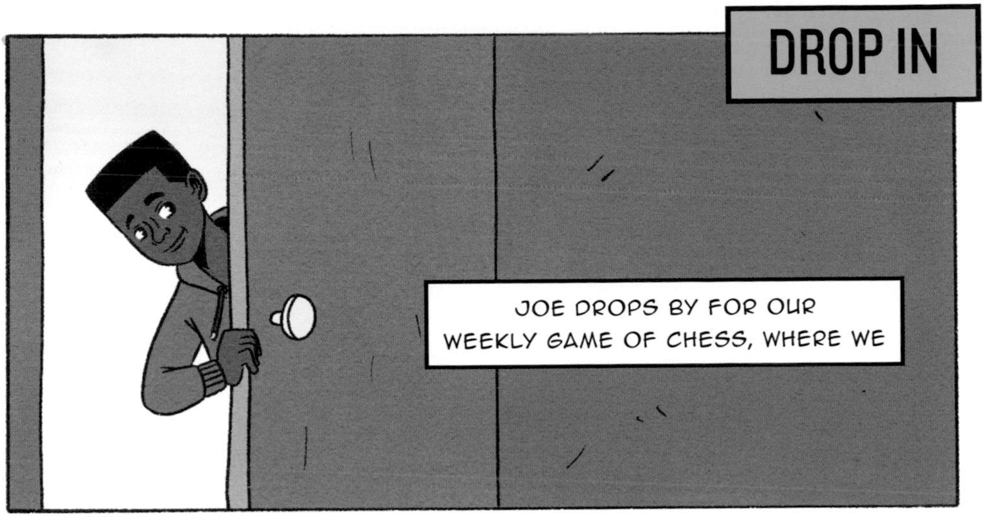
DROP IN
JOE DROPS BY FOR OUR WEEKLY GAME OF CHESS, WHERE WE

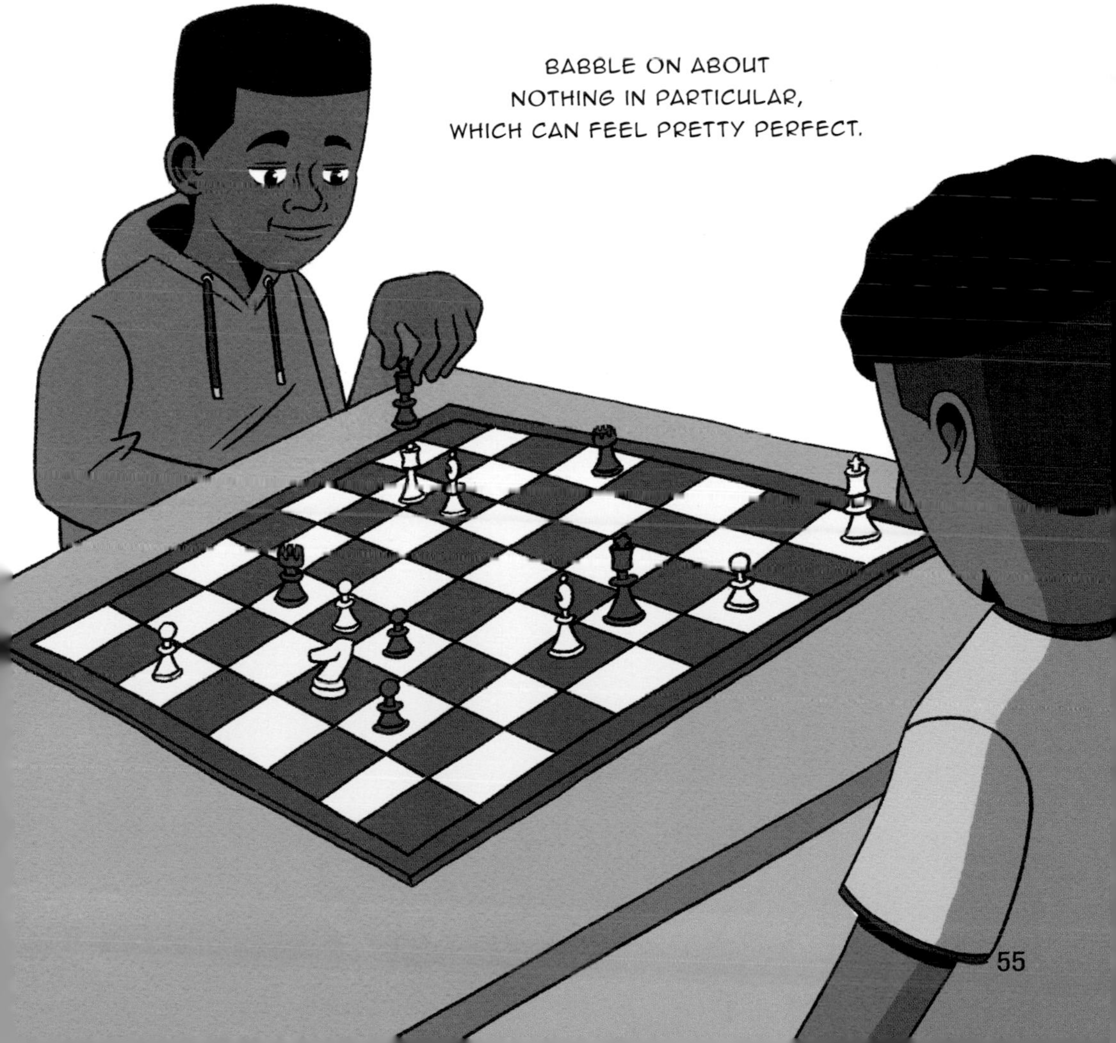
BABBLE ON ABOUT NOTHING IN PARTICULAR, WHICH CAN FEEL PRETTY PERFECT.

SHOULDER-PAD SEASON

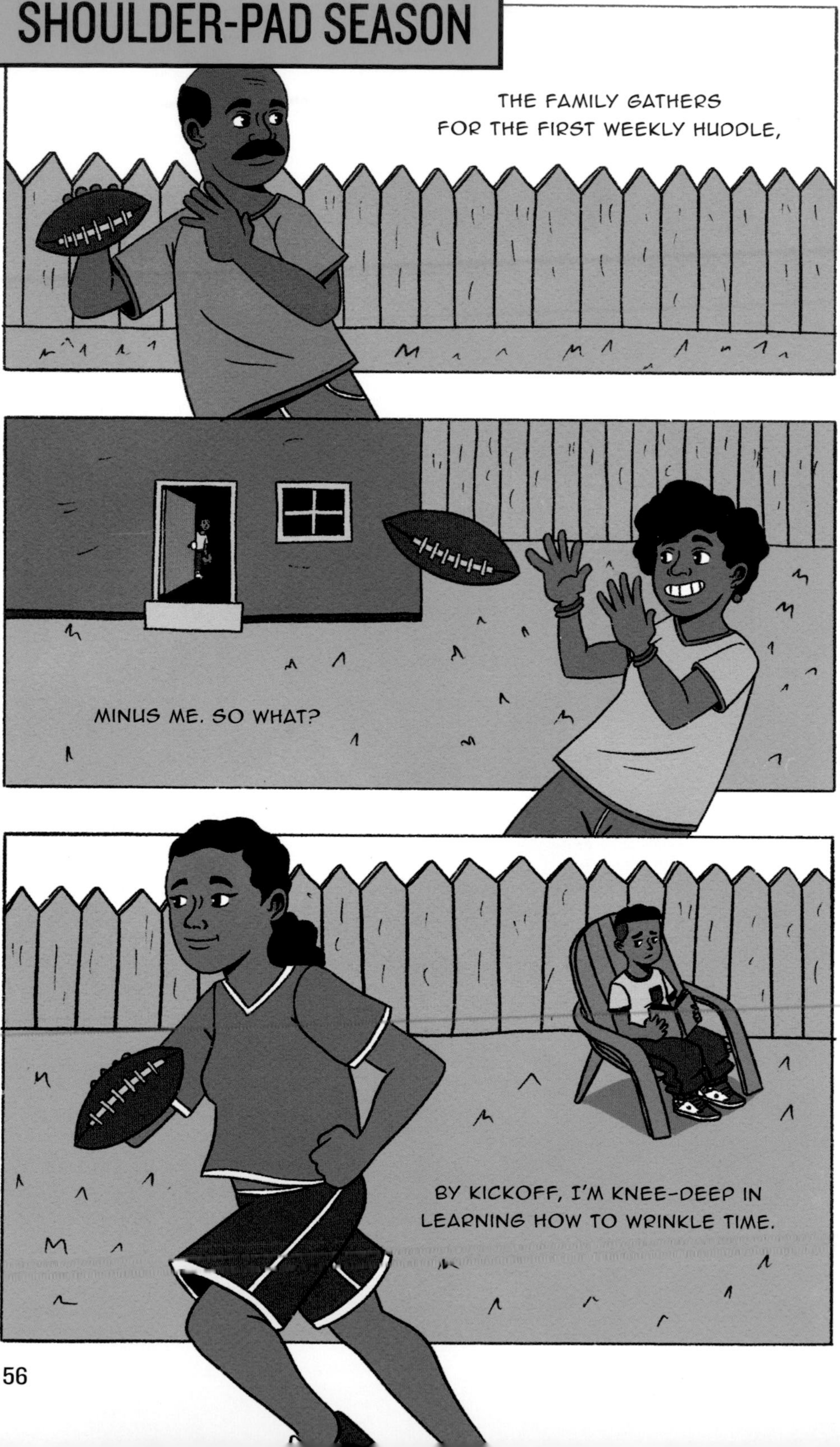
THE FAMILY GATHERS FOR THE FIRST WEEKLY HUDDLE,
MINUS ME. SO WHAT?
BY KICKOFF, I'M KNEE-DEEP IN LEARNING HOW TO WRINKLE TIME.

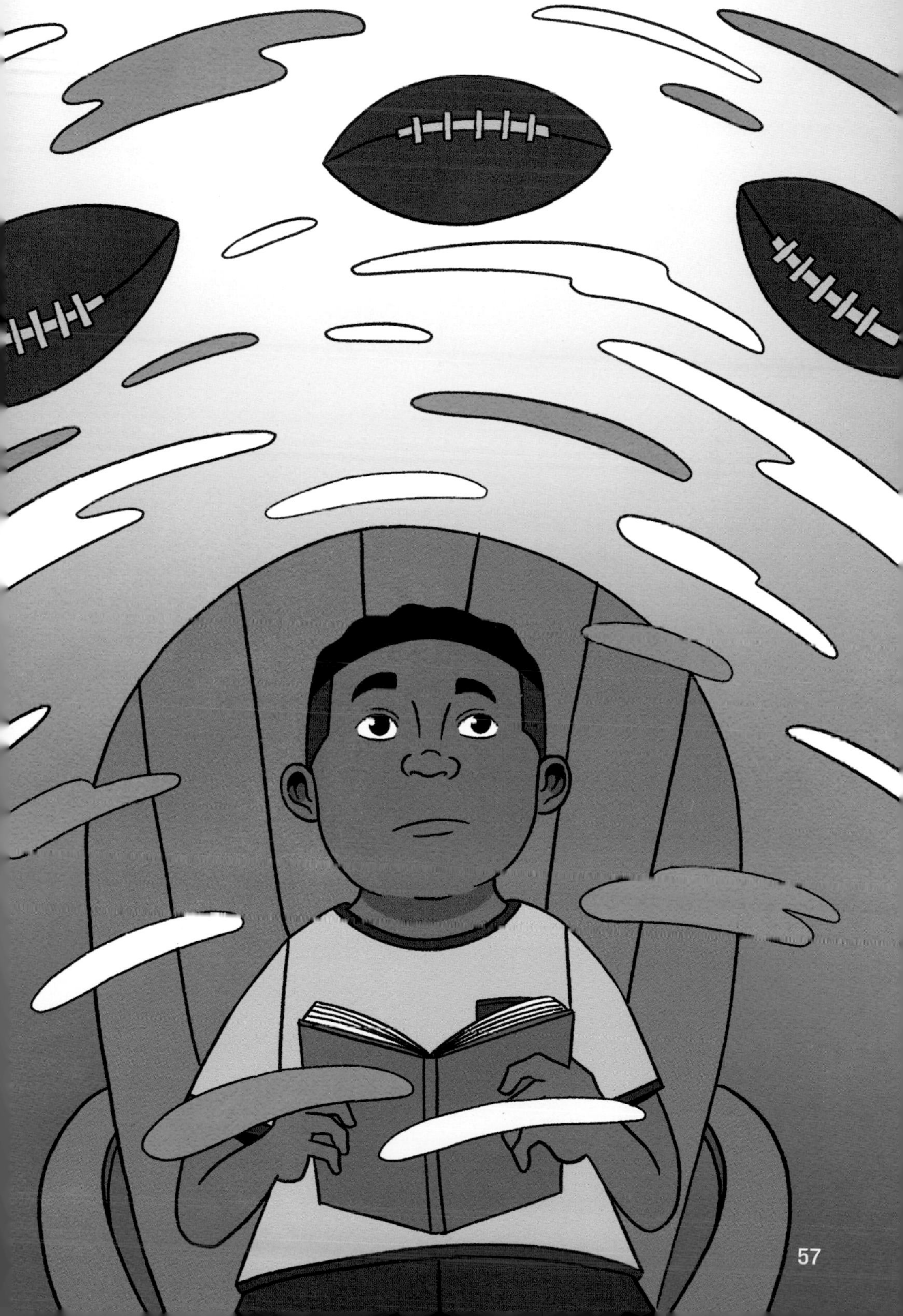

LATE-NIGHT SNACK

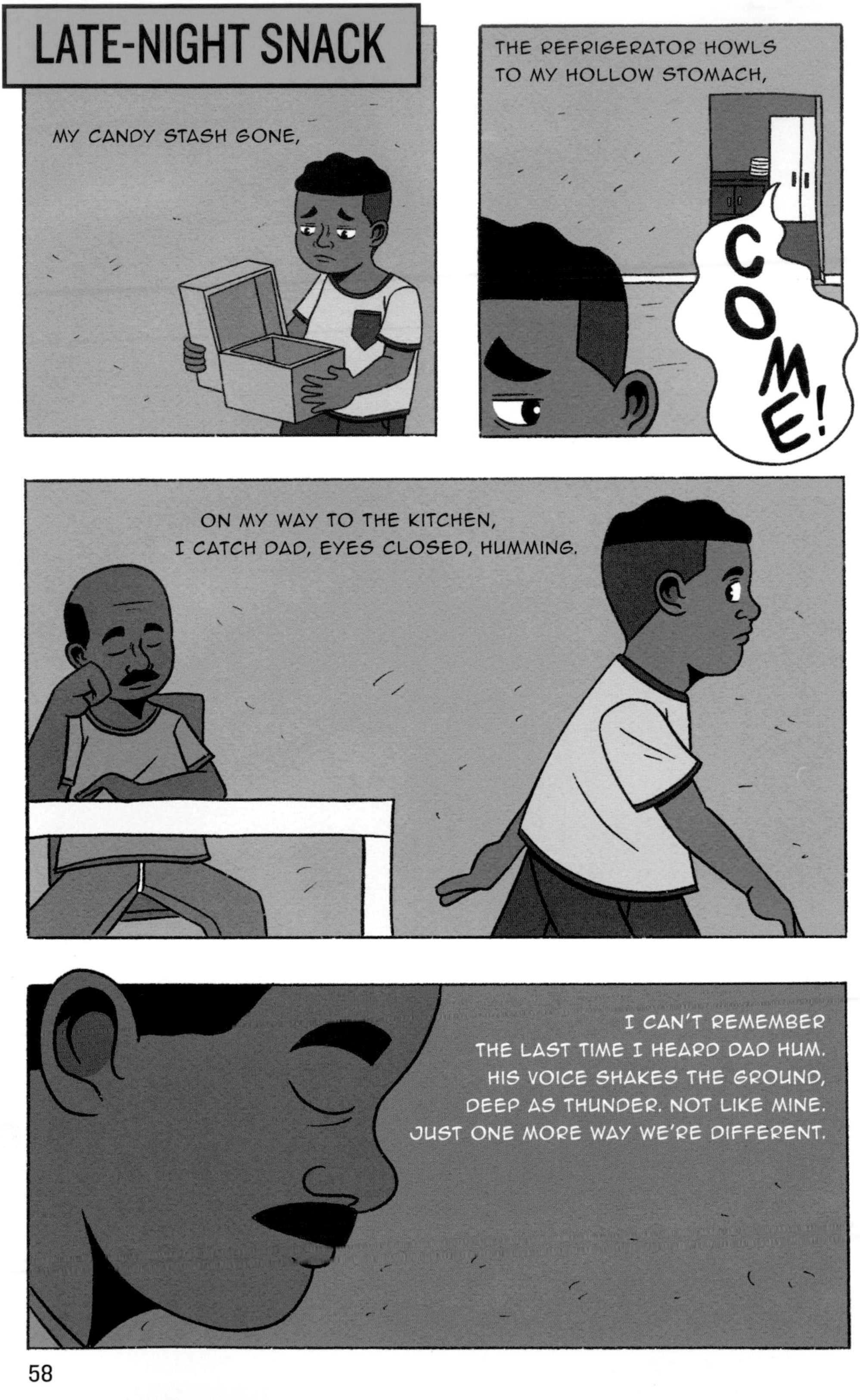
MY CANDY STASH GONE,
THE REFRIGERATOR HOWLS
TO MY HOLLOW STOMACH,
COME!
ON MY WAY TO THE KITCHEN,
I CATCH DAD, EYES CLOSED, HUMMING.
I CAN'T REMEMBER
THE LAST TIME I HEARD DAD HUM.
HIS VOICE SHAKES THE GROUND,
DEEP AS THUNDER. NOT LIKE MINE.
JUST ONE MORE WAY WE'RE DIFFERENT.

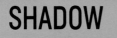

SHADOW

MY MOM, DAD, AND SIS
COULD FIT INSIDE MY SHADOW
AND—*POOF*—DISAPPEAR.
WHENEVER I STAND NEAR, THAT'S
HOW IT FEELS. THEY'RE ALL SO SMALL.

I COULD BE SMALLER,
I THINK, *IF I WANTED TO,*
IF I REALLY TRIED.

I SWALLOW THOSE WORDS WITH A
TALL GLASS OF WATER, AND SLEEP.

DIET

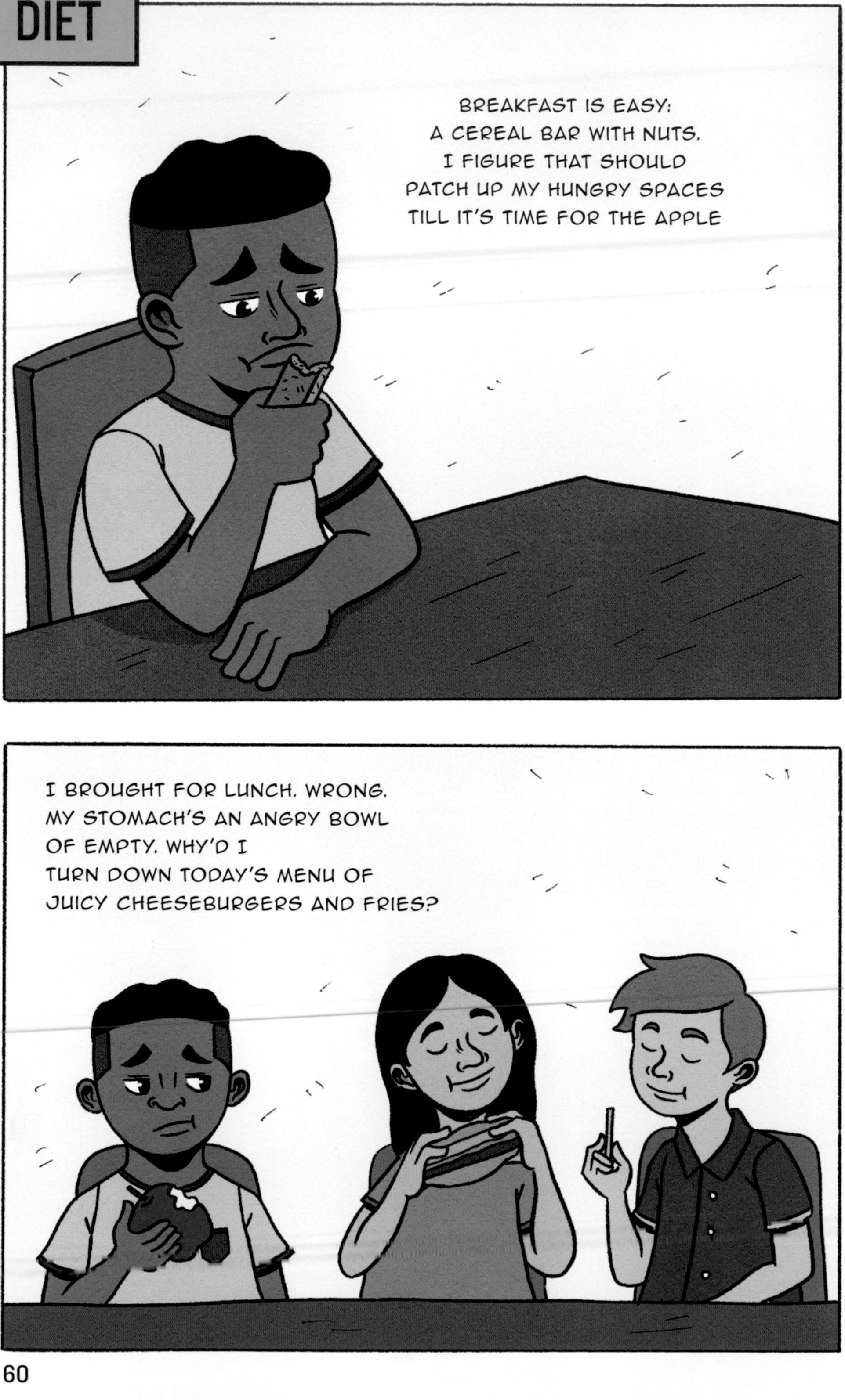
BREAKFAST IS EASY:
A CEREAL BAR WITH NUTS.
I FIGURE THAT SHOULD
PATCH UP MY HUNGRY SPACES
TILL IT'S TIME FOR THE APPLE
I BROUGHT FOR LUNCH. WRONG.
MY STOMACH'S AN ANGRY BOWL
OF EMPTY. WHY'D I
TURN DOWN TODAY'S MENU OF
JUICY CHEESEBURGERS AND FRIES?

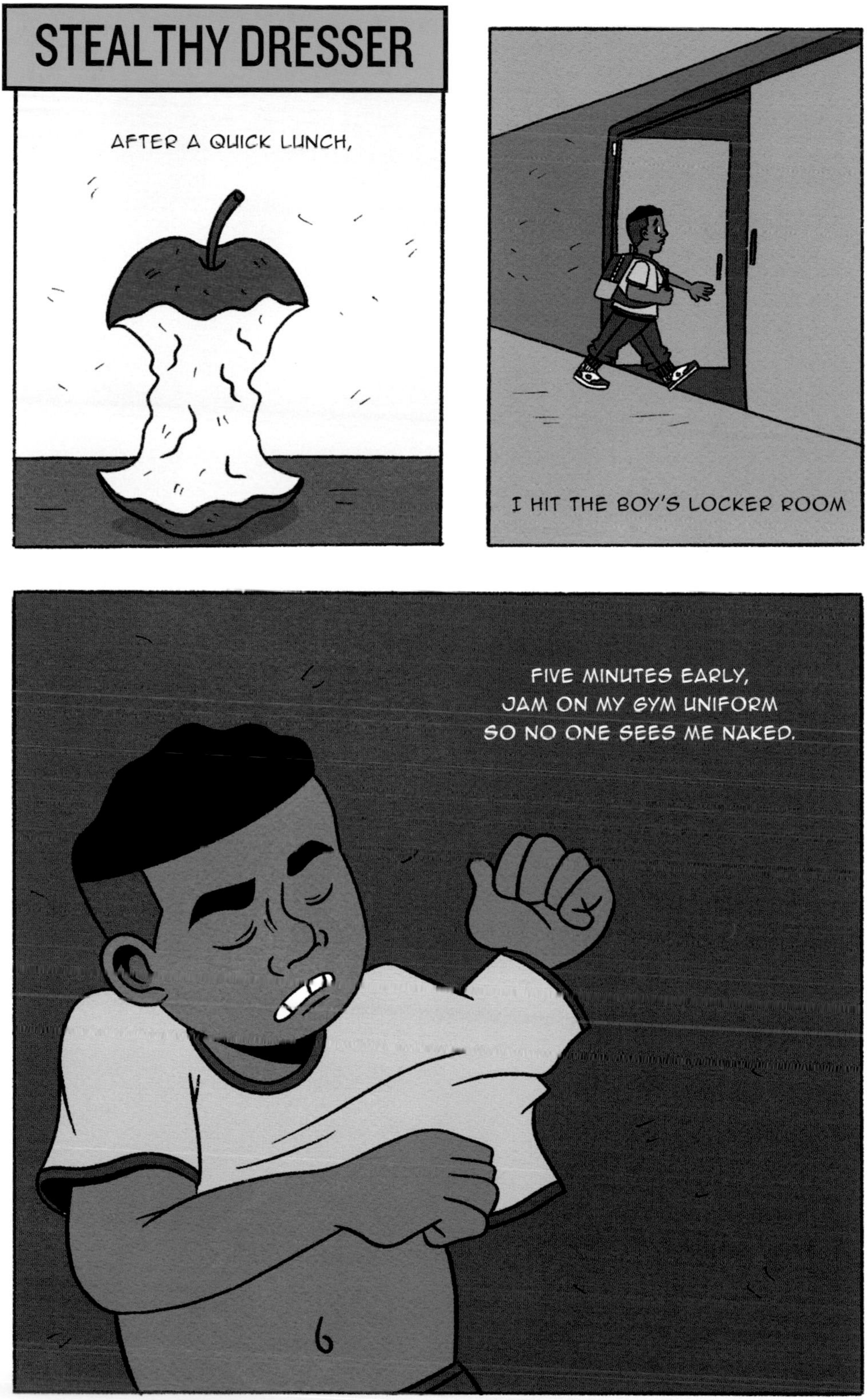
STEALTHY DRESSER
AFTER A QUICK LUNCH,
I HIT THE BOY'S LOCKER ROOM
FIVE MINUTES EARLY,
JAM ON MY GYM UNIFORM
SO NO ONE SEES ME NAKED.

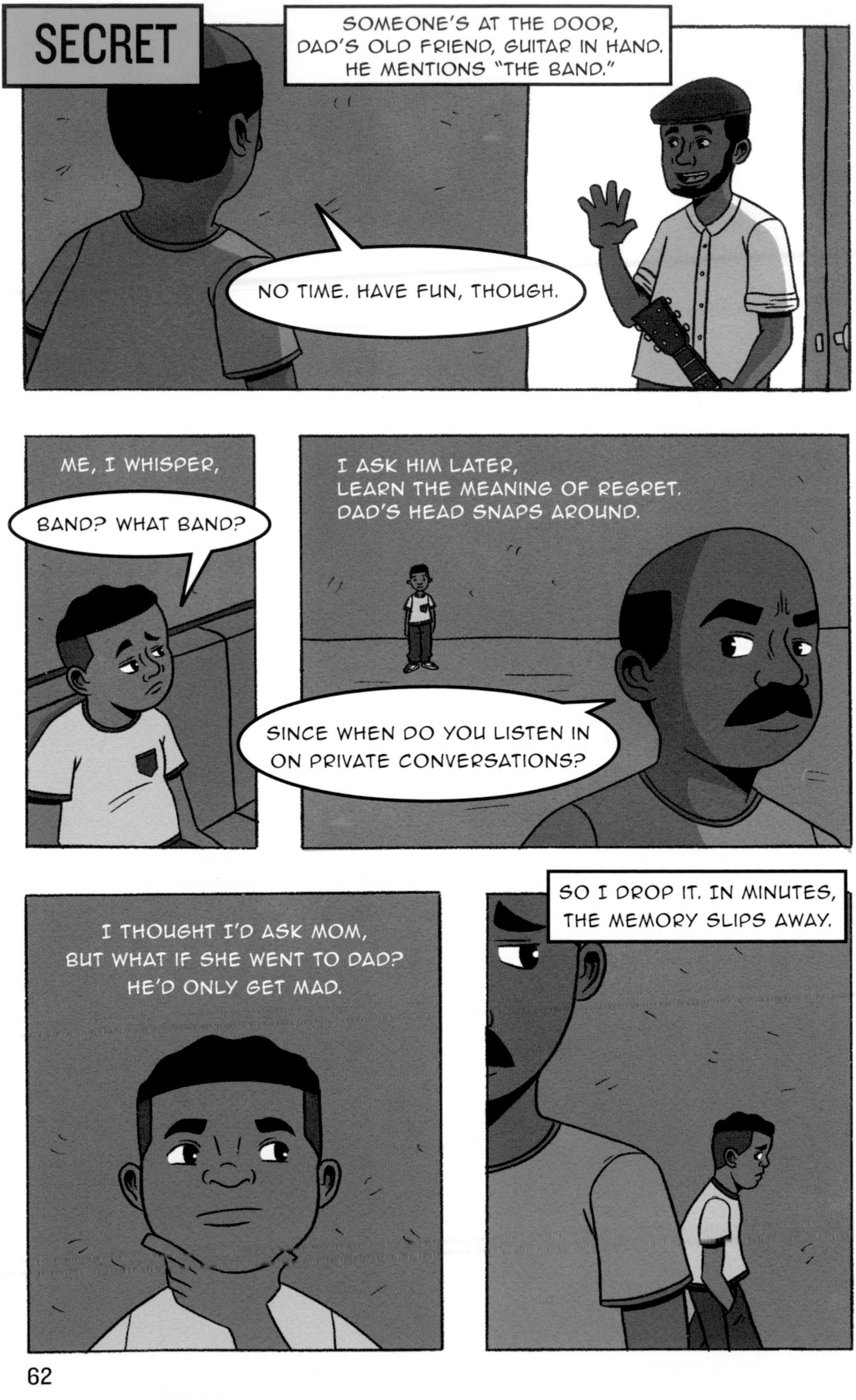
SECRET
SOMEONE'S AT THE DOOR, DAD'S OLD FRIEND, GUITAR IN HAND. HE MENTIONS "THE BAND."
NO TIME. HAVE FUN, THOUGH.
ME, I WHISPER,
BAND? WHAT BAND?
I ASK HIM LATER, LEARN THE MEANING OF REGRET. DAD'S HEAD SNAPS AROUND.
SINCE WHEN DO YOU LISTEN IN ON PRIVATE CONVERSATIONS?
I THOUGHT I'D ASK MOM, BUT WHAT IF SHE WENT TO DAD? HE'D ONLY GET MAD.
SO I DROP IT. IN MINUTES, THE MEMORY SLIPS AWAY.

FUN RUN

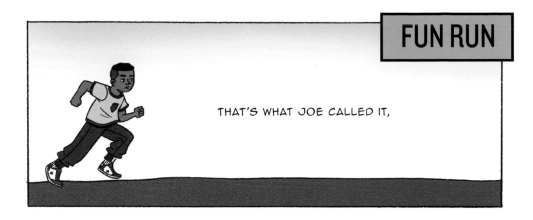

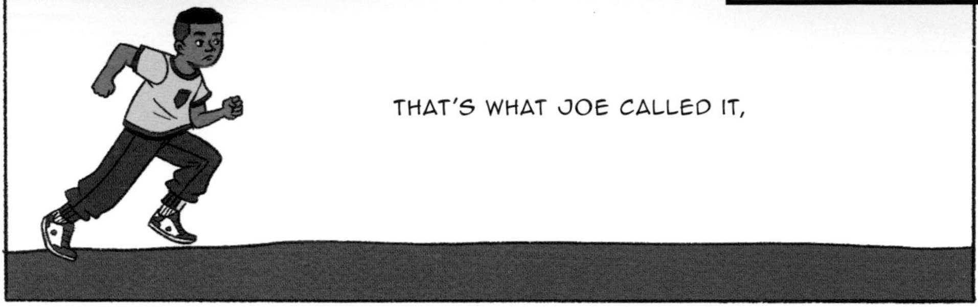
THAT'S WHAT JOE CALLED IT,

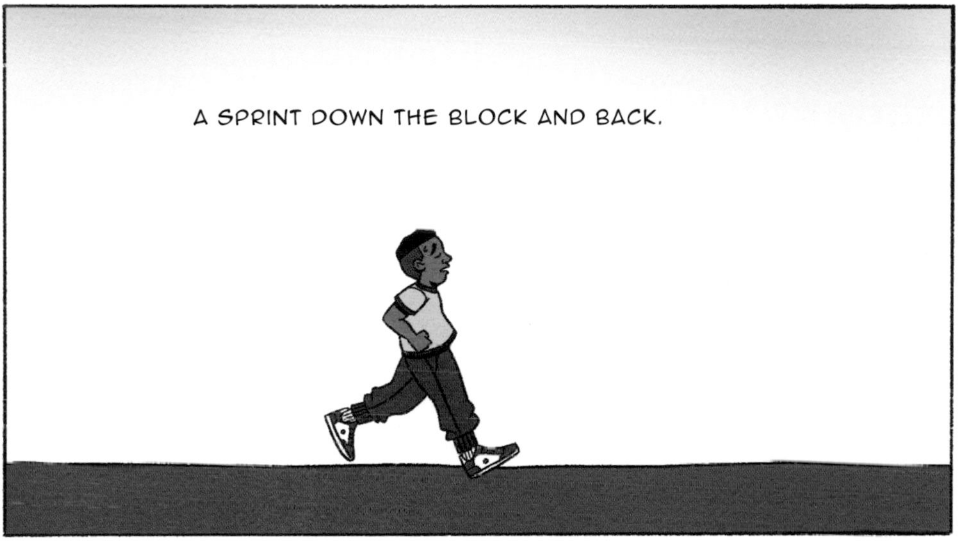
A SPRINT DOWN THE BLOCK AND BACK.

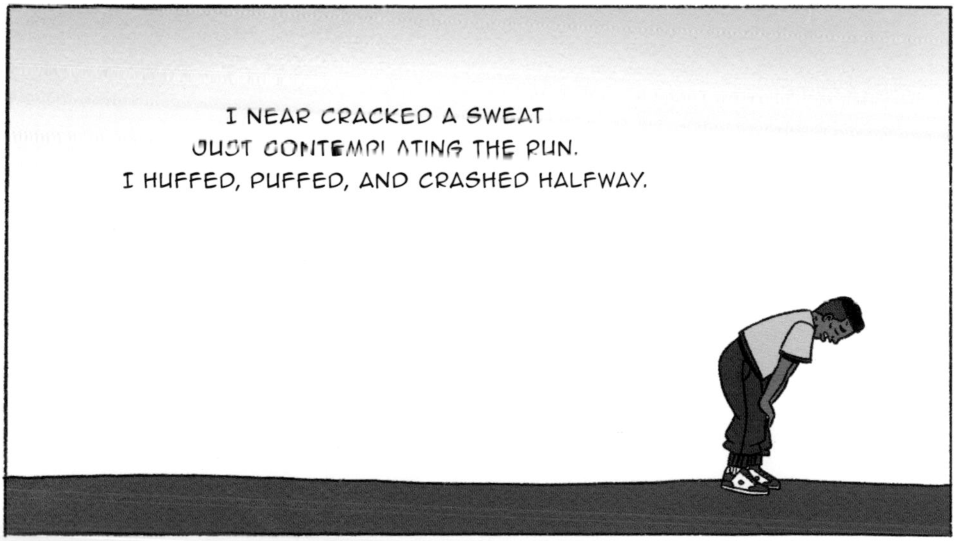
I NEAR CRACKED A SWEAT
JUST CONTEMPLATING THE RUN.
I HUFFED, PUFFED, AND CRASHED HALFWAY.

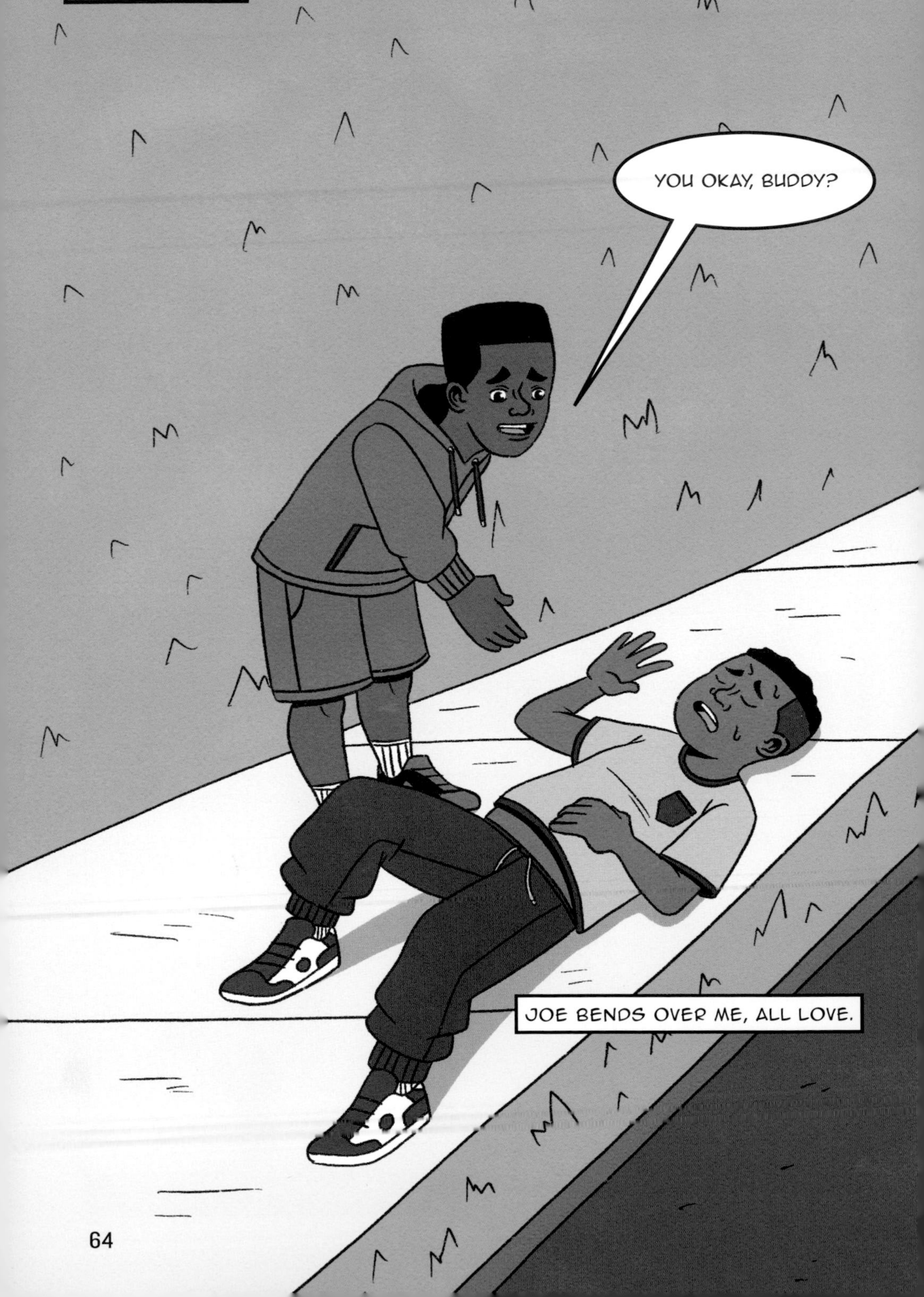
YOU OKAY, BUDDY?
JOE BENDS OVER ME, ALL LOVE.

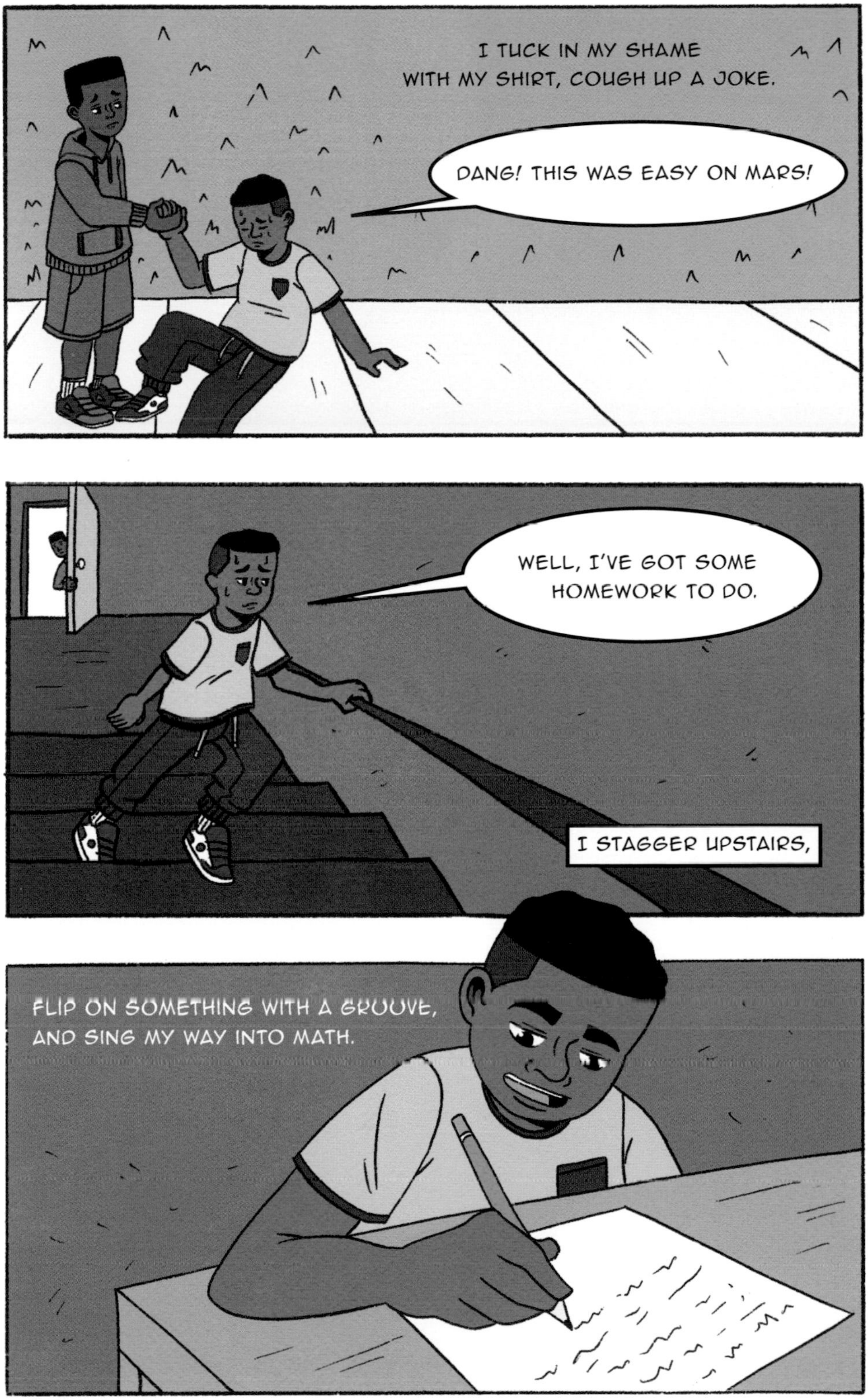
I TUCK IN MY SHAME
WITH MY SHIRT, COUGH UP A JOKE.
DANG! THIS WAS EASY ON MARS!
WELL, I'VE GOT SOME HOMEWORK TO DO.
I STAGGER UPSTAIRS,
FLIP ON SOMETHING WITH A GROOVE,
AND SING MY WAY INTO MATH.

A SLICE OF TRUTH

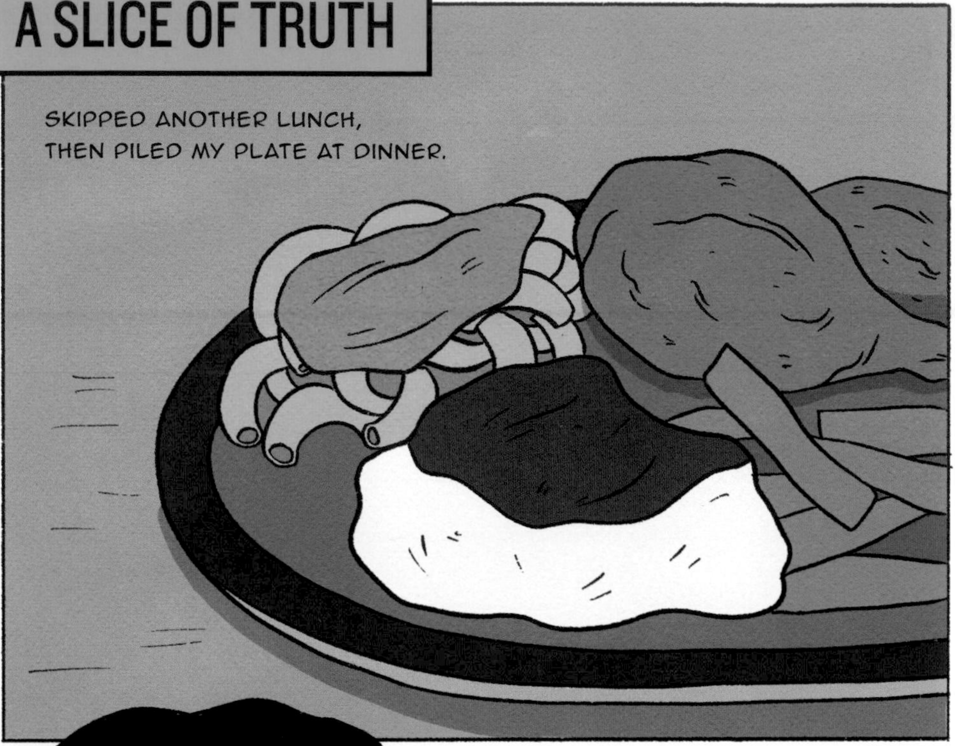
SKIPPED ANOTHER LUNCH,
THEN PILED MY PLATE AT DINNER.

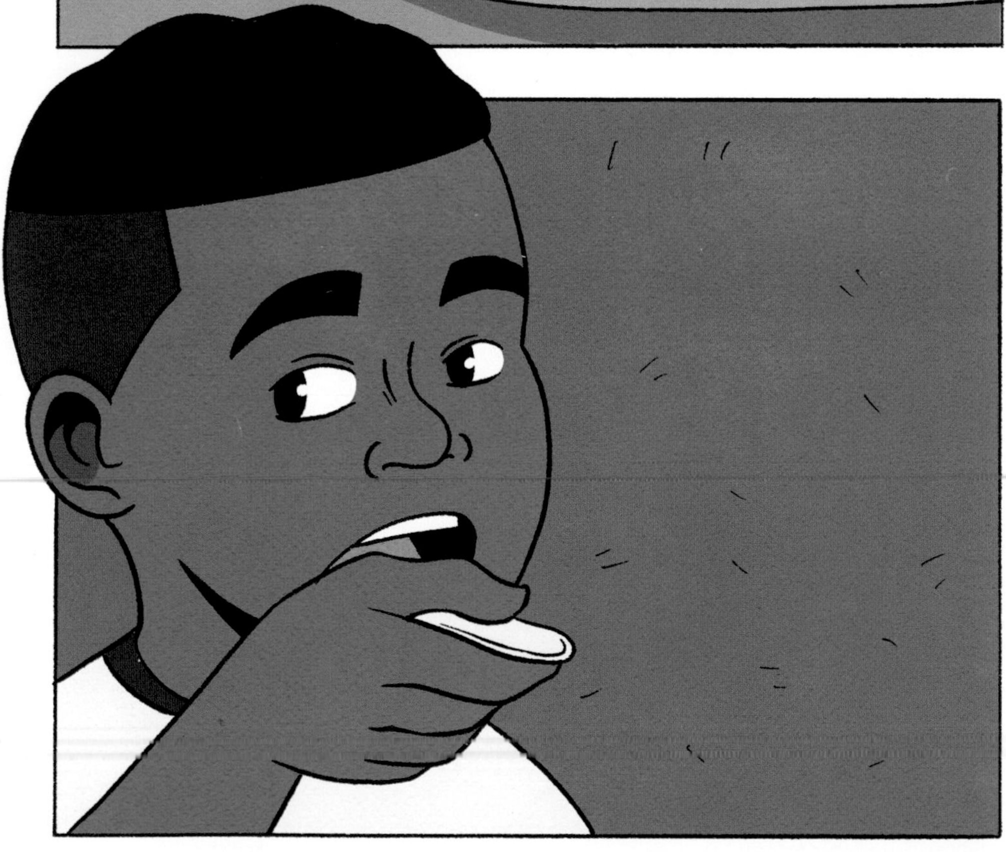

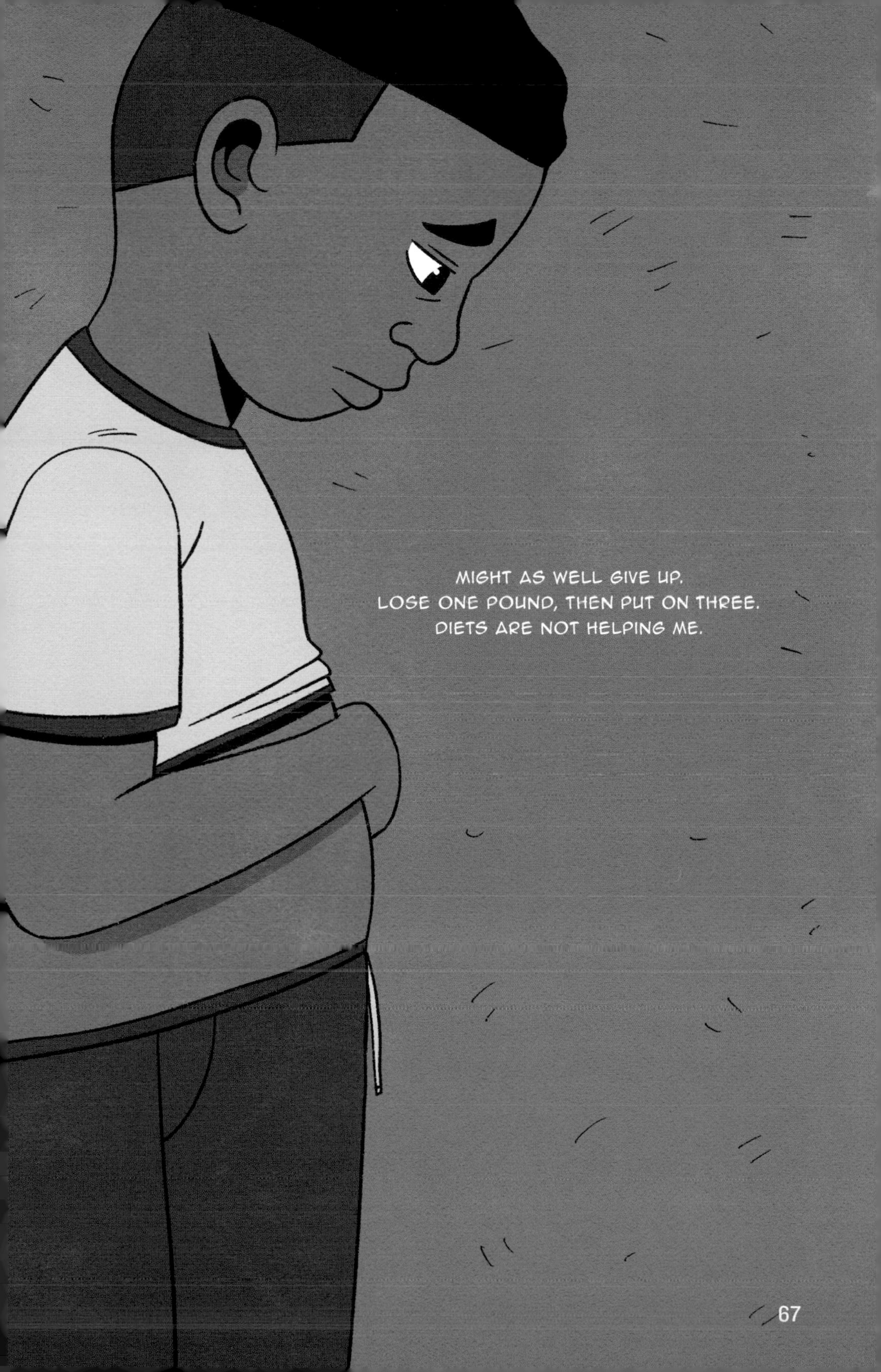
MIGHT AS WELL GIVE UP.
LOSE ONE POUND, THEN PUT ON THREE.
DIETS ARE NOT HELPING ME.

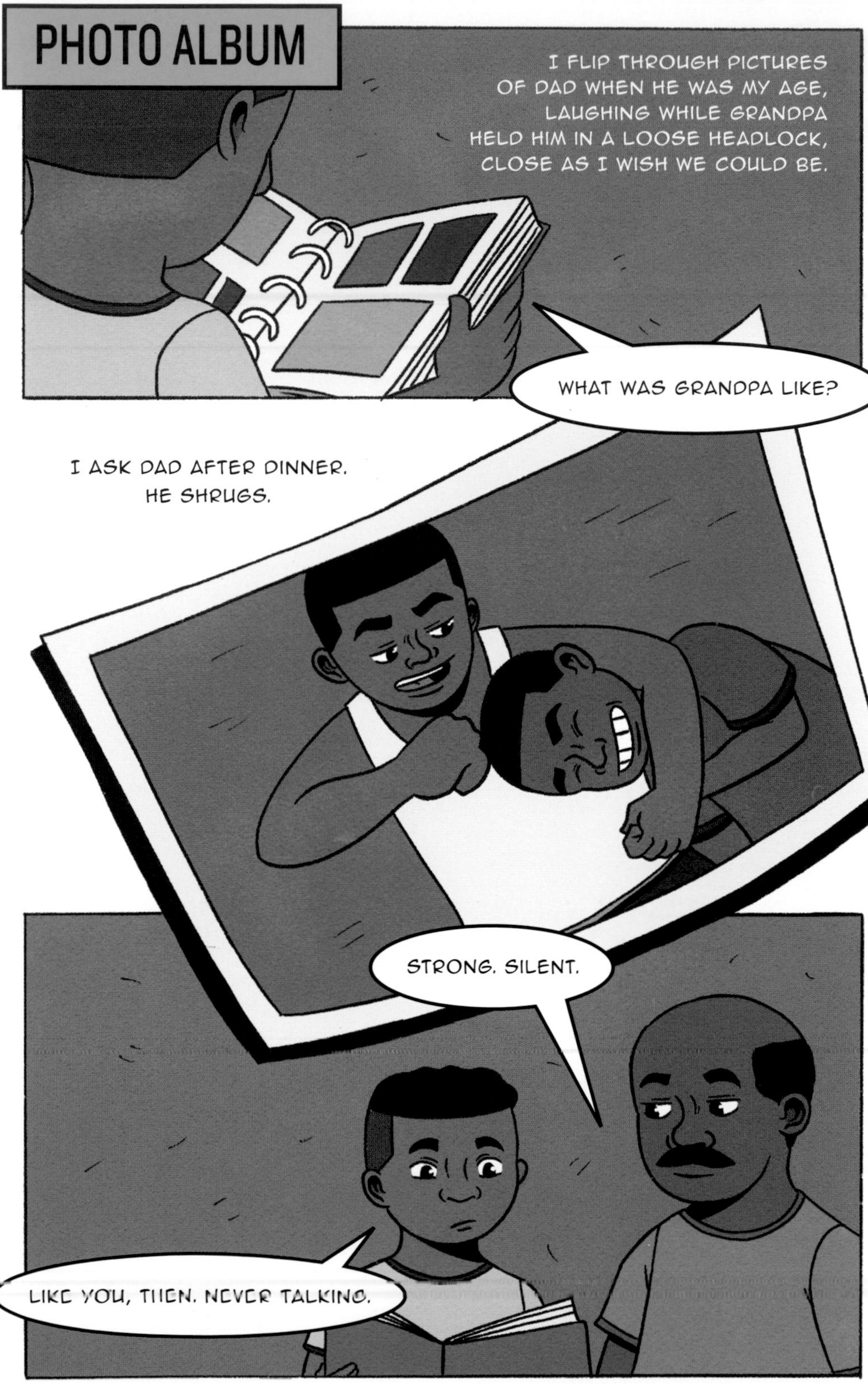
PHOTO ALBUM
I FLIP THROUGH PICTURES OF DAD WHEN HE WAS MY AGE, LAUGHING WHILE GRANDPA HELD HIM IN A LOOSE HEADLOCK, CLOSE AS I WISH WE COULD BE.
WHAT WAS GRANDPA LIKE?
I ASK DAD AFTER DINNER. HE SHRUGS.
STRONG. SILENT.
LIKE YOU, THEN. NEVER TALKING.

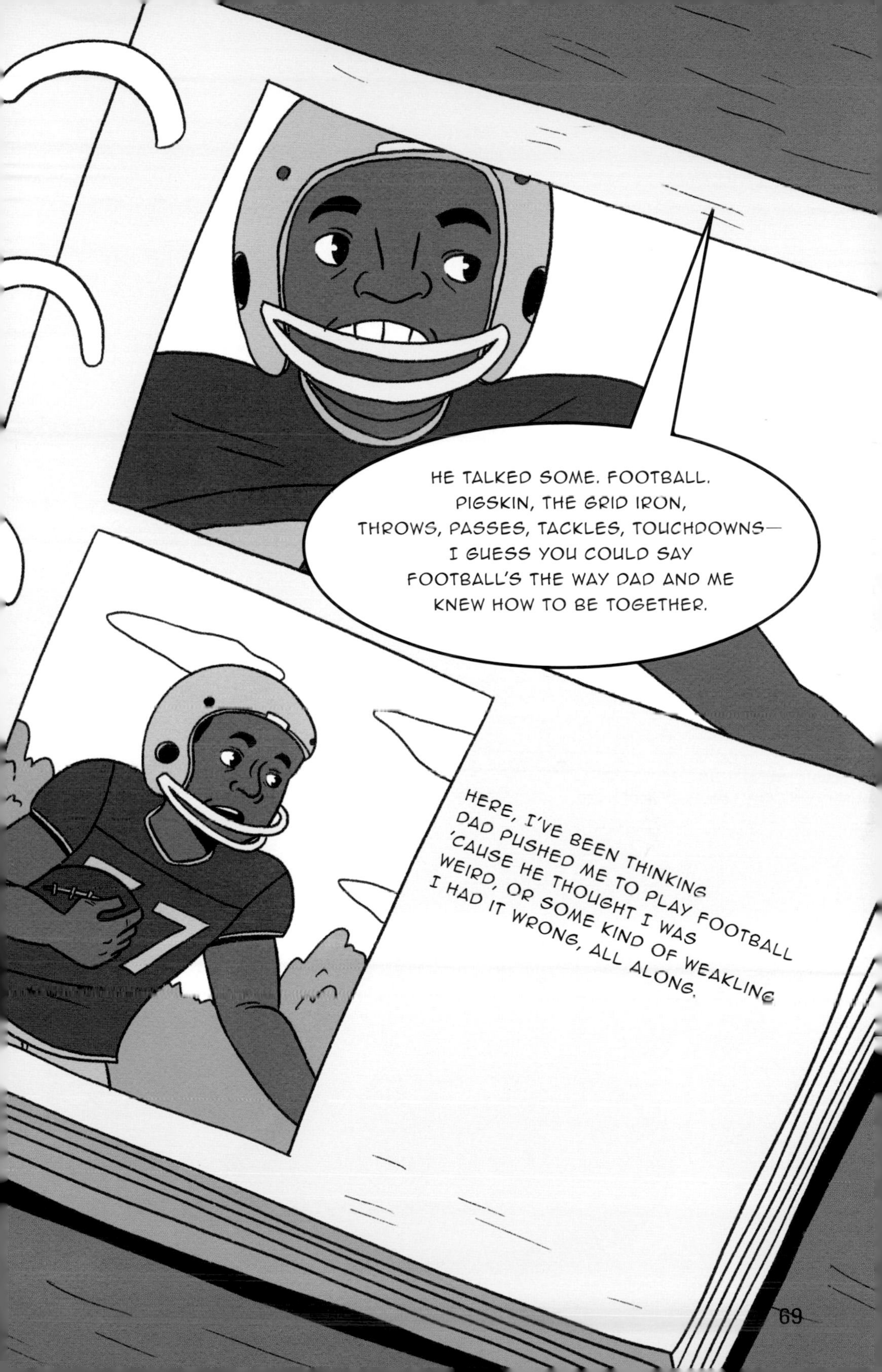
HE TALKED SOME. FOOTBALL. PIGSKIN, THE GRID IRON, THROWS, PASSES, TACKLES, TOUCHDOWNS— I GUESS YOU COULD SAY FOOTBALL'S THE WAY DAD AND ME KNEW HOW TO BE TOGETHER.
HERE, I'VE BEEN THINKING DAD PUSHED ME TO PLAY FOOTBALL 'CAUSE HE THOUGHT I WAS WEIRD, OR SOME KIND OF WEAKLING. I HAD IT WRONG, ALL ALONG.

LUTHER'S SAD SONG, AGAIN

"DANCE WITH MY FATHER"
PLAYS IN THE KITCHEN WHILE I
CHOKE ON EGGS, MISSING
MY RIGHT-HERE DAD LIKE LUTHER
MISSED HIS OWN GONE-SO-LONG DAD.

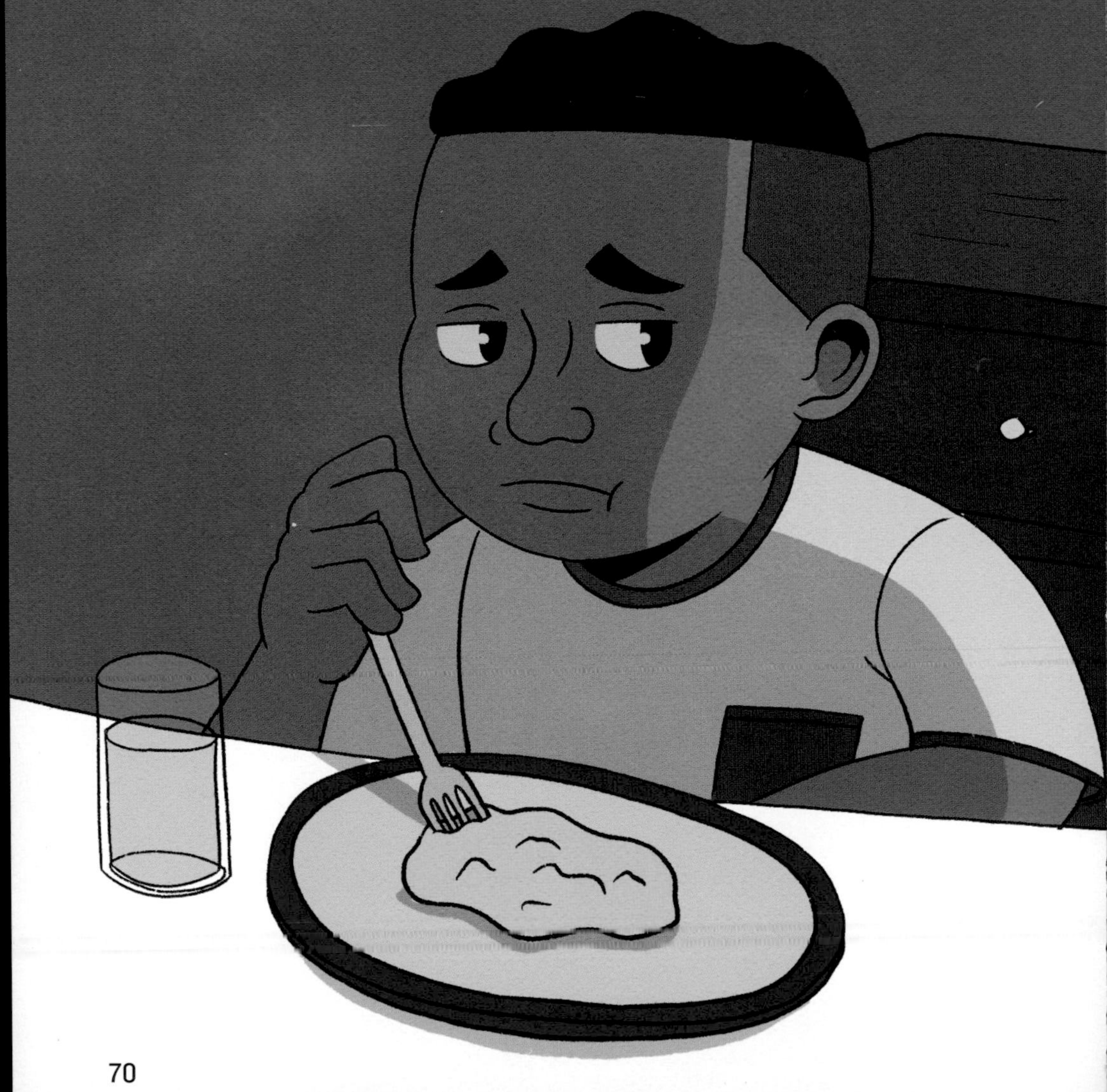

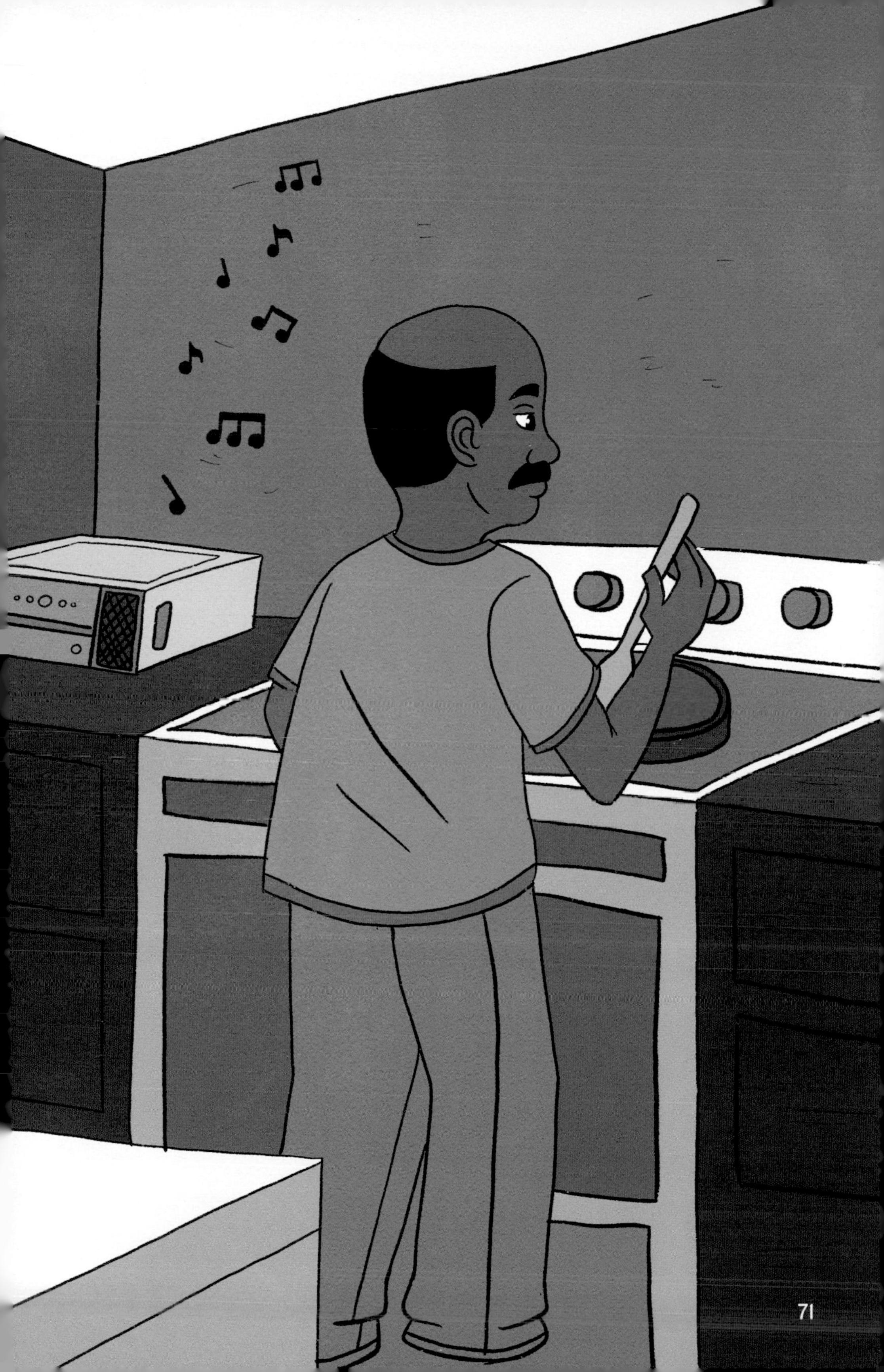

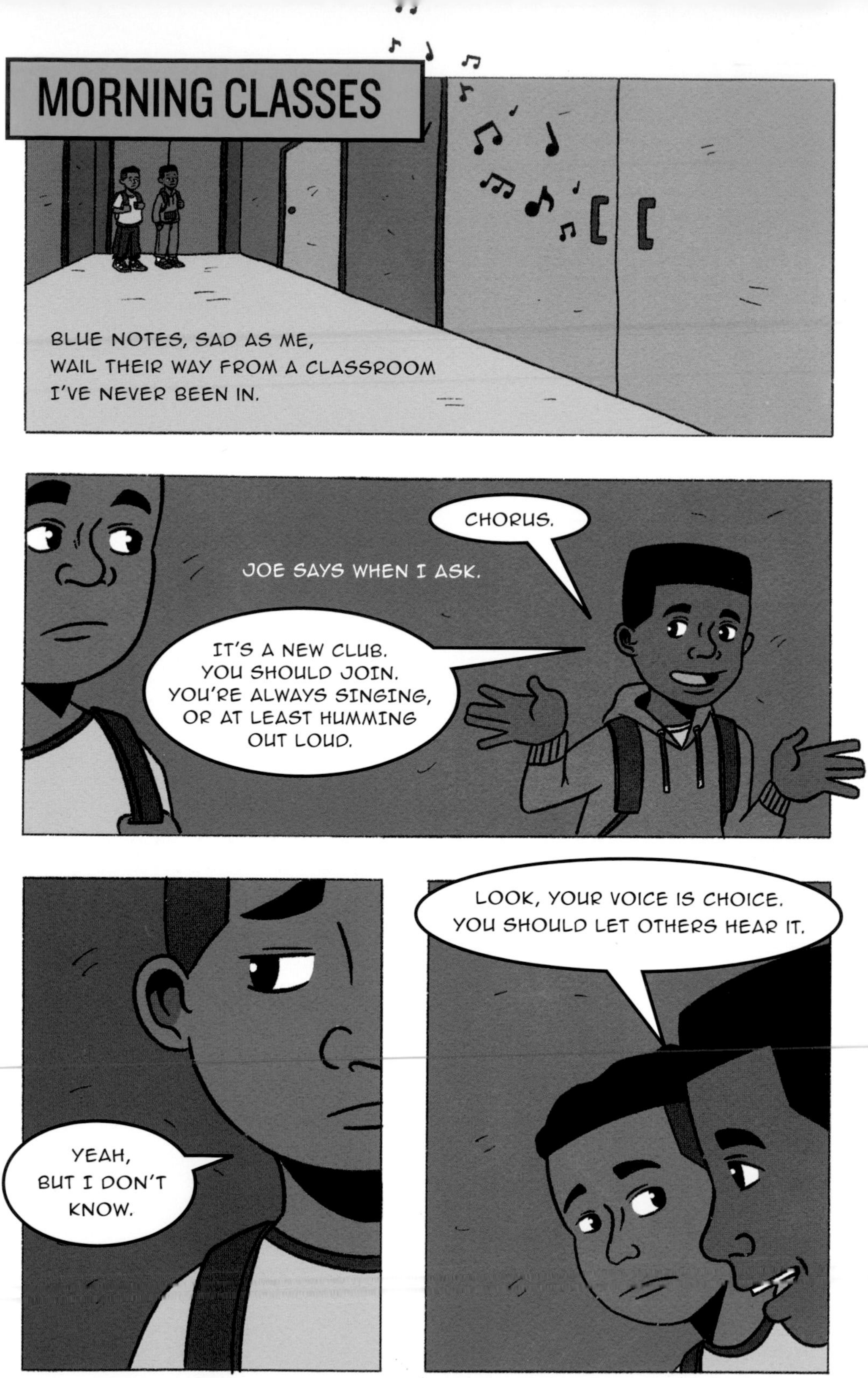
MORNING CLASSES
BLUE NOTES, SAD AS ME,
WAIL THEIR WAY FROM A CLASSROOM
I'VE NEVER BEEN IN.
CHORUS.
JOE SAYS WHEN I ASK.
IT'S A NEW CLUB. YOU SHOULD JOIN. YOU'RE ALWAYS SINGING, OR AT LEAST HUMMING OUT LOUD.
YEAH, BUT I DON'T KNOW.
LOOK, YOUR VOICE IS CHOICE. YOU SHOULD LET OTHERS HEAR IT.

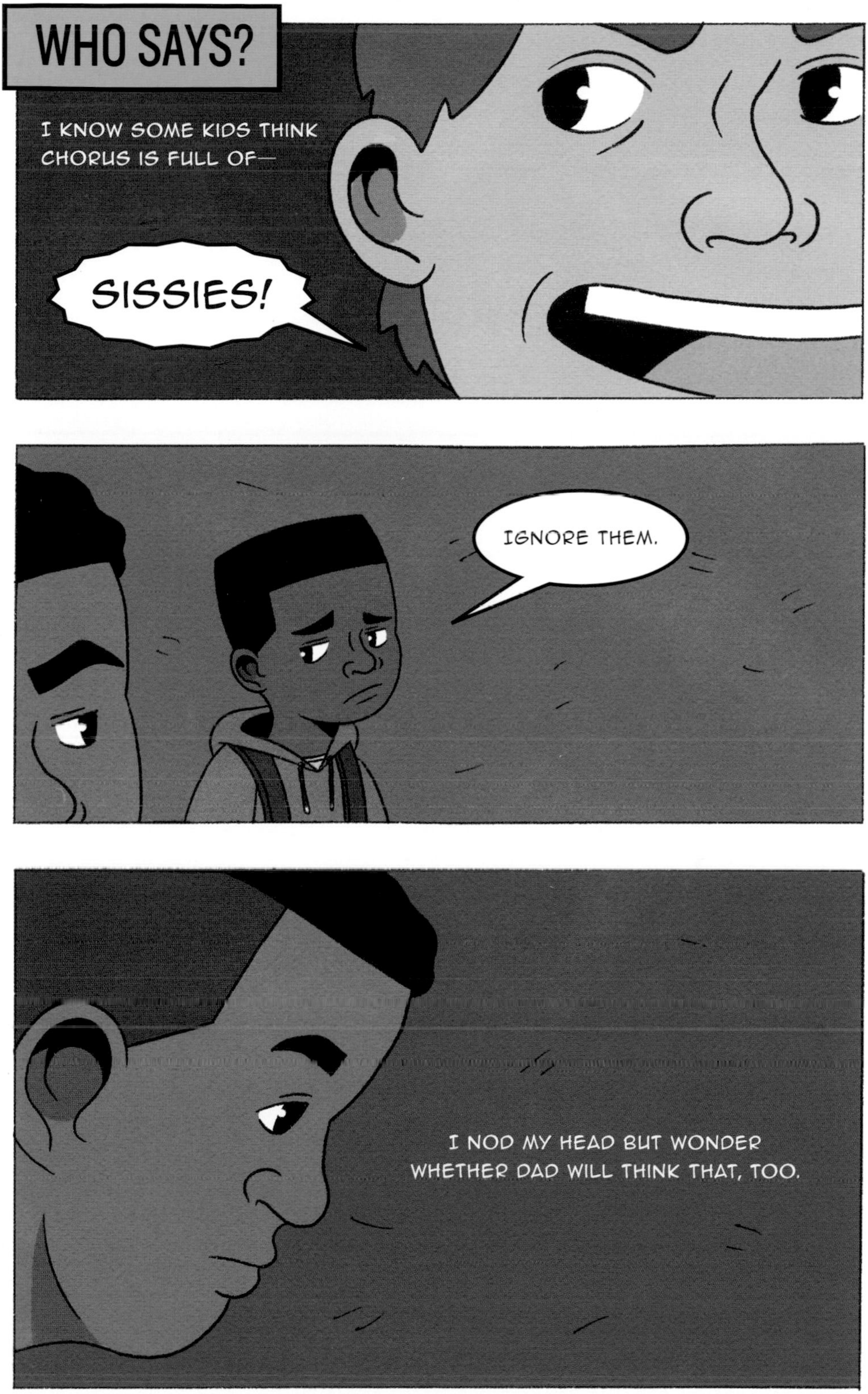
WHO SAYS?
I KNOW SOME KIDS THINK CHORUS IS FULL OF—
SISSIES!
IGNORE THEM.
I NOD MY HEAD BUT WONDER WHETHER DAD WILL THINK THAT, TOO.

SECOND THOUGHTS

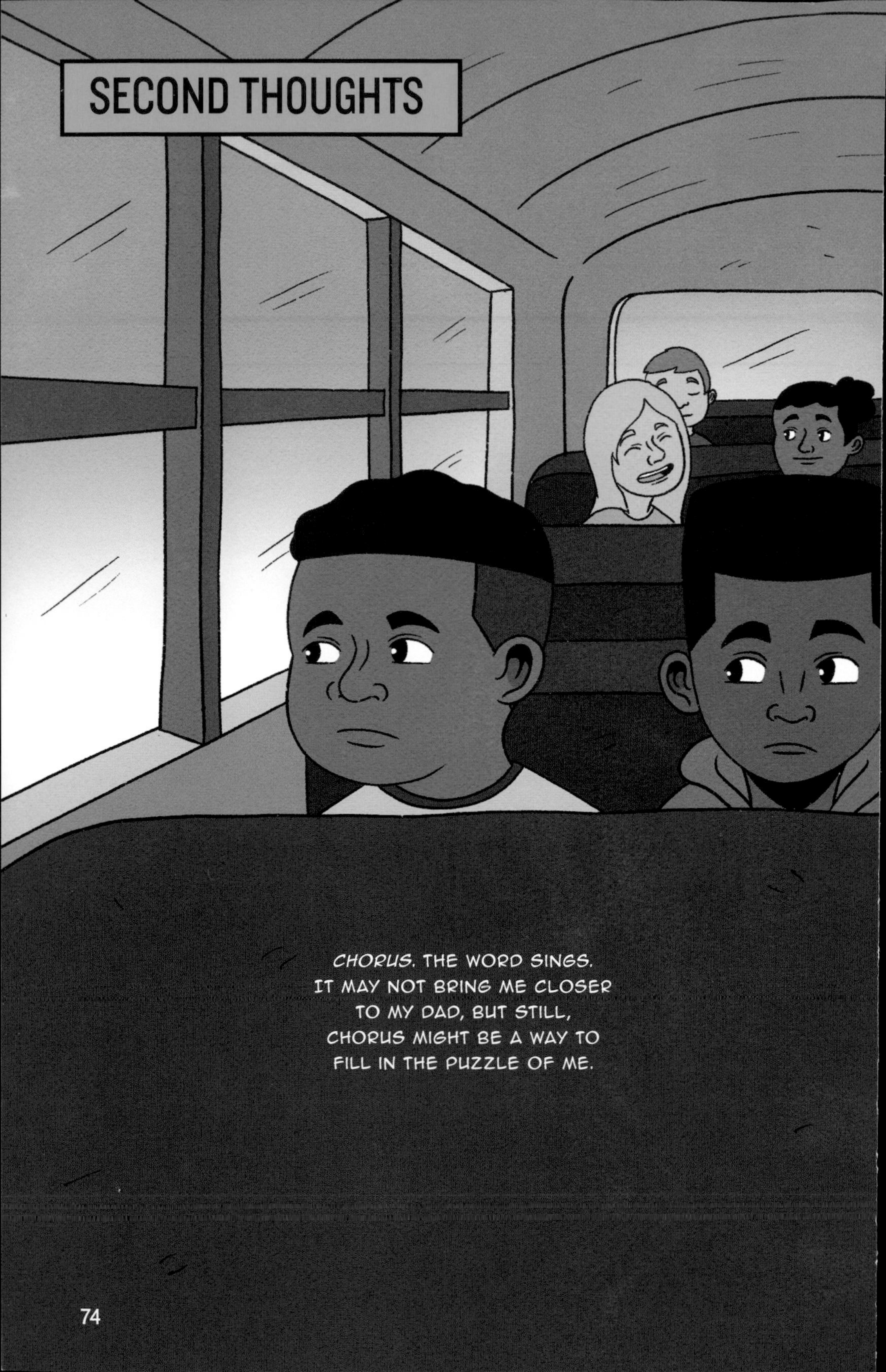
CHORUS. THE WORD SINGS.
IT MAY NOT BRING ME CLOSER
TO MY DAD, BUT STILL,
CHORUS MIGHT BE A WAY TO
FILL IN THE PUZZLE OF ME.

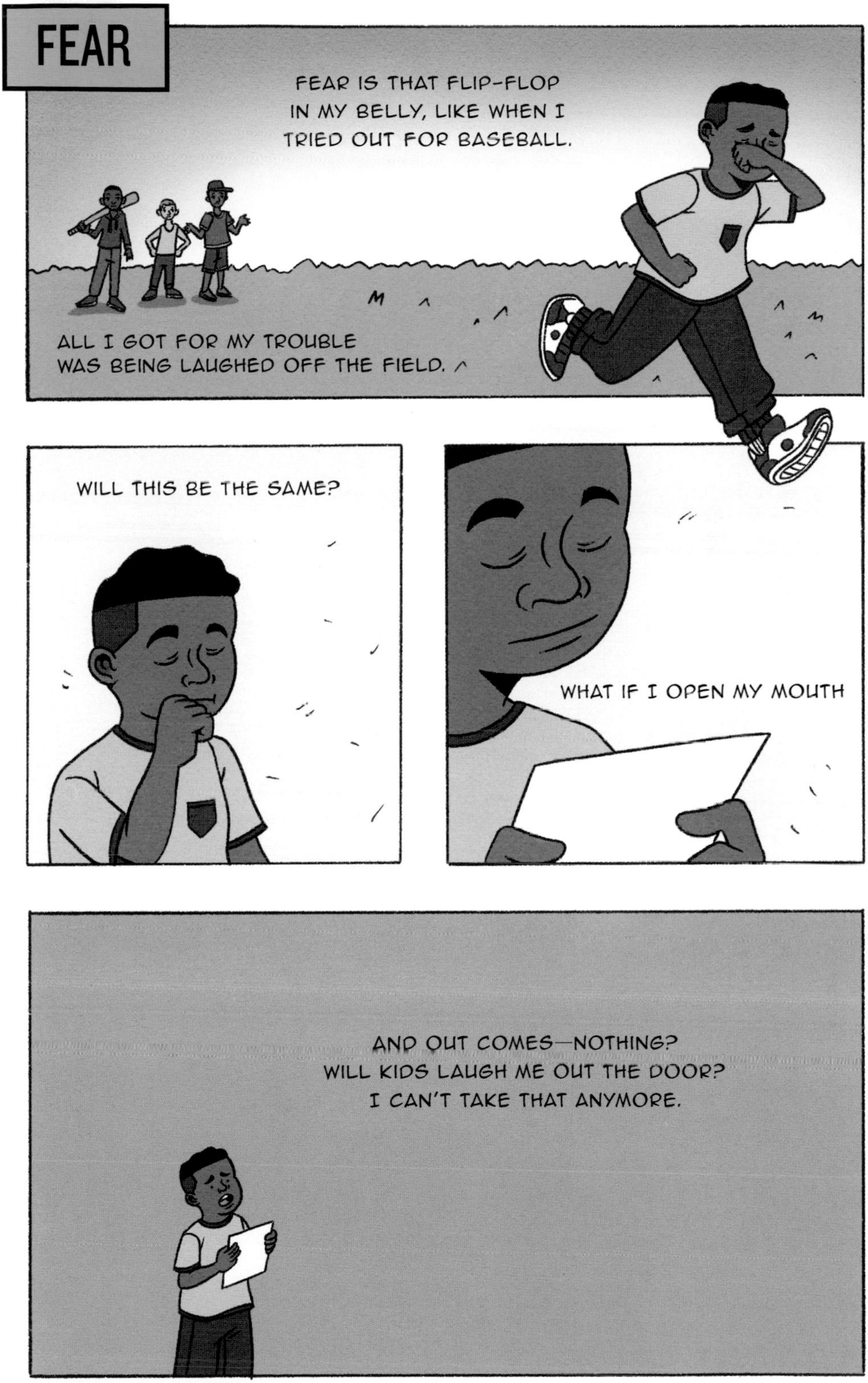
FEAR
FEAR IS THAT FLIP-FLOP IN MY BELLY, LIKE WHEN I TRIED OUT FOR BASEBALL.
ALL I GOT FOR MY TROUBLE WAS BEING LAUGHED OFF THE FIELD.
WILL THIS BE THE SAME?
WHAT IF I OPEN MY MOUTH
AND OUT COMES—NOTHING? WILL KIDS LAUGH ME OUT THE DOOR? I CAN'T TAKE THAT ANYMORE.

TURTLE

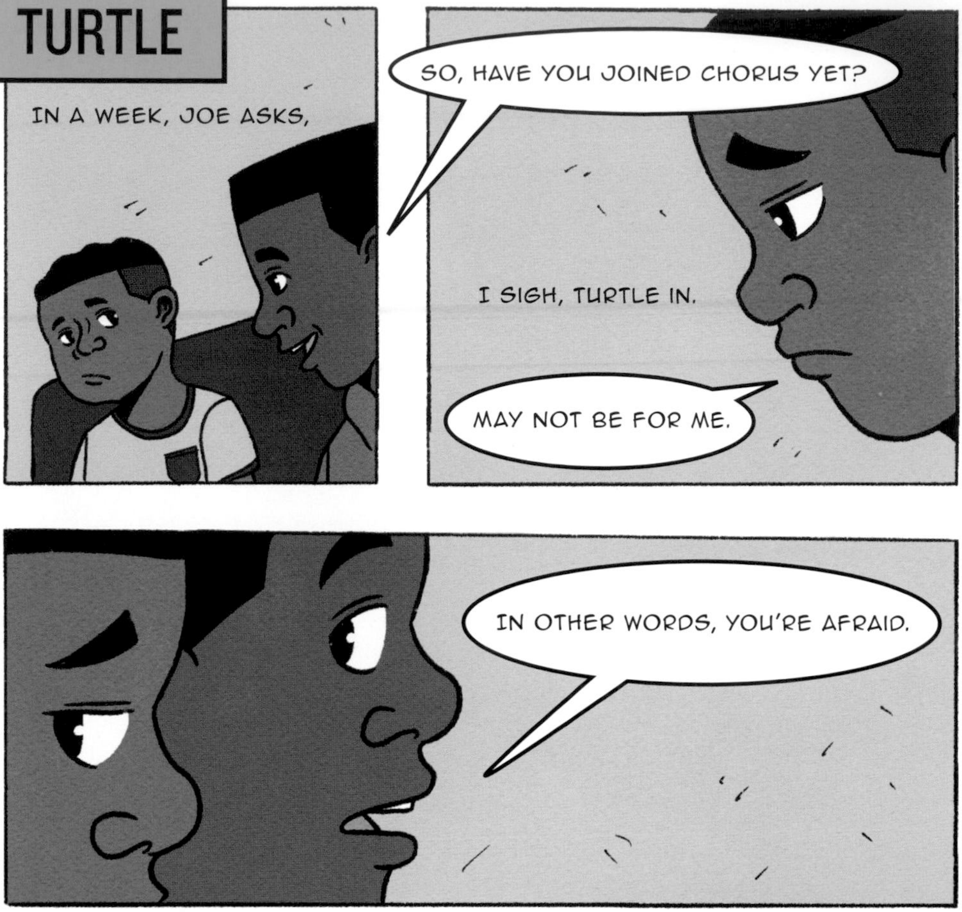
IN A WEEK, JOE ASKS,
SO, HAVE YOU JOINED CHORUS YET?
I SIGH, TURTLE IN.
MAY NOT BE FOR ME.
IN OTHER WORDS, YOU'RE AFRAID.

BUSTED

BEST THING ABOUT FRIENDS:
THEY KNOW YOU INSIDE AND OUT.
WORST THING ABOUT FRIENDS:
THEY KNOW YOU INSIDE AND OUT.
MY TURTLE SHELL IS USELESS.

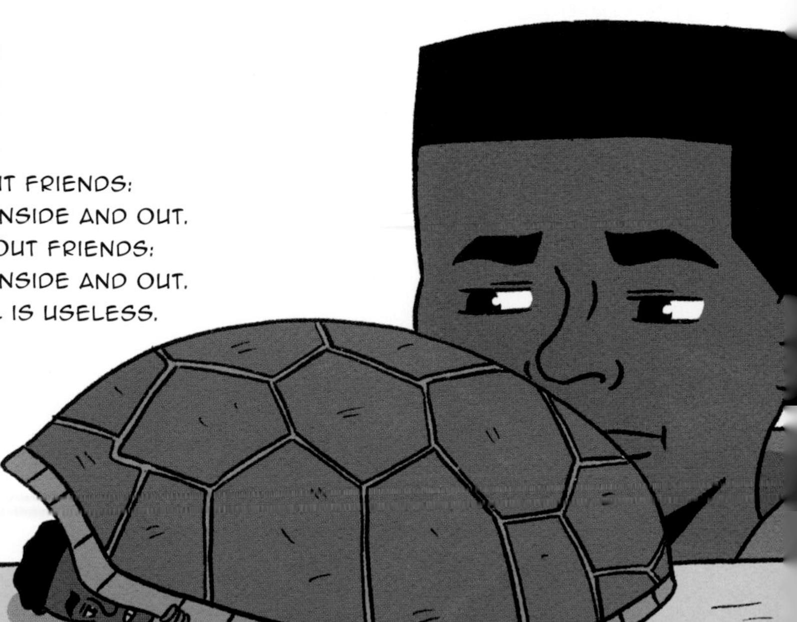

SHIFT

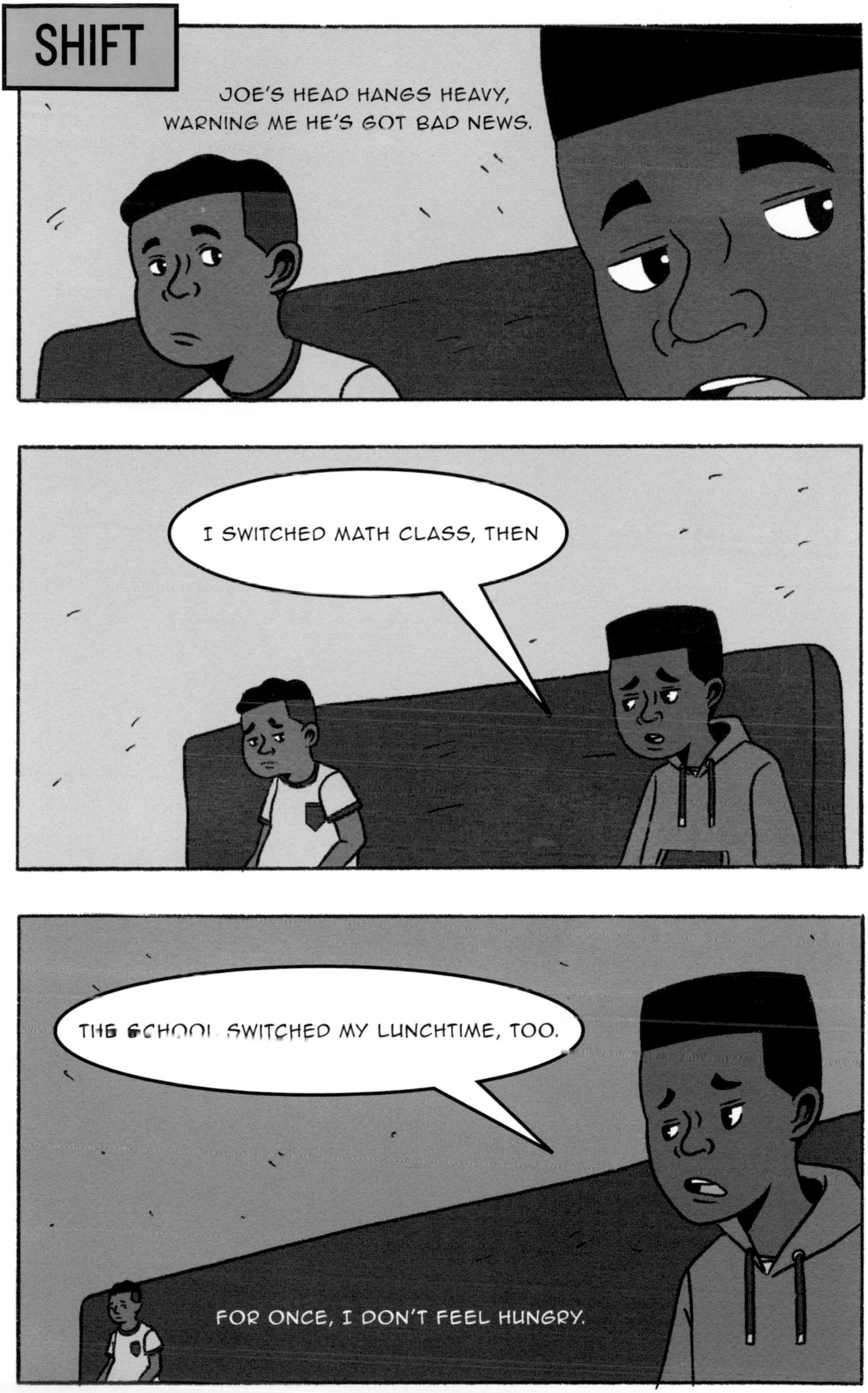

JOE'S HEAD HANGS HEAVY, WARNING ME HE'S GOT BAD NEWS.
I SWITCHED MATH CLASS, THEN
THE SCHOOL SWITCHED MY LUNCHTIME, TOO.
FOR ONCE, I DON'T FEEL HUNGRY.

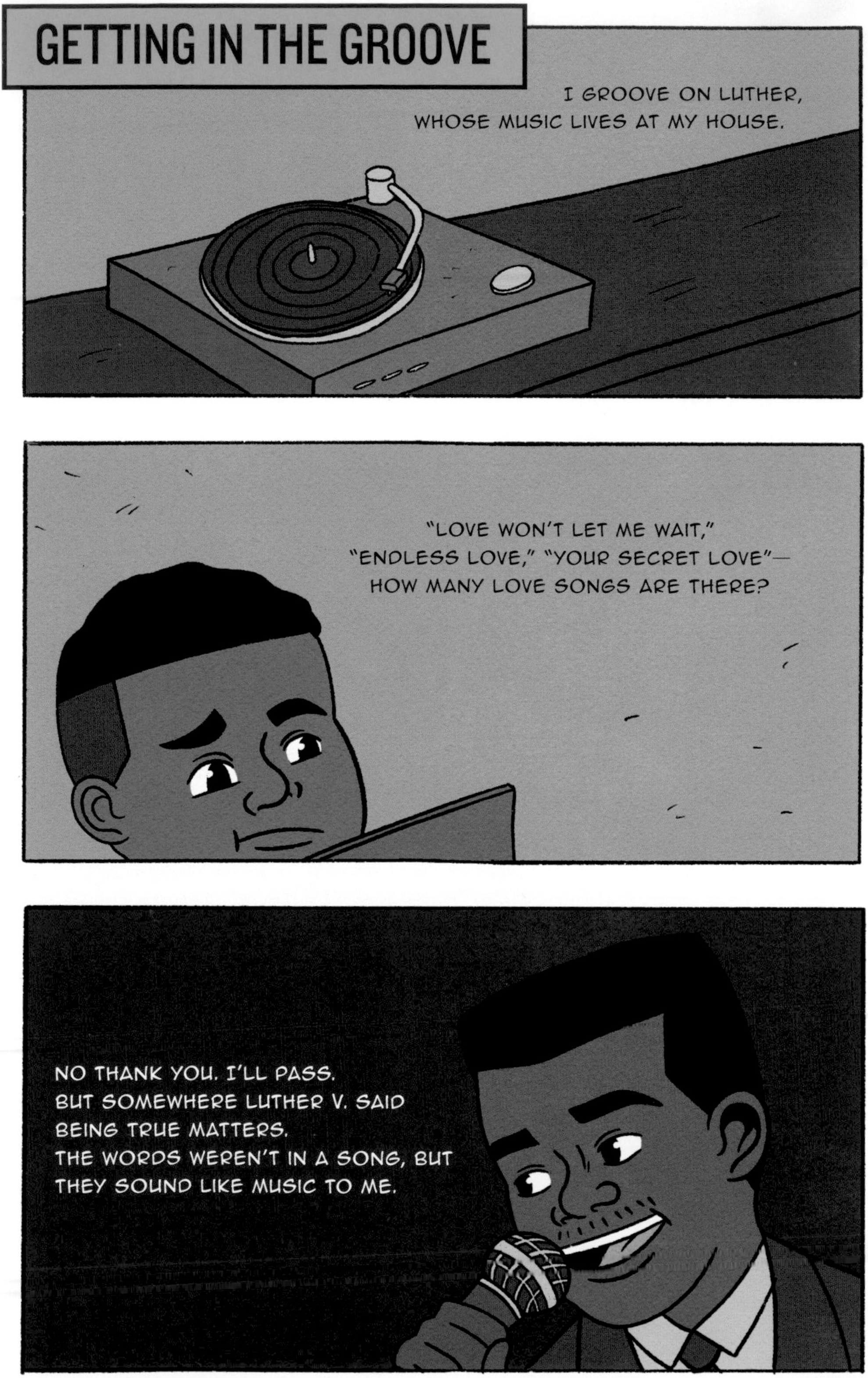
GETTING IN THE GROOVE
I GROOVE ON LUTHER,
WHOSE MUSIC LIVES AT MY HOUSE.
"LOVE WON'T LET ME WAIT," "ENDLESS LOVE," "YOUR SECRET LOVE"— HOW MANY LOVE SONGS ARE THERE?
NO THANK YOU. I'LL PASS. BUT SOMEWHERE LUTHER V. SAID BEING TRUE MATTERS. THE WORDS WEREN'T IN A SONG, BUT THEY SOUND LIKE MUSIC TO ME.

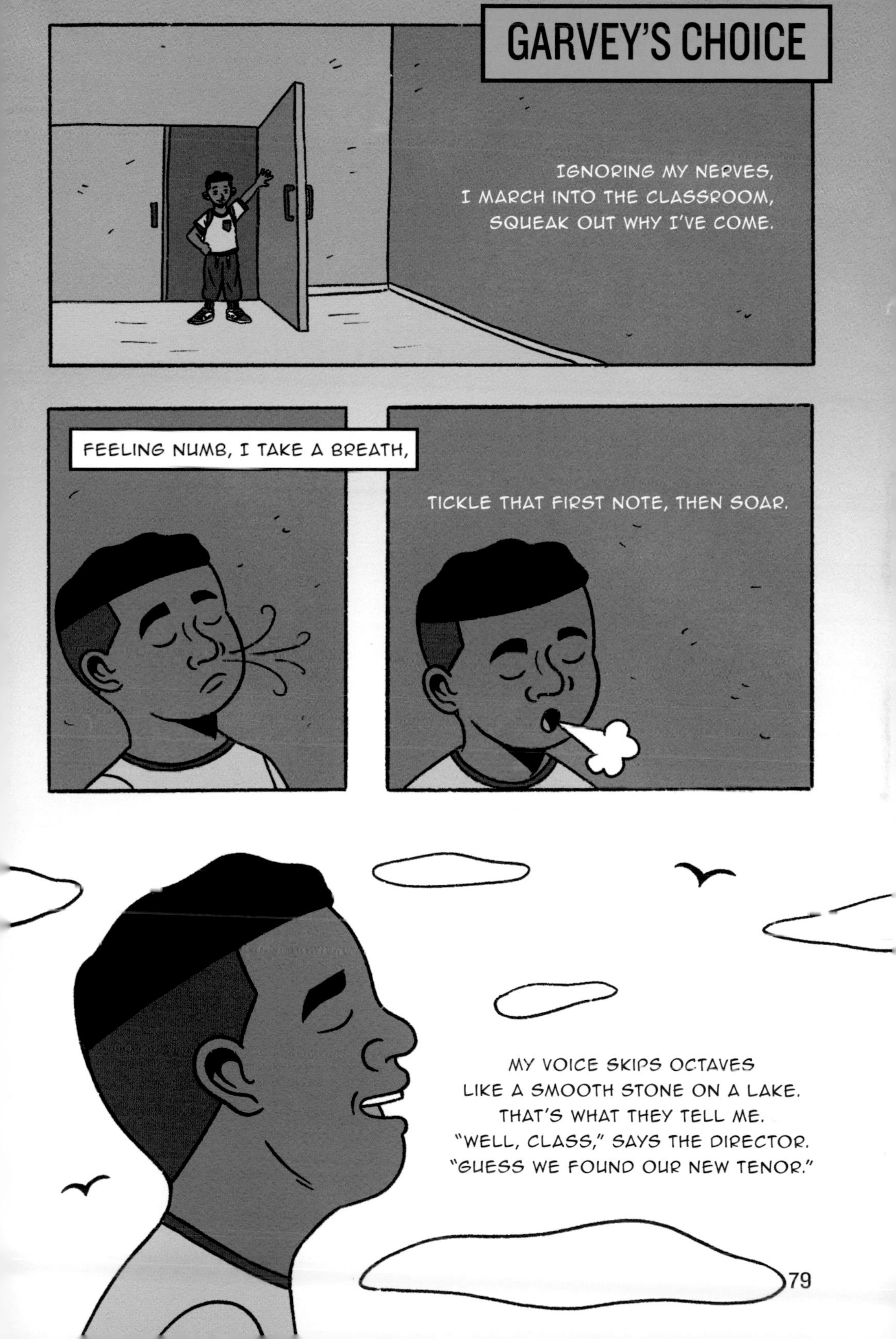
GARVEY'S CHOICE
IGNORING MY NERVES,
I MARCH INTO THE CLASSROOM,
SQUEAK OUT WHY I'VE COME.
FEELING NUMB, I TAKE A BREATH,
TICKLE THAT FIRST NOTE, THEN SOAR.
MY VOICE SKIPS OCTAVES
LIKE A SMOOTH STONE ON A LAKE.
THAT'S WHAT THEY TELL ME.
"WELL, CLASS," SAYS THE DIRECTOR.
"GUESS WE FOUND OUR NEW TENOR."

LIGHTER THAN AIR

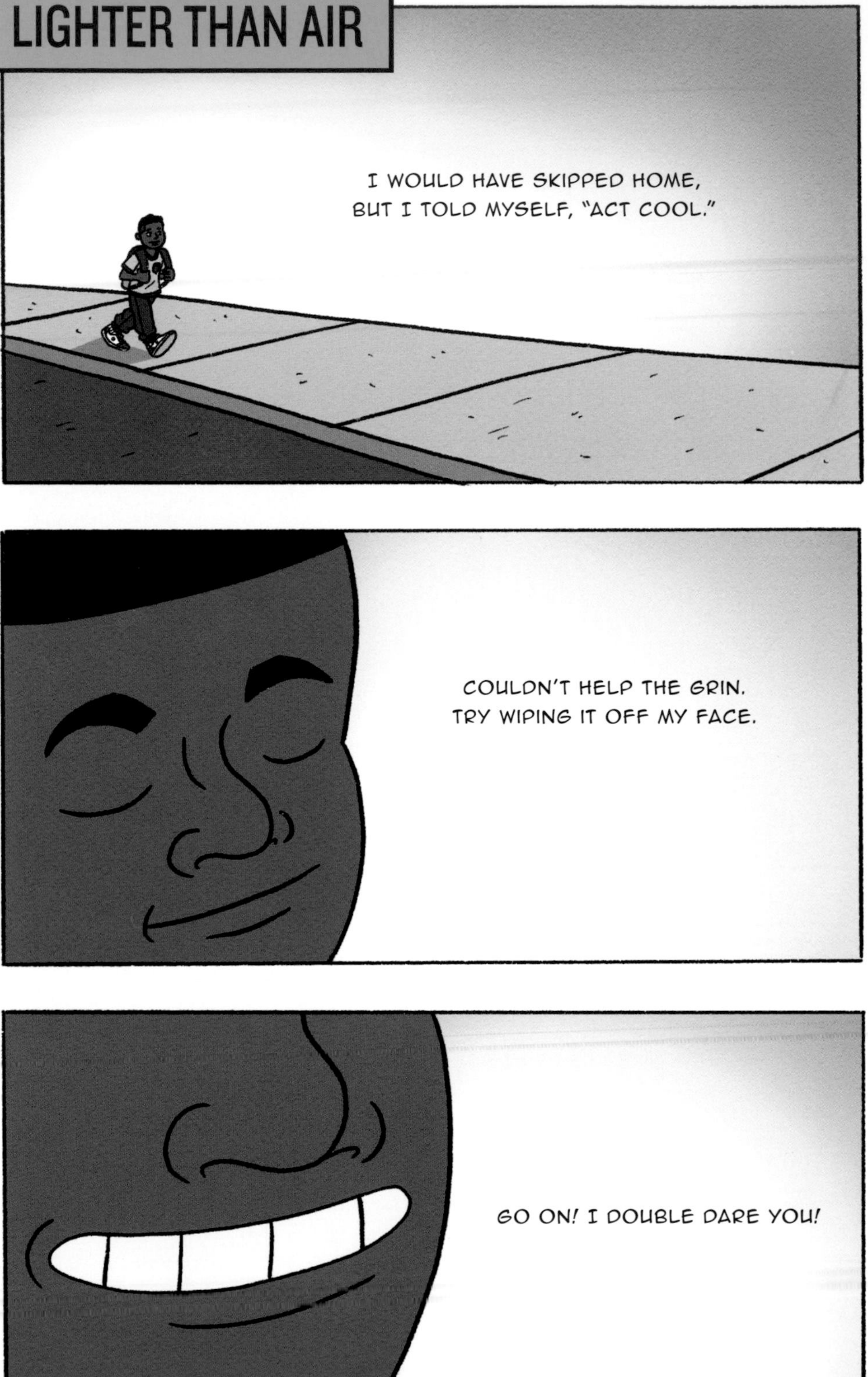
I WOULD HAVE SKIPPED HOME,
BUT I TOLD MYSELF, "ACT COOL."
COULDN'T HELP THE GRIN.
TRY WIPING IT OFF MY FACE.
GO ON! I DOUBLE DARE YOU!

PACT

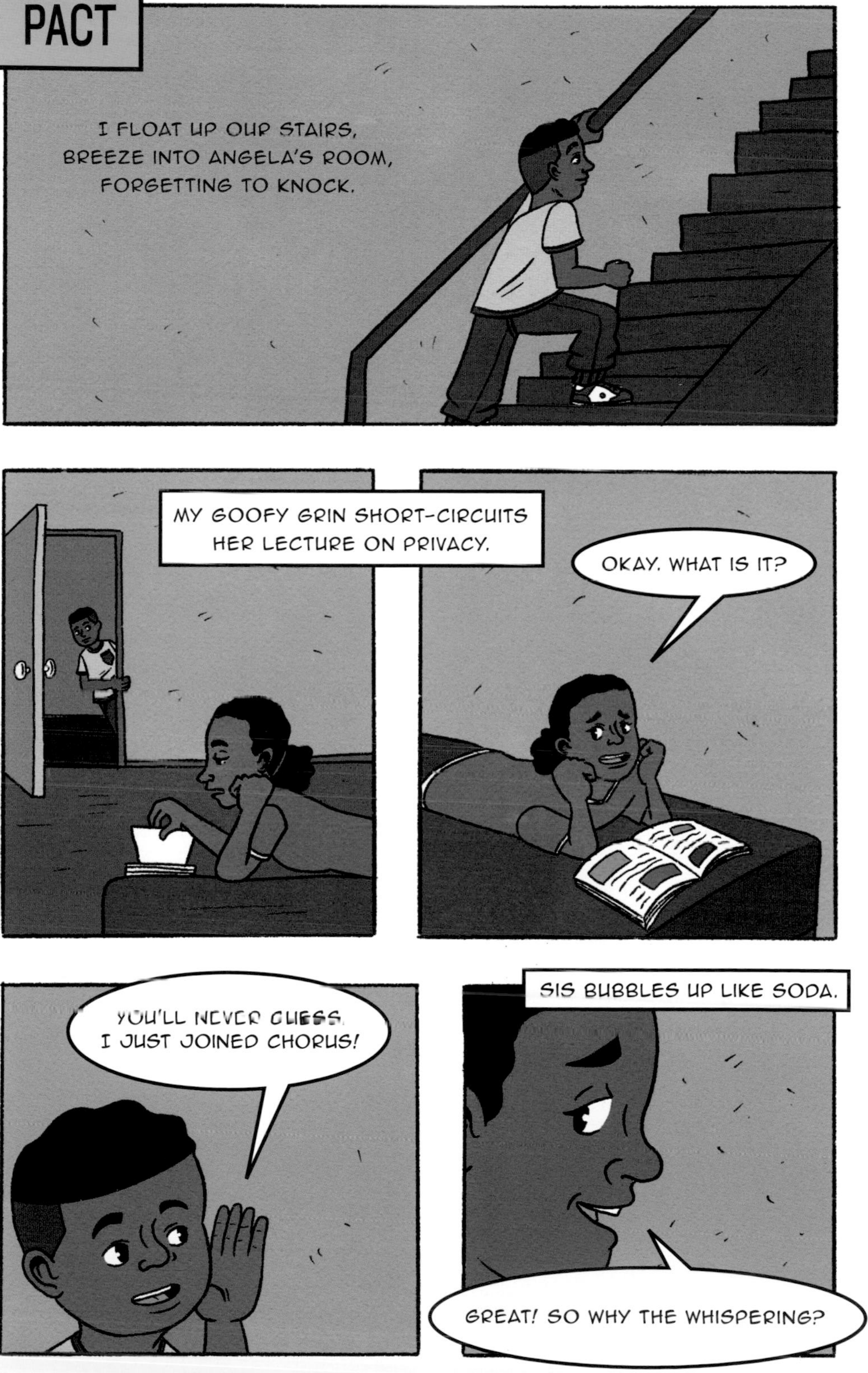
I FLOAT UP OUR STAIRS, BREEZE INTO ANGELA'S ROOM, FORGETTING TO KNOCK.
MY GOOFY GRIN SHORT-CIRCUITS HER LECTURE ON PRIVACY.
OKAY. WHAT IS IT?
YOU'LL NEVER GUESS. I JUST JOINED CHORUS!
SIS BUBBLES UP LIKE SODA.
GREAT! SO WHY THE WHISPERING?

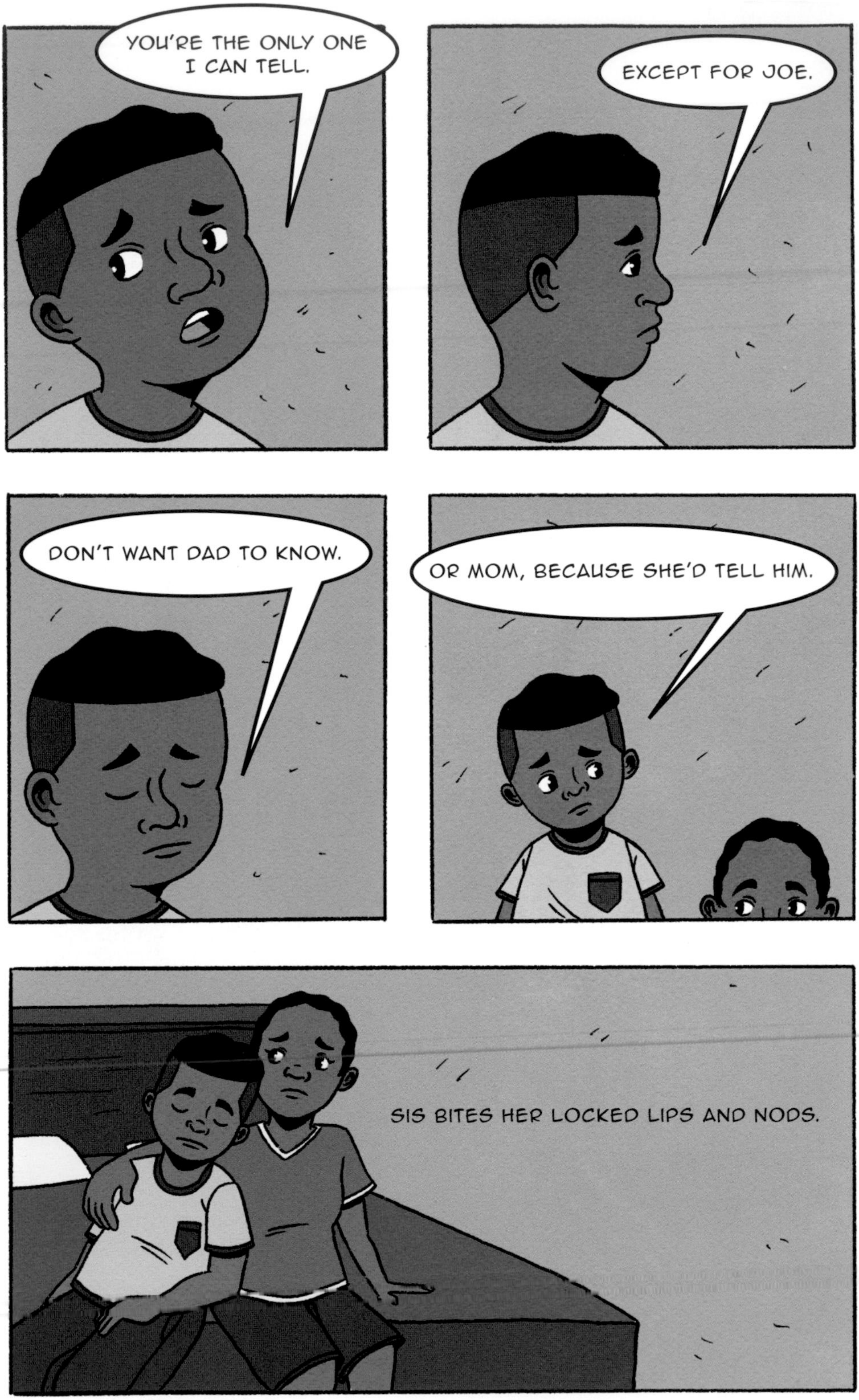
YOU'RE THE ONLY ONE I CAN TELL.
EXCEPT FOR JOE.
DON'T WANT DAD TO KNOW.
OR MOM, BECAUSE SHE'D TELL HIM.
SIS BITES HER LOCKED LIPS AND NODS.

FIRST WARM-UPS

ASK ME WHAT SCALES ARE.
YESTERDAY, I'D SAY, "FISH SKIN."
NOW, I PUSH MY VOICE
TO CLIMB A NEW KIND OF STAIR:
DO, RE, MI IN F AND G.

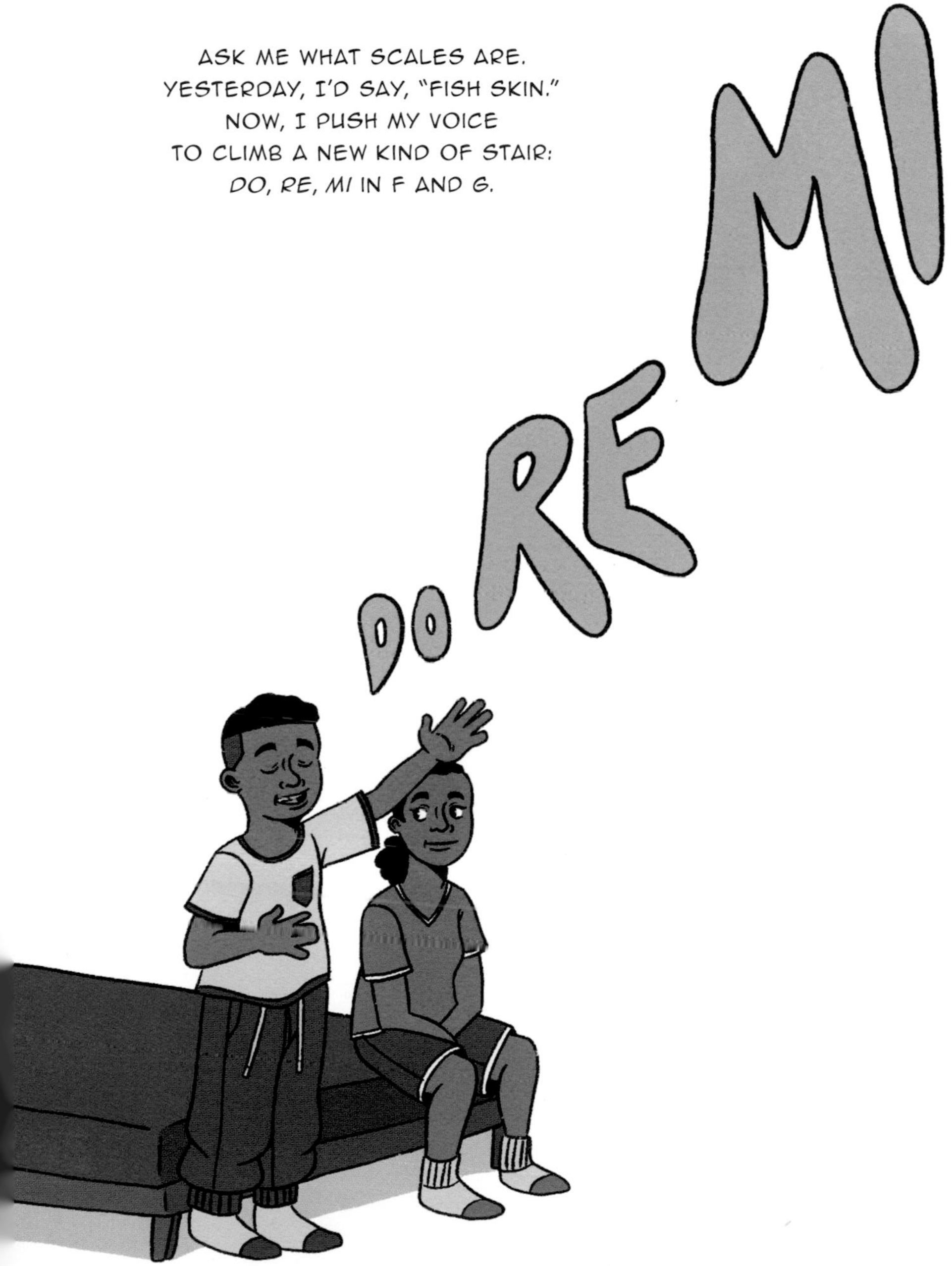
DO
RE
MI

CHORUS CALAMITY

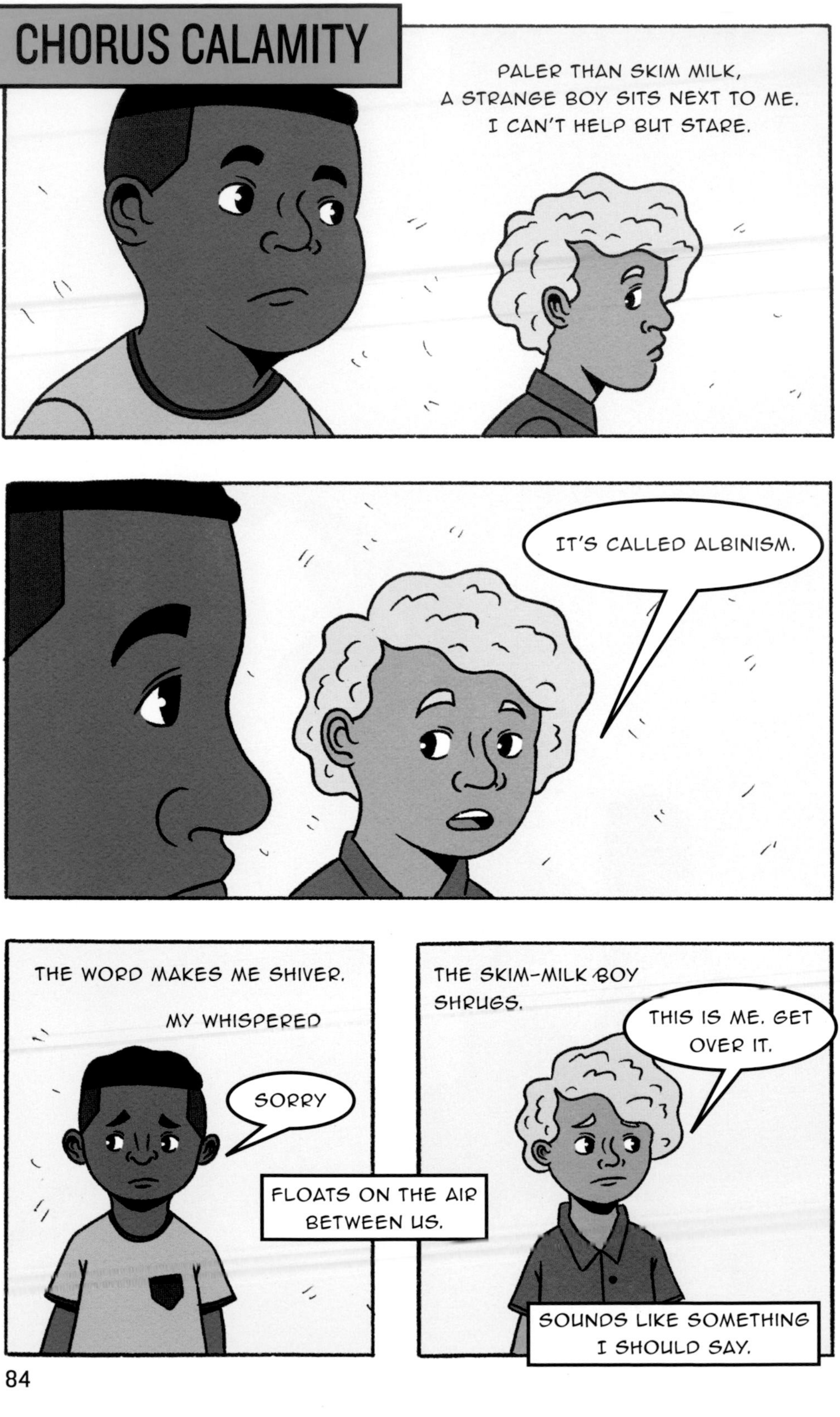

PALER THAN SKIM MILK,
A STRANGE BOY SITS NEXT TO ME.
I CAN'T HELP BUT STARE.
IT'S CALLED ALBINISM.
THE WORD MAKES ME SHIVER.
MY WHISPERED
SORRY
FLOATS ON THE AIR BETWEEN US.
THE SKIM-MILK BOY SHRUGS.
THIS IS ME. GET OVER IT.
SOUNDS LIKE SOMETHING I SHOULD SAY.

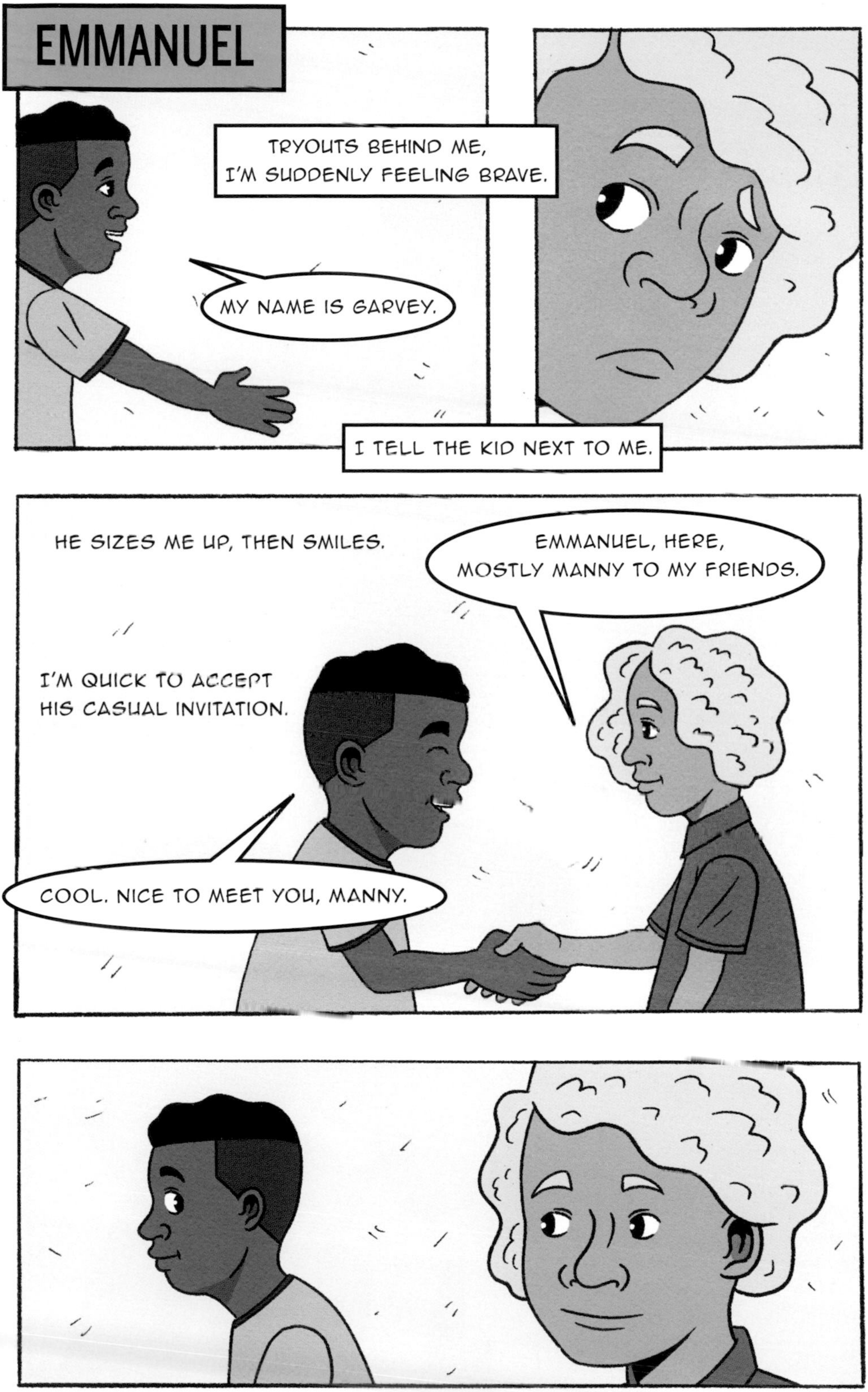
EMMANUEL
TRYOUTS BEHIND ME, I'M SUDDENLY FEELING BRAVE.
MY NAME IS GARVEY.
I TELL THE KID NEXT TO ME.
HE SIZES ME UP, THEN SMILES.
EMMANUEL, HERE, MOSTLY MANNY TO MY FRIENDS.
I'M QUICK TO ACCEPT HIS CASUAL INVITATION.
COOL. NICE TO MEET YOU, MANNY.

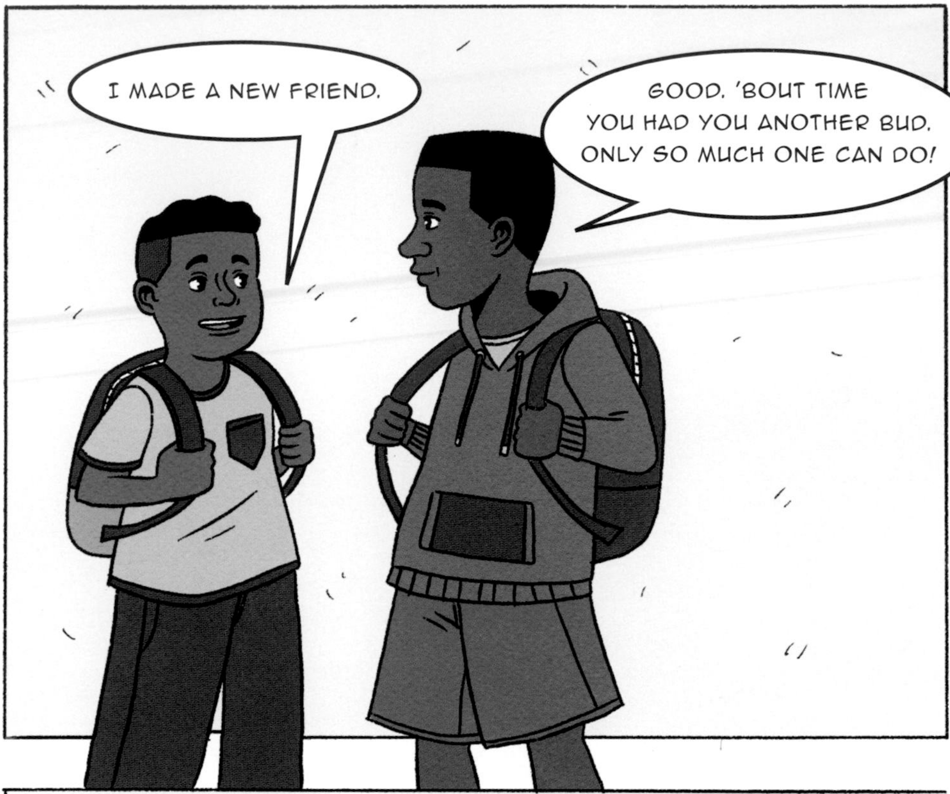
I MADE A NEW FRIEND.
GOOD. 'BOUT TIME YOU HAD YOU ANOTHER BUD. ONLY SO MUCH ONE CAN DO!

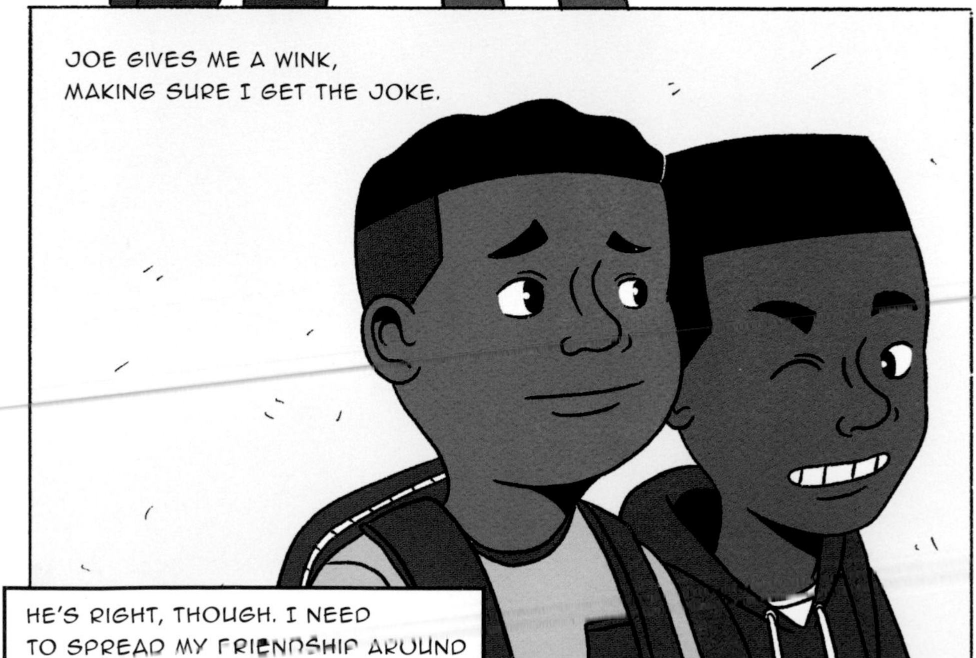
JOE GIVES ME A WINK, MAKING SURE I GET THE JOKE.
HE'S RIGHT, THOUGH. I NEED TO SPREAD MY FRIENDSHIP AROUND SO IT WON'T GET TOO HEAVY.

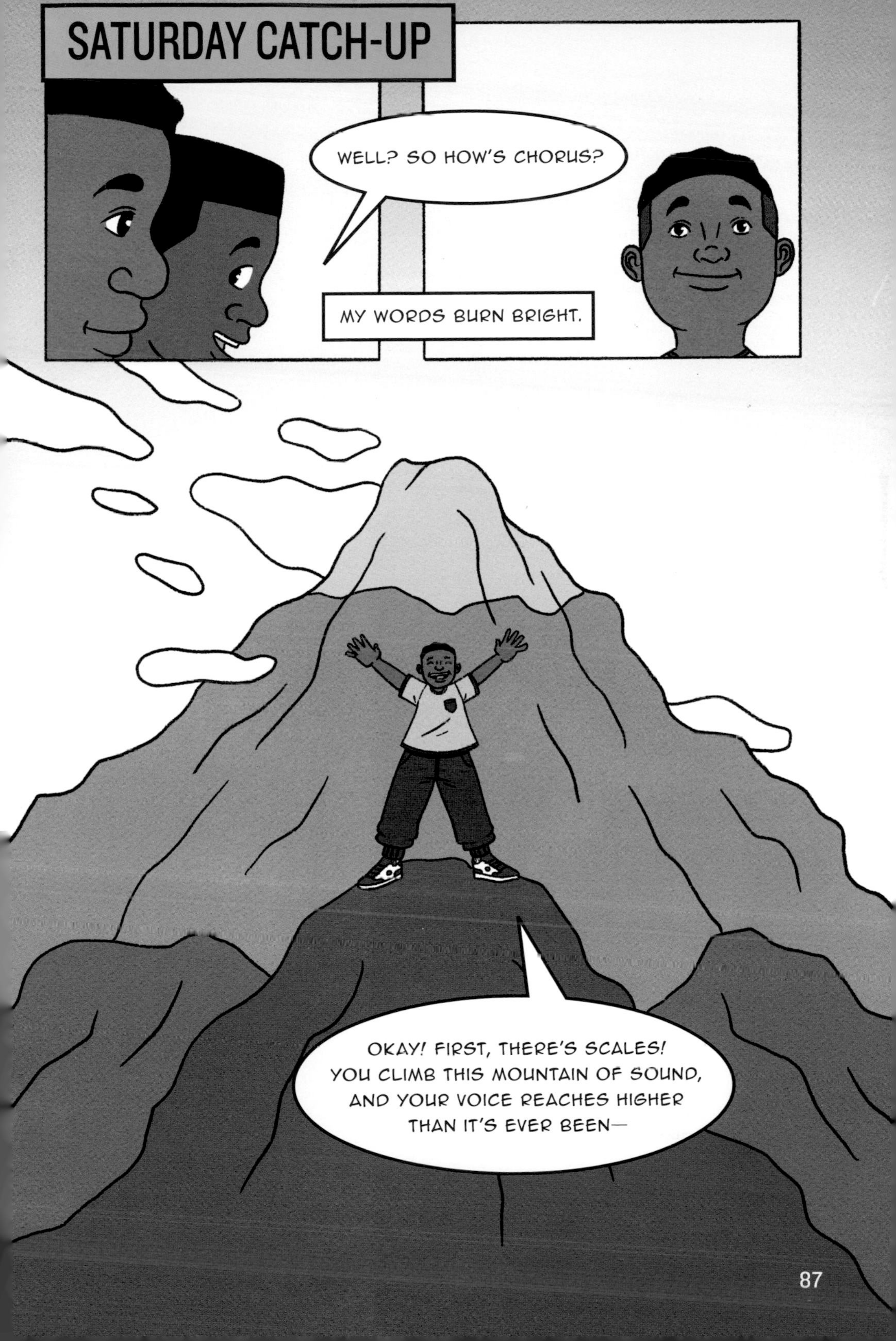
SATURDAY CATCH-UP
WELL? SO HOW'S CHORUS?
MY WORDS BURN BRIGHT.
OKAY! FIRST, THERE'S SCALES! YOU CLIMB THIS MOUNTAIN OF SOUND, AND YOUR VOICE REACHES HIGHER THAN IT'S EVER BEEN—

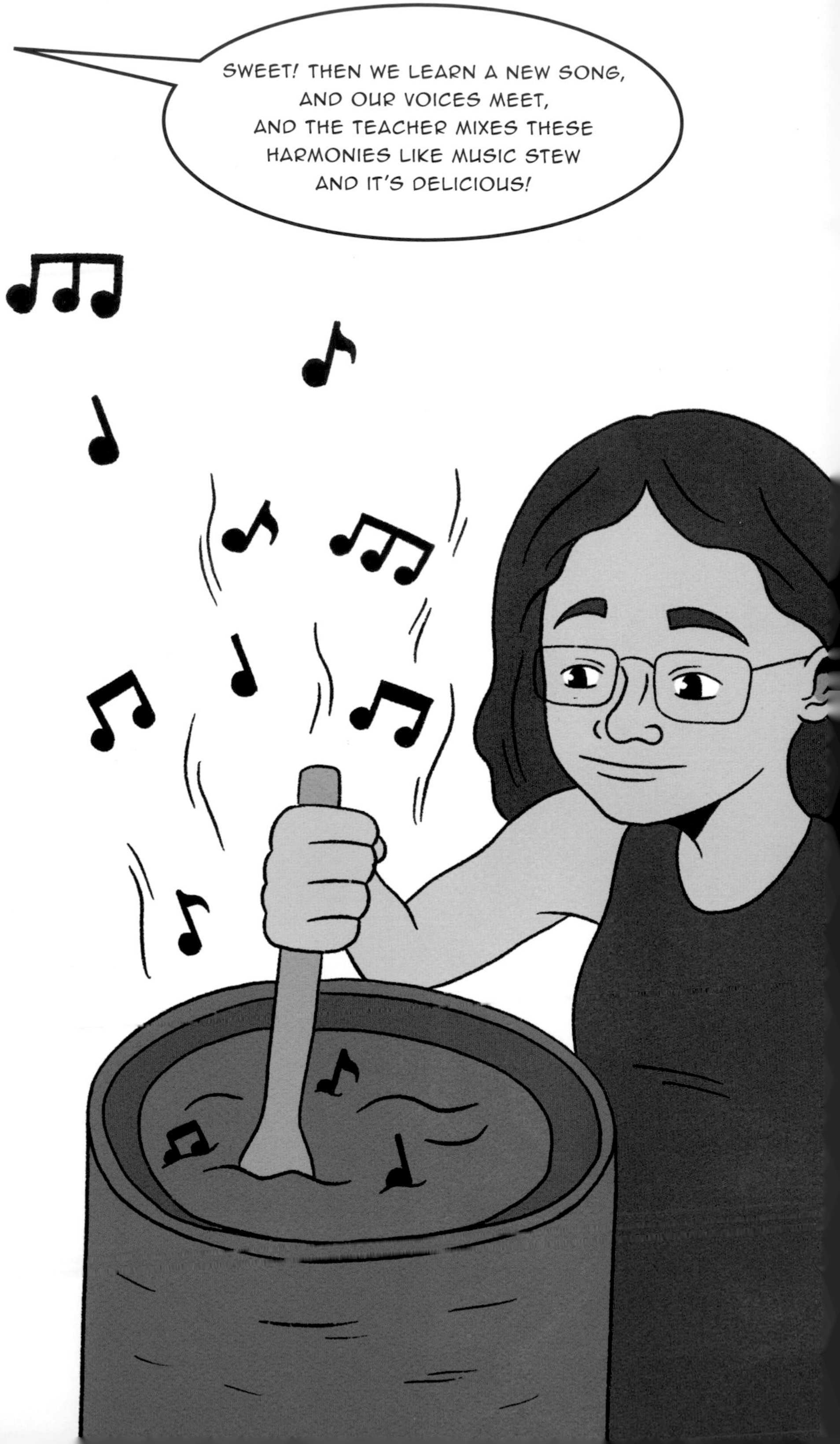
SWEET! THEN WE LEARN A NEW SONG, AND OUR VOICES MEET, AND THE TEACHER MIXES THESE HARMONIES LIKE MUSIC STEW AND IT'S DELICIOUS!

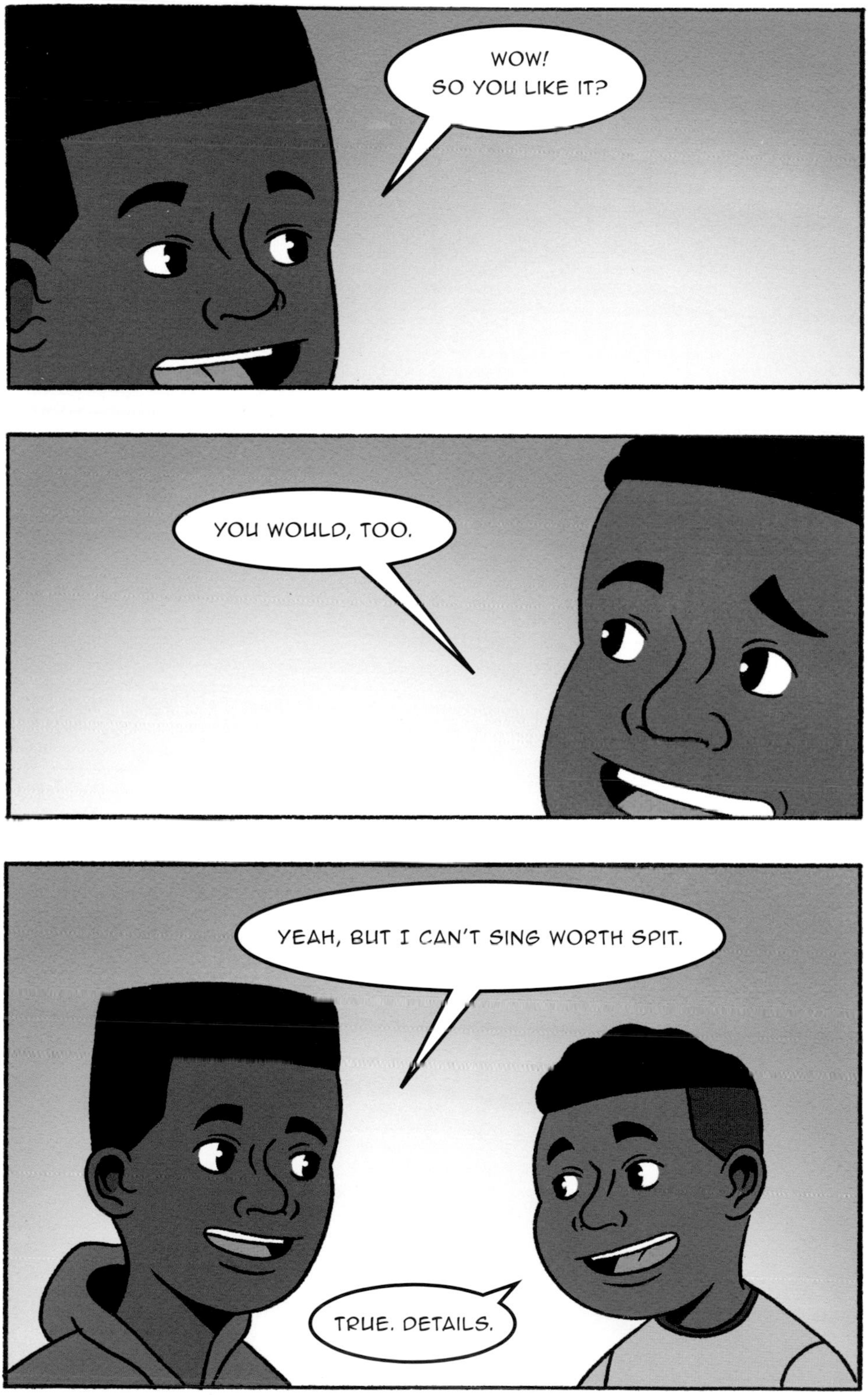
WOW!
SO YOU LIKE IT?
YOU WOULD, TOO.
YEAH, BUT I CAN'T SING WORTH SPIT.
TRUE. DETAILS.

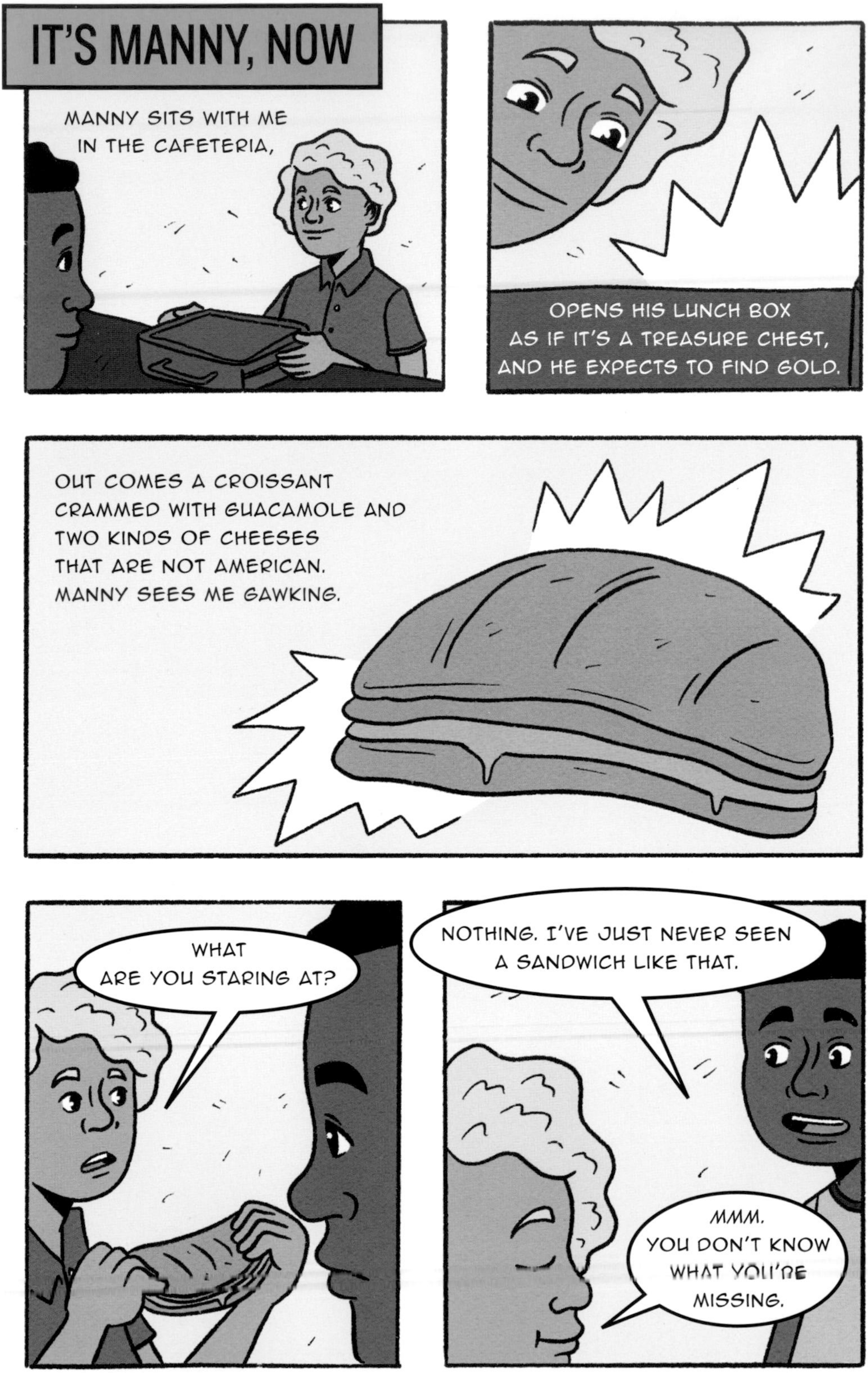
IT'S MANNY, NOW
MANNY SITS WITH ME IN THE CAFETERIA,
OPENS HIS LUNCH BOX AS IF IT'S A TREASURE CHEST, AND HE EXPECTS TO FIND GOLD.
OUT COMES A CROISSANT CRAMMED WITH GUACAMOLE AND TWO KINDS OF CHEESES THAT ARE NOT AMERICAN. MANNY SEES ME GAWKING.
WHAT ARE YOU STARING AT?
NOTHING. I'VE JUST NEVER SEEN A SANDWICH LIKE THAT.
MMM. YOU DON'T KNOW WHAT YOU'RE MISSING.

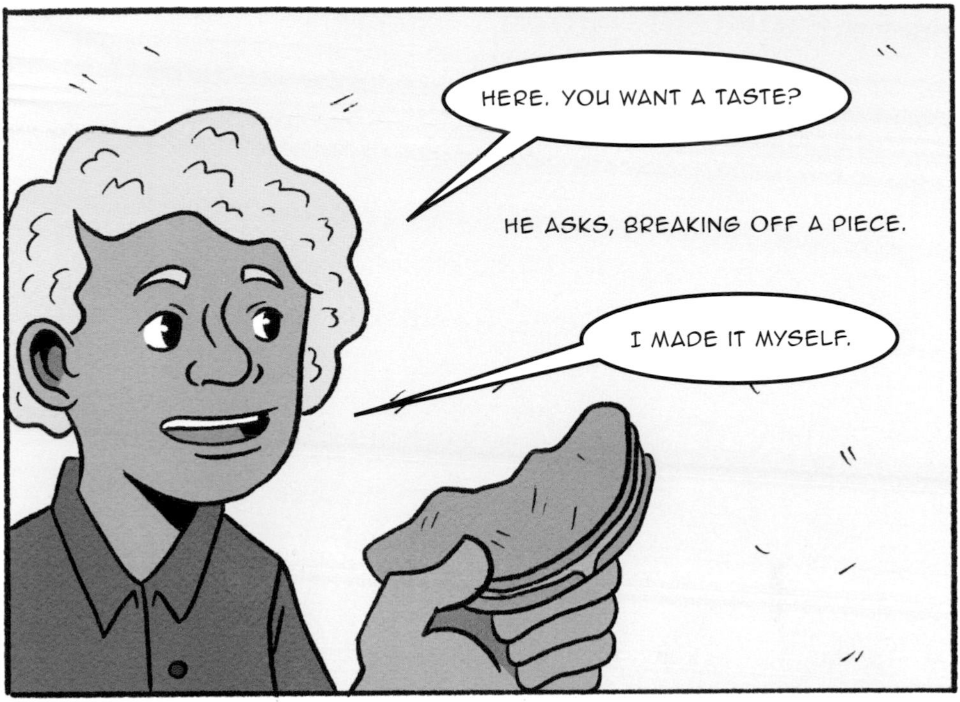
HERE. YOU WANT A TASTE?
HE ASKS, BREAKING OFF A PIECE.
I MADE IT MYSELF.

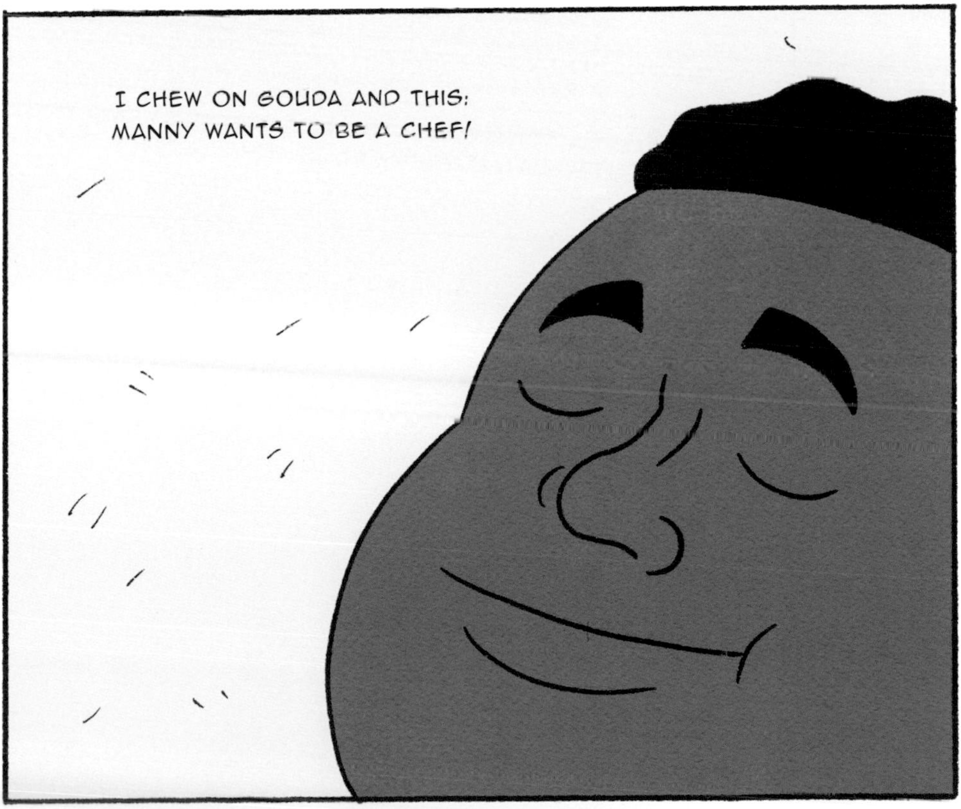
I CHEW ON GOUDA AND THIS:
MANNY WANTS TO BE A CHEF!

NO WORDS NEEDED

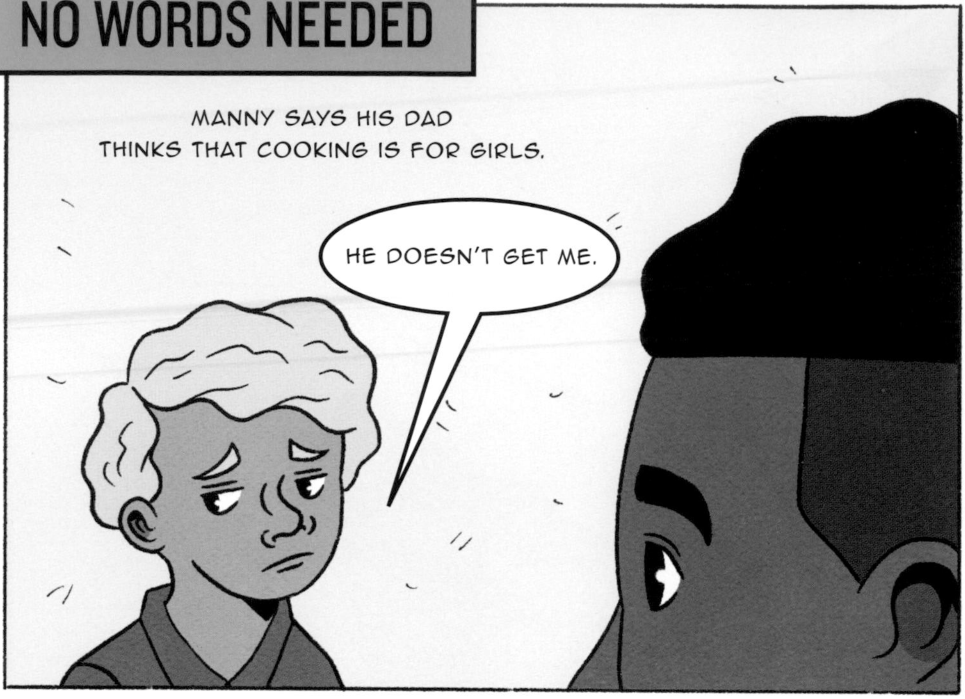
MANNY SAYS HIS DAD
THINKS THAT COOKING IS FOR GIRLS.
HE DOESN'T GET ME.

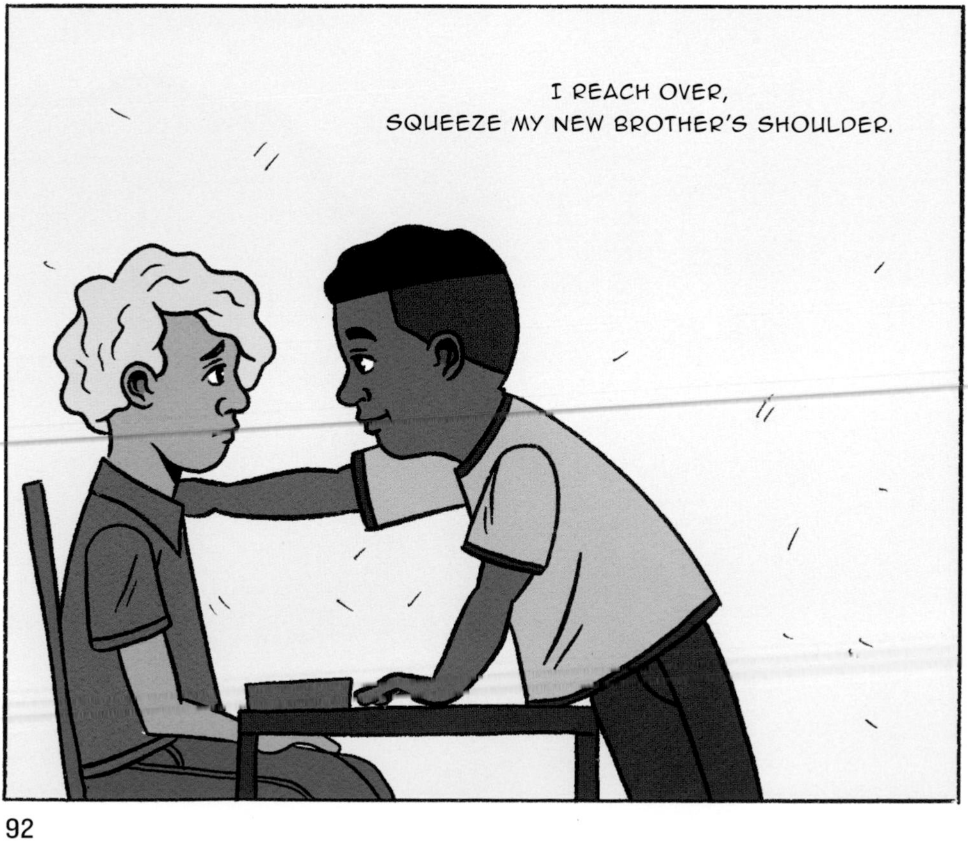
I REACH OVER,
SQUEEZE MY NEW BROTHER'S SHOULDER.

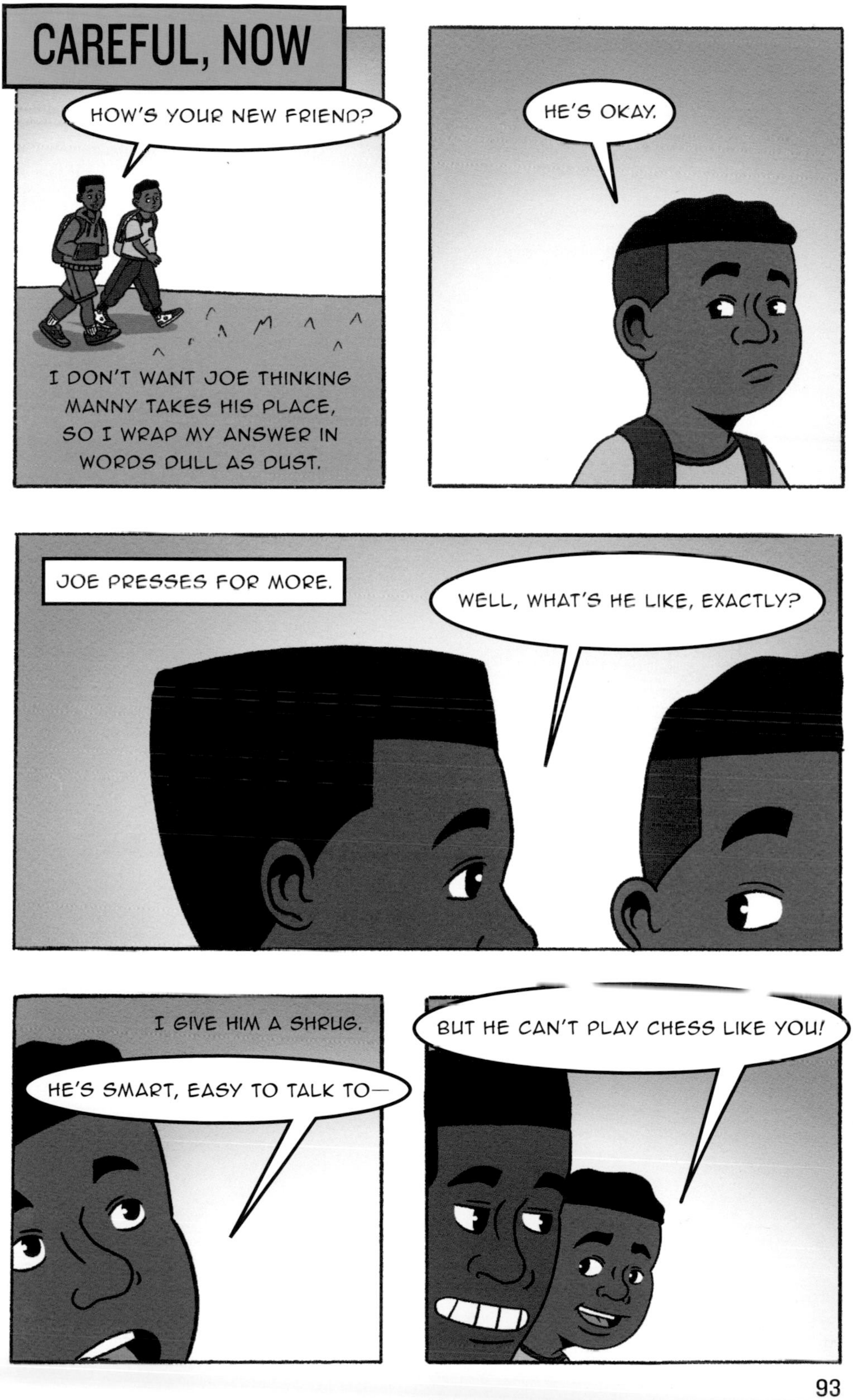
CAREFUL, NOW
HOW'S YOUR NEW FRIEND?
I DON'T WANT JOE THINKING MANNY TAKES HIS PLACE, SO I WRAP MY ANSWER IN WORDS DULL AS DUST.
HE'S OKAY.
JOE PRESSES FOR MORE.
WELL, WHAT'S HE LIKE, EXACTLY?
I GIVE HIM A SHRUG.
HE'S SMART, EASY TO TALK TO—
BUT HE CAN'T PLAY CHESS LIKE YOU!

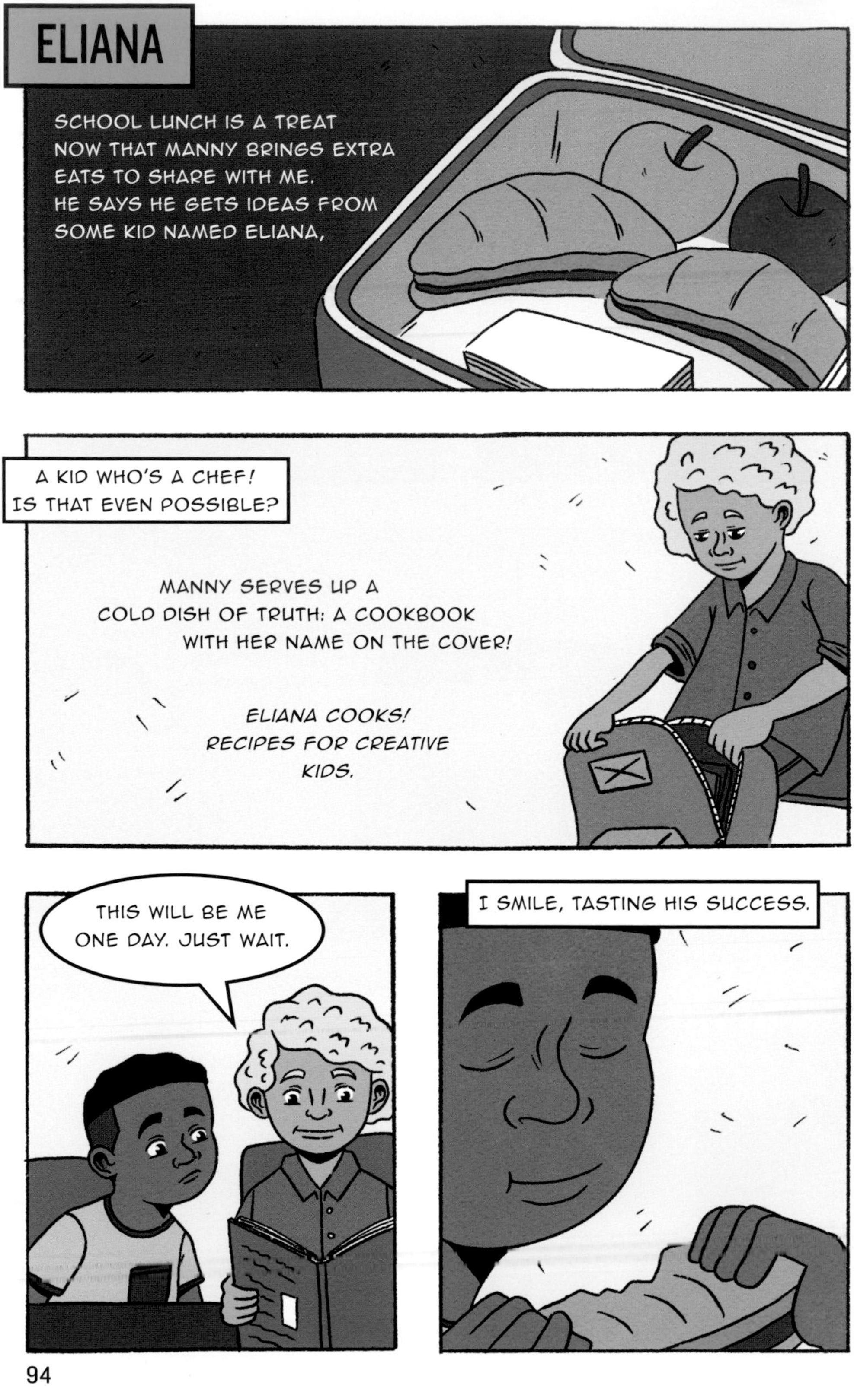
ELIANA
SCHOOL LUNCH IS A TREAT NOW THAT MANNY BRINGS EXTRA EATS TO SHARE WITH ME. HE SAYS HE GETS IDEAS FROM SOME KID NAMED ELIANA,
A KID WHO'S A CHEF! IS THAT EVEN POSSIBLE?
MANNY SERVES UP A COLD DISH OF TRUTH: A COOKBOOK WITH HER NAME ON THE COVER!
ELIANA COOKS! RECIPES FOR CREATIVE KIDS.
THIS WILL BE ME ONE DAY. JUST WAIT.
I SMILE, TASTING HIS SUCCESS.

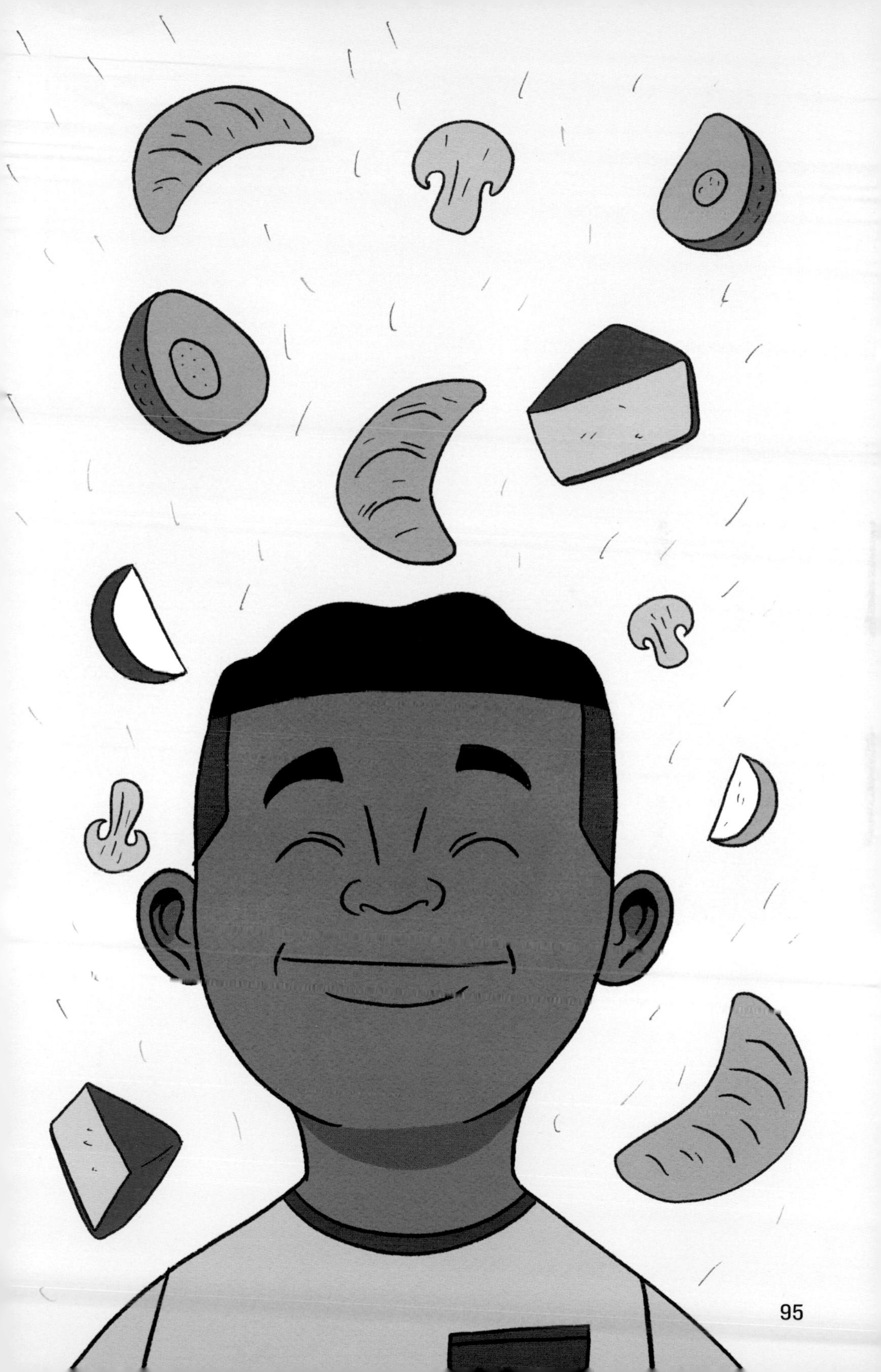

WHERE'D THAT COME FROM?

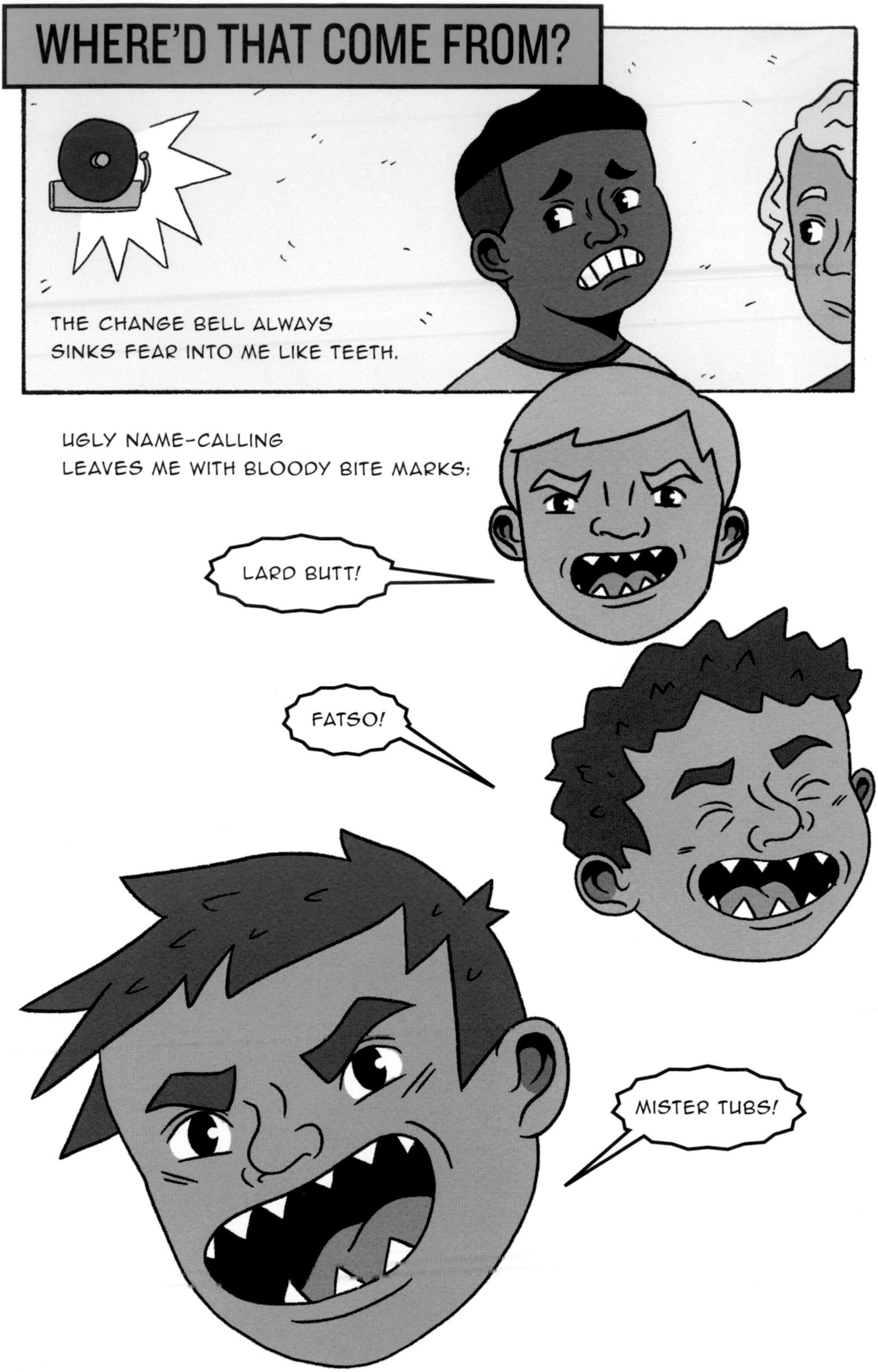
THE CHANGE BELL ALWAYS
SINKS FEAR INTO ME LIKE TEETH.
UGLY NAME-CALLING
LEAVES ME WITH BLOODY BITE MARKS:
LARD BUTT!
FATSO!
MISTER TUBS!

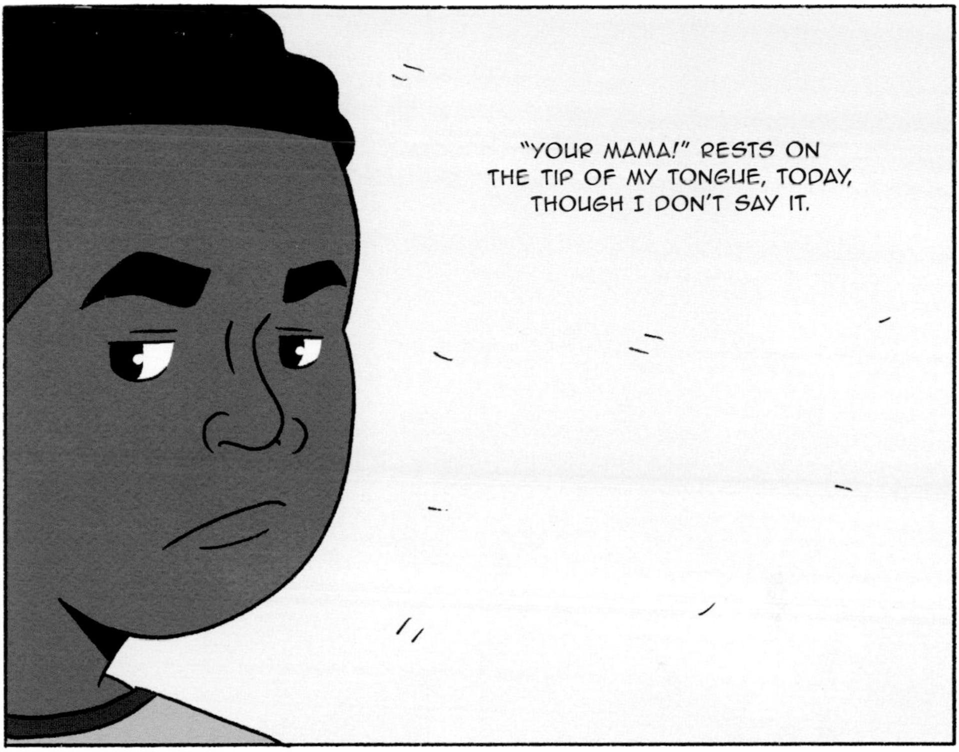
"YOUR MAMA!" RESTS ON THE TIP OF MY TONGUE, TODAY, THOUGH I DON'T SAY IT.

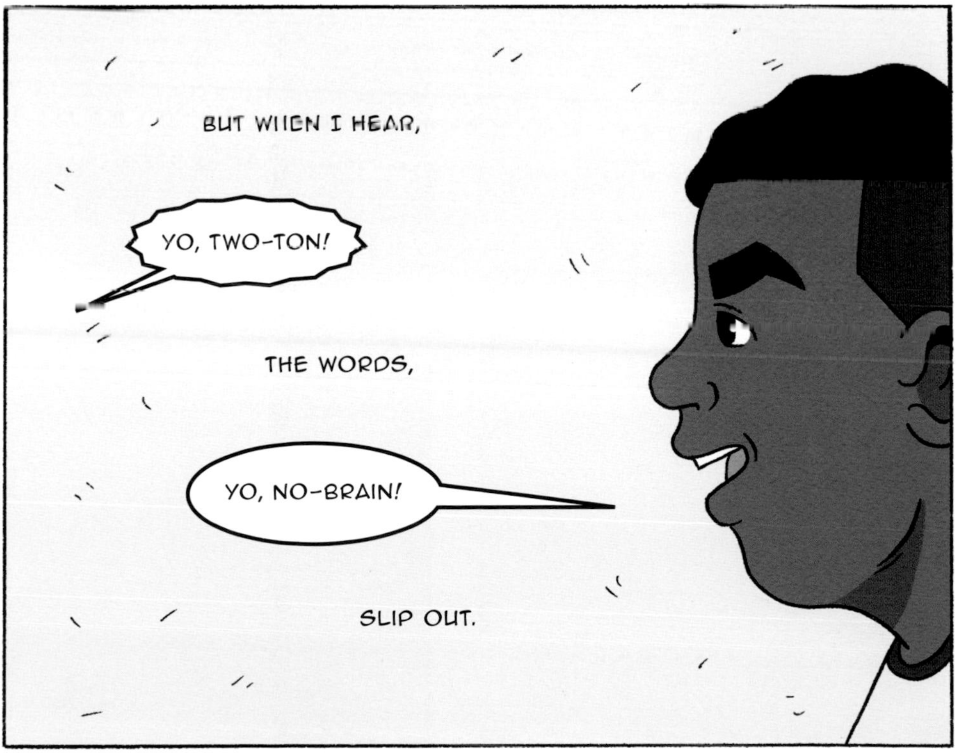
BUT WHEN I HEAR,
YO, TWO-TON!
THE WORDS,
YO, NO-BRAIN!
SLIP OUT.

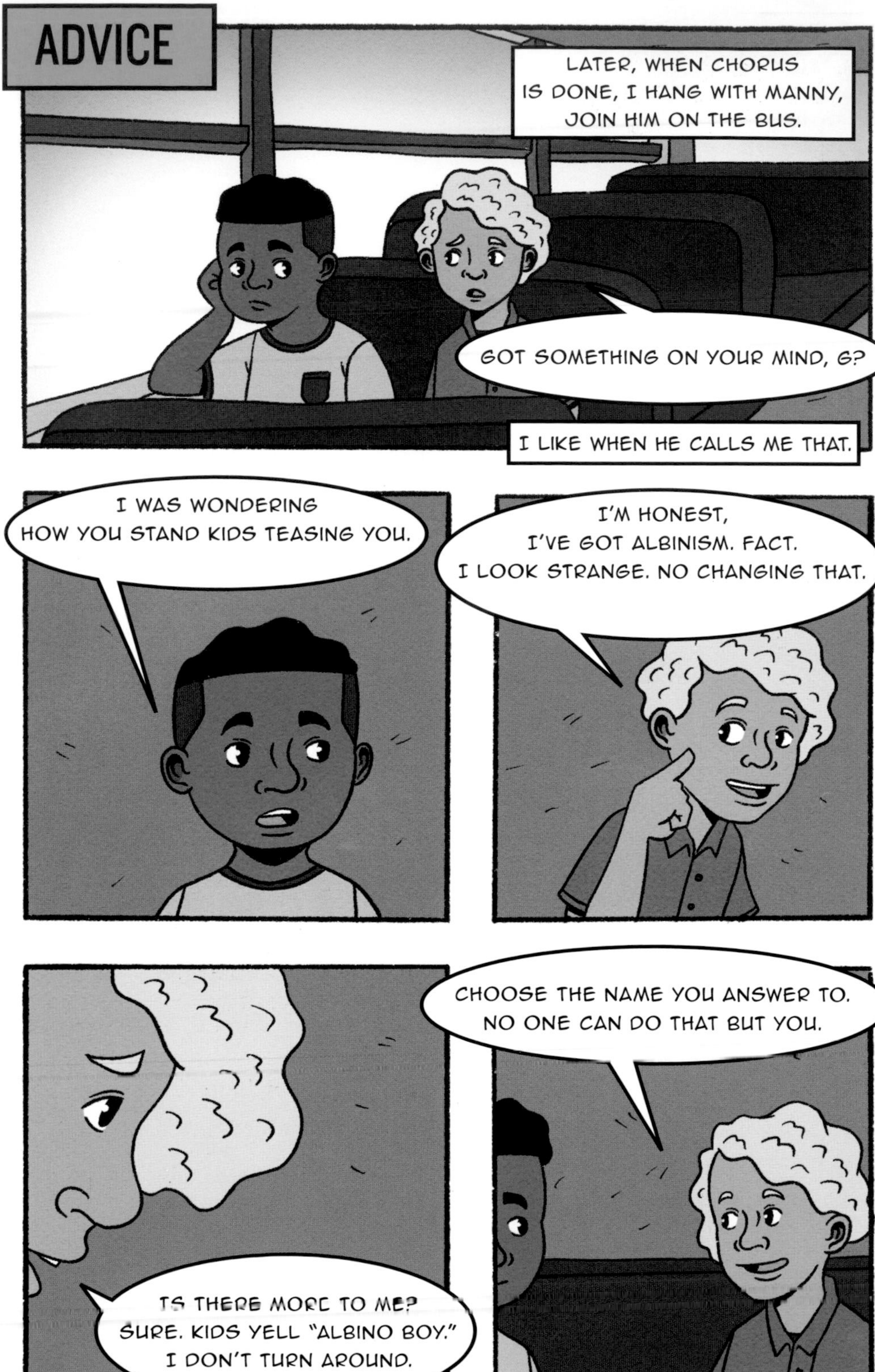
ADVICE
LATER, WHEN CHORUS IS DONE, I HANG WITH MANNY, JOIN HIM ON THE BUS.
GOT SOMETHING ON YOUR MIND, G?
I LIKE WHEN HE CALLS ME THAT.
I WAS WONDERING HOW YOU STAND KIDS TEASING YOU.
I'M HONEST, I'VE GOT ALBINISM. FACT. I LOOK STRANGE. NO CHANGING THAT.
IS THERE MORE TO ME? SURE. KIDS YELL "ALBINO BOY." I DON'T TURN AROUND.
CHOOSE THE NAME YOU ANSWER TO. NO ONE CAN DO THAT BUT YOU.

HIS WORDS

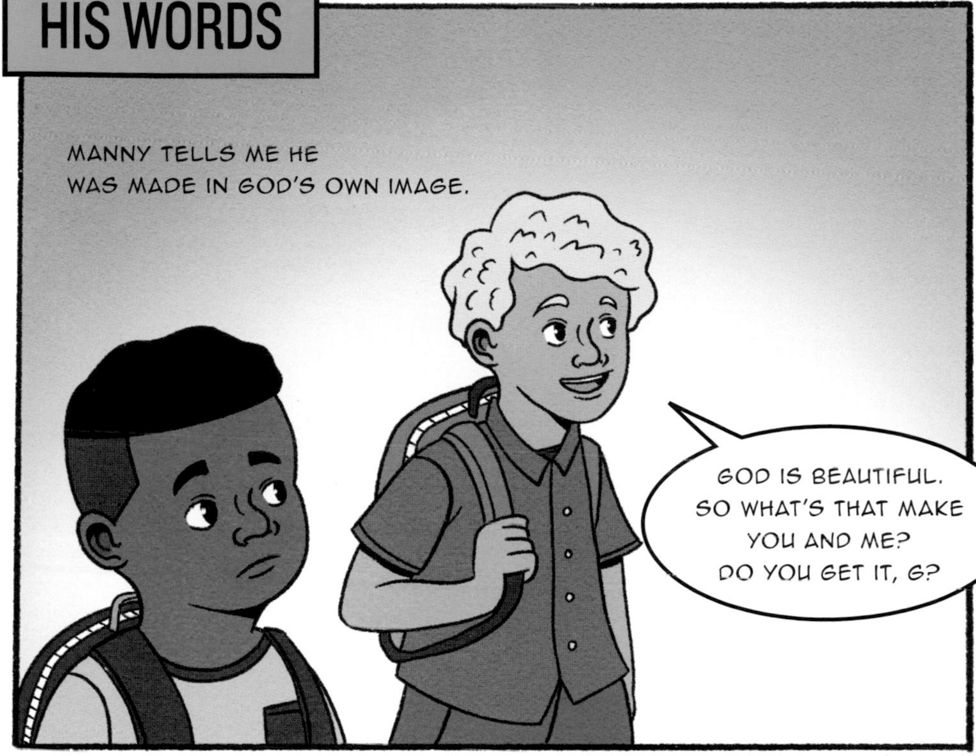
MANNY TELLS ME HE
WAS MADE IN GOD'S OWN IMAGE.
GOD IS BEAUTIFUL.
SO WHAT'S THAT MAKE
YOU AND ME?
DO YOU GET IT, G?

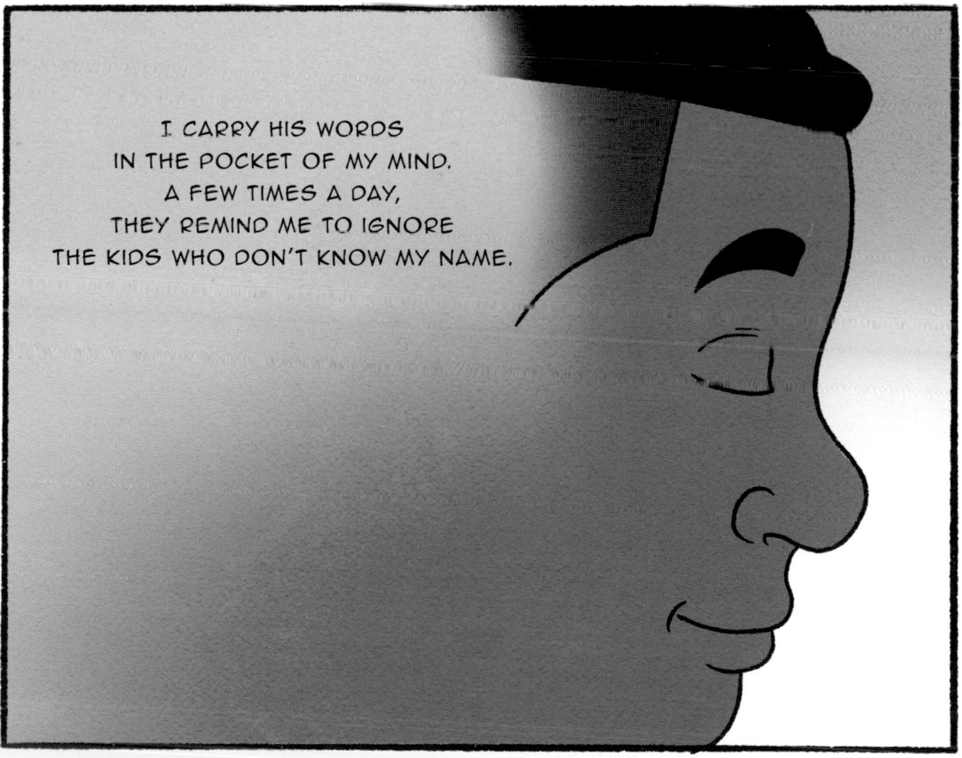
I CARRY HIS WORDS
IN THE POCKET OF MY MIND.
A FEW TIMES A DAY,
THEY REMIND ME TO IGNORE
THE KIDS WHO DON'T KNOW MY NAME.

COME TO THINK OF IT

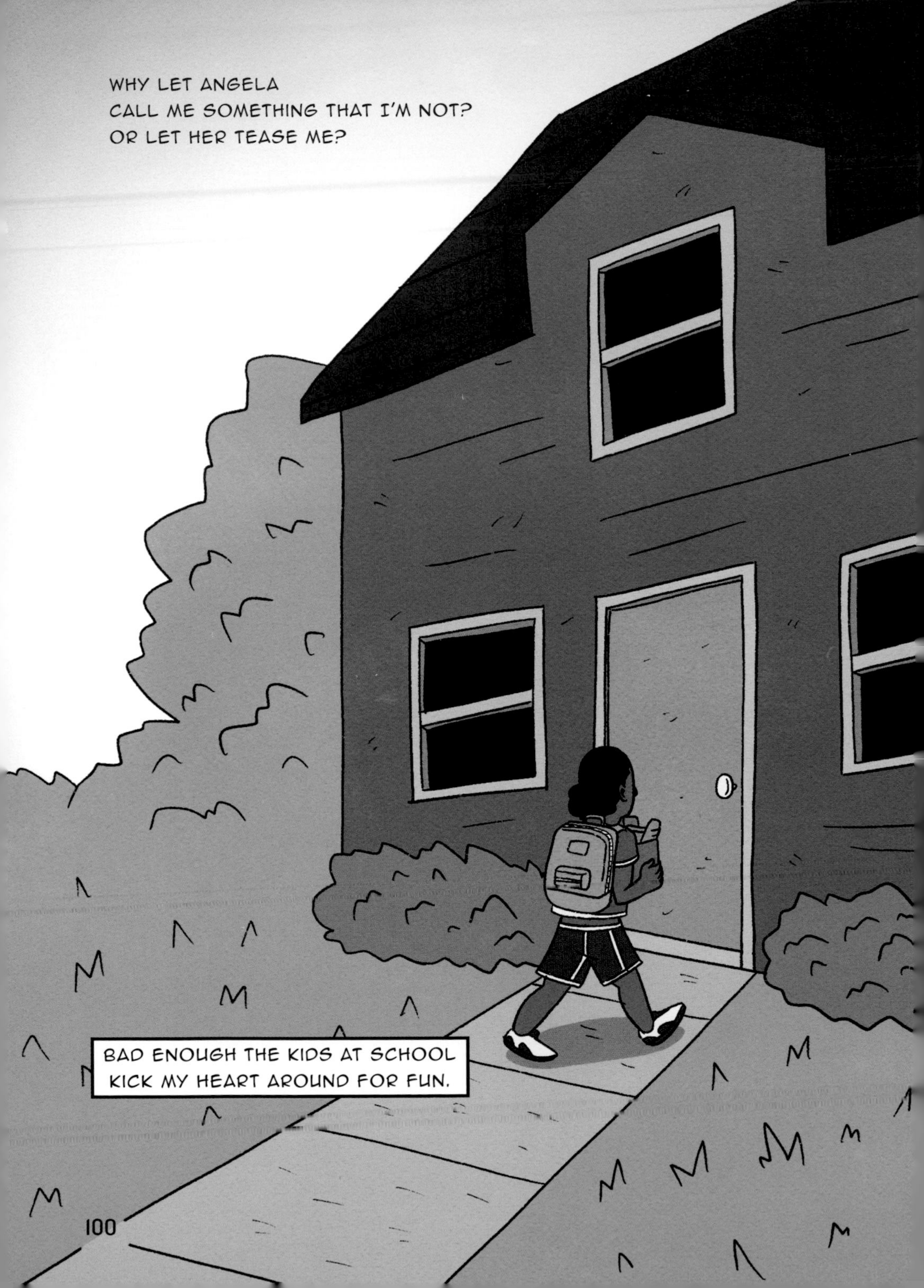
WHY LET ANGELA
CALL ME SOMETHING THAT I'M NOT?
OR LET HER TEASE ME?
BAD ENOUGH THE KIDS AT SCHOOL
KICK MY HEART AROUND FOR FUN.

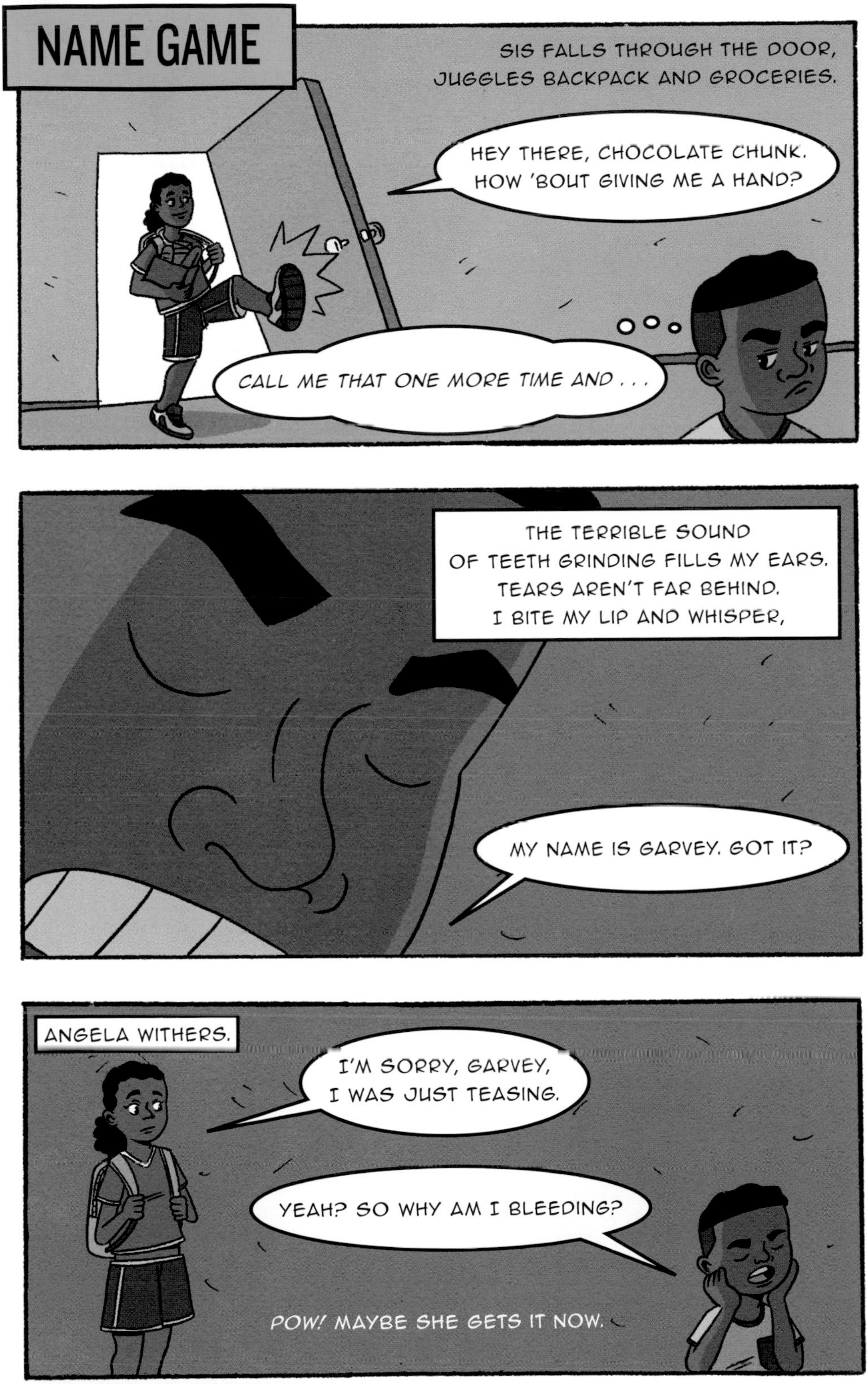
NAME GAME
SIS FALLS THROUGH THE DOOR, JUGGLES BACKPACK AND GROCERIES.
HEY THERE, CHOCOLATE CHUNK. HOW 'BOUT GIVING ME A HAND?
CALL ME THAT ONE MORE TIME AND . . .
THE TERRIBLE SOUND OF TEETH GRINDING FILLS MY EARS. TEARS AREN'T FAR BEHIND. I BITE MY LIP AND WHISPER,
MY NAME IS GARVEY. GOT IT?
ANGELA WITHERS.
I'M SORRY, GARVEY, I WAS JUST TEASING.
YEAH? SO WHY AM I BLEEDING?
POW! MAYBE SHE GETS IT NOW.

PERKS

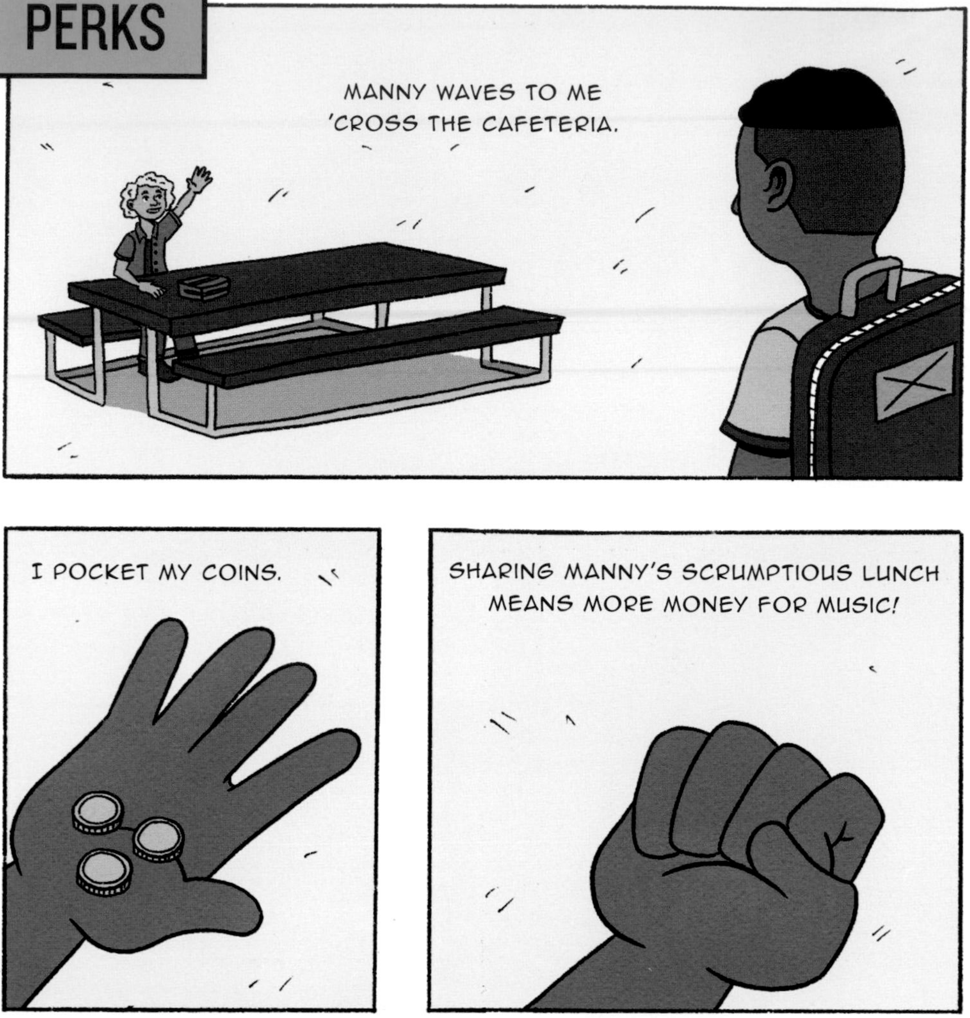
MANNY WAVES TO ME 'CROSS THE CAFETERIA.
I POCKET MY COINS.
SHARING MANNY'S SCRUMPTIOUS LUNCH MEANS MORE MONEY FOR MUSIC!

WEEKEND WONDER: MANNY'S SPICY PORTOBELLO BURGER SUPREME

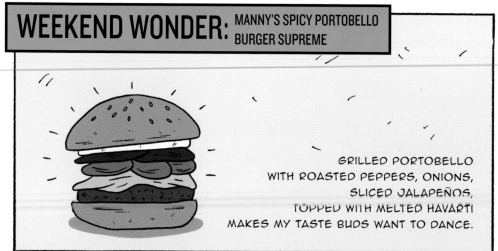

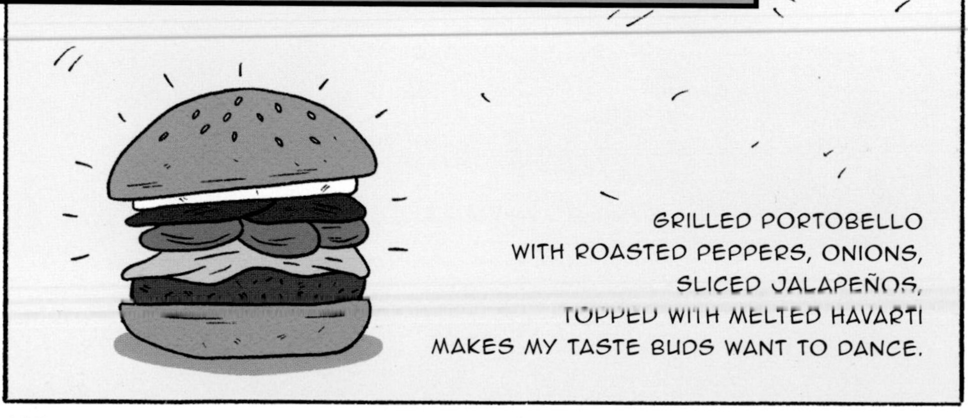
GRILLED PORTOBELLO
WITH ROASTED PEPPERS, ONIONS,
SLICED JALAPEÑOS,
TOPPED WITH MELTED HAVARTI
MAKES MY TASTE BUDS WANT TO DANCE.

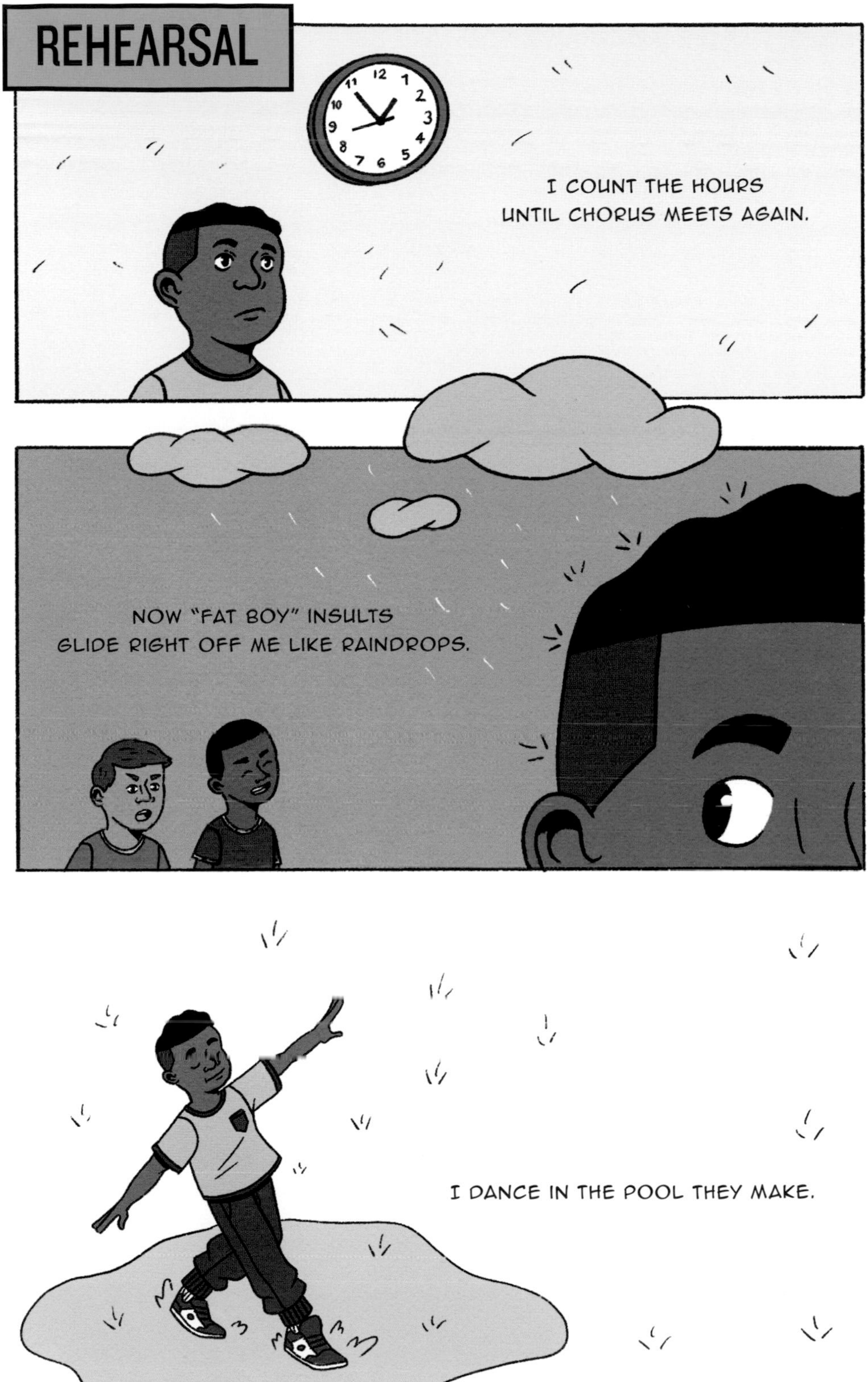
REHEARSAL
I COUNT THE HOURS
UNTIL CHORUS MEETS AGAIN.
NOW "FAT BOY" INSULTS
GLIDE RIGHT OFF ME LIKE RAINDROPS.
I DANCE IN THE POOL THEY MAKE.

THREE BEARS

IT DOESN'T MATTER
HOW WIDE I AM WHEN I SING.
LIKE GOLDILOCKS, I
HAVE FINALLY FOUND WHAT FITS:
MY HIGH TENOR IS JUST RIGHT.

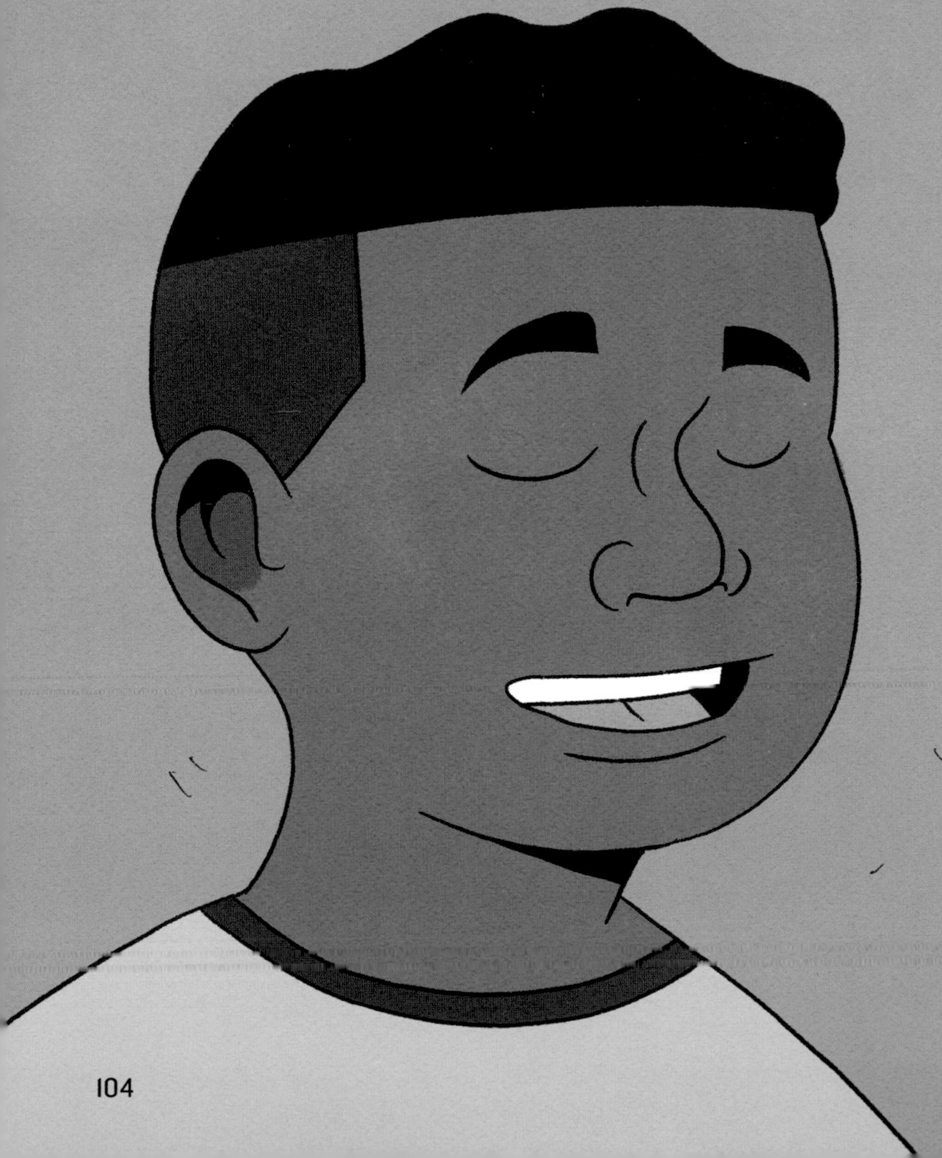

NATASHA BEDINGFIELD SINGS MY SONG

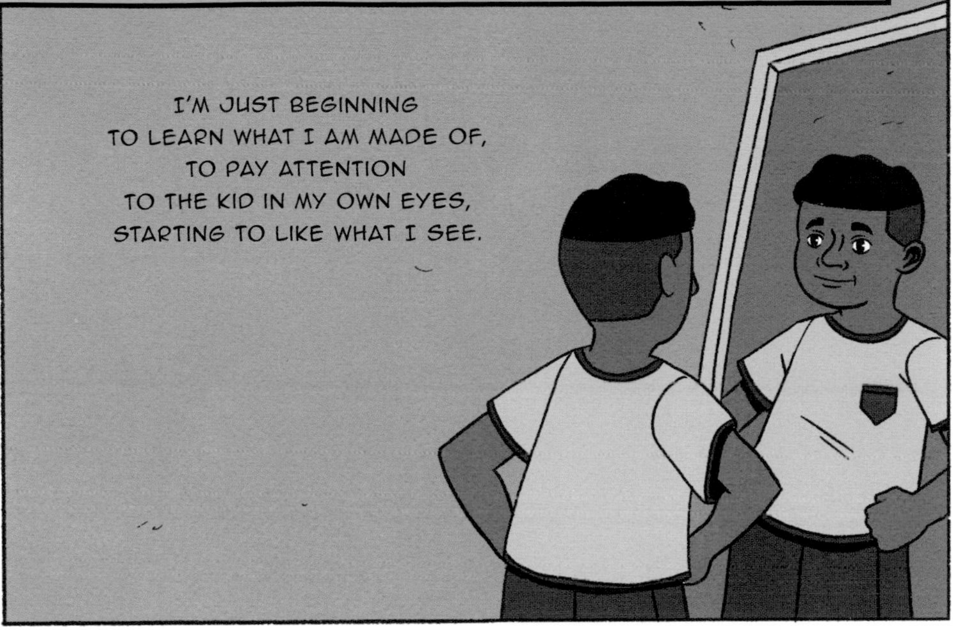
I'M JUST BEGINNING
TO LEARN WHAT I AM MADE OF,
TO PAY ATTENTION
TO THE KID IN MY OWN EYES,
STARTING TO LIKE WHAT I SEE.

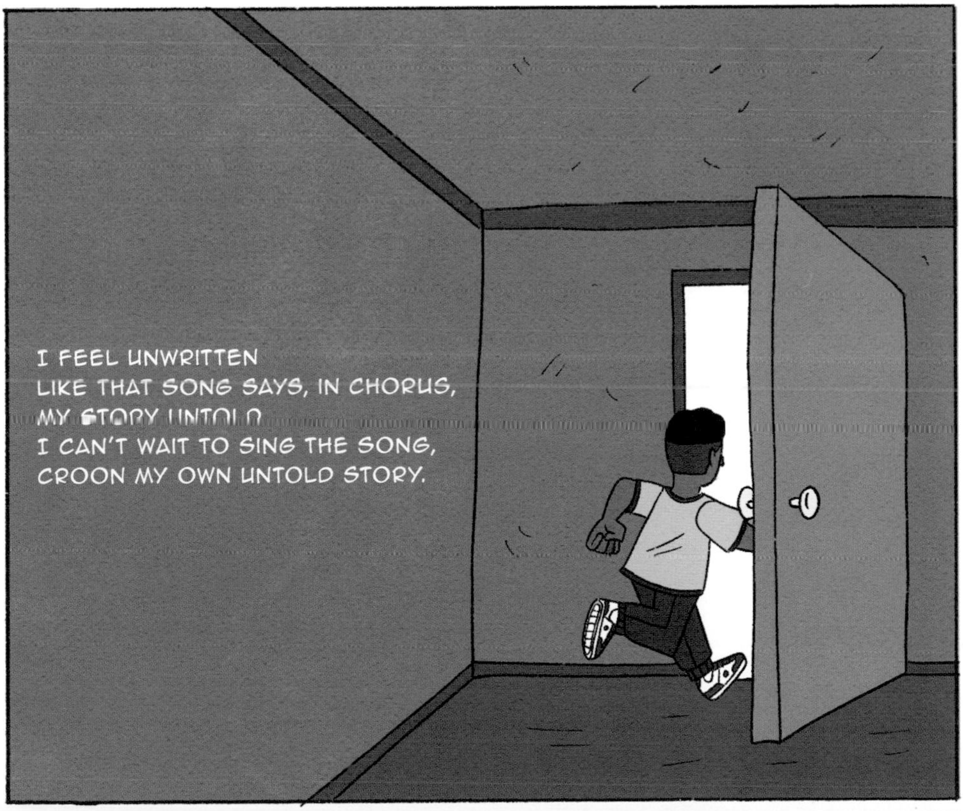
I FEEL UNWRITTEN
LIKE THAT SONG SAYS, IN CHORUS,
MY STORY UNTOLD.
I CAN'T WAIT TO SING THE SONG,
CROON MY OWN UNTOLD STORY.

WHEN I SING

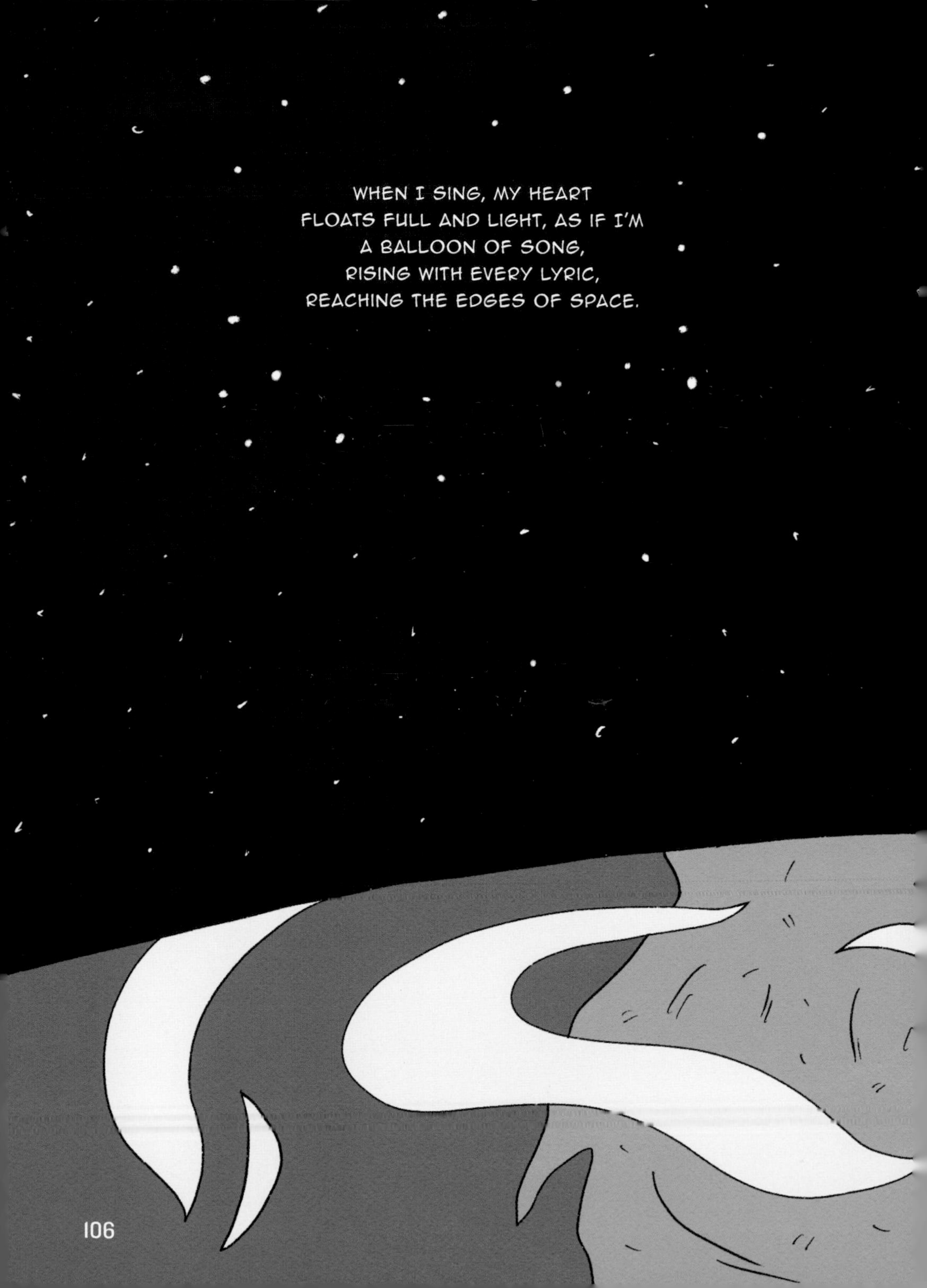
WHEN I SING, MY HEART
FLOATS FULL AND LIGHT, AS IF I'M
A BALLOON OF SONG,
RISING WITH EVERY LYRIC,
REACHING THE EDGES OF SPACE.

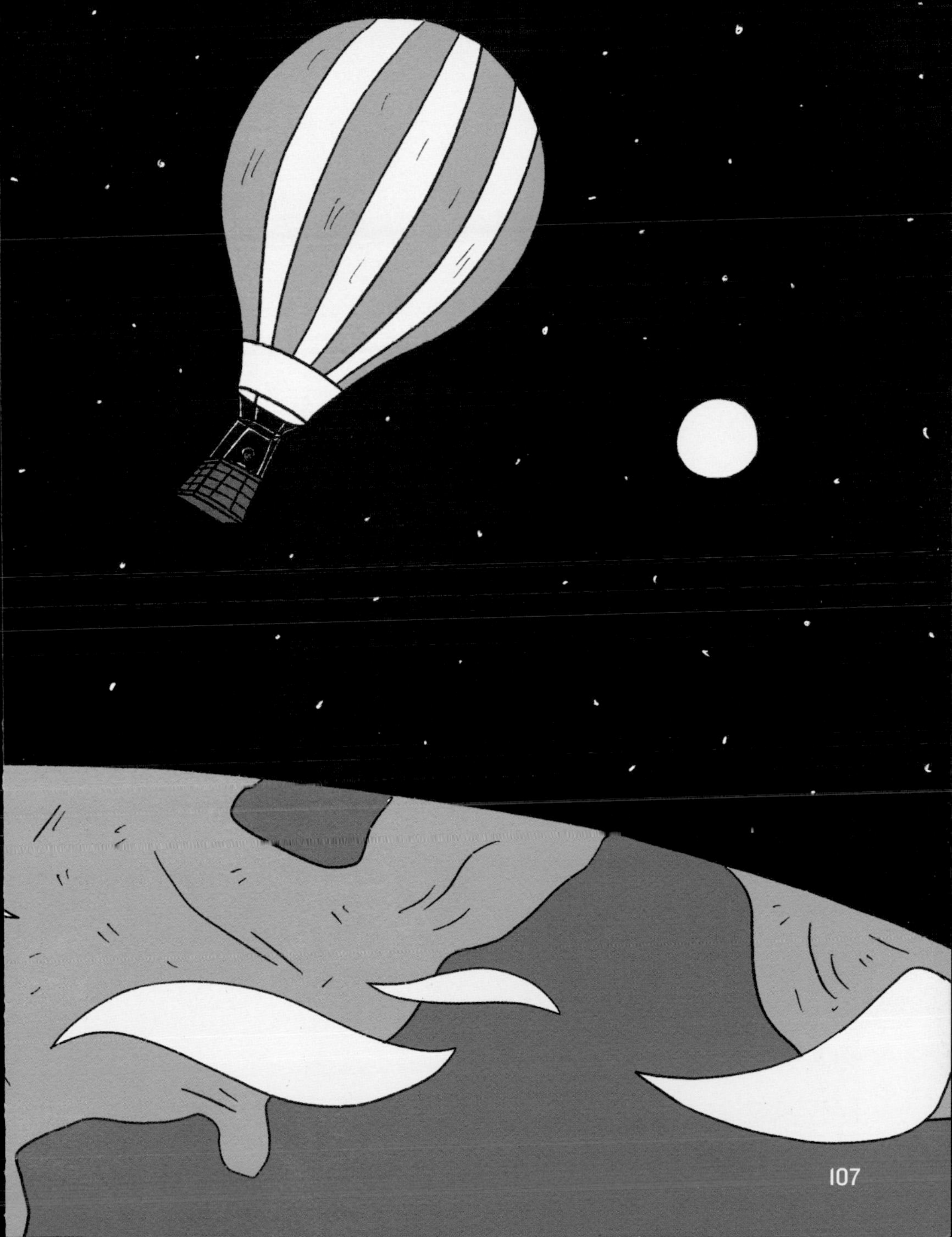

A SPOONFUL OF SONG

MY CHOCOLATE STASH
IS LASTING ME MUCH LONGER.

THESE DAYS, NOTHING TASTES
SWEET AS FOUR-PART HARMONY.
SOMEHOW, MUSIC MAKES ME FULL.

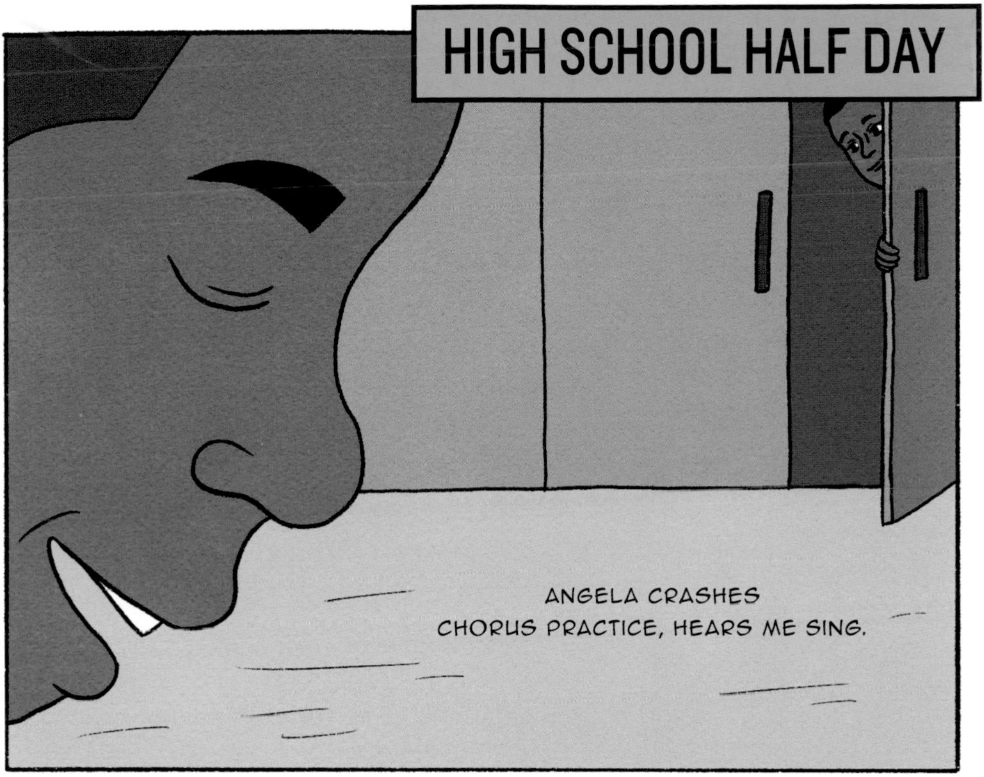
HIGH SCHOOL HALF DAY
ANGELA CRASHES CHORUS PRACTICE, HEARS ME SING.

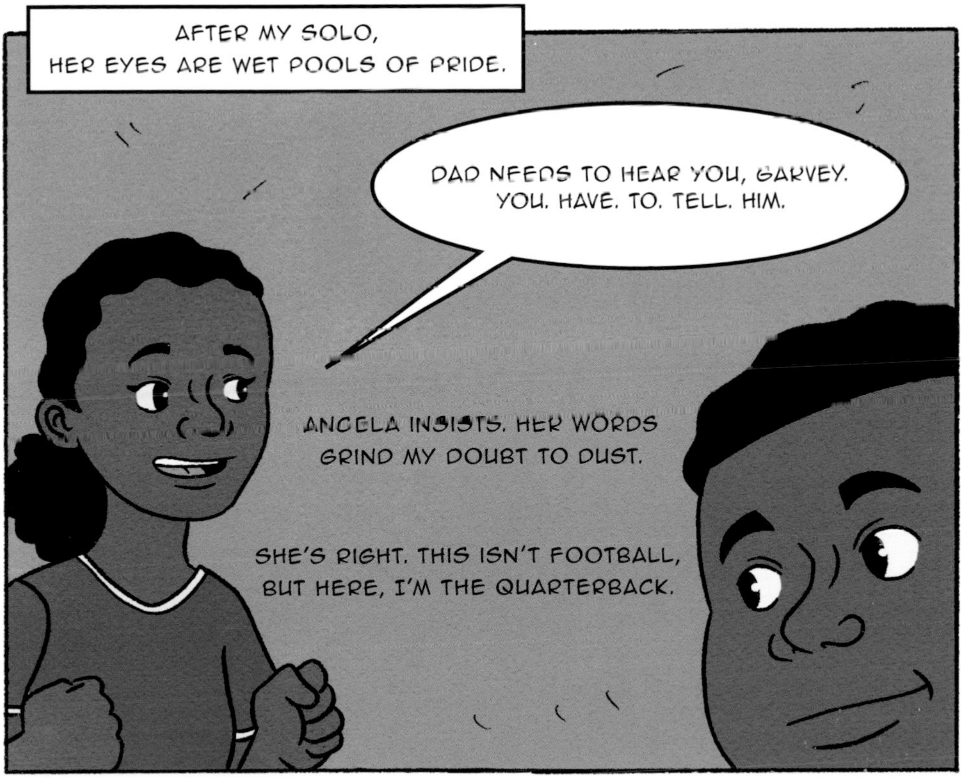
AFTER MY SOLO, HER EYES ARE WET POOLS OF PRIDE.
DAD NEEDS TO HEAR YOU, GARVEY. YOU. HAVE. TO. TELL. HIM.
ANGELA INSISTS. HER WORDS GRIND MY DOUBT TO DUST.
SHE'S RIGHT. THIS ISN'T FOOTBALL, BUT HERE, I'M THE QUARTERBACK.

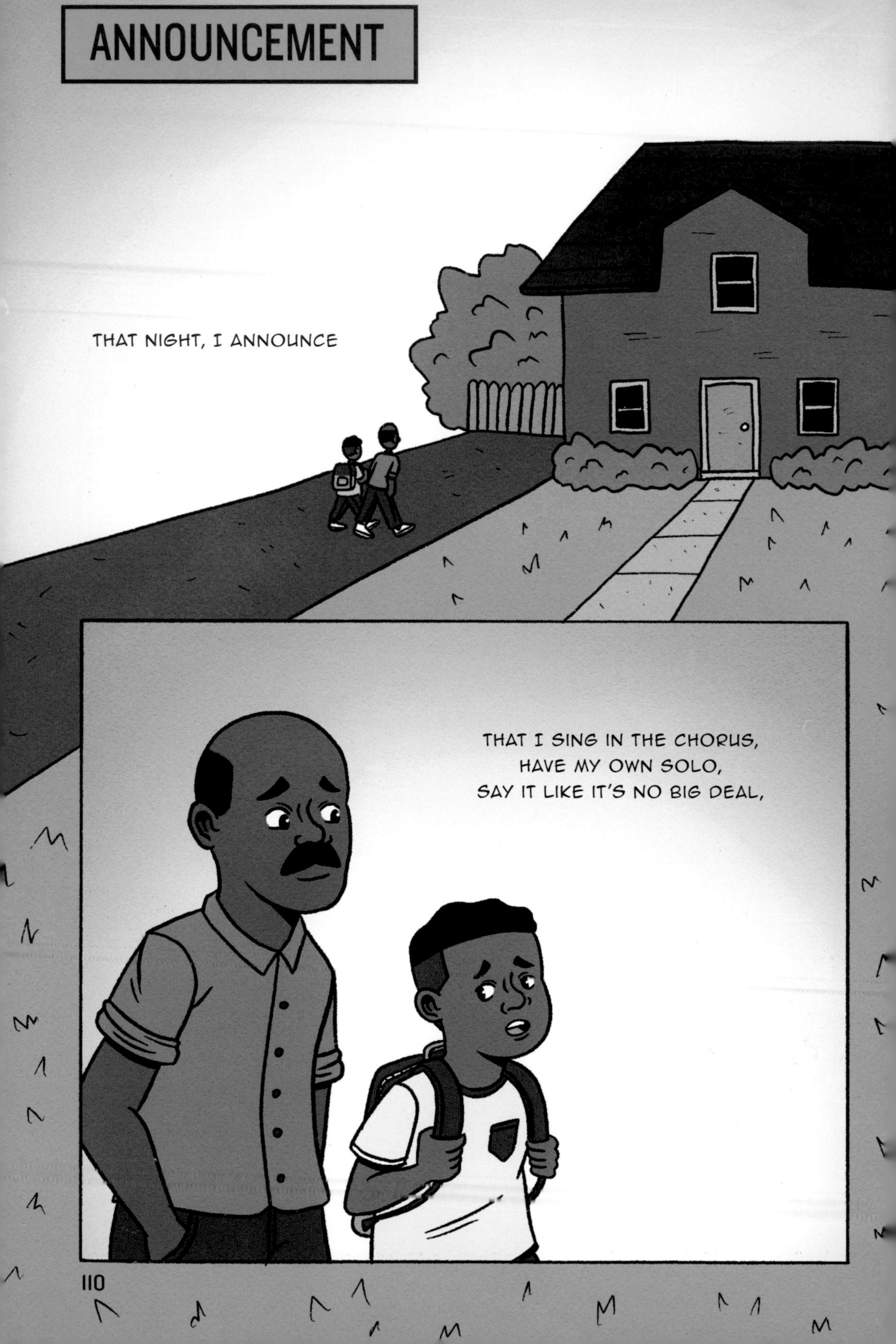
ANNOUNCEMENT
THAT NIGHT, I ANNOUNCE
THAT I SING IN THE CHORUS,
HAVE MY OWN SOLO,
SAY IT LIKE IT'S NO BIG DEAL,

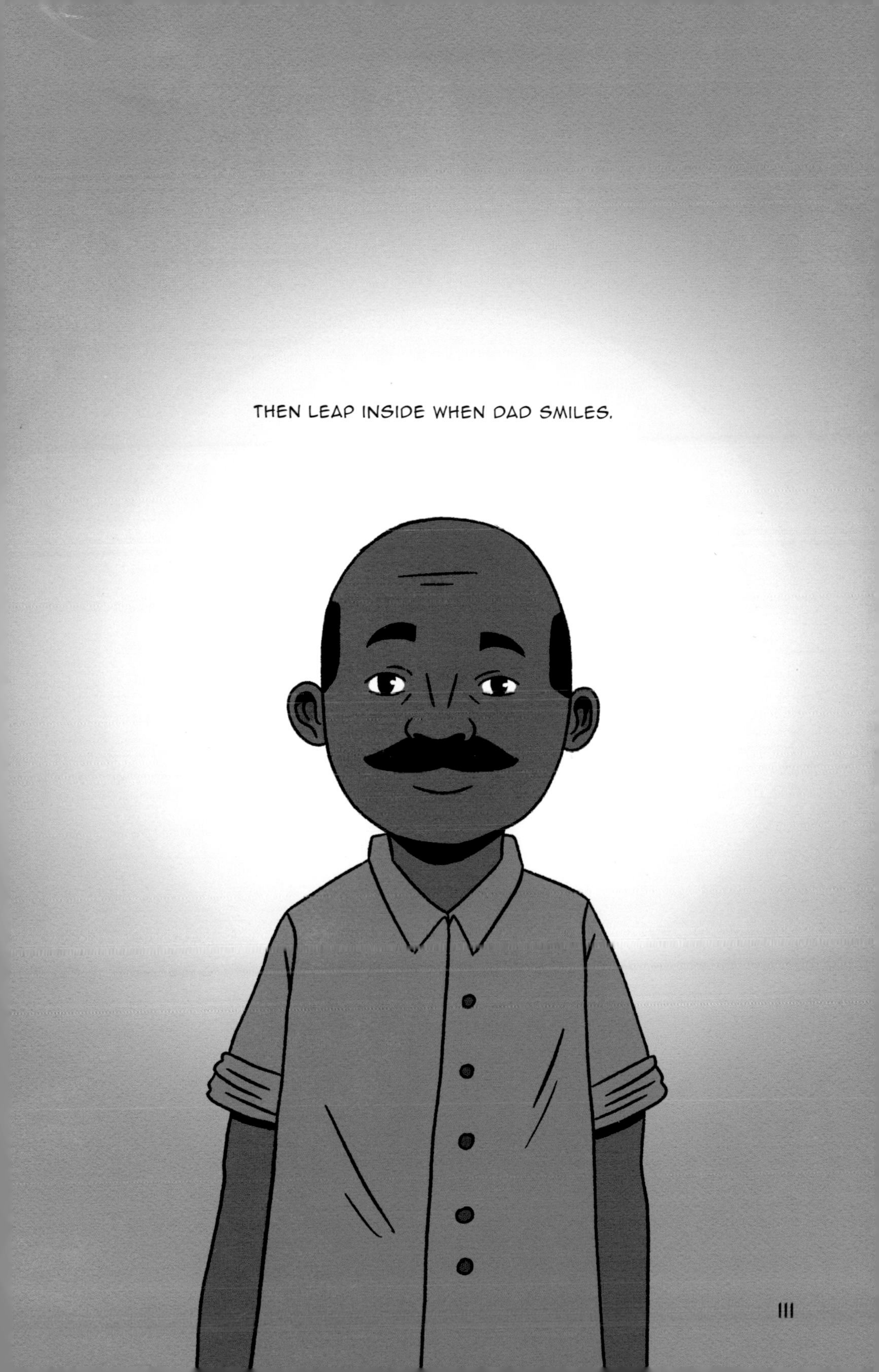
THEN LEAP INSIDE WHEN DAD SMILES.

MANNY'S TURN TO BE BRAVE

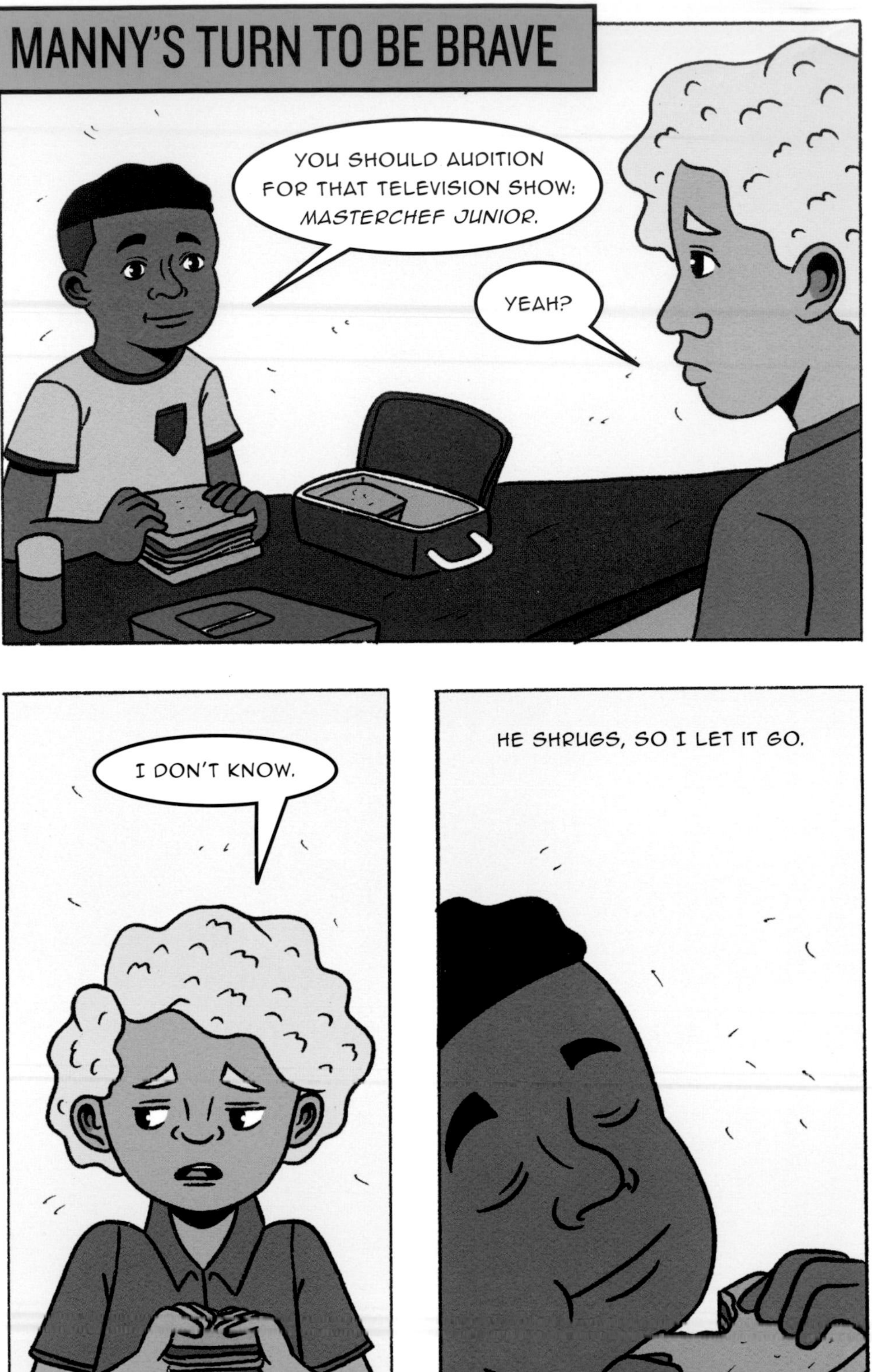
YOU SHOULD AUDITION FOR THAT TELEVISION SHOW: *MASTERCHEF JUNIOR*.
YEAH?
I DON'T KNOW.
HE SHRUGS, SO I LET IT GO.

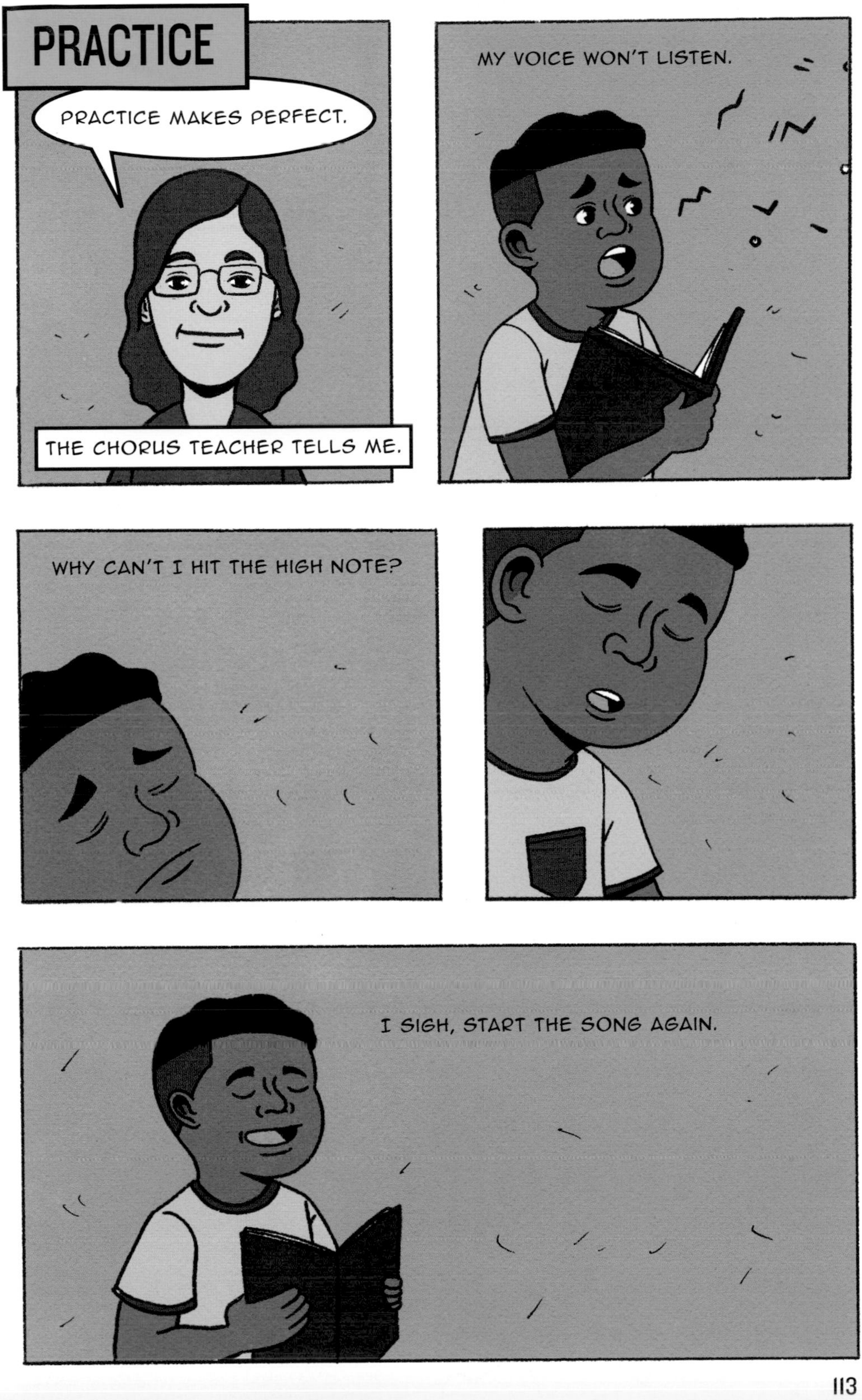
PRACTICE
PRACTICE MAKES PERFECT.
THE CHORUS TEACHER TELLS ME.
MY VOICE WON'T LISTEN.
WHY CAN'T I HIT THE HIGH NOTE?
I SIGH, START THE SONG AGAIN.

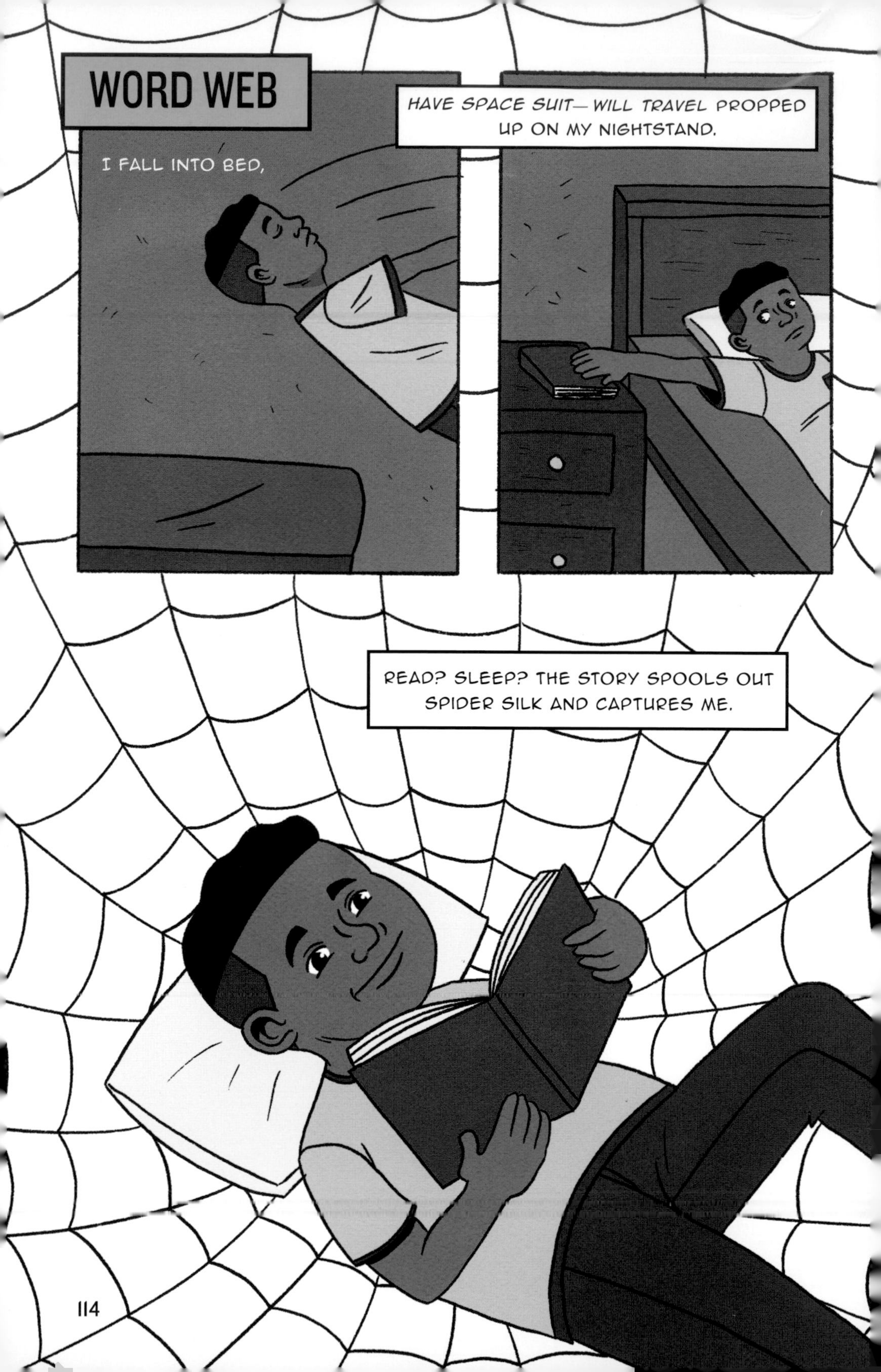
WORD WEB
I FALL INTO BED,
HAVE SPACE SUIT— WILL TRAVEL PROPPED UP ON MY NIGHTSTAND.
READ? SLEEP? THE STORY SPOOLS OUT SPIDER SILK AND CAPTURES ME.

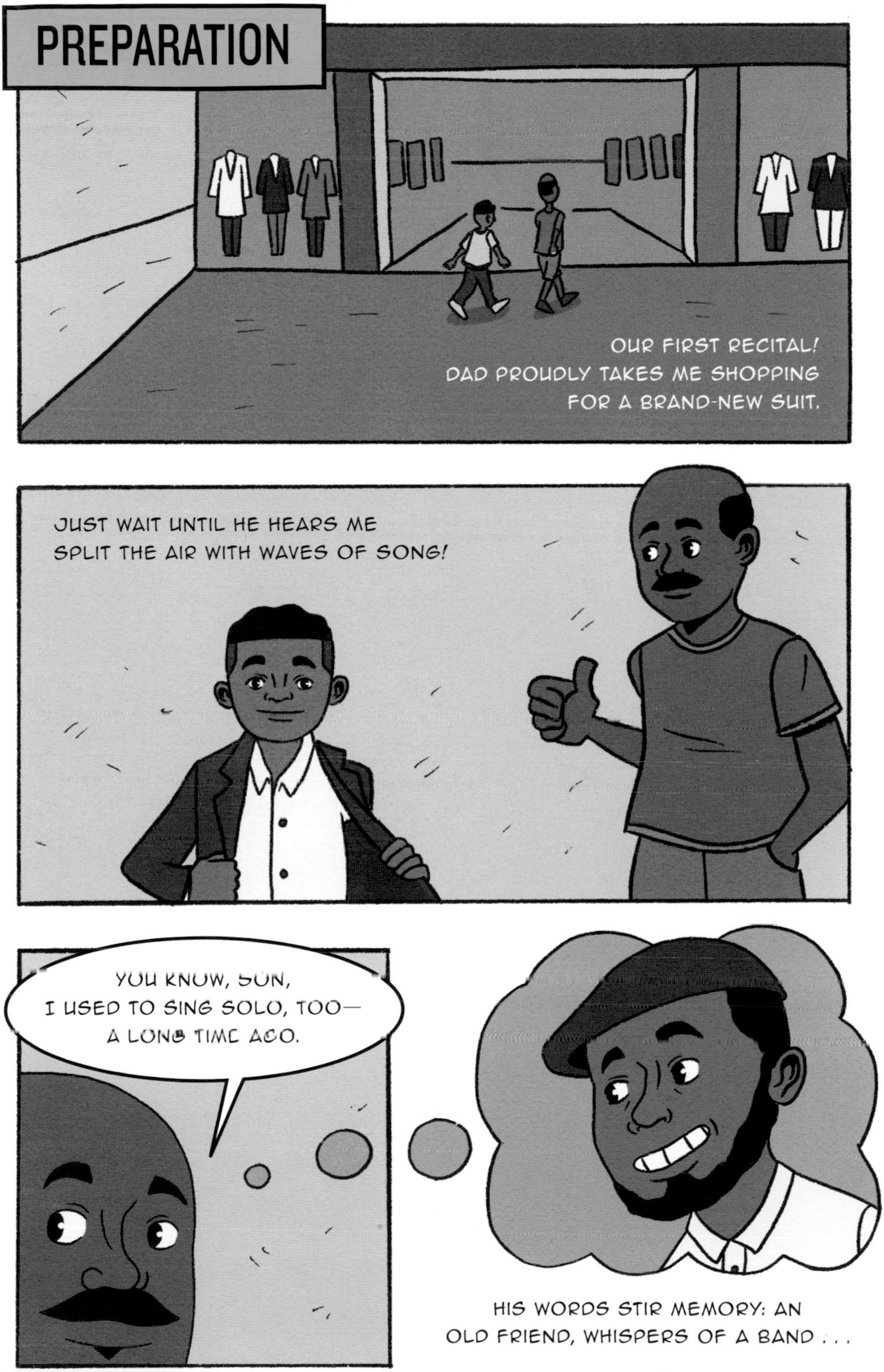
PREPARATION
OUR FIRST RECITAL!
DAD PROUDLY TAKES ME SHOPPING
FOR A BRAND-NEW SUIT.
JUST WAIT UNTIL HE HEARS ME
SPLIT THE AIR WITH WAVES OF SONG!
YOU KNOW, SON,
I USED TO SING SOLO, TOO—
A LONG TIME AGO.
HIS WORDS STIR MEMORY: AN
OLD FRIEND, WHISPERS OF A BAND . . .

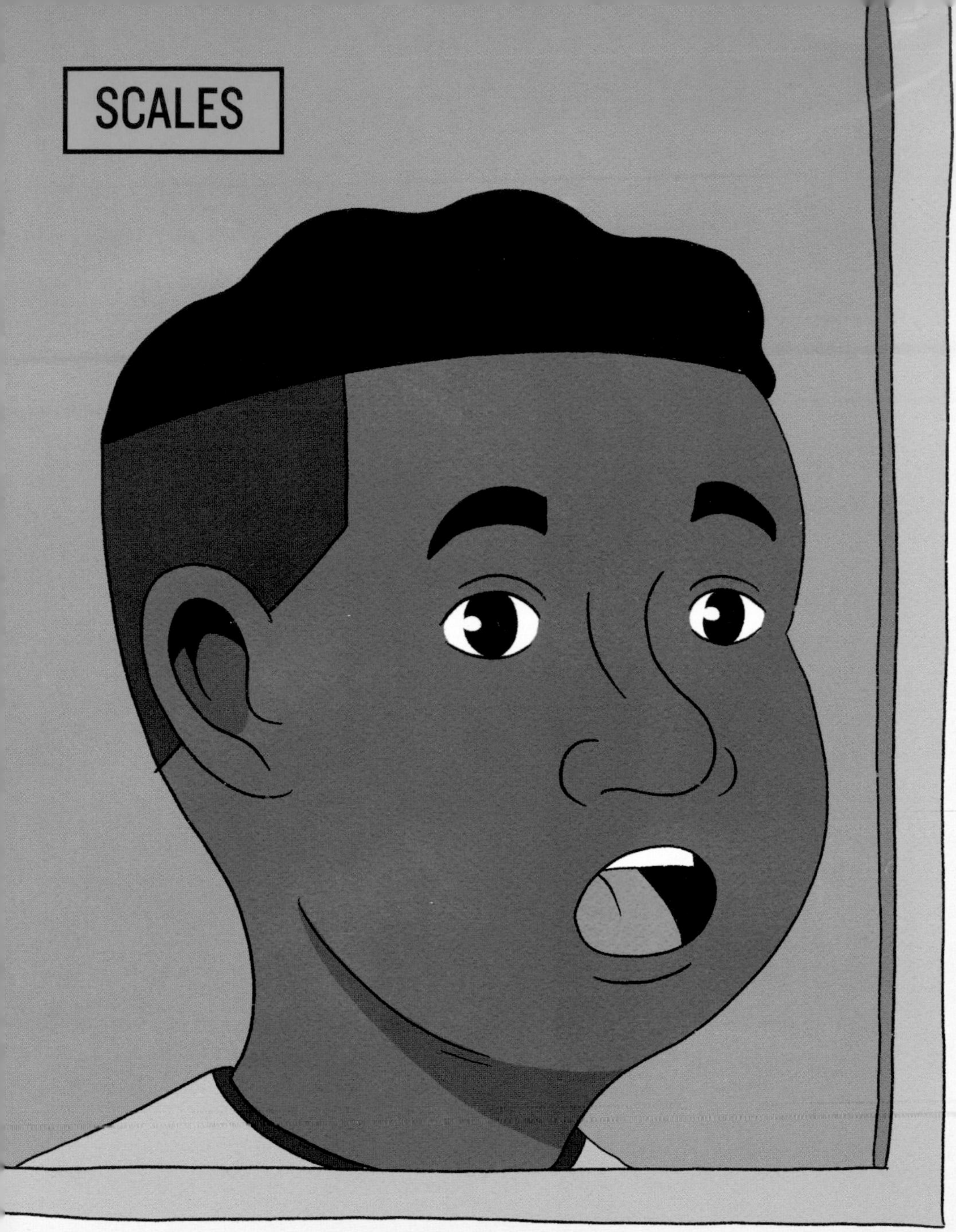
SCALES

EACH NIGHT, I RUN SCALES,
LOOKING INTO MY MIRROR,

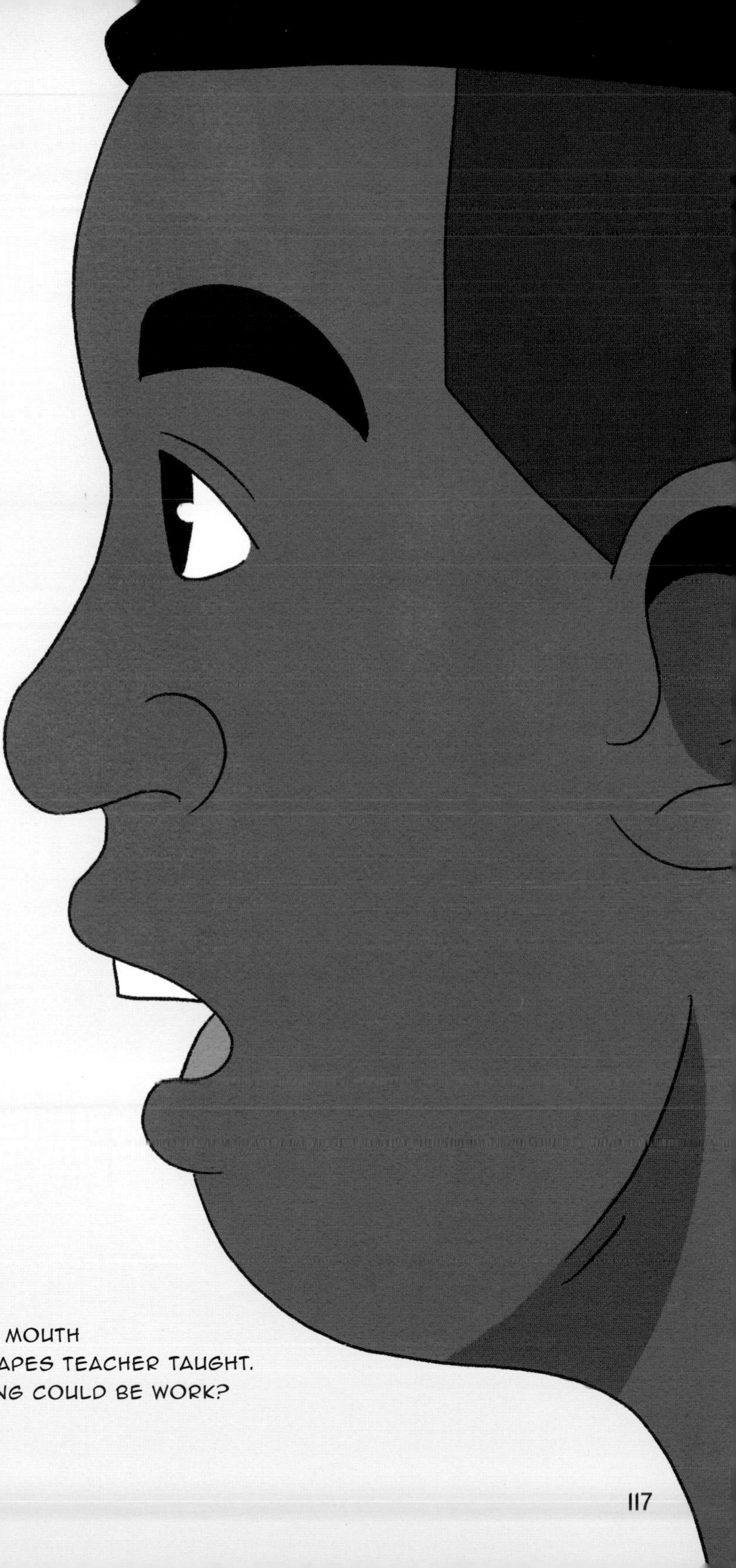

MAKING SURE MY MOUTH
MATCHES THE SHAPES TEACHER TAUGHT.
WHO KNEW SINGING COULD BE WORK?

THE CHANGE BELL

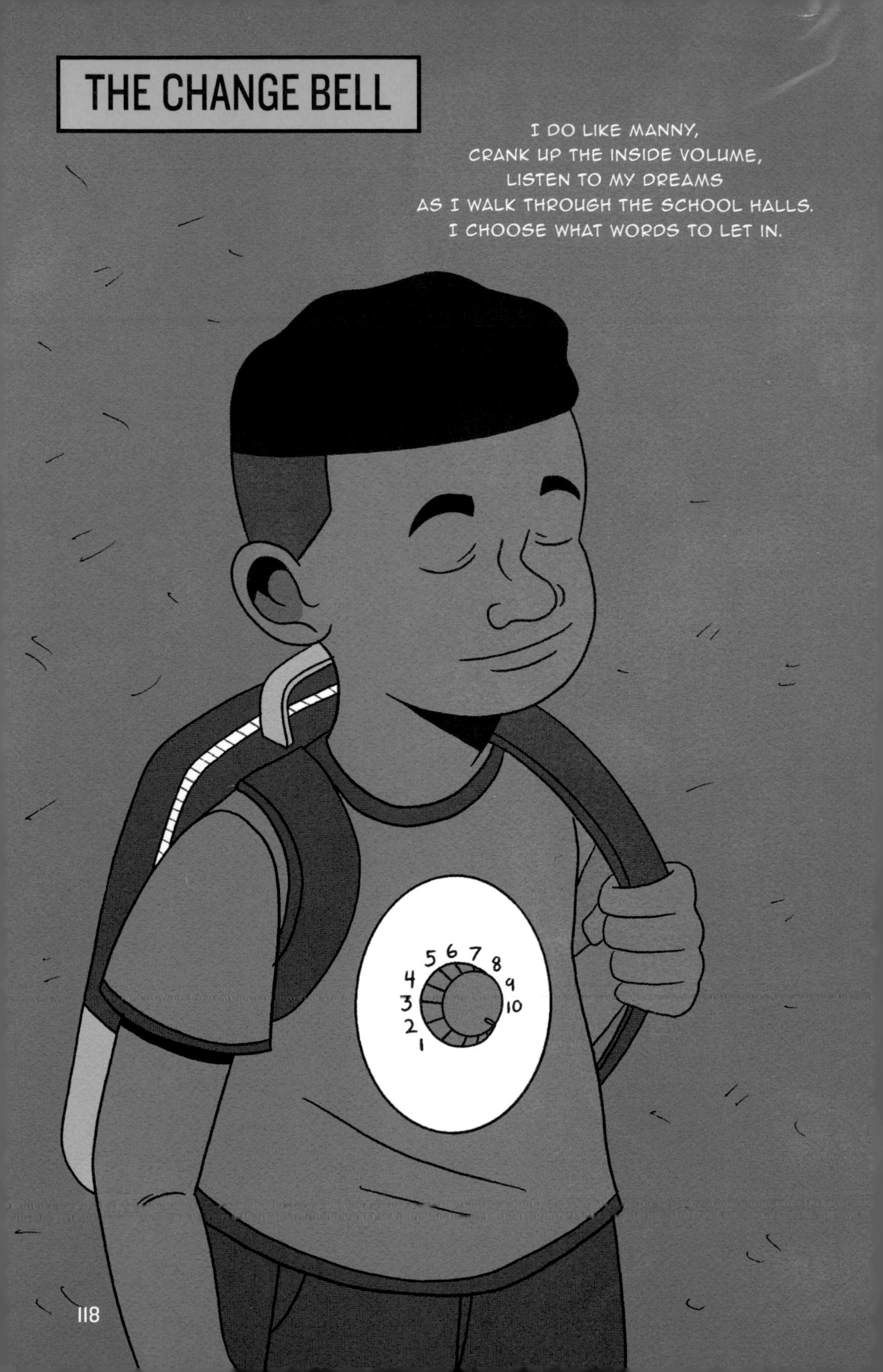
I DO LIKE MANNY,
CRANK UP THE INSIDE VOLUME,
LISTEN TO MY DREAMS
AS I WALK THROUGH THE SCHOOL HALLS.
I CHOOSE WHAT WORDS TO LET IN.
1
2
3
4
5
6
7
8
9
10

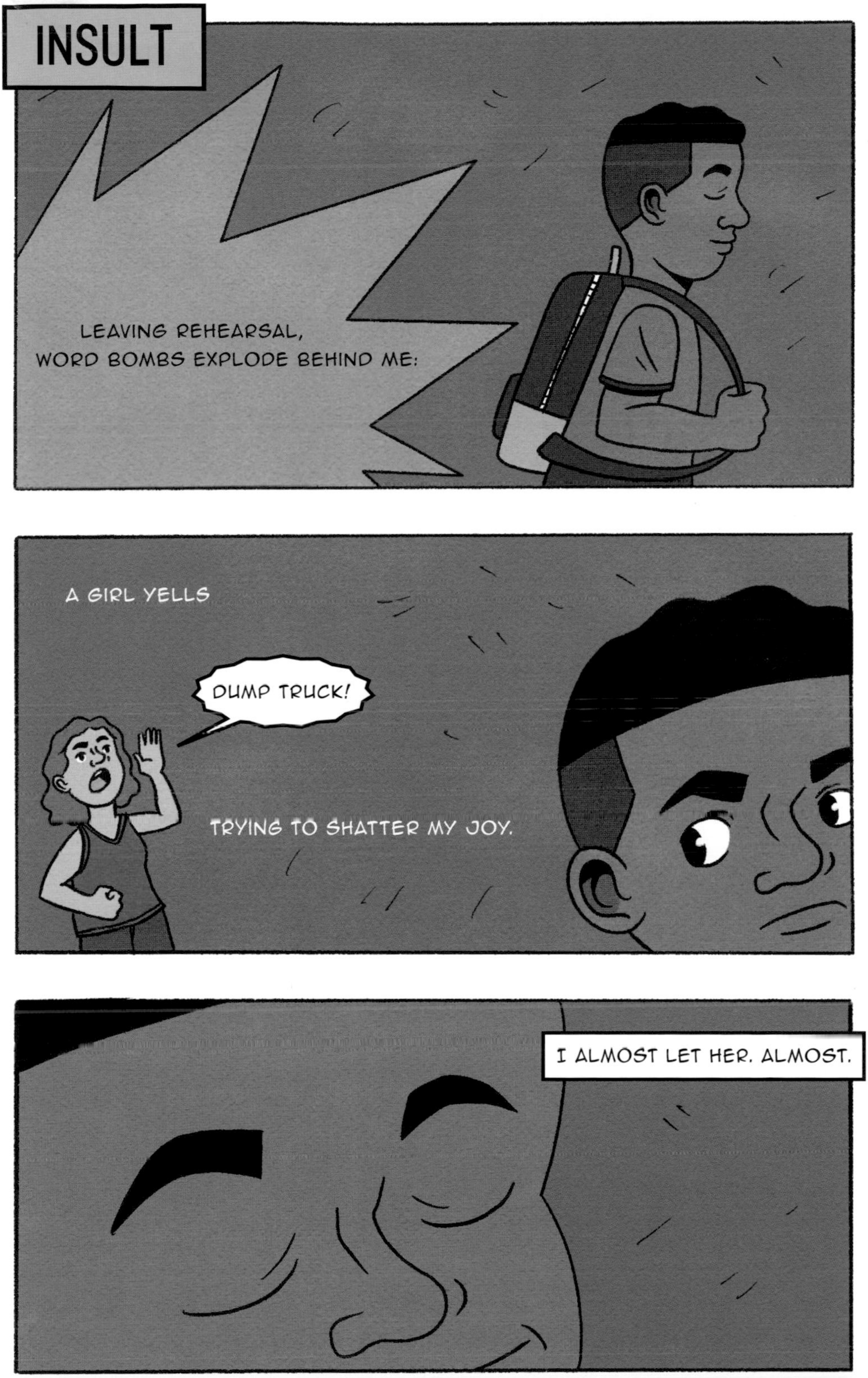
INSULT
LEAVING REHEARSAL,
WORD BOMBS EXPLODE BEHIND ME:
A GIRL YELLS
DUMP TRUCK!
TRYING TO SHATTER MY JOY.
I ALMOST LET HER. ALMOST.

GOOD COMPANY

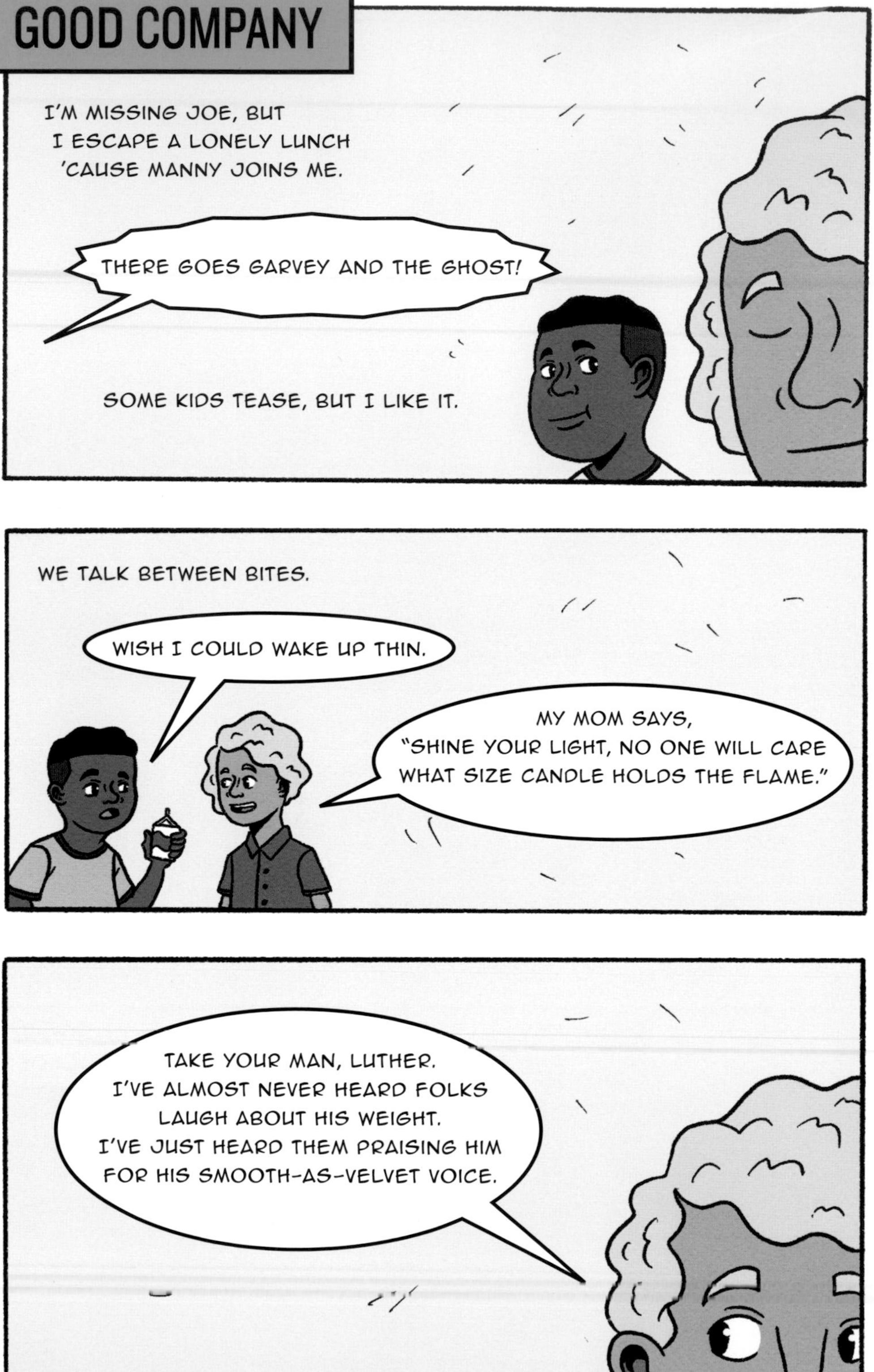
I'M MISSING JOE, BUT I ESCAPE A LONELY LUNCH 'CAUSE MANNY JOINS ME.
THERE GOES GARVEY AND THE GHOST!
SOME KIDS TEASE, BUT I LIKE IT.
WE TALK BETWEEN BITES.
WISH I COULD WAKE UP THIN.
MY MOM SAYS, "SHINE YOUR LIGHT, NO ONE WILL CARE WHAT SIZE CANDLE HOLDS THE FLAME."
TAKE YOUR MAN, LUTHER. I'VE ALMOST NEVER HEARD FOLKS LAUGH ABOUT HIS WEIGHT. I'VE JUST HEARD THEM PRAISING HIM FOR HIS SMOOTH-AS-VELVET VOICE.

I CHEW ON HIS WORDS,
WASH THEM DOWN WITH CHOCOLATE MILK.
MAYBE SOMEDAY I'LL
LIFT MY VOICE TO THE HEAVENS
AND HAVE PRAISE RAIN DOWN ON ME.

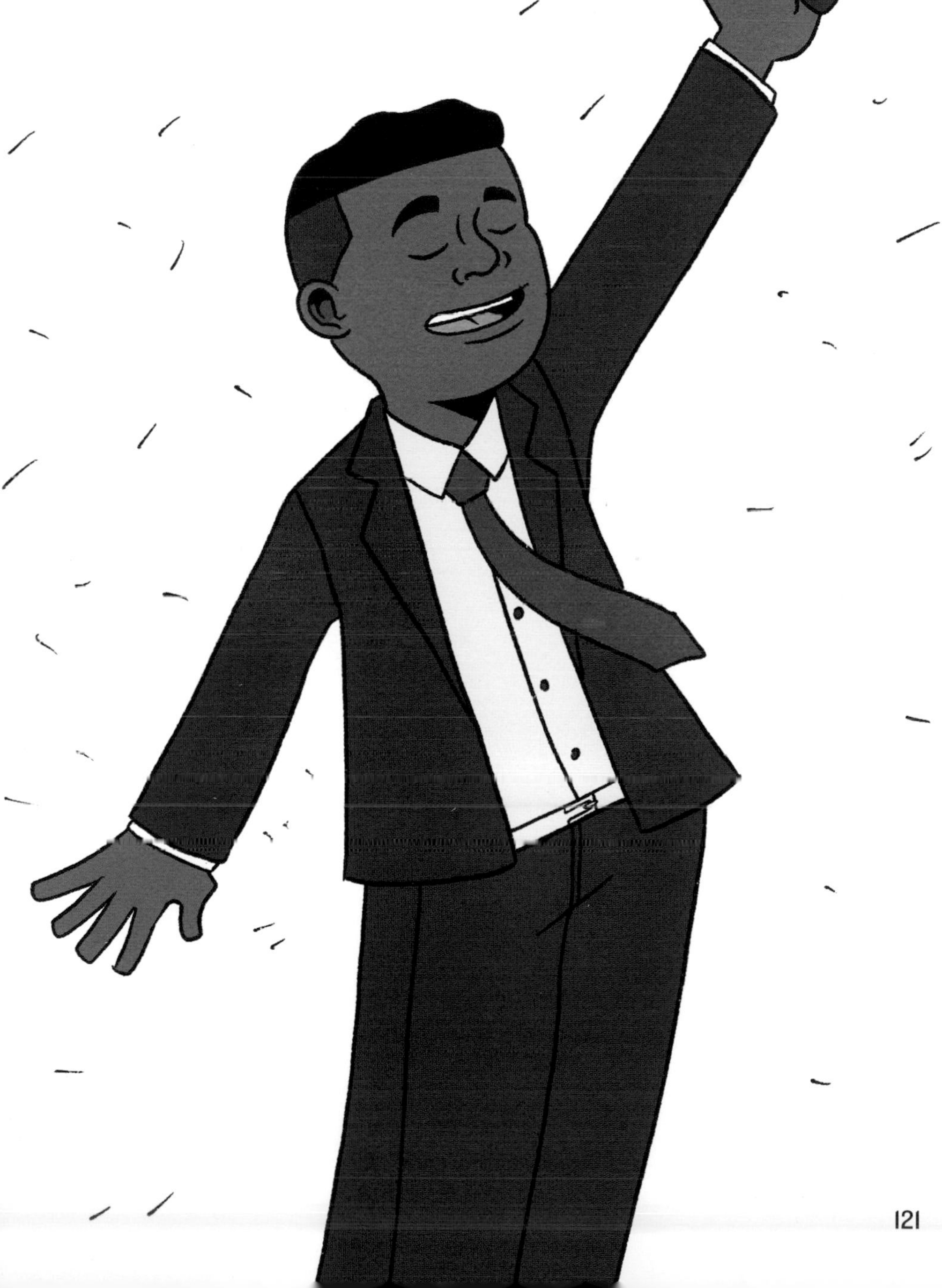

FACING THE MIRROR

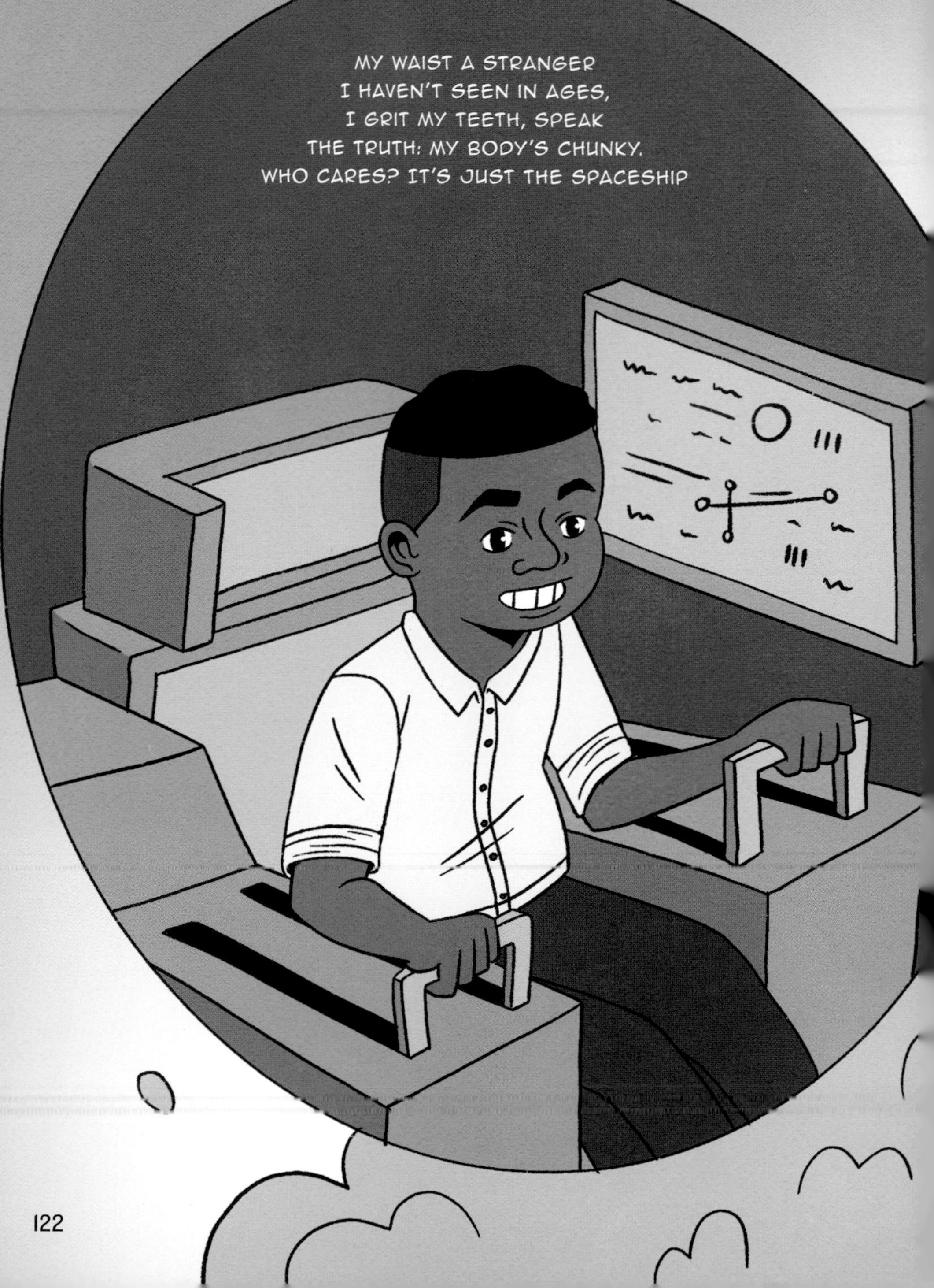
MY WAIST A STRANGER
I HAVEN'T SEEN IN AGES,
I GRIT MY TEETH, SPEAK
THE TRUTH: MY BODY'S CHUNKY.
WHO CARES? IT'S JUST THE SPACESHIP

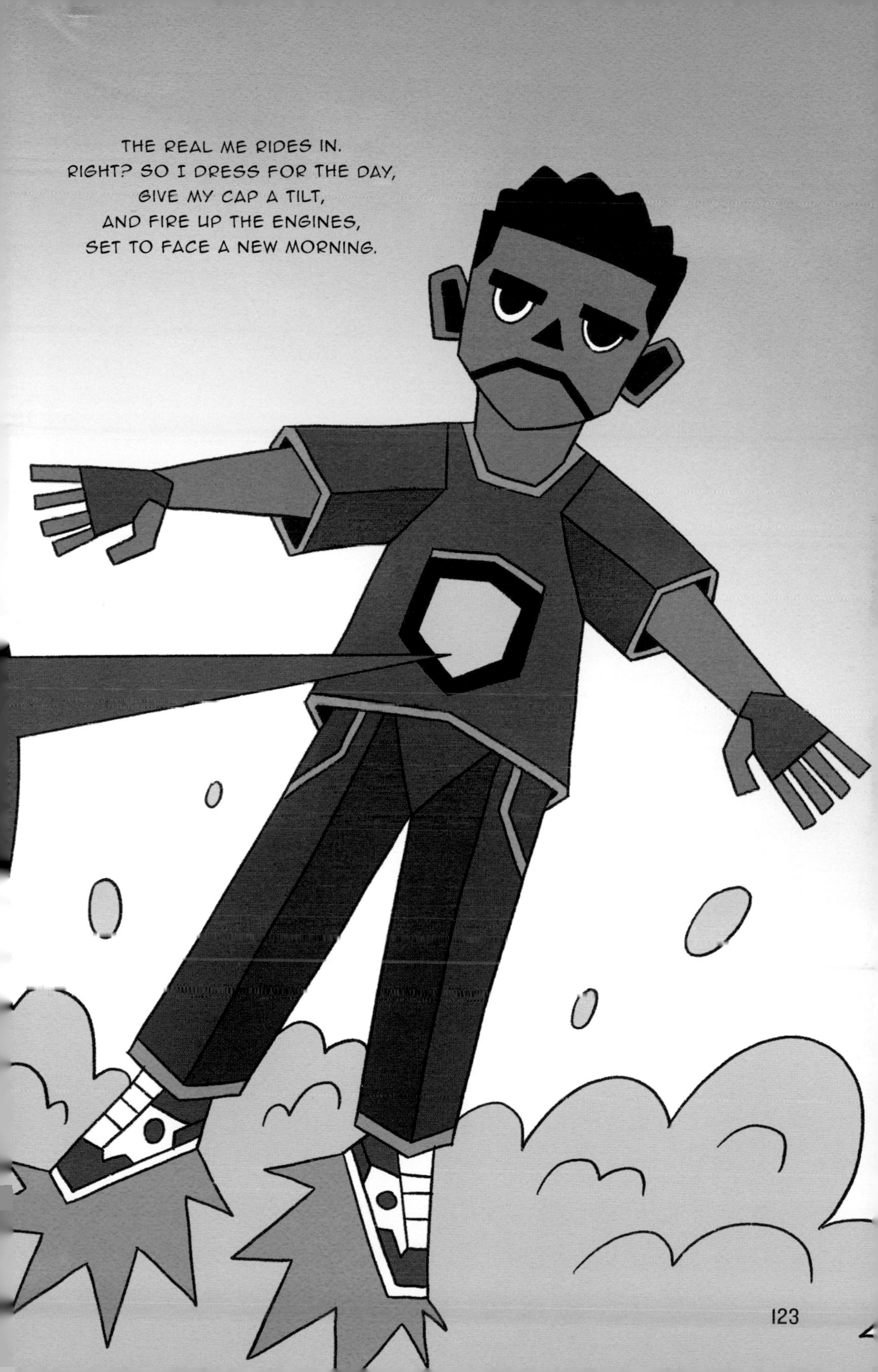
THE REAL ME RIDES IN.
RIGHT? SO I DRESS FOR THE DAY,
GIVE MY CAP A TILT,
AND FIRE UP THE ENGINES,
SET TO FACE A NEW MORNING.

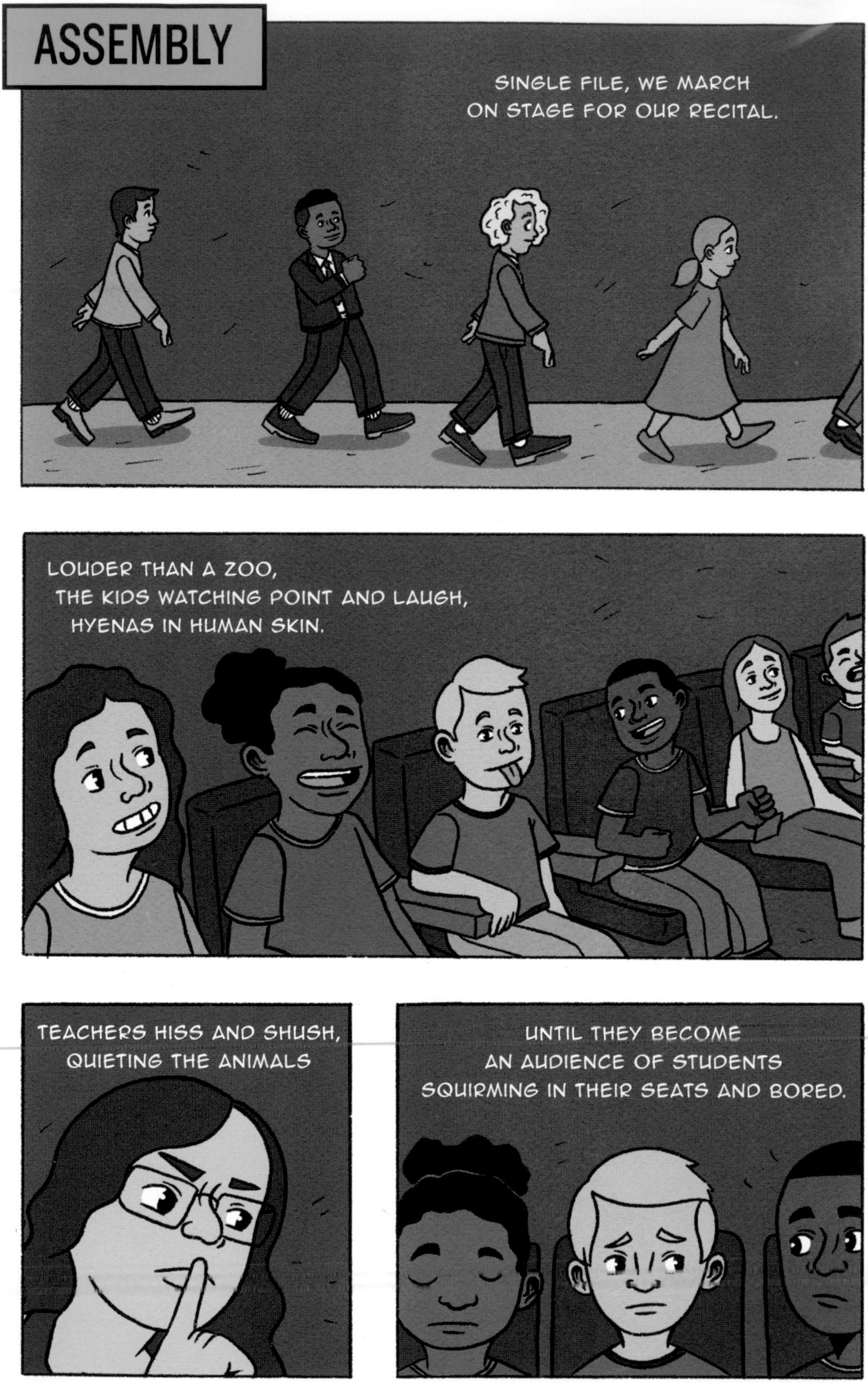
ASSEMBLY
SINGLE FILE, WE MARCH ON STAGE FOR OUR RECITAL.
LOUDER THAN A ZOO, THE KIDS WATCHING POINT AND LAUGH, HYENAS IN HUMAN SKIN.
TEACHERS HISS AND SHUSH, QUIETING THE ANIMALS
UNTIL THEY BECOME AN AUDIENCE OF STUDENTS SQUIRMING IN THEIR SEATS AND BORED.

LIKE WATER RIPPLES,
OUR FIRST NOTES SPREAD HARMONY
FROM FRONT ROW TO BACK.
I SEE MY CLASSMATES FLOATING
IN SOUND, AND I STAND TALLER.

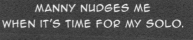

MANNY NUDGES ME
WHEN IT'S TIME FOR MY SOLO.

LEGS LIKE SPAGHETTI,
I WORRY THAT I MIGHT FAINT.
EYES CLOSED, I WAIT FOR COURAGE.

A WHISPER AT FIRST,
THE MUSIC IN ME RISES.
LIVE INSIDE THE SONG,
I TELL MYSELF. AND I DO.

THEN COMES THE HUSH, AND APPLAUSE.

LET DOWN

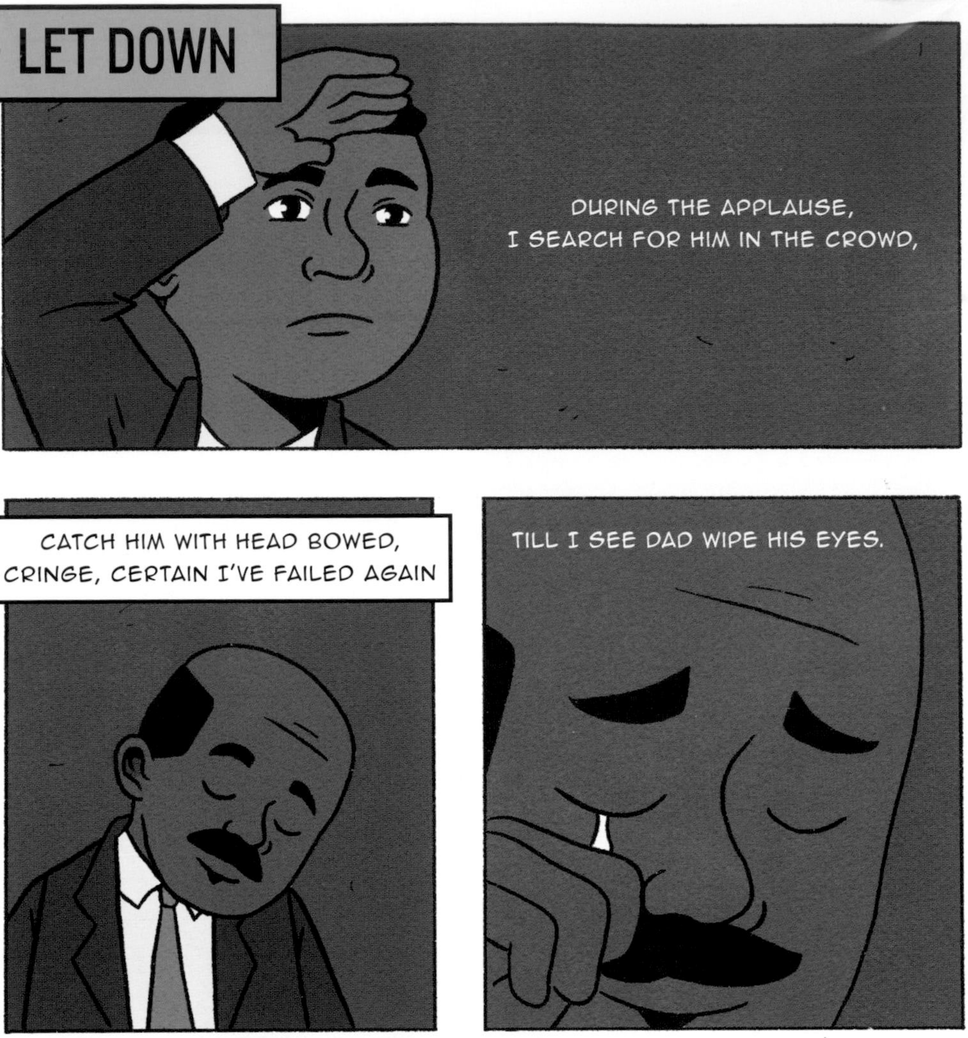
DURING THE APPLAUSE,
I SEARCH FOR HIM IN THE CROWD,
CATCH HIM WITH HEAD BOWED,
CRINGE, CERTAIN I'VE FAILED AGAIN
TILL I SEE DAD WIPE HIS EYES.

THANKS FOR THE PUSH

LIKE HARD CANDY, "THANKS"
STICKS IN MY THROAT, MELTS SLOWLY.
WAITING FOR THE WORDS,
I JAB MANNY IN THE ARM,
MIMICKING MOVIE TOUGH GUYS.

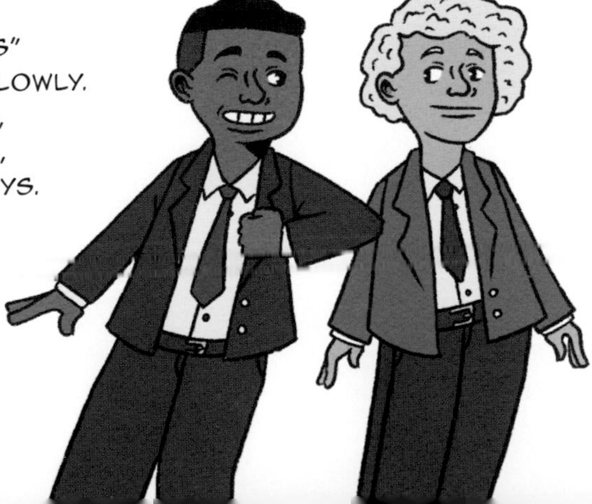

AFTERMATH

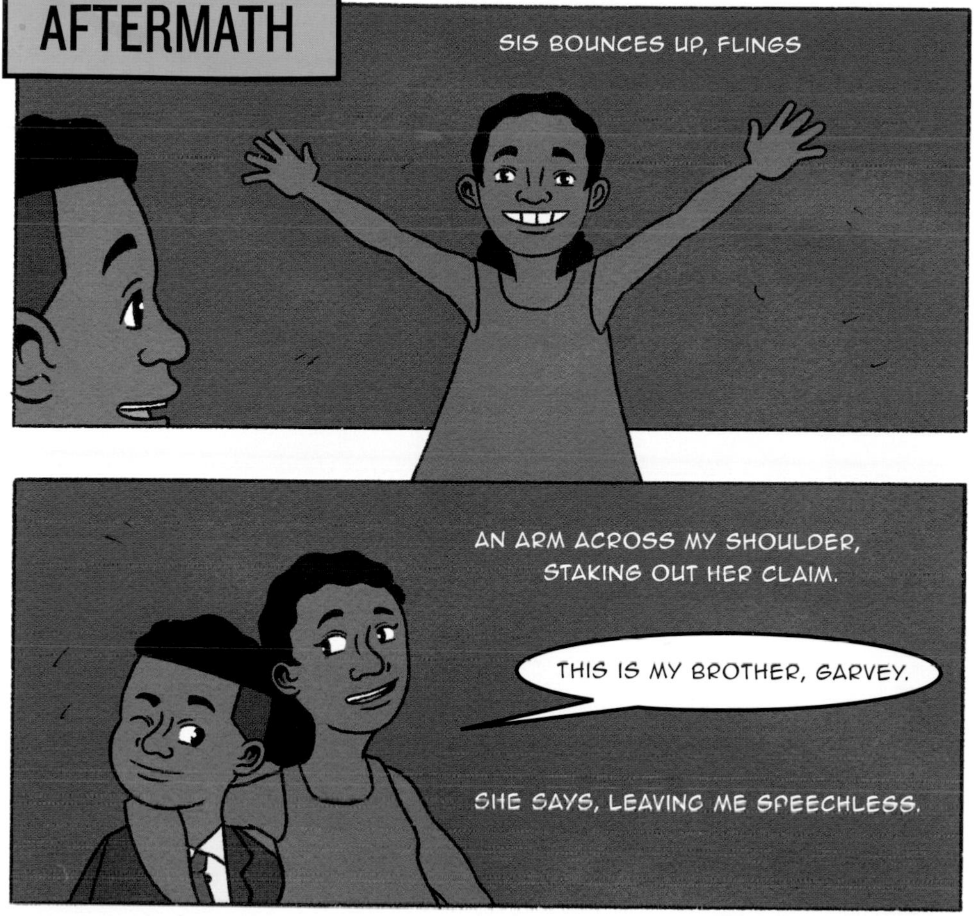
SIS BOUNCES UP, FLINGS
AN ARM ACROSS MY SHOULDER,
STAKING OUT HER CLAIM.
THIS IS MY BROTHER, GARVEY.
SHE SAYS, LEAVING ME SPEECHLESS.

NEW FAN

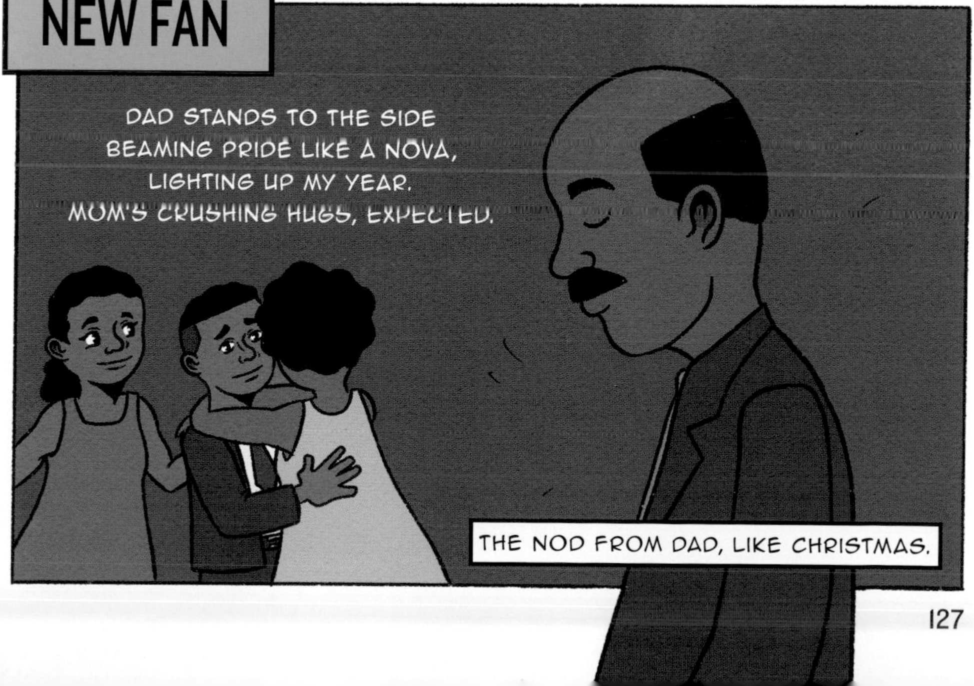
DAD STANDS TO THE SIDE
BEAMING PRIDE LIKE A NOVA,
LIGHTING UP MY YEAR.
MOM'S CRUSHING HUGS, EXPECTED.
THE NOD FROM DAD, LIKE CHRISTMAS.

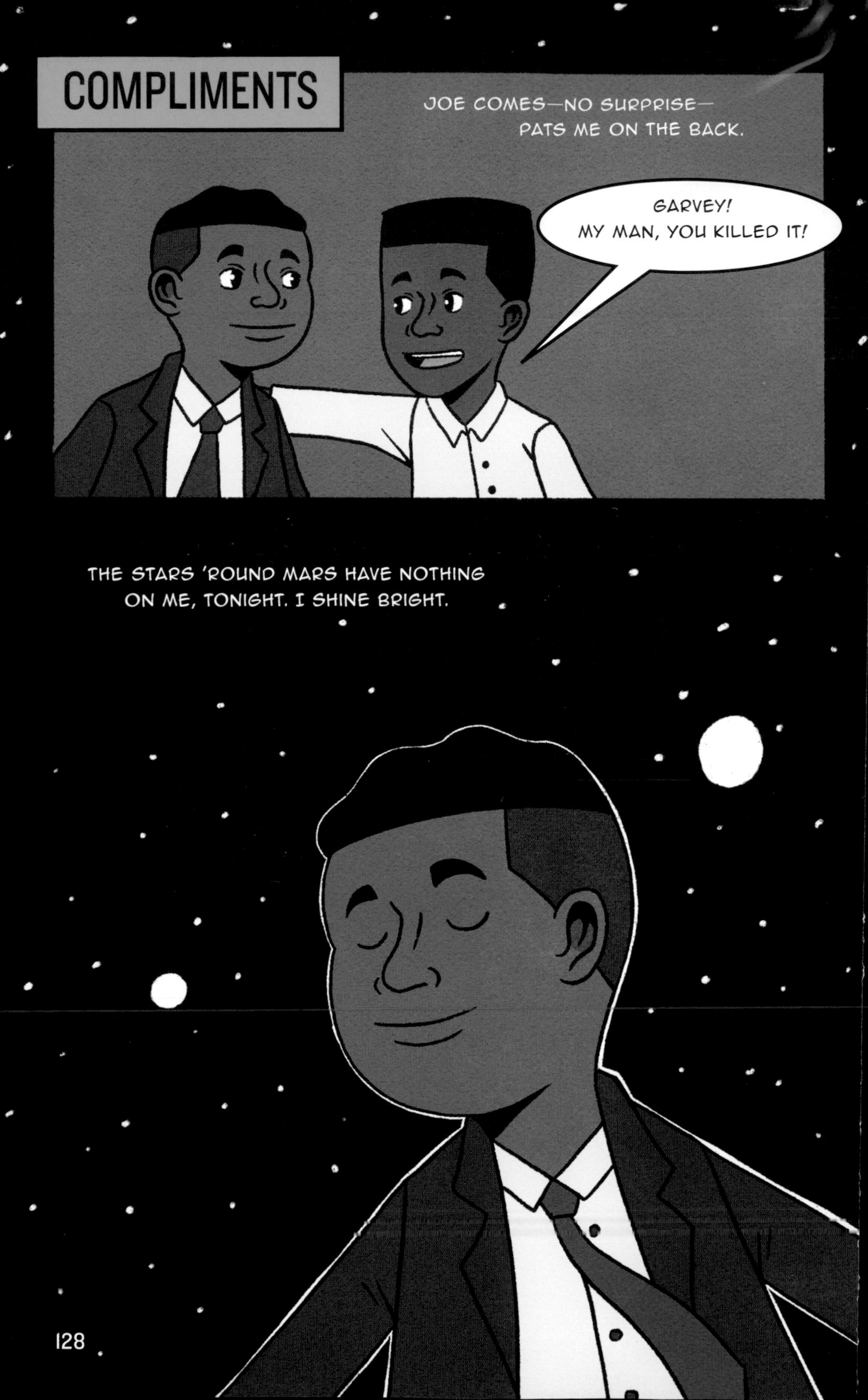
COMPLIMENTS
JOE COMES—NO SURPRISE—
PATS ME ON THE BACK.
GARVEY!
MY MAN, YOU KILLED IT!
THE STARS 'ROUND MARS HAVE NOTHING
ON ME, TONIGHT. I SHINE BRIGHT.

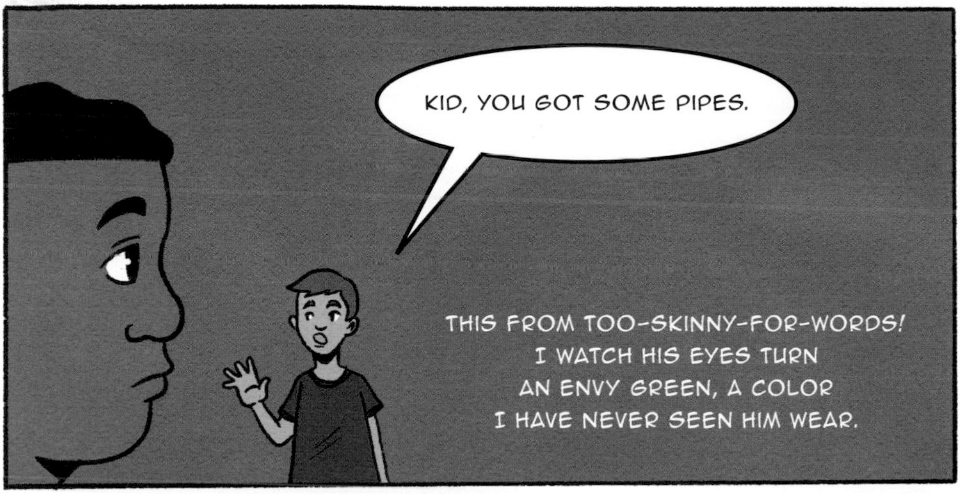
KID, YOU GOT SOME PIPES.
THIS FROM TOO-SKINNY-FOR-WORDS!
I WATCH HIS EYES TURN
AN ENVY GREEN, A COLOR
I HAVE NEVER SEEN HIM WEAR.

LESS THAN PERFECT

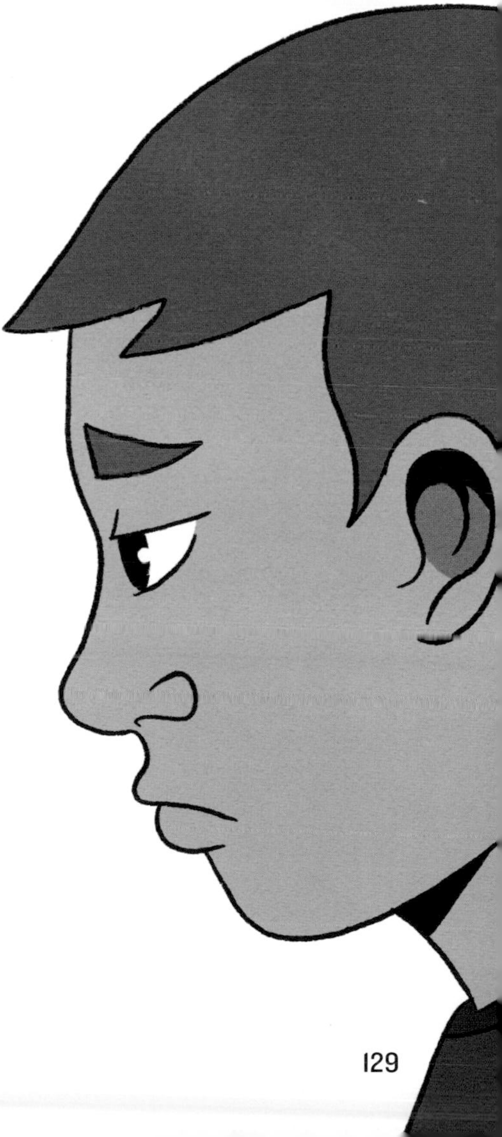

GRIM SHADOWS, PROBLEMS
HAUNT US ALL—ROUND, THIN, SHORT, TALL.
TOO-SKINNY-FOR-WORDS
IS UNHAPPY TO THE CORE.
NEVER NOTICED THAT BEFORE.

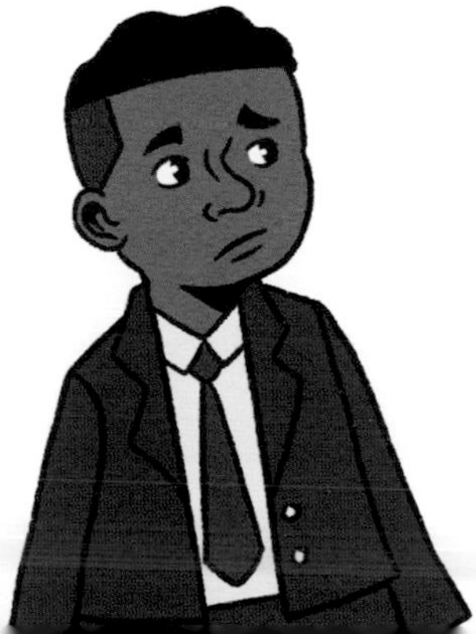

INTRODUCTIONS

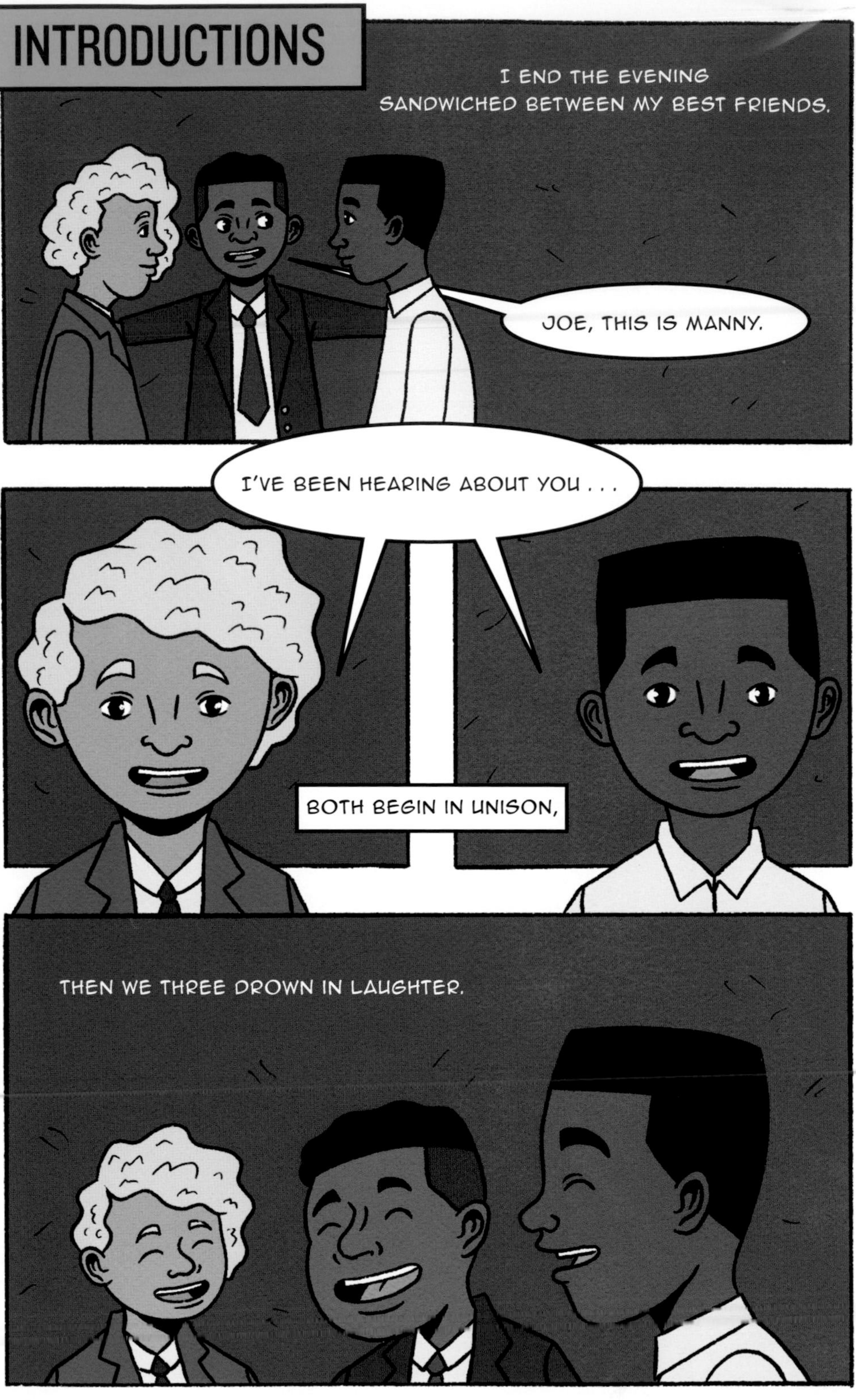
I END THE EVENING SANDWICHED BETWEEN MY BEST FRIENDS.
JOE, THIS IS MANNY.
I'VE BEEN HEARING ABOUT YOU . . .
BOTH BEGIN IN UNISON,
THEN WE THREE DROWN IN LAUGHTER.

TOO SOON GOOD-BYE

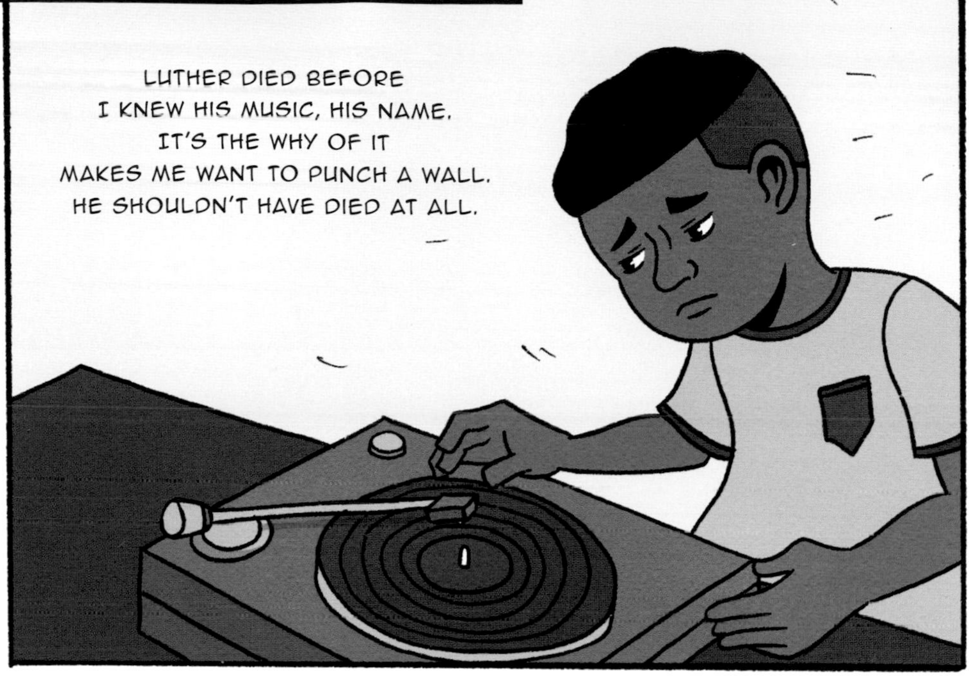
LUTHER DIED BEFORE
I KNEW HIS MUSIC, HIS NAME.
IT'S THE WHY OF IT
MAKES ME WANT TO PUNCH A WALL.
HE SHOULDN'T HAVE DIED AT ALL.

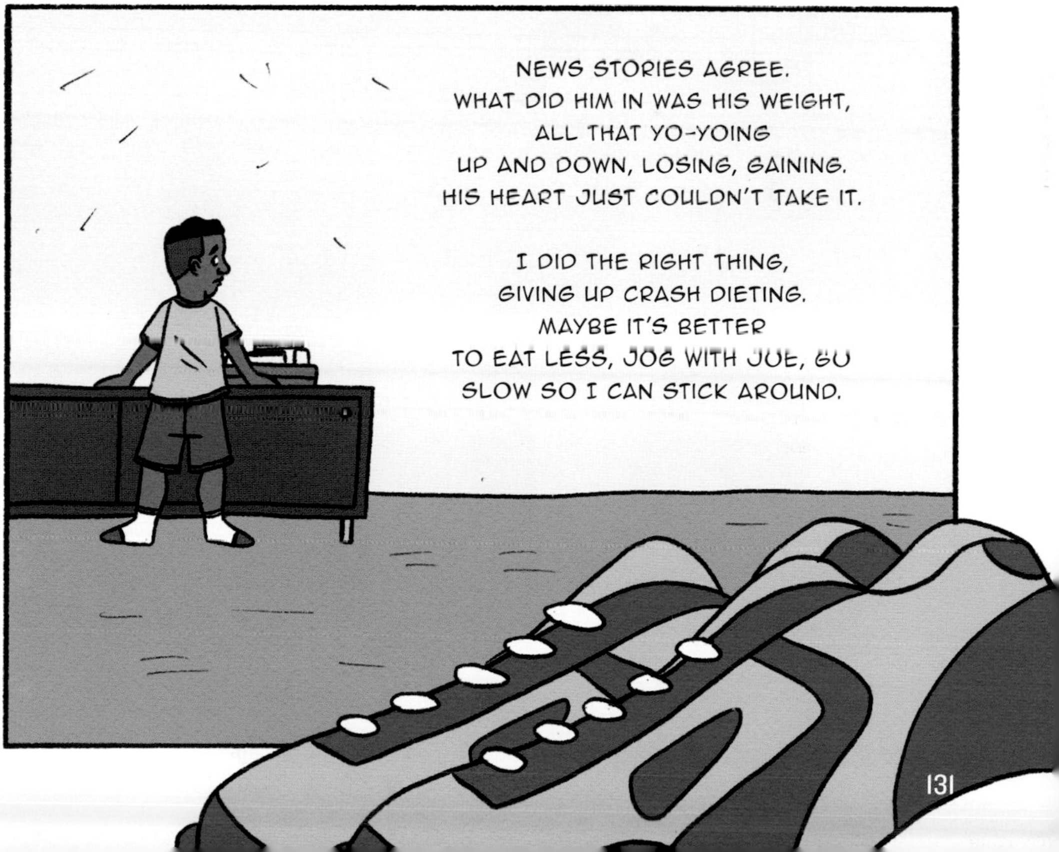
NEWS STORIES AGREE.
WHAT DID HIM IN WAS HIS WEIGHT,
ALL THAT YO-YOING
UP AND DOWN, LOSING, GAINING.
HIS HEART JUST COULDN'T TAKE IT.

I DID THE RIGHT THING,
GIVING UP CRASH DIETING.
MAYBE IT'S BETTER
TO EAT LESS, JOG WITH JOE, GO
SLOW SO I CAN STICK AROUND.

ON THE MOVE

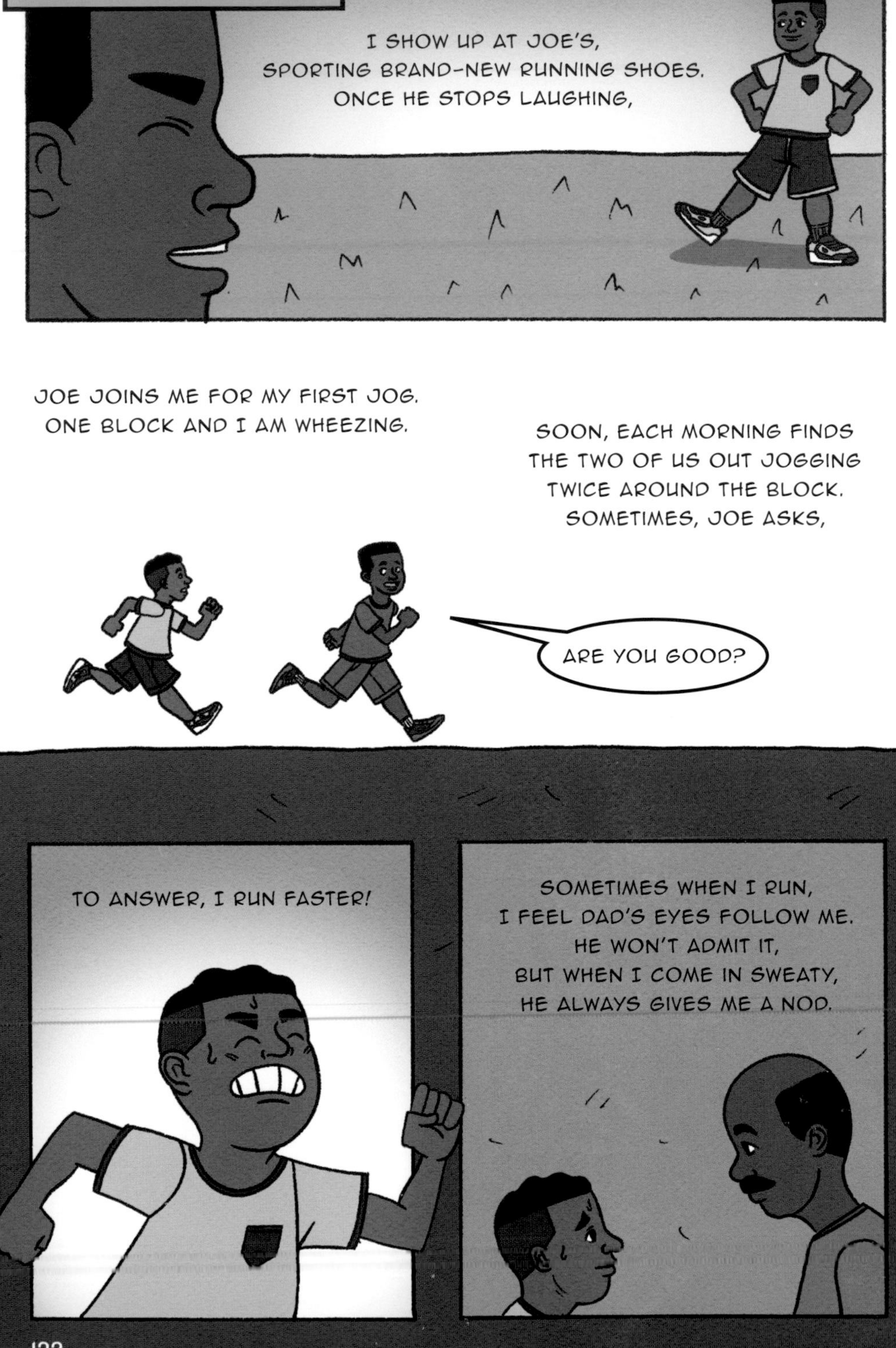
I SHOW UP AT JOE'S, SPORTING BRAND-NEW RUNNING SHOES. ONCE HE STOPS LAUGHING,
JOE JOINS ME FOR MY FIRST JOG. ONE BLOCK AND I AM WHEEZING.
SOON, EACH MORNING FINDS THE TWO OF US OUT JOGGING TWICE AROUND THE BLOCK. SOMETIMES, JOE ASKS,
ARE YOU GOOD?
TO ANSWER, I RUN FASTER!
SOMETIMES WHEN I RUN, I FEEL DAD'S EYES FOLLOW ME. HE WON'T ADMIT IT, BUT WHEN I COME IN SWEATY, HE ALWAYS GIVES ME A NOD.

SPRING THAW

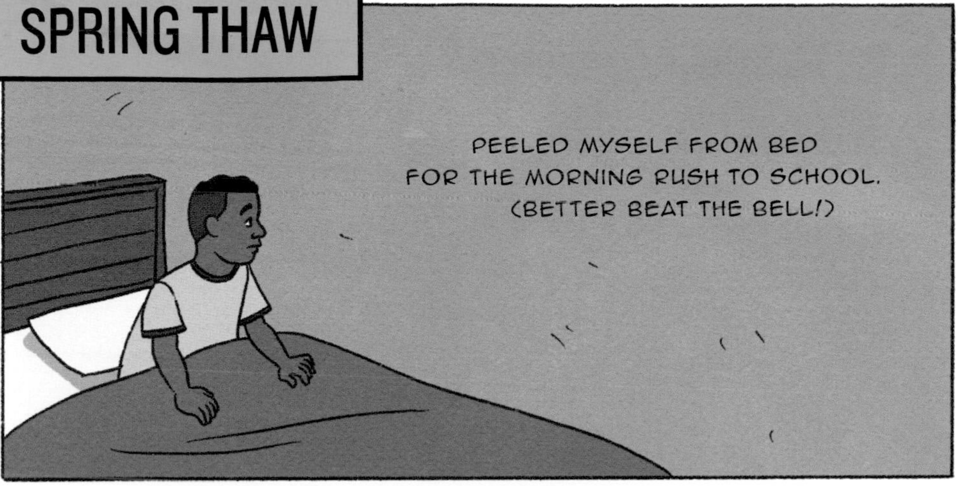
PEELED MYSELF FROM BED
FOR THE MORNING RUSH TO SCHOOL.
(BETTER BEAT THE BELL!)

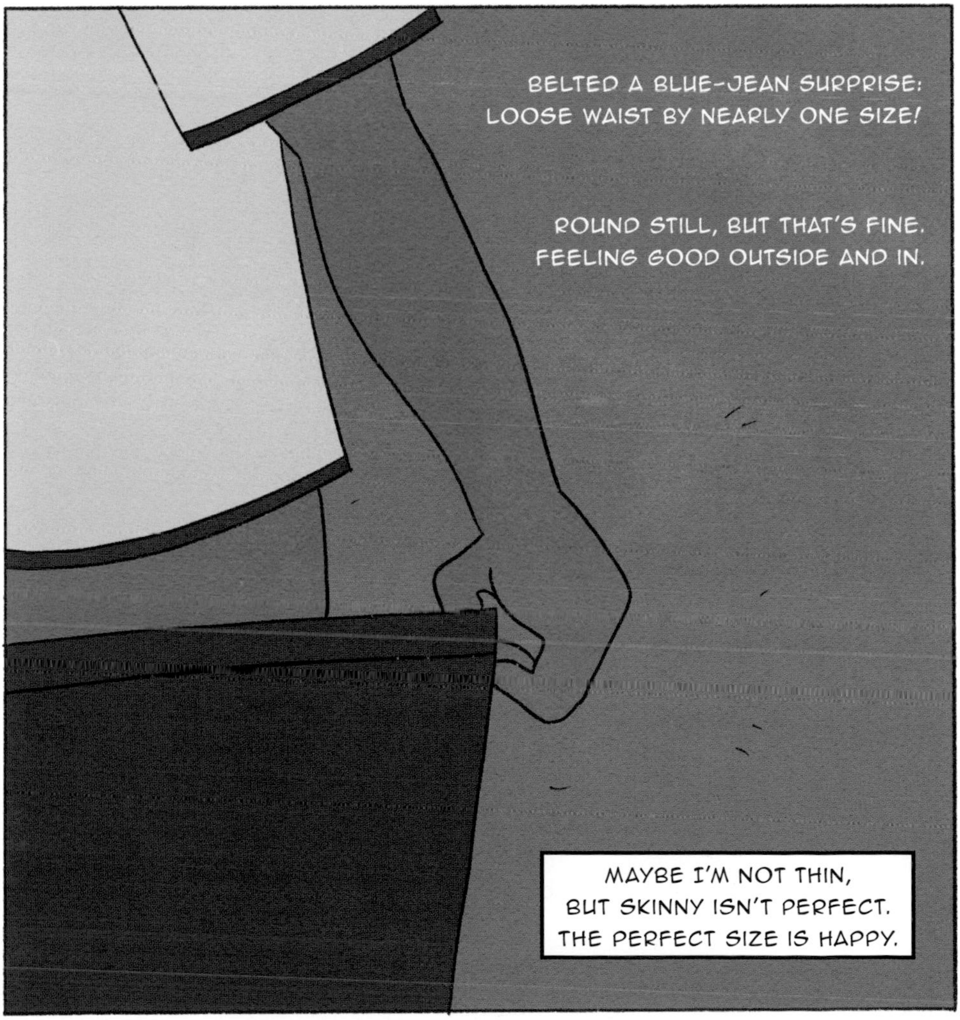
BELTED A BLUE-JEAN SURPRISE:
LOOSE WAIST BY NEARLY ONE SIZE!
ROUND STILL, BUT THAT'S FINE.
FEELING GOOD OUTSIDE AND IN.
MAYBE I'M NOT THIN,
BUT SKINNY ISN'T PERFECT.
THE PERFECT SIZE IS HAPPY.

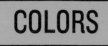

COLORS

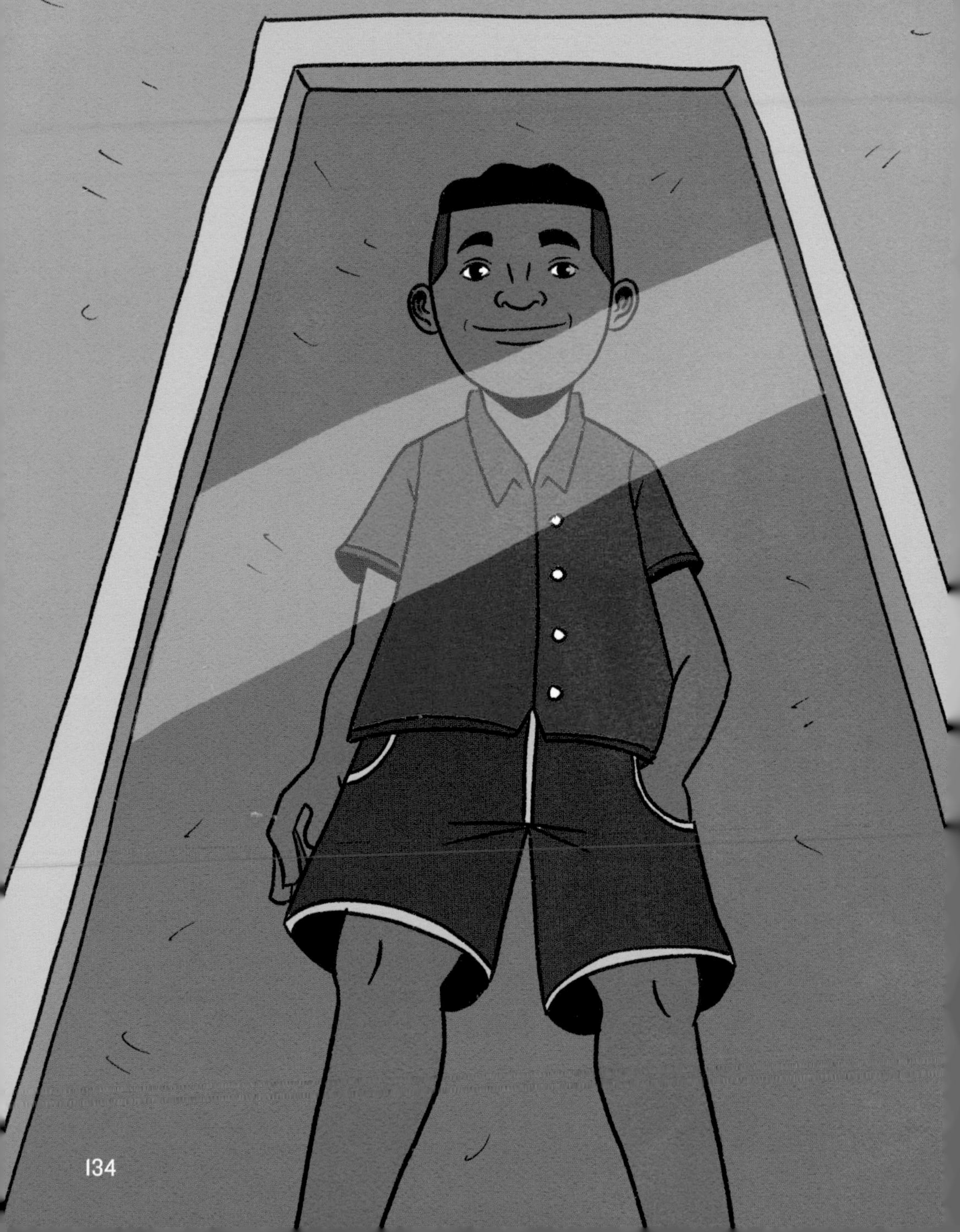
MY SHIRT RED AS FLAME,
I STAND BEFORE THE MIRROR,
SMILING AT A BOY
WHOSE FRAME IS FAMILIAR
BUT CHANGED, UNFINISHED—ALL ME.

TURN AROUND

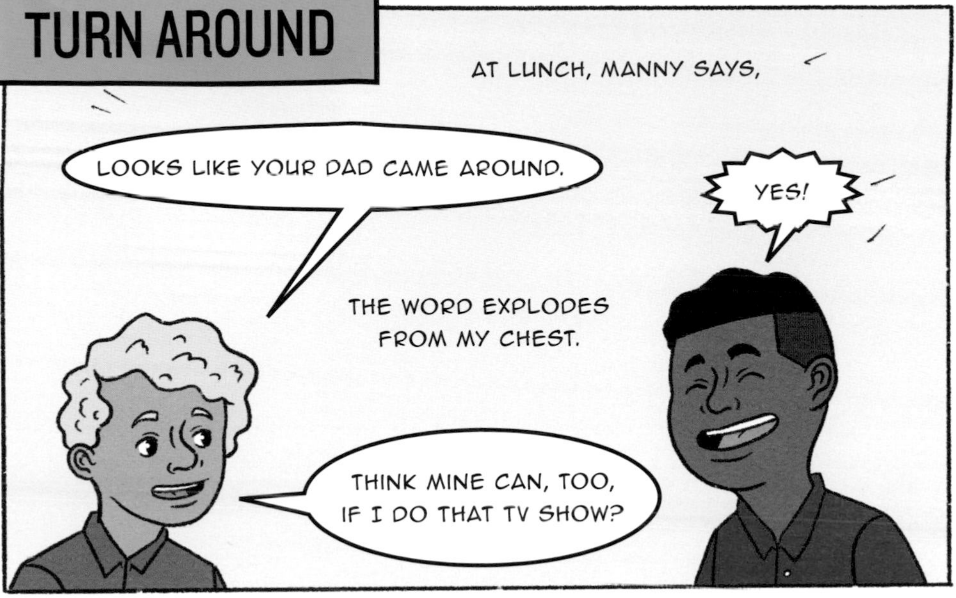
AT LUNCH, MANNY SAYS,
LOOKS LIKE YOUR DAD CAME AROUND.
YES!
THE WORD EXPLODES FROM MY CHEST.
THINK MINE CAN, TOO, IF I DO THAT TV SHOW?

THIS TIME, I CHEW ON
HOPE FOR MY GOOD FRIEND.

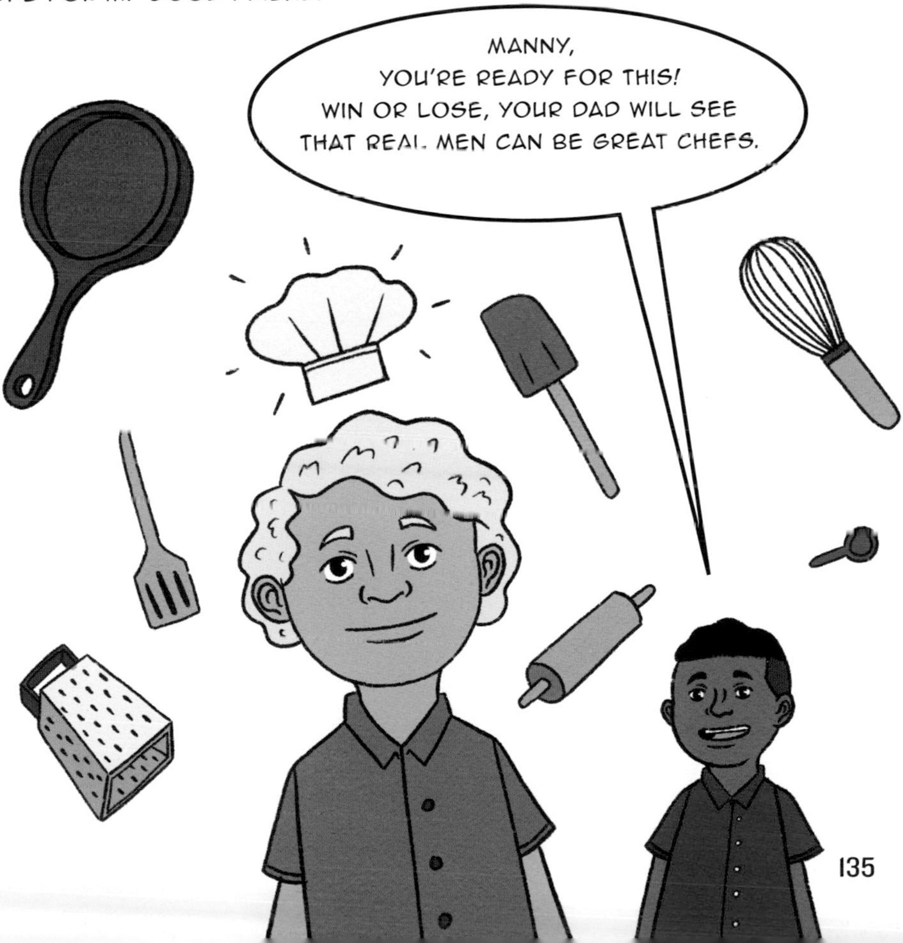
MANNY, YOU'RE READY FOR THIS! WIN OR LOSE, YOUR DAD WILL SEE THAT REAL MEN CAN BE GREAT CHEFS.

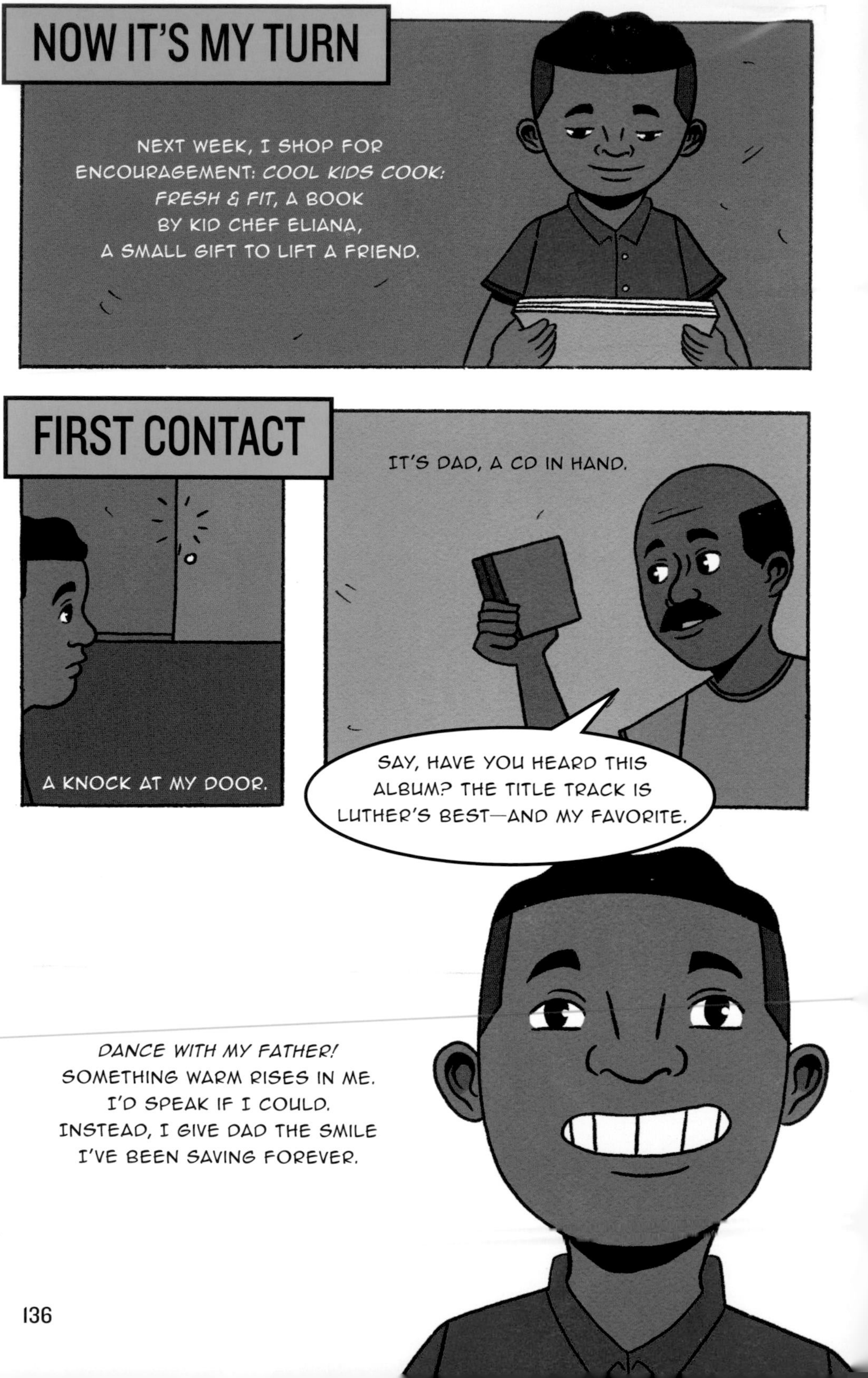
NOW IT'S MY TURN
NEXT WEEK, I SHOP FOR ENCOURAGEMENT: *COOL KIDS COOK: FRESH & FIT*, A BOOK BY KID CHEF ELIANA, A SMALL GIFT TO LIFT A FRIEND.
FIRST CONTACT
A KNOCK AT MY DOOR.
IT'S DAD, A CD IN HAND.
SAY, HAVE YOU HEARD THIS ALBUM? THE TITLE TRACK IS LUTHER'S BEST—AND MY FAVORITE.
DANCE WITH MY FATHER! SOMETHING WARM RISES IN ME. I'D SPEAK IF I COULD. INSTEAD, I GIVE DAD THE SMILE I'VE BEEN SAVING FOREVER.

THE TALK

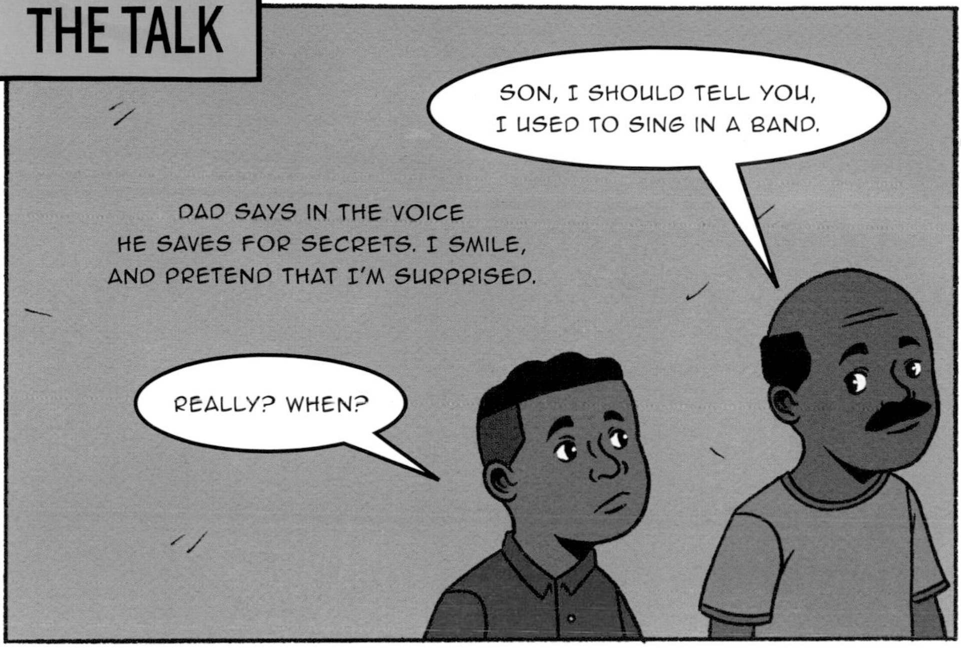
SON, I SHOULD TELL YOU,
I USED TO SING IN A BAND.
DAD SAYS IN THE VOICE
HE SAVES FOR SECRETS. I SMILE,
AND PRETEND THAT I'M SURPRISED.
REALLY? WHEN?

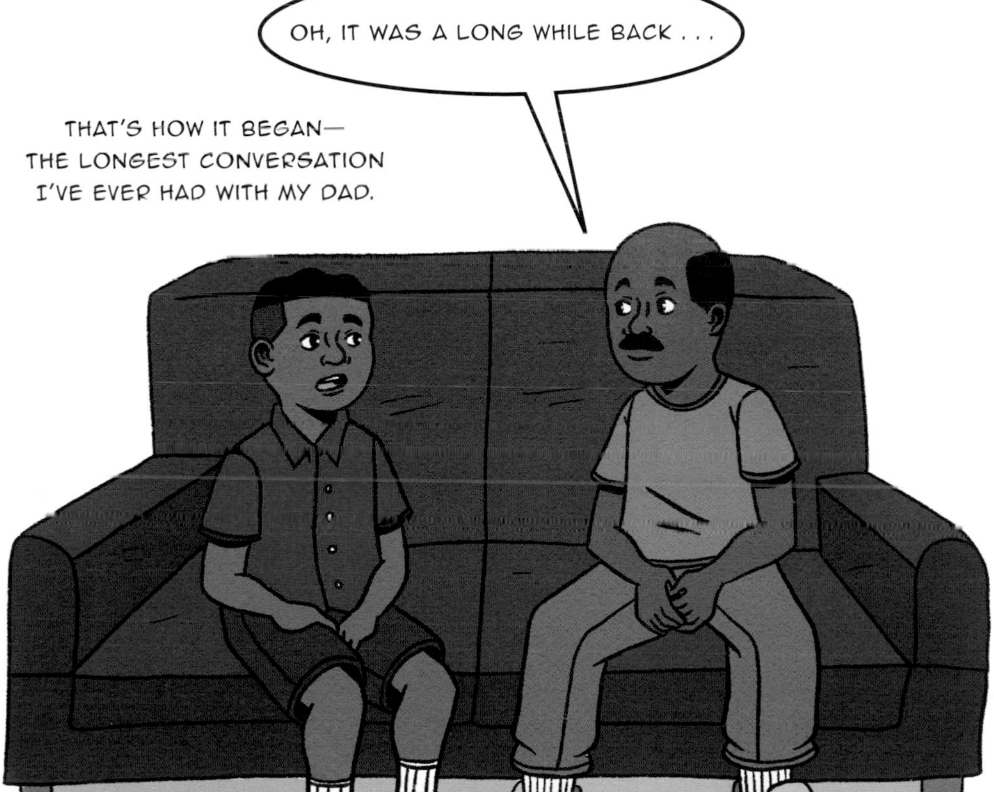
OH, IT WAS A LONG WHILE BACK . . .
THAT'S HOW IT BEGAN—
THE LONGEST CONVERSATION
I'VE EVER HAD WITH MY DAD.

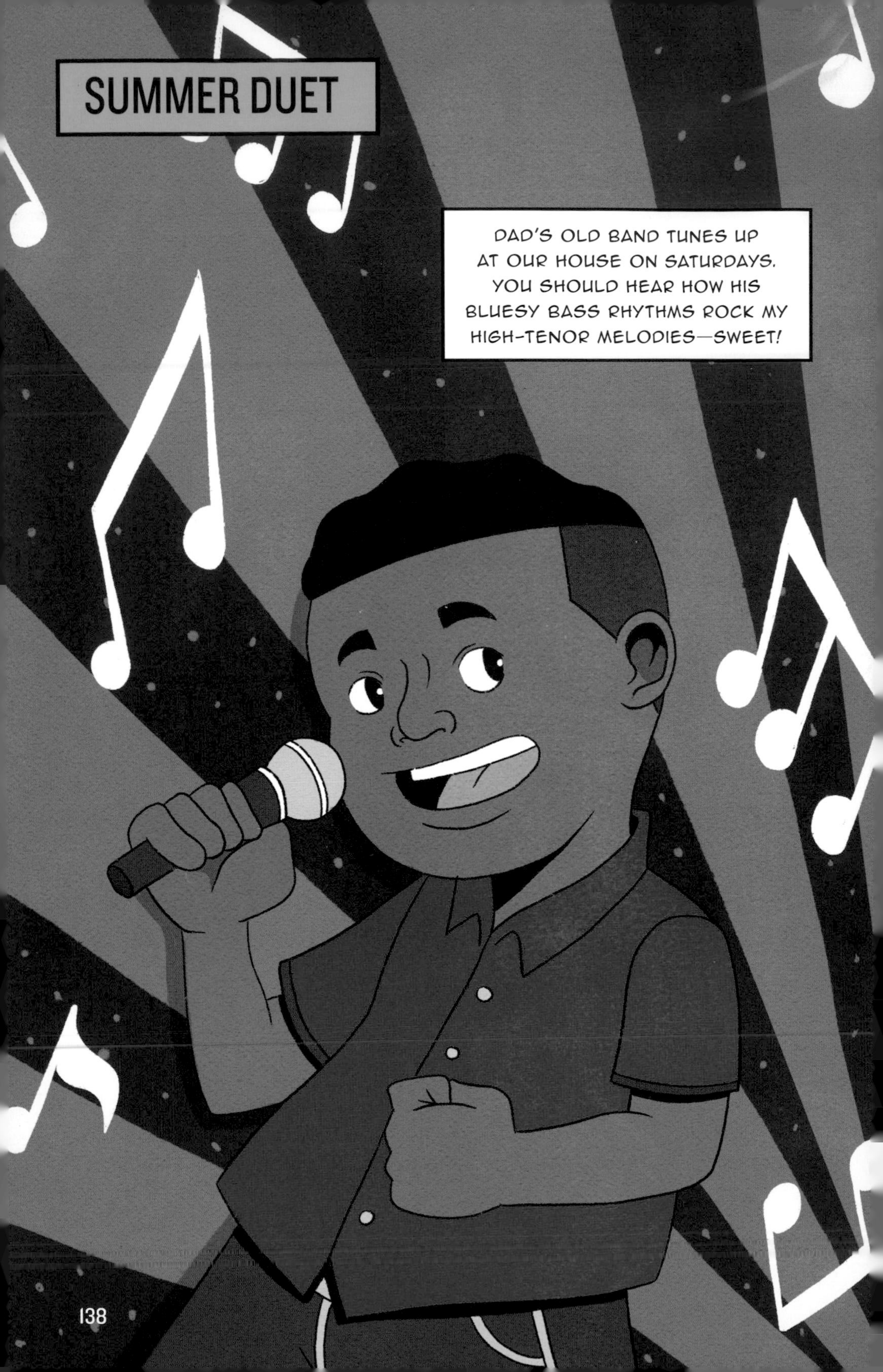
SUMMER DUET
DAD'S OLD BAND TUNES UP AT OUR HOUSE ON SATURDAYS. YOU SHOULD HEAR HOW HIS BLUESY BASS RHYTHMS ROCK MY HIGH-TENOR MELODIES—SWEET!

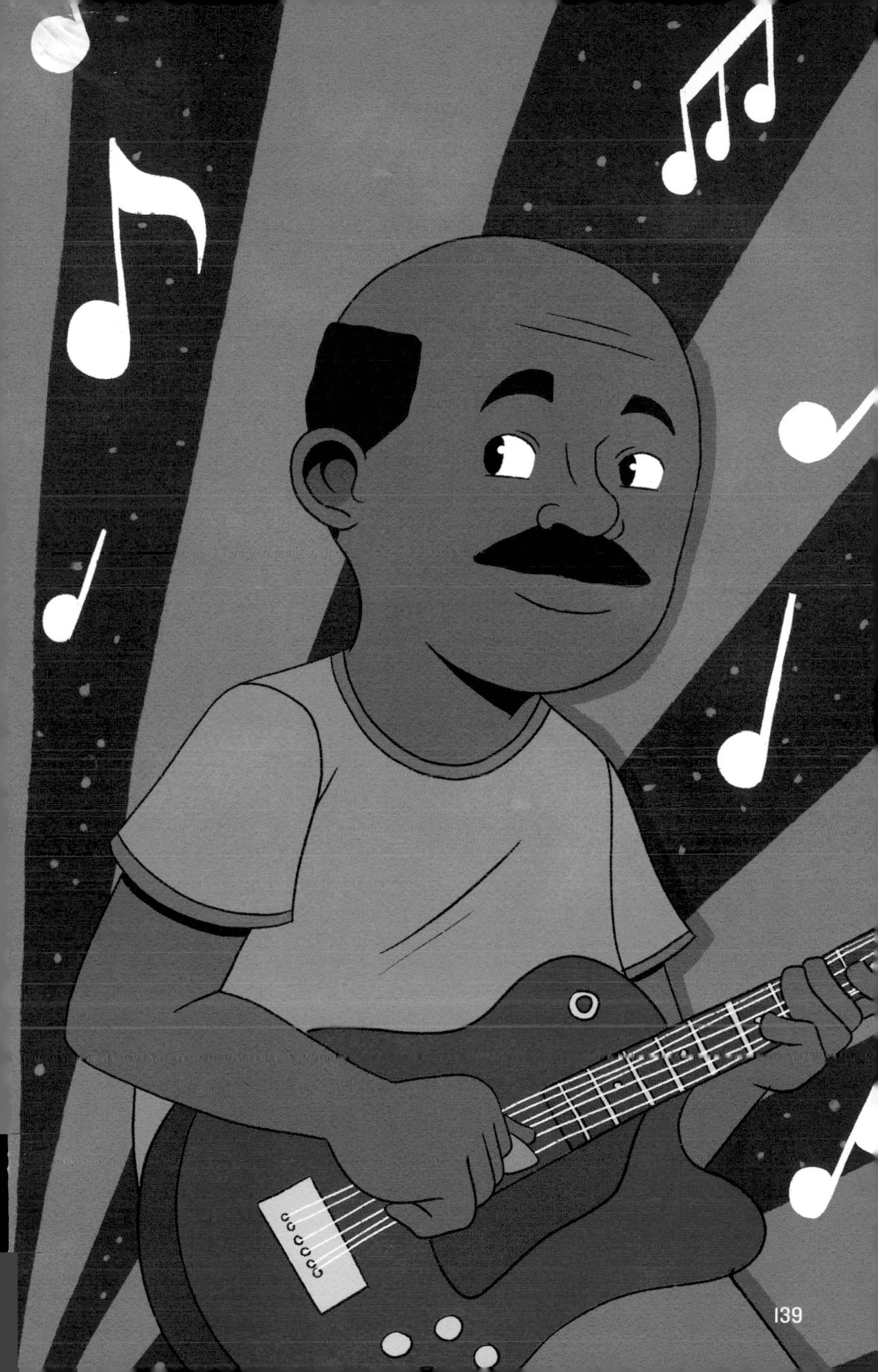

TANKA

All the poems in the original *Garvey's Choice* were written in tanka. About two-thirds of the tanka poems remain intact in *Garvey's Choice: The Graphic Novel*. Others have been adjusted either because lines had to be broken between narrative text and speech balloons or across two speech balloons, or because dialogue tags like "he said" and "she said" were deleted since the art makes it clear who is speaking.

Tanka is an ancient poetry form, originally from Japan. The word *tanka* means "short poem" in Japanese. The basic tanka is five lines long. The line-by-line syllable count varies in the modern English version, but the number of lines is always the same.

The modern form of tanka I chose to use for *Garvey's Choice* is broken down as follows:

Line 1: 5 syllables

Line 2: 7 syllables

Line 3: 5 syllables

Line 4: 7 syllables

Line 5: 7 syllables

Not every American poet follows a syllable count for tanka poems, but I think of a syllable count like a puzzle. Each word is a puzzle piece, and I like figuring out which words fit best!

Traditional tanka poems focus on mood. They are often poems about love, the four seasons, the shortness of life, and nature. In my tanka, I include mood, but in each poem, my focus is more centered on telling a story.

I hope you have enjoyed the stories I told!

—*NG*

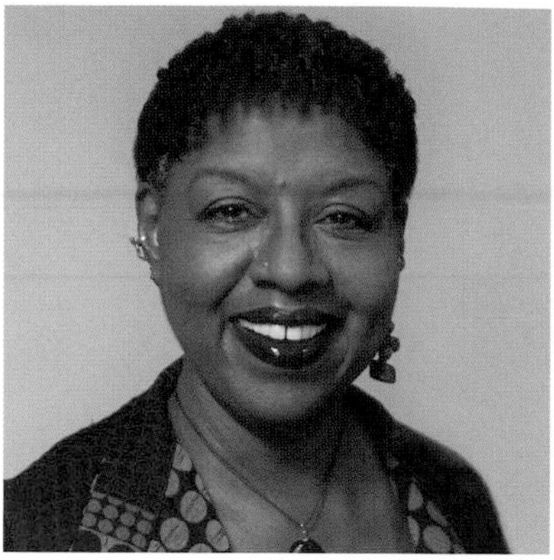

Photograph by Aaron Lemen

NIKKI GRIMES is the recipient of the Coretta Scott King–Virginia Hamilton Award for Lifetime Achievement, the ALA Children's Literature Legacy Award, the ALAN Award for outstanding contributions to young adult literature, and the NCTE Award for Excellence in Poetry for Children. Her books include her critically acclaimed memoir-in-verse *Ordinary Hazards* and the *New York Times* bestsellers *Kamala Harris: Rooted in Justice* and *Barack Obama: Son of Promise, Child of Hope*. She won the Coretta Scott King Award for *Bronx Masquerade* and earned a Coretta Scott King Author Honor five times—for *Words with Wings*, *Jazmin's Notebook*, *Dark Sons*, *Talkin' About Bessie*, and *The Road to Paris*. She lives in Corona, California. Visit nikkigrimes.com.

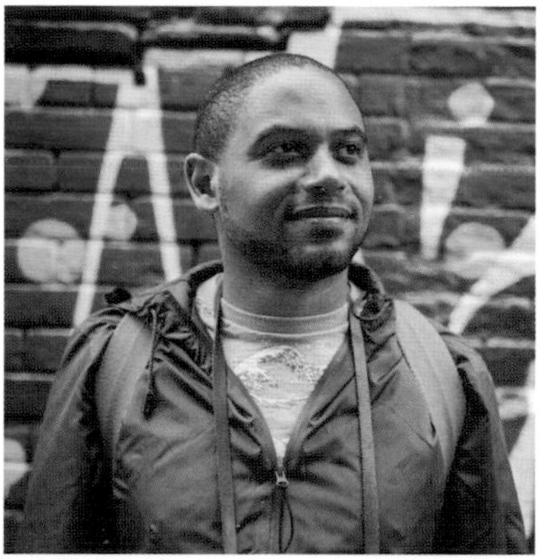

Photograph by Sarah Schultz-Taylor

THEODORE TAYLOR III is the illustrator of multiple children's books, including Shaquille O'Neal's Little Shaq series and the picture books *Buzzing with Questions: Thc Inquisitive Mind of Charles Henry Turner* and *When the Beat Was Born: DJ Kool Herc and the Creation of Hip Hop*, for which he received the Coretta Scott King John Steptoe New Talent Award. His work is inspired by his love of music, comics, animation, video games, street art, and more. He lives in Richmond, Virginia, with his wife and son.

Visit theodore3.com.

DON'T MISS

NIKKI GRIMES
New York Times Bestselling Author
GARVEY IN THE DARK

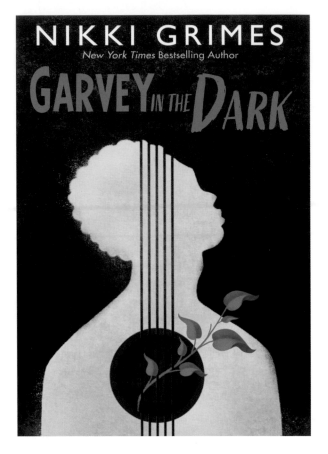

Capturing the shock and impact of the COVID-19 pandemic through the eyes of her beloved character Garvey, Nikki Grimes's newest novel in verse shows readers how to find hope in difficult times.

"This sequel is as much a triumph as *Garvey's Choice*—a stunning example of how much can be accomplished with few words in the hands of a masterful poet."

—Padma Venkatraman, Walter Award-winning author of *The Bridge Home*

"A must-read for young people who lived through the early days of the outbreak as well as those who will be curious about it in years to come."

—Kate Messner, *New York Times* bestselling author